The Book of Obeah

A Novel

First published by O Books, 2010
O Books is an imprint of John Hunt Publishing Ltd., The Bothy, Deershot Lodge, Park Lane, Ropley,
Hants, SO24 0BE, UK
office1@o-books.net
www.o-books.net

Distribution in:

UK and Europe
Orca Book Services
orders@orcabookservices.co.uk
Tel: 01202 665432 Fax: 01202 666219
Int. code (44)

USA and Canada
NBN
custserv@nbnbooks.com
Tel: 1 800 462 6420 Fax: 1 800 338 4550

Australia and New Zealand
Brumby Books
sales@brumbybooks.com.au
Tel: 61 3 9761 5535 Fax: 61 3 9761 7095

Far East (offices in Singapore, Thailand,
Hong Kong, Taiwan)
Pansing Distribution Pte Ltd
kemal@pansing.com
Tel: 65 6319 9939 Fax: 65 6462 5761

South Africa
Stephan Phillips (pty) Ltd
Email: orders@stephanphillips.com
Tel: 27 21 4489839 Telefax: 27 21 4479879

Text copyright Sandra Carrington-Smith 2008
sandracarringtonsmith.com

Design: Stuart Davies

ISBN: 978 1 84694 299 0

A CIP catalogue record for this book is available
from the British Library.

Printed by Digital Book Print

O Books operates a distinctive and ethical publishing philosophy in
all areas of its business, from its global network of authors to
production and worldwide distribution.

The Book of Obeah

A Novel

Sandra Carrington-Smith

BOOKS

Winchester, UK
Washington, USA

ACKNOWLEDGEMENTS

I still remember the night I sat down to write the first words of *The Book of Obeah*. It was a muggy night in July 2006, and a powerful storm was brewing in the southwest. I had woken that very morning with the beginning words of the story ringing in my head, and I promised myself, throughout the day, that I was going to jot them down on paper. That stormy night sealed the beginning of a new journey – one I never regretted embarking on.

Once the first draft was complete, I began looking for an agent. Alas, I had no idea just how hard that was going to be. I received rejection after rejection and truly began to feel discouraged, but when I was almost ready to throw in the towel, something amazing happened.

A friend introduced me to Dena Patrick, my editor. Dena was the answer to my prayers – with her coaching, and the merging of her mind-blowing skills with my own, the manuscript was enriched and polished, and *The Book of Obeah* was born.

Many people have been instrumental to the evolution of this project, so I hope I am not forgetting anyone. I would like to thank my family, Diego, Cosetta and Patrizia Faiazza, my in-law family – especially Bob and Ann Carrington-Smith – for their undying love and support, and all the friends who have read the manuscript and have volunteered their valuable opinions - Pam and Fred Scarboro, Leslie Long, Susan Clark, Natalie Kimber, Garreth Griffin, Cherie Lassiter, Lorie Best and Riccardo Panessa.

Special thanks to my copy editor and friend, Dara Lyon Warner, who saved the day at the eleventh hour when *The Book of Obeah* needed a drastic cut, and of course, thanks to my children Stephen, Michael and Morgan, and to my husband John Carrington-Smith, who never ceased to believe in me and supported me from the beginning of this venture.

I would like to thank my agent, Krista Goering, for her

encouragement and vision; my publisher, John Hunt. Thanks to my GOLO friends - especially Lolly - for the ongoing online support.

Thank you so much, everybody, for without your help I would not be writing this page. You've all been unique pieces of a beautiful puzzle that is finally complete.

Ultimately, I would like to dedicate this book to Dena Patrick. Her ongoing dedication to my message has united us beyond anything words can express, and her constant encouragement has built my confidence as an author. Needless to say, *The Book of Obeah* would not be where it is today without her energetic input.

Dena, I feel that we gave birth to this child together, and I don't know that I can ever entirely convey to you how grateful I am - *The Book of Obeah* will always be "our" book, and I look forward to many more projects we can work on together. Destiny connected our paths, and all I can see in front of us is a beautiful, long, straight road we will always somehow travel side by side.

PREFACE

"There will come a time when powerful signs herald a crossroads for Humanity. Events affecting one part of the Earth will instantly be known to the rest of the world and shall be recognized by a chosen few as the prophesied signs. Consequences of action and inaction will be apparent, cause and effect manifesting faster as this cycle draws toward conclusion. Inequities and imbalance will be painfully evident on individual, regional and global levels. Feelings of isolation, disconnection, and confusion will be widespread. Few will express these feelings, most choosing to mindlessly walk through their daily tasks, numbing themselves in countless ways. Hardships will flood the vast majority of people from every direction, creating a rising sea of anxiety. This will be reflected in Mother Earth being out of balance, with cataclysmic events taking place more regularly and more intensely as She strives to attain equilibrium.

A long-ago gathering of elders who revered and held sacred our connection to Mother Earth foresaw the time of this crossroads. A divinely inspired plan was conceived to counteract this state of imbalance, to be put into place at this crucial time. Over a preordained period, four distinct, devastating conflicts among societies throughout history will be confronted—one at a time—so as to heal suffering at the core, bringing about a state of wellness and balance. The prophetic elders knew they must protect this knowledge, for there would always be those who would seek to maintain control of the power. The elders' descendants became protectors of this ancient wisdom tradition—sometimes knowingly, sometimes not—with their lives intrinsically entwined in guardianship of the sacred prophecy.

The painful disparities of the past and present must be exhumed to be honored and healed. Accountability will be imperative once a shift toward stability is initiated. The fate of All rests with a universal awakening..."

Translation of Choctaw tribal shaman proclamation; Bayou-Lacombe, LA; Circa 1878

PROLOGUE

Giselle never forgot the day she fled Louisiana.

It began as a fairly normal day, with the morning sun peeking through yellow gingham curtains framing the window above her bed. They were a recent gift from her mother, who had sewn them by hand as a surprise for her thirteenth birthday.

"Giselle, I'm going out for a little while," Yvette announced from the hallway. "There's food in the kitchen. I'll be back as soon as I can."

Her mom was already gone by the time Giselle woke enough to reply. She didn't know where her mother was going or what was happening, but could sense something was very wrong. Yvette had always been cheerful and affectionate but lately was withdrawn.

Reluctantly, Giselle got out of bed and quickly dressed. Once again, it was left to her to take care of her little brother. She hoped eight-year-old Francois hadn't felt the tension surrounding them lately.

She was worried about her father rarely being home; even more alarming was her mother's physical condition. Yvette seemed to worsen by the minute, with dark circles under her blue eyes, blending with an increasingly gray complexion.

Throughout the day Giselle did her best to entertain Francois and distract herself at the same time. They were in the middle of a card game when Yvette burst through the front door in a frenzy, panting as she ran to her bedroom and locked the door.

Francois looked at his big sister, silently pleading for answers. Giselle had no answers but knew better than to ask. Although mother and daughter were normally close, Yvette had grown secretive and moody in the last few days.

The two children sat motionless, afraid to breathe. It wasn't long before the bedroom door was flung open, revealing a wildly disheveled Yvette, clearly terrified, with eyes darting in all directions looking for threats only she could see.

"Mama, please tell me what's wrong!"

Giselle ran over and Yvette clutched her hands in desperation, as if the girl could somehow save her from madness.

"We must leave now, child! There's no time to lose!"

Giselle looked into her mother's frightened eyes. "What are you saying, Mama? Why do we have to leave—what about Daddy?"

"There's no time, Giselle. We have to leave now. Pack a few things for yourself, and I'll take care of the rest."

Giselle went to Francois, huddled in a far corner, his little body shaking. She wanted to scoop him up in her arms and comfort him, shielding them both from what was happening, but knew she must do as she was told. Yvette needed her now more than ever.

The children followed close behind as their mother led them through the thick vegetation of the swamp, stopping only to catch their breath.

The evening shadows had just begun their dance with the waning sun when Yvette paused at the base of an ancient oak tree. Giselle and Francois watched curiously as Yvette reached into the hollow of the trunk. Her back was to the children, but Giselle saw her carefully place something large and square into a cloth bag.

Yvette motioned for them to once again follow her through the winding paths among the trees. Eyes fixed straight ahead, she was lost in her own world, oblivious to the growing distress of her children.

Giselle carried Francois several times and did her best to soothe his cries. They continued this way through the endless darkness for many hours until they reached Morgan City.

They went directly to the railroad station where the children collapsed onto a wooden bench, and Yvette proceeded to buy tickets to take them away from the only home they had ever known.

The memory of their flight from the bayou was still vivid in Giselle's mind and continued to evoke intense feelings within her, now seventy years later.

Sitting at her kitchen table, gaze fixed on a spellbound moth dancing around the ceiling light, Giselle knew time was running out.

Melody must be told the truth; an explosive chain of events was about to unfold around her granddaughter. She deeply regretted the decision to harbor such a secret her entire life.

Is there anyone in this world without regret when death is near?

This question hovered in her mind all afternoon. Giselle dreaded the effect her passing would have on her beloved Melody, already too familiar with grief and loss. Even more she dreaded the impact of the revelations which lay ahead. The world as Melody knew it would soon crumble. Not being able to shelter the child weighed heavily on Giselle.

At least I was born into this clandestine world; Melody will now be thrust into it with no warning, no preparation.

It was no surprise that her granddaughter had been chosen to fulfill the prophecy. Melody had an inner strength, with a core of integrity and sound judgment. Over the years Giselle had also observed Melody's intuitive abilities. Her granddaughter scoffed at the idea of having intuition, but Giselle knew otherwise.

It was troubling that Melody repressed so much of herself, but her grandmother understood why she kept the world at a distance.

You can't do that much longer, child. The walls are coming down; the veil exists and is growing more transparent with every breath.

Giselle had waited years for the dream—a message—and it came to her three nights ago. The prophecy was clear, and

Melody was the next link in this chain. Giselle was charged with revealing this legacy to her granddaughter but had no idea where to begin.

It suddenly dawned on her how to open this door. *Of course! It was the only way.*

Upon her death, Melody would receive a letter instructing her to go where it had all started for their family. This is where she would be guided to discover the ancient web of mystery at the heart of the legacy.

Giselle knew that, Annie, her own daughter, wouldn't support Melody during the trials to come. But Melody would be fine; she was accustomed to her mother being emotionally absent.

Her granddaughter would stay busy in the weeks after her death, attending to all the details without outwardly questioning anything. She would do so out of love and respect, but also to keep the pain at bay.

There was no alternative.

She removed a colorful pouch from the pocket of her housecoat and withdrew an unusual, exquisite string of rosary beads. As she clutched the rosary to her heart, the pale, bony fingers of her right hand closed around the pen. She again looked up at the delicate moth, fervently praying Melody wouldn't have to be sacrificed to the light.

"Please God, protect Melody and guide her on this path. Help her stay open...help guide her to the truth."

Giselle began to write, knowing her granddaughter's life was soon to be changed forever.

CHAPTER ONE

Although she arrived at the hotel only hours earlier, Melody Bennet awoke at daybreak and walked to the rain-spattered window, gazing at the courtyard several floors below. Having never been to New Orleans, this image was as she had always imagined: a decorative wrought iron balcony overlooking an elegant Victorian garden, with a verdigris-encrusted gargoyle fountain in the center.

She was especially enamored of the exposed brick walls in her room which conveyed an earthiness that was sensuous, tactile. She assumed they were part of the original structure and must have absorbed centuries of sounds, smells and emotions of New Orleans.

Melody now found it curious that her grandmother rarely spoke of this area, given her final request to return here.

Grandmama's letter surprised everyone. They were certain Giselle would have chosen to be buried beside her late husband, who died two years earlier. To everyone's dismay Giselle instead left instructions for her granddaughter to take her ashes to the Louisiana bayou, where they could be scattered and blessed by a mysterious woman by the name of Marie Devereux.

Melody walked briskly to the elevator, eyes still burning from lack of sleep, and jumped when the elevator door opened.

Her fatigue was reason enough for the nervousness, not to mention the task at hand. It also troubled her that there would be no resting place where she could visit her grandmother once the ashes were scattered.

She was too tired to be overly self-conscious about appearance but tried to smooth out the wrinkles in her khaki pants and white cotton shirt before reaching the lobby.

As the doors opened, she cleared her throat rather abruptly, stifling the deep emotion lurking just beneath the surface.

At the reception area an attractive young woman bearing the name tag "Olivia" was talking on the phone. She appeared to be in her mid-twenties, a few years younger than Melody, and was rather stunning with cognac eyes and sleek ash-brown hair. Melody wasn't sure what Creole meant, but that word popped into her mind to describe the mildly exotic look.

Melody often wished she had such striking looks. Her own brown hair seemed drab compared to Olivia's. Her eyes were the only feature she wouldn't call drab: normally hazel-green, they became a vivid emerald shade when she cried.

She caught herself staring at Olivia and quickly turned around to survey the lobby.

Located on the fringe of the historic French Quarter, she was lucky to have gotten a reservation on such short notice. It was close to tourist spots yet not directly in their midst. She hoped to at least get a taste of "The City That Care Forgot" while here, in memory of Grandmama Giselle.

It had been remodeled extensively since Hurricane Katrina, but maintained an air of antiquity. Rumored to be one of the few truly haunted spots in New Orleans, its previous incarnations were quite diverse. Throughout much of the 1800s, the hotel was home to an enigmatic order of African-Caribbean nuns. The attached smaller building, now the hotel's restaurant, had been a well-known brothel. *What a contrast! The tales these old brick walls could tell.*

She heard the phone call come to an end and returned to the front desk.

As she approached she saw a peculiar movement behind Olivia. It was another person, but not really…more like a faint holographic image of the young girl, with different hair and clothes.

No, not again. Melody closed her eyes and held her breath, knowing exhaustion must be playing tricks on her.

When she opened her eyes again the ghostly apparition was gone. The only person she saw was Olivia, smiling and waiting patiently.

"May I help you, Miss?"

"Yes, please," Melody answered.

"I need to schedule a swamp tour. To be more specific, I need to find someone who will take me to a particular point in the swamp."

"Do you have the name?"

"Yes, my grandmother was originally from that area and it's called the Atcha...um..."

"The Atchafalaya Basin?"

"Yes! I'm sorry. I knew I would destroy that name."

"No problem," Olivia said. "Do you have the name of the specific bayou? There are thousands in Southern Louisiana, though most tours are of the Atchafalaya Basin."

"This is my first time in Louisiana. My grandmother left a map but it means absolutely nothing to me. I saw something labeled 'Bear Bayou,' but I couldn't find a thing online." Melody laid the hand-drawn map on the counter. "Maybe someone who lives in the area would know where it is, if I showed them this map?"

"Here it's most frequently called 'Bayou des Ourses,' the French name." Olivia said. "That's why you couldn't find anything online. Let me make a few phone calls, and I'll see if I can find a local guide willing to take you. Most of them know the bayous like the backs of their hands. It may take a few hours to find someone."

"That's fine, I appreciate your help."

"Why don't you explore our fine city and come back to see me in a while? I'll be on duty until three this afternoon. I should know something by then."

"Sounds great. By the way, I'm also supposed to get in touch with my grandmother's friend, a lady by the name of Marie

Devereux. I believe she lives somewhere near the bayou as well. I tried to see if she had a number in the local directory but couldn't find her."

"She may not have a phone." Olivia explained. "A lot of the older folks, especially the ones living in the bayou, don't believe in telephones. It may be a real challenge to find her but hopefully the guide can help you with that as well."

"Okay, I'll check back in a couple of hours. Thanks for your help".

Melody had traveled quite a bit throughout the States, but nothing prepared her for New Orleans. Like most Americans, she was familiar with the city's image: Bourbon Street, Mardi Gras, voodoo dolls, jazz, delicious food, coffee.

She was also painfully aware of the images of destruction brought to this region by Hurricane Katrina.

Stepping out of the lobby was jarring to the senses. The air was palpably heavy and moist after the steady overnight rain, with steam rising from the street and sidewalk. She was glad she put her hair up this morning.

It wasn't only the change in climate; there was an entirely different energy here than anywhere she had been.

No particular plan or destination in mind, she headed east, breathing in the aromas pouring forth from the French Quarter.

Summer is the traditional off-season, so she was surprised by the number of people out and about. There seemed to be a mix of residents and visitors, one easily distinguished from the other.

She turned north, away from the intersection of Bourbon and Orleans—away from The Quarter—onto another busy street lined with stores and cafés. Some seemed untouched post-Katrina while others were still in the process of mending their wounds.

It amazed her that, despite its bruises and daily reminders of buildings scarred by flood, the vibrant spirit of the city lived on.

People were everywhere, some working to rebuild the city's charming smile, while others were embracing the role of tourist.

Moist air captured the aromatic cloud of coffee and beignets. Suddenly famished, she found a table at the nearest outdoor café and ordered two large croissants with preserves and coffee; she then sat back in the patio chair to take in the scene.

Across the street, an older black gentleman leaned against a wall, playing his harmonica as though he hadn't a care in the world. White hair stood out starkly from the deep coffee color of his skin, and long, graceful fingers closed gently around the harmonica. She noted a red scarf threaded through the belt buckles of his white slacks, matching a single red carnation stylishly tucked in the pocket of his black shirt.

The tune had a melancholy, yearning tone, and his eyes remained closed as he poured his heart into the song. A small dish was on the ground at his feet for those who were inclined to leave a token of appreciation. Occasionally he would stop playing for a moment to smile at a passerby, tipping his invisible hat.

After paying, Melody walked across the street, where she bent down and placed a dollar in the small dish.

"Thanks, little lady." His extraordinary smile radiated from the heart. She smiled in return but her eyes were drawn to the opening in his shirt, where a strange pendant glimmered in the hazy sunshine.

Melody walked on, allowing the city's ambience to envelop her every step.

A small jazz band strolled by, followed by a group of rowdy tourists celebrating life. There was something magical about this place, something which challenged visitors to find the joy in each moment.

For the first time Melody wondered why her great-grandmother fled Louisiana with her children. Granted, she hadn't been to the swamp—and no doubt it was vastly different from

New Orleans—but to grow up so close to this amazing place and then leave so abruptly?

She regretted not knowing more of her family history, and had a feeling anything truly of interest would be buried with Grandmama, forever protected by the swamp.

Melody glanced at her watch. Almost two-thirty. She had to hurry back to the hotel before Olivia went off duty.

"Good news, Ms. Bennet! A shuttle will take you to the edge of Atchafalaya Basin tomorrow morning at five. A man named Jean Pierre will take you where you need to go. If you don't see him when you get off the shuttle, walk to the local emporium. It's run by a gentleman — his name is Paul. He'll know where to find this Jean Pierre. He may even know where to find your grand-mother's friend."

Melody wasn't sure how to spend the rest of the afternoon but knew she had to stay busy. She sifted through the brochures on local attractions displayed neatly in the lobby and left the hotel again.

This walking tour took her past streets with such wonderful, New Orleans-esque names as Bienville, Toulouse, Dauphine, and Saint This-That-and-The-Other streets. Melody hadn't realized there was such a strong Catholic influence.

As the afternoon wore on the streets became more congested and the noise level increased. Performers and street vendors filled the sidewalks as café staff generated an orchestra of clinking sounds as they set the outdoor tables for dinner.

The smells in the air had also changed. Now mixed with the scent of coffee, there were deeper aromas of spices and seafood. An increasingly sumptuous mélange of stimuli bombarded her as the afternoon progressed.

Melody found the corner where the harmonica man had been playing but was disappointed when she didn't see him there.

She walked on, taking in the city and wondering if Grandmama Giselle had spent similar afternoons here when she was young.

After awhile, strolling through the French Quarter began to wear on Melody. She wasn't used to such a constant festive atmosphere and needed to take it in small doses.

As she approached Rampart Street the crowd seemed to thin. The atmosphere was noticeably different: quiet, subdued, with only a few people gathered at shop windows, peering inside. These buildings showed the true impact of Katrina; some had considerable damage, with flood lines above Melody's head. There were more and more abandoned shops as she continued into this remote section. She remembered reading how the flood levels varied throughout the city, with the center of the French Quarter—and center of the tourist economy—being the least affected. She was now seeing one of the areas not so blessed.

Many residents had been permanently relocated to other parts of the country, voluntarily or out of necessity.

The "Katrina Diaspora" was a label some had given the mass exodus. Some of those displaced after the storm understandably opted to rebuild their lives on higher ground; the stories of others who still longed to return home but had no way of doing so broke Melody's heart.

She continued her exploration, most appreciative of the shade and breezeway effect of the alley. Some of the shops that were open looked dark inside, their small windows allowing very little light to enter. She observed two women with colorful headdresses exiting one of the storefronts. Their clothing called to mind African garb, the bright colors standing in contrast to the dark tone of their skin. Melody recognized the store name as one of the voodoo shops she had seen listed in the hotel directory, located near the Voodoo Spiritual Temple.

Once inside her eyes immediately fell on a wall plaque that piqued her curiosity. "Magick to all who enter here." She was attracted to a small table adorned with a black statue, shells, and a small cup of what appeared to be espresso on a saucer with several packets of sugar beside it.

A young woman with mocha skin and eyes of smoldering tar approached. She wore a yellow dress draped off one shoulder, her head wrapped in a silk yellow scarf from which jet black wisps of curly hair escaped. Melody was drawn to her gold necklace: a pierced heart enclosed in a five-pointed star.

"Hello, I'm Stephanie, and that's Anastasia," the woman said, gesturing toward the statue. "She helps with divination."

Bending over to smell the contents of the cup, Melody's mouth watered, confirming it was indeed coffee. "What are the coffee and sugar for?"

"Legend has it that Anastasia was a slave who loved sweet coffee—she couldn't stand the bitterness of black coffee. She could read people's destinies, but sugar was always denied to her in life. Now fortunetellers call on her spirit to help them in their readings. To thank her, they bring offerings of sugar and coffee."

"What kind of shells are these?" Melody asked.

"They are cowrie shells. Used for prosperity and love roots — what you may call spells."

"Really?" Melody cringed inwardly at the idea of "spells"; she didn't understand the "roots" comment but left that alone as well.

"Yes. Do you see the shape of the shell? It resembles a woman's sexual center, so it is linked to creation, since a woman gives birth and creates new life. In love spells, it is used to attract the man you want."

"People still perform spells?" Melody quickly added, "No offense, I'm just so unfamiliar with all of this."

"Yes, many people still work roots – or tricks as some call them", the girl replied with a gentle, knowing smile. "And they are quite effective, unless your belief system denies it altogether and neutralizes the effect of the spell."

"Well, I don't have a man in my life and don't see one on the horizon," Melody said.

"You might have one soon. Would you like a reading?"

"A reading? You mean with cards?"

The young woman nodded and smiled. "Yes, tarot cards. We can also cast the shells."

"Cast the shells?"

"It's an ancient method of divination, the Oracle of Ifa. It is said to have originated in Africa—Benin, West Africa to be precise. Originally people would cast coconut shells but today many cast cowrie shells. Your answer lies in the way they fall, open or closed."

Seeing she had Melody's attention, she continued.

"Voodoo legend teaches that a marvelous human was very aligned with the Creator's energy. Upon his death, he was elevated as an Orisha, and—"

"I'm sorry, a what?"

"An Orisha. A god or goddess. If you are familiar with the Catholic faith, perhaps you can compare Orishas to the saints."

"Okay, that I understand. I attended Catholic school."

She enjoyed listening to this woman and felt an odd sense of curiosity she normally wouldn't indulge beyond the limits of her computer.

"With this new Orisha status, he gradually lost the very quality which had first elevated him. His ego side took over, and he became arrogant and uncharitable. He focused on becoming the highest Orisha. Nothing mattered to him more than his individual position. One night Olodumare, the Creator, appeared to him as a beggar, and the Orisha slammed the door in his face. Immediately, he was trapped inside a coconut and condemned to answer questions for eternity. He would be—how would you say?—the spokesperson for the other Orishas."

Melody nodded, understanding the basics.

"The coconut pieces have to be broken into specific sizes, and it requires quite a bit of skill to do that. Coconuts aren't plentiful here as they are in Africa, so most of us use cowrie shells instead. Would you like a reading?"

Deciding this was certainly a distraction from the reality at hand and a way to pass time, Melody agreed. "Why not?"

She followed Stephanie into a smaller room, separated from the larger one by a curtain of multi-colored beads. Dozens of candles provided the only light. Inside, she was greeted by the strong smell of incense. A heavyset, older black woman sat against the back wall, clad in hues of orange and gold. Around the woman's neck was a gold chain, on which hung a charm of a snake biting its own tail and a small chamois bag.

Melody had never seen such intriguing jewelry: first the harmonica player, then Stephanie, and now the fortuneteller.

"Sit down, child," the older woman said with an unmistakable Caribbean accent.

Melody sat at a small table covered with a purple cloth on top of which sat a deck of large cards. Placed around the room were several religious icons Melody recognized from her years in Catholic school. A large statue of Saint Michael stood near the door, surrounded by fruit, cigars, and toys. At his feet sat a large red candle and four bananas, plus another saucer filled with an orange oily substance.

"What would you like to know?"

"I....I don't really know. Can you just give me a general reading?"

As Melody met the woman's gaze, she saw something unsettling lurking in her eyes.

"As you wish, child. Are you sure you have no specific questions? Your heart is very heavy."

Melody was surprised; she didn't think her pain was visible. "I'm here to scatter my grandmother's ashes...we were extremely close."

The old woman said nothing. She shuffled the cards and

handed them to Melody. After instructing her to shuffle them seven times, she then closed her eyes, hands resting on the edges of the purple cloth, palms upward. Melody shuffled the cards in silence.

After a few moments, the woman opened her eyes, took the cards from Melody's hand, and laid them on the center of the cloth.

"Cut the deck for me," she said, lightly touching Melody's hand, "then hand me eleven of them, one at a time."

Melody watched intently as the old woman laid out the first three cards, left to right, and the other eight in groups of two, arranged at the cardinal points—North, East, South and West—around the group of three. She paused and looked at the three central cards, then raised her head to meet Melody's gaze.

"You say your grandmother died and I see this is so. Here's the Death card in your recent past." She pointed to a card showing a skeleton, clad in black and carrying a scythe. "But look at these two other cards. The three of diamonds, which represents a gift, is beside the Death card." She paused. "Your grandmother left you a gift, a legacy."

"A gift? I don't think so. Her will mentioned nothing unusual, other than the burial instructions."

"Any family left down this way?"

Melody shook her head. "I don't know much of anything right now. I don't know where she came from or where her family is."

"You must find them, child. They have something or know something. But I urge you to beware. The next card, representing the future, is the Tower. This forewarns of a breakdown of something, usually beliefs or values. Whatever system your life is built on will crumble like ashes once you receive this legacy."

Melody laughed nervously. "Simply being here having a reading is a breakdown of my belief system. What about the other cards?"

"They are the circumstances which allow the other cards to manifest, the wheel of choice which enables their existence. The two in the North represent your life now, in relation to the legacy. Let's see, we have the seven of swords and the eight of staves. These cards talk of deception—hidden, dangerous things from long ago—and a trip to escape darkness."

"My great-grandmother fled Louisiana ages ago with her two young children, but no one knows why. Grandmama never discussed it."

Nodding but never looking up, the old woman continued. "Let's look at the cards in the South. They represent the motivating hidden factors, the passions beneath the blanket of morals. We have the nine and the king of spades. Your great-grandmother was running from a man...someone she was close to. She was afraid. She knew she had to make a decision but also knew there was pain with either choice. The nine of swords involves a decision of life and death."

"The man could have been my great-grandfather. As far as I know she never saw her father again, and her brother moved back here as a young man; I don't know if she ever heard from him. Every time I asked about her family, she'd always change the subject.

The woman again nodded, eyes still fixed on the cards.

"Inheriting this legacy will create conflict. It will bring much out of the shadows, into the light. You must be strong. You *are* strong, Melody. Your grandmother wouldn't have left you such a gift otherwise."

Melody tensed, certain she hadn't given her name.

"How do you know my name?"

"You told me your name, child, when you came in."

Melody thought back to the moment when she walked into the room. She remembered thinking it odd that they *hadn't* exchanged names when they met.

The woman continued. "The three of swords in the West

speaks of something that must be released. It has been locked away too long and has become poisonous, like an abscess. It needs to be opened and released, so the wound can heal. In the East, for things to come, you have the nine and the ten of cups. The nine represents a reunion, a communion of sorts; the true fusion after the veil has been lifted. The ten represents bliss of the heart, love and prosperity, true connection. Please, get another card out for me and lay it on top of the group of three."

Melody drew another card with shaky hands. She saw a card with a snake biting its own tail—*like the necklace!*—creating an egg shape. A man and woman were in the middle of the egg, naked, holding hands.

The woman looked up and smiled, her eyes softening. "You have the world, child. This is the card that wraps the whole reading and talks of the final outcome. Your grandmother left you a very powerful gift indeed—powerful enough to shake the foundation of what people believe. Its unfolding will cause conflict and strife, but it will give you something very potent: a key to a hidden door with the potential to change the world as you know it, as well as your role within it."

"What kind of gift can that be?"

"Probably something very different from what you expect. True gifts cannot be touched and have no price, but they are real. You cannot hold air, but you would die without it. Remember, you already have a gift: the gift of sight. You know this, your grandmother knew it...there's no need to be afraid."

The old woman sat back, hands folded on her lap, signaling the end of the reading.

Melody reached for her purse, not wanting to make eye contact nor acknowledge what was just said. As she stood, the woman reached across the table.

"Wait, take this gris-gris bag." She handed Melody a small key charm and little bag of dried herbs. "The key is the symbol of Elegba—Saint Michael. He'll lead you to the inner doors you must open to reach your truth."

Melody had always resonated with Saint Michael, The Warrior of Heaven.

"What should I do with this?" Melody asked, holding up the bag.

"When you feel confused or scared, pour a pinch in a warm bath, lie in it, and recite the Twenty-Third Psalm. Do you know it?"

Melody nodded.

"Good. Recite it four times, or in increments of four. Use prayer beads to help keep track, as the vibration of the repetition is vital. It will give you clarity and strength."

"Thank you...thank you very much." Melody awkwardly bowed her head and walked through the curtain of beads, back into the main room of the store.

"Can I help you with anything else?" Stephanie asked from behind the counter.

"Yes, I have a question: Is there a special meaning to the word magick, spelled with a 'k'?"

"Ah, yes. Magic is what we think of as stage illusion, while magick is spiritual manifestation based on the power of intention and prayer, often combined with sacred rituals."

Slightly embarrassed, Melody continued, "What kind of offerings does Saint Michael prefer? You know, like you were telling me about the slave, Anastasia."

"He likes red and black candles, strong liquor, cigars, fruit and toys. One of his manifestations is that of a child, so it is customary to offer him small toys. He also loves coconut. His offerings are usually left at a four-way crossroad, on a Monday."

Melody smiled, not comprehending what the girl meant by "one of his manifestations." She had many questions but instead simply thanked the girl, paid for the reading, and walked back into the street.

The waning sunshine breaking through the clouds felt good on her skin. The events of the past hour had left her disconcerted. On one hand she felt she should forget everything the old woman said; on the other, she had the strange feeling her grandmother wanted her to pay attention. What kind of powerful legacy could Grandmama have left her?

As she headed back toward the French Quarter, she longed to feel the same carefree abandon of those around her. She didn't want to think of legacies and secrets, guilt and death; she wanted to listen to music and have a glass of wine, and know that no one knew her name unless she told them.

After walking a few blocks she chose another small sidewalk café, sat in the corner under an awning, and tried to blend with the underlying beat of the city. After placing her order, she looked through the literature she brought along. One brochure was quite helpful, as it clarified a few common misconceptions: the difference between Creole and Cajun; the difference between a swamp and a bayou; the tourist industry version of voodoo versus the sacred religion.

She was fascinated by the history of this area.

After finishing the crawfish quesadilla and glass of wine, she headed back to the hotel. By the time she returned to her room, Melody was physically and mentally exhausted.

That night, her dreams were confusing and frightening. In one of them, Grandmama Giselle was smiling at her, though Melody could sense her sadness.

"I'm sorry, Melody. It's up to you now. Always remember that even when you doubt yourself, I shall always believe in you. Draw strength from that."

In the dream, Grandmama's face slowly faded, turning to dust which blew away in a violent wind.

CHAPTER TWO

It was four forty-five Thursday morning when Melody walked out of the hotel lobby to catch the shuttle to the Atchafalaya Basin. Instead of bringing her purse, she put her belongings in a backpack, along with the ashes.

She tried to be prepared but didn't know what one wears, or takes, to the swamp. She went with capri pants and sneakers, and layered with a tank top and shirt. Her hair would remain pulled back in a ponytail throughout this trip.

She didn't feel up to the task of finding this Devereux woman. Since arriving in Louisiana, she felt so odd, as though everything was happening in slow motion: landing in the wee hours of the morning, the hallucination in the lobby, the card reading. She seemed to be moving through a fog.

Part of this oddness was a sense of liberation that she couldn't quite explain, given her reason for being here.

The shuttle was nowhere in sight, so Melody sat on a small bench in front of the hotel to wait. She craved a cup of coffee but didn't want to risk missing the shuttle.

It was comforting that the city was still awake and she wasn't alone at this hour. *Does this place ever sleep?* Picking up the delicious scent of beignets and roasted coffee, her mouth watered instantly. One could tell time here by the different smells permeating the air throughout the day.

A passenger van pulled up in front of the hotel. A young black man stepped out and looked her way. He looked sleepy but offered a contagious smile when he spotted Melody sitting on the bench.

Tucking his shirt into black slacks, he asked "You Ms. Bennet?"

"That's me."

"Any luggage?"

"No, just the backpack."

"Mind if I get coffee while y'get settled?"

"Not at all. Would you be so kind as to get me a cup, too?"

"My pleasure, ma'am. Regular?"

"Yes, please." She didn't want to put him out further by asking for cream and sugar. She turned to get money from her backpack but he had already darted across the street.

In a matter of minutes he returned, and Melody couldn't wait to take her first sip, even if she had to take it black. Much to her delight, it had sugar and cream—the perfect amount of each! She then remembered reading that "regular" down here meant with sugar and cream, not black as she was used to.

Melody flashed back to the statue of Anastasia at the voodoo shop and smiled, feeling a connection through their mutual dislike of bitter coffee.

They left immediately, just the two of them; after a few minutes driving silently, the driver spoke.

"Ever been to the bayou before? Pretty impressive it is to see snakes and gators, but the bugs take all the fun out of it for me."

"Unfortunately, this isn't a pleasure trip. I'm going to scatter my grandmother's ashes."

The driver lifted the visor of his cap and looked at her through the rearview mirror.

"Pardon me?"

"My grandmother was from the bayou." Melody couldn't recall if "bayou" or "swamp" was the correct word. "But she lived most of her life in North Carolina."

"That where you're from?"

"Yes. Lived there my whole life," Melody answered. "I'm just here to honor her last wish."

"My, my. That's nice what you doin'. Most people these days, they don't honor their old folks no more. My grandfather raised me and taught me how important it is."

"Me, too. Grandmama practically raised me and taught me

17

the same thing. Respect your elders, both alive and in spirit..."

Melody broke the lingering silence.

"What is your name?"

"James. I was raised in the bayou but moved to the city when I was twenty 'cause I got tired of fishin'."

Melody laughed. "I also have to find a lady my grandmother mentioned in her letter. They were friends, I think. The instructions say to find this lady before releasing the ashes."

James looked at her again through the mirror.

"What's this lady's name?"

"Marie Devereux. I have an address for her but don't know if it's current."

"Probably is. Folks never move 'round there. Don't know her, though. It's a generation or two before me. Ole Man Paul probably know her.

"Is he the owner of the emporium?"

"That him. Ain't nobody Ole Man Paul don't know."

"I'll check with him. Thanks, James."

Melody relaxed against the seat. Outside, the city was disappearing as the sun began to rise, casting a buttercup glow through the back window of the van. The further they got out of town, the fewer cars and trucks they encountered. She rested her eyes for only a moment, tuning in to the drone of the motor; in few minutes, she was asleep.

Much to her surprise, she woke as James was pulling up to an old country store.

"Here's Ole Man Paul's shack. I'll wait here while you find who you lookin' for."

Melody got out of the van and looked around. The store was a weathered wood shack sitting on pillars. The left side was heavily damaged, and a thick blue tarp still covered part of the roof. She had followed the newscasts about Hurricane Katrina which mainly covered New Orleans and coastal Mississippi, but

18

she now wondered how people here were affected, away from the reporters and relief workers.

Melody saw three small boats in the water and wondered if one of them belonged to the man Olivia contacted on her behalf.

Two men exited the small store, chatting away. One was young, wearing a baseball cap over unkempt blond hair and had a wad of chew in his left cheek. The second man was older, his bellying tested the strength of both his jeans and shirt.

They saw Melody standing by the van looking rather lost, so they ambled over her way.

"If you're waiting for a tour, they don't start 'til eight-thirty," the older man informed her.

"I'm looking for Jean Pierre. I believe this is where I'm supposed to meet him."

"He should be in soon to bring in last night's catch. Go on inside to wait and get yourself a cold drink."

"Thanks, I'll do that."

She pulled her backpack out of the van and tipped James generously.

"Thanks for everything, James. Have a safe trip back."

"Thank *you*, Ms. Bennet. Hope y'find your granny's friend. Just call the hotel when y'wanna be picked up."

As she walked into the store, a small bell attached to the door handle announced her entrance. A large, burly man was watching her from behind the counter. His bushy gray beard, laced with traces of red, covered most of his ruddy face; the rest was shadowed by the visor of his fishing hat.

Melody removed her sunglasses and glanced around. The store had a little bit of everything, from groceries to hardware to over-the-counter medications.

"Can I help you?" The man's voice was deep, almost guttural.

"Yes, please. You're Mr. Paul, right?"

The man didn't respond other than eyeing her suspiciously.

"I'm looking for a man named Jean Pierre. I was told I could find him here."

"What you want with him? You a police officer or somethin'?" He crossed his arms in front of his chest defiantly and stood there, challenging an answer.

"No! Heavens, no! The receptionist from my hotel in New Orleans called yesterday, looking for someone who would take me into the bayou, to a certain spot. I was supposed to meet him here to show him a map."

The old man relaxed his arms but still looked wary.

"He should be in shortly. You can sit over there and wait for him." He pointed to an old chair in the corner, next to a huge jar of pickled eggs.

"Thank you. I'm also looking for an old woman who is supposed to live in this area. Marie Devereux. I have an address but don't know if it's current. Do you know anyone by that name around here?"

"Maman Marie? She don't come 'round that much no more, but she don't live far from here."

"Would you know how I can get in touch with her? It's very important that I talk to her before..."

"She don't do tricks no more. At least not for other people."

"Excuse me?" Melody was confused, then remembered "roots" or "tricks" are like spells.

"Ain't it what you're looking her up for?"

"No, my grandmother just passed away and wanted her ashes brought back here, where she was born. She wanted me to find this Maman Marie first."

The old man relaxed for the first time.

"Who's your grandmother?"

"Giselle Baton."

"Giselle Baton? Wasn't she the young girl who left with her mother and brother in a hurry a long time ago?"

"I don't know much about it, but that sounds about right."

"I was just a young'un then. Her father had a lot of men

searchin' for them, but they vanished without a trace. People said her mother had a lover, a rich man in N'Orleans, and ran off with him."

"That's not true. Well, I don't think it was; I think something scared her away. From what I understand, they didn't stay in New Orleans. They moved away."

"Scared her away? What scared her?"

"I don't know, but it seems to me a mother of two wouldn't have just run away back then—not without a good reason."

"You got a point there, young lady. Tell you what. Forget Jean Pierre. I close shop at lunchtime. I'll take you to see Maman— don't mind seeing that ole devil myself. Ain't seen her in a while."

His voice softened and became almost melancholic. "I'll take you myself to scatter Giselle's ashes. A beauty, she was. All the boys 'round here had a crush, but she never gave nobody a chance."

Maybe he wasn't as tough as he tried to appear. A lot of people like him resented outsiders and were afraid of anything spoiling their corner of paradise. Even Charlie, her grand-parents' farmhand, was like that.

"Thank you very much. I'd appreciate that."

"I bet one of them ole boys out there wouldn't mind takin' you for a little boat ride while you wait."

Melody followed his gaze and saw the two men she talked to when she first arrived. Both were bent over one of the boats, tending to a net.

Paul stepped out from behind the counter, and Melody realized what a giant of a man he really was. At five-six she felt like a child next to him.

Melody trailed behind as he went to speak to the two men, not wanting to intrude. The older of the two fishermen again spoke first.

"So your grandmother was from 'round here, was she?"

"Yes, sir. I don't know exactly where from, but I know she lived in this area until she was around thirteen."

"Yeah, I heard the story from my pop. Strange thing though."

"Strange? What do you mean?" Melody asked.

"I always heard—"

Old Paul interrupted. "Don't you listen to him, child. He don't know what he's sayin'...probably been drinkin' already."

The man started to protest, but Old Paul shot him another look and the words died in his mouth.

Old Paul smiled and said, "Joe here will take you to visit our swamp for awhile, 'til I close shop."

The younger man took a hesitant step forward. "The pee'row is all ready to go, ma'am. You ready?"

"As ready as I'll ever be, I guess."

The same odd, uncharacteristic sense of abandon she felt in New Orleans returned. She didn't want to think or feel; she just wanted to let one moment flow into the next with as little thought as possible.

Joe helped Melody into the boat and opened a folding seat. He wiped it off with an old cloth he kept inside a small toolbox and gestured for her to sit down. As the boat pulled away from the dock, Melody watched the two older men on the bank. They appeared to be arguing, but were already too far away for her to hear what they were saying.

Melody wondered what the older fisherman had meant when he said that something was strange. She thought back to the reading at the voodoo shop, when the fortuneteller told her she was about to uncover a secret.

As the boat glided further into the swamp, Melody noticed the vegetation had become thicker...along with the insects. Her arms already itched from several mosquito bites, and she could have kissed Joe when he handed her a bottle of bug repellent.

After a while he turned off the boat engine, and they were gently carried by the undercurrents. A symphony of nature surrounded them. Melody spotted a blue heron taking off from the water to her right, and watched her fly to the barren branch of a dead tree. As she followed the heron's movements, her eyes caught sight of a snake wrapping its coils around another branch. She didn't know if the snake was poisonous, but was glad she wasn't close enough to find out.

"Lots of wildlife around here, huh?" Melody joked in a feeble attempt to hide her anxiety.

"Yeah, you should see it at night. Snakes really come out then. Most of 'em are harmless, though. Gotta watch out for the water moccasins and white vipers—they got a mean streak in 'em. The worst thing is the skeeters. Them little vampires feast on you like frogs on flies."

Even though her arms were burning from the multiple bites, Melody was less concerned about the mosquitoes than the snakes. She liked the outdoors, taking an occasional hike by a river or lake. But snakes and swamps...well, that was a different story. She had been afraid of snakes for as long as she could remember. Perhaps her aversion came from attending Catholic school, where she was taught serpents represent the devil.

Joe restarted the engine, proceeding slowly enough that Melody could enjoy the breathtaking beauty of her surroundings. It was magnificent! They came to a point where the channel split into three directions.

He took the furthest right turn into a smaller passage canopied by tall trees and vines. It was a natural tunnel. Melody closed her eyes and silently prayed. *Please God, don't let any snakes fall on me!* As the water widened again, the canopy thinned and the boat spilled out of the tunnel to face yet another split. They veered left and came to a point where the water was shallower, with sand banks on each side. She was captivated by the sight of an alligator basking in the sunlight, which grew more intense by the minute.

Joe guided the boat easily between the banks. To Melody, it

seemed a slight mistake could be deadly; she could feel her pulse quicken at the thought of what might happen if their boat ran aground or collided with something. The instinctual fear, mixed with the rawness of the primitive setting, was intoxicating. Though terrified, she had never felt more alive.

The tour went on for a while longer, each turn unveiling a new type of perilous beauty. Melody was surprised when their next turn put them back at the emporium. She had completely lost all sense of direction and time.

She wondered if they had passed the spot where Grandmama's ashes were to be scattered. *Was there something special about that area of the swamp?* Grandmama must have been familiar with it; after all, she was thirteen when she moved and had lived her entire life here before being taken away.

Melody stepped out of the boat, accepting Joe's outstretched hand.

"How much for the tour, Joe?"

"It was a favor to Ole Man Paul, so don't you go worryin' yourself about it. It was my pleasure to show you 'round."

Melody thanked him and walked back to the shack. The clock read noon; they had been on the water longer than she thought.

By now the heat was withering. Even though the shack was not air conditioned, it was a relief to walk into a shaded area. Her clothes were soaked with sweat and embarrassingly pasted to her body. She scolded herself for not planning ahead and bringing a complete change of clothes.

Old Paul was still behind the weathered counter when Melody walked in.

"How'd you like our swamp, little lady?" he asked with a big smile.

"Very impressive, though kind of scary, too. We saw snakes, alligators and about a million other creatures. And there are so many sounds out there—it's incredible!"

Old Paul talked while moving around, readying things to

close up shop. "I agree. I lived in the city for awhile, when I was young. I'd taken a job cookin' in a fancy restaurant in N'Orleans, but after 'while had to run back here. All that city and people noise was killin' me. I'm more at peace here, life makes more sense. All them city folk think they got it all figured out. But really, they got it all wrong."

Paul excused himself for a few minutes to tend to things outside.

His words made Melody think of her childhood at the farm. She reminisced about the times spent with Grandmama. They would explore the farm when the weather was nice, and rock on the front porch when it rained, while pies baked in the oven.

It was the happiest time in her life. Her dad, Grandpa Henry and Grandmama had all been with her then.

After her father passed, she and her mother lived in fairly upper-class neighborhoods with swim clubs and tennis courts. She never had fun, though—not like the fun she had at the farm. She regretted not spending more time there as an adult; she learned so much there...she learned so much from Grandmama.

A roach scurrying across the dirty plank floor triggered another memory.

As a child, she had been terrified of beetles and roaches. Her grandfather wasn't much help in alleviating fears; on the contrary, like her Catholic school teachings, he seemed to feed them.

One day Melody saw a roach in Grandmama's kitchen while she was alone downstairs. She screamed at first, then realized the roach was desperately trying to get away from her. Thinking it was probably more scared than she was, Melody bravely knelt on the ground to get a closer look. The little creature must have sensed that she meant no harm, because it stopped as well.

It was as if they were assessing one another. Melody recalled knowing at that very moment that she and the roach weren't really all that different. Both experienced fear, a hunger to live, and a need to explore. From that day on, she was no longer afraid of roaches. That one incident empowered her, making her feel more connected to the world.

That is, until her dad died.

When Old Paul came back in, she snapped out of her reverie. Famished, she picked up a can of Vienna sausages, sitting next to fishing supplies, and brought it to the counter to pay.

Paul waved her off.

"No charge, but don't you go spoilin' your appetite. When we get out of this joint, you're gonna try some of Ole Paul's famous gumbo."

"What *is* gumbo, exactly? I've never tried it."

"Never had gumbo?! Outside folk don't know good eatin'. Gumbo is soup with all sorts of good things in it: crawdads, Boudin—"

"What's Boudin?"

"Sausage. Good gumbo's gotta have sausage. Also vegetables, chicken feet, and any other good thing you might have lyin' around."

"Chicken feet?!"

"Well, those are mostly for decoration, but they add a little somethin'. Even the small things are important, the ones you think don't matter. In the end, that's what makes the biggest difference. The things that set the fine line between ordinary and special. Sort of like people, y'know?" He winked as he cleaned up around the counter. "Each of us has a bit o' this and a bit o' that in our life recipes. There's the person who's got more salt, more pepper, and then there's the one who got hot pepper or sugar. Folks think if their recipe ain't like everybody else's, then it ain't as good. Everybody's always after what everyone else has got in their gumbo. They never think their own gumbo is quite good enough." Old Paul shook his head sadly. "If they worried less about others and tried to improve their own recipes to their own likin', they'd have a helluva gumbo. Funny animals, humans..."

Melody found Old Paul's life lesson thought-provoking. She was glad she knew how to listen, especially to older people; it was one of the many things Grandmama taught her as a child.

She nibbled on the Vienna sausages, too self-conscious to devour them as she'd like, then went to the cooler and pulled out a can of Mountain Dew. Dom Perignon in a luxury penthouse couldn't provide the pure satisfaction of a cold soda in ninety-eight-degree heat with humidity to match!

When Paul was ready to leave, Melody followed him to his boat. Joe had explained that they called their boats "pee'rows" or "pee-roges" down here. Knowing a little French, she assumed the proper spelling was "pirogue." Old Paul confirmed this and seemed impressed.

Melody thought it was funny that people moved about on boats here, and saw the bayou as a countrified version of Venice. It lacked the fancy palaces and cathedrals, but was charming and breathtaking in its own unpretentious way.

The motor purred softly and she soon found herself back in the midst of the swamp, this time with the temperature in the upper nineties. Sweat liberally rolled down her face and neck.

Old Paul didn't seem too bothered by the heat. Maybe his thick, weathered skin didn't let heat in as much.

Before long they pulled up to another shack, more like a small log cabin, supported by thick pillars which kept it above water. It had a large front porch with a small table set between two old rocking chairs.

Paul rowed to the edge of the water and tied the boat to a pole sticking out of the ground. They stepped on shore and climbed a short stairway to the porch.

Overhead, a ceiling fan whirled at maximum speed.

"I keep the fan on to shoo skeeters and flies. They ain't got a likin' for fans; they get confused by 'em."

The screen door squealed on its hinges, opening to a small living room. The furniture was sparse and simple, but altogether offered a tidy image. The kitchen was tiny but had room at the end for a table and two chairs.

Paul turned the burner on low under a large earthenware pot. "Time for you to try some gumbo."

She was still hungry—the can of Vienna sausages barely made a dent—but wanted to wash up first. There were only two more rooms in the house: Paul's bedroom and a small bathroom with barely enough room for an undersized bathtub.

To Melody's delight, Paul immediately handed her a large glass of iced tea.

All windows were open, protected by thick screens, but there wasn't a hint of a breeze. The heat from the stove rendered the kitchen unbearably hot. Between the heat and hunger, Melody felt her knees tremble. Afraid she would faint, she quickly clutched her glass of tea and took two large gulps. The cold sweet tea tasted wonderful, and after a few more sips she felt better.

"Why don't we go sit on the porch for awhile? It takes some time to get used to this weather. Hot and humid, but I wouldn't live anywhere else." He took a long drink and smacked his lips. "This here tea is the cure. You know, they say 'round here that for everything that makes you ill, there's somethin' that'll heal you from it."

Melody smiled, recalling that Grandmama Giselle had said something very similar.

"Are you familiar with the plants and herbs around here?"

"Who, me? No child, my wife knew some, but the Lord took her ten years ago. Now, Maman...*she* knows all the plants 'round here. She can make you a fixin' for anything. She's a *treateur*."

"Are you talking about Maman Marie?"

"That's her. Lived her whole life in the swamp. Always said that life outside ain't real, just an illusion. Nobody sees her much; she's a hermit. Folks used to say she did evil magic, but they went to see her just the same."

"Why do they call her Maman?"

"Marie and her sister, Louise, learned Voodoo from an ole black woman who called herself Maman Corinne." Paul leaned back in the rocker and drained the last bit of tea from his glass. "Marie was in awe of that ole woman and her way of healin'. Wanted to be strong as her."

He stood up and took Melody's empty glass. "Let me get us a refill, and I'll share a story with you."

Paul returned with two full glasses, leaned back in the chair and explained that in those days, very few people openly practiced Voodoo. It had come to this region by West African slaves who had been taken to the islands, primarily Haiti. It had also seeped into the lives of white slave owners, who left Haiti to escape the revolution in the late 1800s or so. They began to follow the same Voodoo rituals.

For centuries most white people had a strong fear of Voodoo or anything that appeared "primitive," but Louisiana Voodoo is a combination of African and Caribbean Voudou, mixed with Christianity, specifically Catholicism.

"It's been a known way of life in these parts for many, many decades now, not only in white and black folks, but the Hispanics, too, with all the *botanicas* and Spanish supermarkets sproutin' up everywhere."

He took a big gulp of tea before carrying on with his story.

"Marie started using the original African names of the gods and whatnot, probably out of respect for Maman Corinne—now *she* was a traditional high priestess, a spiritual descendant of pure African Voudou," Paul said, obviously impressed. "Before long, people 'round here began calling her Maman Marie. She's a lot like Maman Corinne: very nurturing, yet tough as nails. She was called on to help with everythin' from blessings to cures. Folks always said she was the best at drivin' away the Couchemal."

"Driving away what?" Melody asked.

"Couchemal. The spirit of babies who die before bein'

baptized. Maman used to put a drop of holy water in all standing water around the house." Paul's voice got softer. "She did that here, the night my daughter died. Birth complications, they said. Doc saved my wife but couldn't do nothin' for the baby."

Melody felt a rush of affection as she stared into his weathered face.

"I'm so sorry, Paul. Do you have any other children?"

"It's okay, child. It was a long time ago. No, Edith never could have more children after that. Her body got better but she never was herself again..." He stood and clapped his hands together. "Enough with my stories. Let's go get us some gumbo!"

Paul fixed two huge bowls of gumbo with some cornbread on the side. He also refilled their glasses and pulled two spoons out of a drawer that screeched worse than the front screen door.

They sat at the small kitchen table, enjoying the gumbo in silence. Melody thought it was one of the most heavenly foods she'd ever eaten. The intense heat of the day combined with the spicy heat of the gumbo caused beads of sweat to form on her forehead and upper lip, but she didn't slow down. It was too good.

When the bowl was left without a trace of gumbo, Melody patted her stomach with a satisfied smile

"Wow! My compliments to the chef. It was ab-so-lutely delicious."

"Thank you, child. Why don't you go sit on the porch for awhile and relax? I'll clean this up and join you."

"Please, let me at least clean up. It would make me feel better to help with something."

"Nonsense. I know where everything goes and do things my own way. Just go rest. I'll be right out."

It was hotter than ever outside, though the overhead fan brought a little relief.

The sight from the porch was hypnotizing; the water appeared motionless yet the pirogue was rocking from side to side ever so gently. Melody sat down and closed her eyes, allowing herself to completely relax, rocking in unison with the boat.

Her eyes flew open when she heard heavy steps on the staircase. An older black man in cut-off jeans and t-shirt was already at the top of the stairs walking toward her. He was tall and wiry, and his head was shaved, revealing a peculiar tattoo over his right ear.

"So, you're Giselle Baton's granddaughter."

Melody was surprised the news had spread so fast.

"Yes, I am," she said rather timidly. "Are you a friend of Paul's?"

"Actually, I'm a friend of your great-grandfather. Let's just say Giselle and I were close. Related in a way."

Even though he was smiling, there was nothing friendly about this man. Every hair on Melody's body stood on end. Her senses were suddenly sharper, the fight-or-flight instinct on high alert.

They stared at one another, both as still as the bayou.

Melody gave in first. "Is this some sort of joke?"

The heat and the man's impertinent grin were getting on her nerves.

"No joke, little lady. I never joke." There was now a hard, threatening tone to his voice. He seemed unstable, his head twitching at times as though he were listening to voices. His eyes never left Melody.

"What do you want?" Melody asked, standing quickly.

The man started to get up as well. She moved toward the door, about to yell for Paul, when the man lunged and grabbed her by the arm.

"You have something that belongs to me—to *my* family—and you're gonna give it back!" he hissed.

Melody yanked her arm away, hitting her elbow on the frame of the screen door.

"I don't know what you're talking about. I have nothing that belongs to you. Leave me alone!"

The man glared at her with unadulterated hatred.

"Your great-grandma stole something a long time ago. Something that belonged to me. I'm sure your grandma has it, and I *will* get it back. Remember me, little lady. You'll be seeing me again very soon."

He disappeared around the side of the house in a matter of seconds. Melody's heart pounded wildly and she was covered in sweat. She fell back into the rocking chair, where Paul found her a few minutes later.

"What's wrong, Melody? You're as white as a sheet, like you've seen a ghost!"

"You could say that. A man just came up here and threatened me. Said I have something of his, and that he's going to get it back."

"A man? Here?" Old Paul knelt down and took her hand into his. "I was looking out here while I was straightening up, and I didn't see nobody. You sure?"

"Yes, of course I'm sure. I dozed off and woke when I heard him coming up the steps."

Paul smiled at her like she was a child. "Well, that explains it. You dozed off. It's easy for things to seem real when you first start dreamin'."

Melody started to protest but stopped. *Could* she have dreamed the whole episode? After all, it would make more sense than what she thought had happened. The only thing she knew at that moment was that she was tired and confused. And hot.

"Maybe the heat did play a trick on me."

"Here, I brought you some more tea. Maybe you're dehydrated a bit." Melody accepted it gratefully.

"You sit a spell and drink this. We'll go see Maman whenever you're ready."

"Does she live far from here?"

"Nah, we could take the truck, but it may be cooler by water now the sun's not directly overhead. You up to it?"

"Is it all right to just barge in on her? She might take naps in the afternoon."

"It don't matter none to Marie. She's up at night with her ceremonies and sleeps in the morning. Old people don't sleep much, you know," he said with a wink.

"We can go, I'm fine. I'm dying to meet her."

"Death is one of Maman's specialties. People here say that the Angel of Death lurks near her house, especially during her rituals."

"What?!"

"Just playing with you...just playing," he chortled, amused by her shocked expression.

CHAPTER THREE

"I wonder if Grandmama ever wrote to Maman Marie. I've never heard her name before." Melody was the first to break the silence as the pirogue slid through the water.

"Likely they just knew each other from a long time ago, and Giselle wanted Marie to bless her ashes before they were scattered. Marie is a few years older than Giselle and was already a root worker before your grandmother left. She's been a full-fledged priestess now for many a year."

"What's a root worker?"

"It's someone who works magick, with herbs and spells. You'd probably call it a witch."

"A witch! Come on…you don't expect me to believe in witches now, do you?"

"You believe what you will. Voodoo and hoodoo are big here," Paul chuckled. "Why don't you tell me what you think you know about Voodoo before we get there."

Melody thought for a minute. "Well, I picture voodoo dolls. And, honestly, only black women and men—mainly women, though—putting curses on people. Seems like they're always from Haiti or some Caribbean island. I hate to admit it, but I don't know much about any of this other than what I've seen in movies. I had no idea I needed to. What on Earth is hoodoo?"

"Okay, Miss Melody. Here's lesson number one: Voodoo is a system of belief, a religion which goes *way* back to ancient times. Some say it's the world's oldest religion, started in West Africa.

"Hoodoo is the root-working part, the practical, hands-on side that deals with hexes and such. There's more Voodoo influence than people know. Black gospel churches, the ones black folks know as 'sanctified churches,' work on the same principle as Voodoo. They dance, shout and drum until the Holy Spirit makes Itself known through the minister or another faithful. Much the same as Voodoo ceremonies, where drumming and dancing summon Orishas.

"The Hispanic community is chock full of Voodoo. The families with Hispanic heritage...most of them have altars in their homes. Of course, they summon spirits in the name of the Catholic saints with novena candles. But for every candle representing a saint, they honor a matching Orisha. Check it out, child. I'm sure you have these *botanicas* and Spanish markets in North Carolina now. You'll even find candles for the Seven African Powers in these stores."

Melody was intrigued.

"So, Hispanics who claim to be Catholic are really into Voodoo?!"

"They would never admit it if you asked them—and some of the younger ones may not know the difference any longer—but yes."

He shared that in Voodoo, like most tribal wisdom, everything was passed down orally from generation to generation. With no written history, the West considered the people and their beliefs primitive.

"White people were afraid of the unknown ways of the natives in other parts of the world. As we know, it is human nature to fear what we don't understand," he said.

Melody wasn't sure if he was making a point about her—like her reaction to the word "witch"—or about people in general.

She found herself not only engrossed in what he was saying, but also impressed by his eloquence. His speech pattern became much less "good ole boy" and more that of a history professor. He was passionate and clearly knowledgeable about this subject.

He explained that, since slave trade and colonization were all about power, the African natives were systematically stripped of everything they knew: their families, their homes, even their religious beliefs and traditions. Native American Indians were subjected to the same atrocities, as were the Mayan Indians by

Spanish conquerors. Fear of the unknown—combined with greed and power—led to ridicule and disdain, then outright cruelty and contempt.

Melody noted how hurt and offended Paul sounded when describing the mockery and demonization of these customs. He said Cajuns and Louisianans suffer the same ridicule, with most outsiders having more preconceptions, misconceptions, and stereotypes in their heads than he could begin to list.

"If something is written down, people tend to believe it, even if it's been translated hundreds of times and interpreted hundreds of different ways since it was first written. Wisdom shared through telling stories, through oral tradition—passed on that way through the generations—is viewed as uneducated, backward," he said, shaking his head in disgust.

When he finished, Melody wasn't sure what to say other than "thank you." She'd always bristled when people were judgmental, especially in matters about which they knew little to nothing...and the hypocrisy that often accompanied that behavior had always frustrated her.

She had to admit it; before this conversation she had harbored some of those same "outsider" misconceptions. She sat quietly for the remainder of their journey to Maman Marie's, rather ashamed of herself.

Old Paul pulled his pirogue onto the sand bank behind Maman Marie's house. Melody was about to get off the boat when she spotted a snake near a bush.

"Watch out, Paul!" She tried to control the hysteria in her voice. "There's a snake!"

"There's always snakes 'round Marie. I bet she keeps 'em fed so they'll stay and scare off intruders. She don't like people to intrude on her."

"Isn't that what we are doing right now? Is she going to call her snakes on us?"

He burst out laughing. "No, snakes ain't pets you train. Besides, she'll be happy to see you once she knows who you are. I told you, she and Giselle were friends, back in the day."

"Paul, I know it's not polite, but I have to ask: Is Maman black or white or Hispanic or what?"

"Maman is white, Melody. That's why she's sometimes referred to as a *treateur*: a white, Cajun healer practicing Voodoo. Quite a few white people been practicing Voodoo in these parts for a long while now. But, like I already told you, Voodoo here— like everything else in Southern Louisiana—has been influenced by so much: African slaves, people from the islands, Spanish Catholicism...we've got our own Voodoo gumbo!"

"Was my grandmother involved in Voodoo?" Melody stalled again, afraid to get out of the boat.

"I don't know if Giselle worked roots. Don't think she did. But I'd bet it formed a big part of her belief system, even if she didn't practice hoodoo. Her mother...now, she used to practice."

Melody was intrigued. "My great-grandmother was a root worker?"

"Yep, Yvette learned Voodoo from Maman Corinne as well. But let's get on and not keep Maman waiting; I'm sure she's been watchin' us since we pulled up. You can learn anything and everything you want about this from her."

Melody glanced around to make sure the snake was gone. The coast seemed clear, so she scrambled out of the boat and followed Paul, making sure to stomp as she walked for fear of any "pets" extending their welcome. She'd always heard that snakes respond to vibration and scurry away.

Paul knocked loudly on the front door.

"She's a bit hard of hearing," he explained.

Melody wondered what this Maman would look like. She still couldn't picture a white Voodoo priestess, even after all the talk.

She was surprised to see a very attractive older white woman appear at the door, gazing at her curiously. She was taller than

Melody expected, standing eye-to-eye, with a piercing blue gaze. Her thick gray-white hair was perfectly coiffed, reminiscent of Grandmama.

She looked from Paul to Melody. After pausing for a moment, Maman said in an unexpectedly cultured, velvety voice, "I see Paul brought you along. He knows that I don't work roots for people any more. I'm sorry, young lady."

Paul remained silent, so Melody spoke up.

"I don't need a spell, Ma'am. My grandmother recently passed away. Giselle Baton. Do you remember her?"

Maman Marie just stood there, no change in expression.

"She left instructions for me to bring her ashes here, to the bayou, and to contact you before doing so. I thought you might know why she asked this."

For a split second Melody saw a strange flicker in the woman's eyes; as quickly is it came, it disappeared. Her face gradually softened, as though recalling fond memories from long ago. She broke into a radiant smile

"Come on in, Chère. What did you say your name was?"

"Melody, Melody Bennet. It's nice to meet you."

"The pleasure is mine, Melody. I didn't even know Giselle had a granddaughter."

"Yes, I'm her only grandchild."

"Is that a fact? Come in and sit...let's get to know one another a bit. I'd like the company."

Paul seemed surprised by the warmth of Maman's welcome.

"I'd like that very much, but I don't want to intrude."

"No intrusion. I'd love to find out what Giselle has been up to all these years."   She exchanged a glance with Paul. "If that's all right with you, Paul? I assume the young lady is your guest."

Paul put his hands in his pockets and shifted on his feet a bit.

"We just met at my store. I offered to take her to release Giselle's ashes in the swamp."

"Giselle wanted to be back here..." Maman said, more a

statement than a question. "All those years away from the swamp didn't spoil her then. You've got the ashes with you?"

"I do. I've carried them in my backpack."

"Very well. We'll bless them tonight, at sundown. It may be late before we are done; would you like to stay the night?"

Maman turned toward Paul. "Will you be staying, Paul? You are welcome to."

"Nope. None of that mess for me, Maman. I respect what you do, but what can I say? I just can't get into all that stuff."

That surprised Melody; he seemed to know so much. He actually seemed a bit afraid of the old woman. She thought it strange that such a skeptic would allow a healer to perform a ritual on his child. Maybe it had been his wife's idea and he had just gone along with it; or, maybe his views and beliefs had changed over time. Regardless, he certainly seemed to have a lot of respect for Maman.

Melody was a little spooked. Everything was happening so fast. And there was so much to understand. Being in the swamp was like being in a foreign land; and now to learn that Voodoo was part of what her grandmother requested. *Why did Grandmama keep so much from me? What did she really believe in?*

"I'm sorry. I don't really understand…and I obviously didn't come prepared. I didn't know what Grandmama wanted you to do, I just…I just knew I had to bring the ashes to you. I thought I'd be back in my hotel by late tonight."

Maman Marie smiled patiently. "It's fine. Not to worry. There is a process we must follow, a particular ritual. I'll explain as much as I can but, yes, you will be here all evening and part of the night."

Melody was uncomfortable but didn't feel she had much of a choice. This is what she came here to do. It was what her grandmother wanted.

"It will be fine. Thanks for bringing me here, Paul. Will you still take me to the place in the swamp tomorrow?"

Paul nodded. "I'll be back after lunch, then. See you both tomorrow." He turned around and added, with a mischievous grin, "Melody, have a good night and don't let Maman and her snakes spook you none."

Just the mention of snakes sent a shiver down Melody's spine. She hoped she didn't have to go outside; how could she spot them in the dark?

"I'll be all right. Grandmama wouldn't have sent me here otherwise."

"That's the attitude, Chère. That's the attitude." Maman put her arm around Melody's shoulder and led her into the living room while Paul let himself out.

Heavy black curtains blocked the sun, and a low-wattage bulb in a corner lamp was the only source of light. Two large pillar candles, one black and one white, stood prominently on a table in the center of the room, separated by a bowl of crystalline water.

The room was comfortable even without air conditioning, thanks to the drapes. The walls were mostly bare, adorned sparingly with African art. On the far wall was a sheet of parchment with a strange symbol drawn on it; on each side of the parchment were two sconces with red candles. Maman walked in ahead of Melody and sat down on a red velvet couch, in front of the table with the pillar candles. She lit both, and then turned to Melody, who sat in a matching red velvet chair facing her.

"So, Melody, tell me all about your Grandmama."

"Well, she left with her mother and brother over sixty years ago and ended up in North Carolina."

"North Carolina?"

"Yes, she met my grandfather, Henry, there when she was around twenty. They soon had my mother, Annie. They never had other children, though I'm not sure if that was by choice or not."

"Were they happy?"

"I think so. Grandpapa Henry was a bit cranky, not nearly as carefree as Grandmama, but he truly loved her. They were sweet together." Melody briefly described the farm and things she thought might be of interest to an old friend of her grandmother's. "That farm is still my favorite place. I loved my time there with Grandmama...we were very close," Melody said, her voice breaking a little.

"And what of Giselle's family here?" Maman asked.

"She rarely mentioned anything about her family or her childhood. From what I've heard over the years, her brother moved back here with his father when he was in his teens, but I don't know anything about him. I don't even know if he's still here. I think his name is Francois."

Maman nodded. "Yes, I think that's what it was. I didn't know he had moved back."

"For all I know, he may have ended up somewhere else altogether. He could have passed by now. Grandmama never spoke of him."

"Did your grandmother ever tell you why they left?"

"Not in detail. She just said they ran off in the middle of the night."

"Well, there's been a lot of talk through the years about why they ran off. This has always been a tight-knit community, more so back then. Bertrand Baton, your great-grandfather, wasn't the pick of the litter. Yvette was warned against marrying him. You know already that she was a root worker, don't you?"

Melody nodded.

"She was warned, but she didn't listen; she thought she could use magick to change him. Unfortunately, she was naive and her efforts didn't pay off. Some said she ran off with some rich businessman in New Orleans, others speculated that her husband had killed her and the children. Nobody knew for sure."

"So, you were never in contact with her or my grandmother?"

"No. I wish we were. I wondered many times through the

years what happened to Giselle, but didn't know where to find her. She came with her mother to see my older sister several times, so we became friends. My sister worked roots, too. She's back in the Spirit pool now." There was a silent pause before Maman continued. "I'm surprised Giselle still remembered me."

"She must have regarded you highly. Coming to you was an important part of her final wish."

Maman smiled tenderly. Giselle's faith in her after all these years warmed her heart.

"Does your family still own that farm in North Carolina?"

"Yes, Grandmama would never agree to sell it. I guess my mother and I will have to decide what to do with it."

"Tell me about your parents, Chère."

Melody's mood darkened as she thought of Annie, and her heart ached instantly thinking of her father. She told Maman about her father's passing many years ago and of her mother remarriage.

"I take it you're not close to your mother."

"No, not really, and I fear it's only going to get worse now that Grandmama is gone."

After her father's death, Melody did her best to take care of her mother for him. But it hadn't been easy. No matter how hard she tried, nothing was ever good enough for Annie. Grandmama did her best to offset Annie's attacks on Melody's self-esteem, but over the years Melody's doubts about herself—personally and professionally—had taken seed and quietly grown, to the point where she was unsure of who she was, what she wanted, or what she had to offer.

Melody was surprised how good it felt to share these things, especially with someone who knew her grandmother.

"When Grandmama died, my mother's anger and agitation surfaced immediately. She was upset about her own mother's passing, but I think she was also bothered about her final requests and how they appeared to others. Appearance is a big deal to my mother. I don't think she's recovered from my dropping out of law school. Working as a paralegal isn't prestigious, so it embarrasses her."

Melody explained that she was essentially alone now: her mother lived in a fantasy world with her new husband, her dad and Grandpapa Henry were already gone, and now Grandmama Giselle was gone.

"I'm not sure why, but I do believe Grandmama bringing me here is some sort of a turning point in my life."

Maman simply nodded.

"What happened to my great-grandfather after Yvette left?"

"We never saw him much after that. He became sort of a recluse and…well, we don't know where he went. Word was he married his housekeeper, a woman from Haiti who already had a son when she went to work for him. People said she was an Obeah woman, a root worker, and worked strong magick. They say he adopted the boy."

The color drained from Melody's face; Maman leaned over, taking her hand into hers.

"Are you all right, Chère? Are you ill?"

Melody felt queasy and weak, and had to wait a few moments before speaking.

"I was sitting on Paul's porch when an older black man came up out of nowhere. He said he and my grandmother were 'related in a way.' He also said my grandmother had something of his, which he wanted back. He didn't say it in a nice way, either. When I told Paul about it, he said I must have dozed off and dreamed the whole thing."

Maman Marie was thoughtful, not dismissive at all. "Are you thinking he's the Haitian woman's son?" Maman asked.

Melody shrugged. "Maybe?"

"Some said the woman knew magickal secrets sent down through generations. My sister said that Haitian woman's claws were in your great-grandfather when he was still married to

Yvette; that she had worked a root against Yvette to get rid of her and clear the way. She wanted a husband and a father for her young son, and she set her sights on Bertrand."

"What kind of thing could my grandmother have that belonged to them?"

Maman was quiet for a moment, and Melody had the distinct impression she might know more than she was willing to share. "I'm not sure, Chère."

"Ms. Marie…"

"Please, call me Maman."

"Okay, Maman," Melody hesitated for a moment, "Is Bertrand Baton still alive?"

"I just don't know. I haven't seen him in many a year. Of course, if he is alive, he's very, very old by now."

"Yes, I suppose he would be." She fidgeted, pushing several loose strands of hair away from her face. "Can you explain how you are going to bless my grandmother's ashes?"

Melody wanted to understand what was going on. She had a sense Giselle was urging her to learn, to be open to a new way of seeing and being in this world.

Maman sat back and closed her eyes, envisioning the ceremony.

"At sundown we begin the ritual. Sunrise and sunset are cracks between the worlds; they are the best times to do magick. People get fixated on clocks and calendars, and don't remember time is man-made. Spirits don't know time as we know it. For them, past, present and future are one. Sunrise and sunset bring on natural shifts of consciousness and allow perceptions to change. Different spirits inhabit these dimensions, requiring different rituals and different offerings." Maman paused to allow Melody to absorb this. "First, we'll summon the ancestors. Some may have left to join the Spirit pool again and be reincarnated, but some choose—or are forced—to remain and work out the chains that keep them in this dimension."

"What kind of chains?"

"Feelings of guilt, anger, unresolved issues. Helping someone else allows them to evolve and dissolve the ego-natured ties they couldn't release during their earthly life."

"Ah, like angels getting their wings." Melody smiled, pleased she understood something.

"Yes, Chère, something of the sort. After calling the ancestors, we'll offer libation to create a sacred space and listen to the drumming."

"Do you drum?" Melody recalled attending a Native American drumming ceremony in college and enjoying it very much.

"I used to, but now I usually play records. It makes it easier for me to fall into trance. Back in the old days, my sister and I took turns drumming, so that the other one could trance out and be possessed by the Loa."

"What do you mean, 'possessed by the Loa'? I'm a product of Catholic school where possession equals the devil." Melody laughed awkwardly.

"Once we are in a semi-trance, we'll call in Elegba to open the doors and let us into the dimension where magick manifests. He'll get us in touch with the appropriate Loa to bless your grandmother, or he'll do it himself. One of his duties is ferrying souls through the River of Death."

Maman was speaking but Melody no longer followed. It was like walking into a lecture being given by someone speaking a completely different language, about a completely unfamiliar subject.

"Did your grandmother have a patron Loa?"

Melody was at a complete loss and was suddenly overwhelmed with confusion, grief, even fear. "I have no idea! I've never even *heard* of a Loa. I don't understand anything you just said!"

"What upsets you so, Chère?"

"I'm so confused and don't understand anything!" she cried out, emotions no longer under control. "I lost the person dearest to me in the entire world. I had no time to process that before learning she had this mysterious last wish, and then I learn so many things about her that I never knew. I don't understand this side of her at all!"

Taking a deep, deliberate breath, she tried to compose herself, ashamed of her outburst. It wasn't Maman she was upset with. "Honestly, all this talk of spirits and magick and Voodoo and root workers—it freaks me out! No offense, Maman..."

"You aren't from here, Chère. You were never brought up with this sort of talk. Giselle obviously kept all this hidden, and we must trust she had her reasons. There are very few people living in this country who *truly* know Voodoo. Just listen to what I'm saying, and try to put what you have heard before aside. Don't let the words throw you. Sometimes language makes things so complicated. So often we use different words and, without realizing it, we're speaking of the same thing. I need for you to keep an open mind, okay?"

Melody listened as Maman calmly spoke. Even though Paul had explained some things about Voodoo, Melody wanted to know what Maman had to say. Her voice was very soothing, her presence reassuring.

"Remember that all religions have evolved through time—none are in their pure state. They've borrowed from one another; often merged with one another. Catholicism combined with ancient African traditions created Voodoo as we know it. Voodoo has so very many different interpretations now, as it has evolved. Similar to how the Christian faith evolved into different branches and ways of interpreting the founding beliefs. Do you under-stand this much?"

Melody nodded.

"Voodoo is a religion followed by millions of people, with a basic belief similar to other religions, especially Earth-based or indigenous practices, viewing nature and our connection to nature as sacred. Louisiana Voodoo has been influenced by many things. We believe in one Creator, spirit in form. God Energy. You believe this, too, yes?"

Melody nodded.

"This God Energy exists in a myriad of manifestations called Orishas. Orishas are like your saints. They have an elevated status, yet we all have God Energy. Voodoo teaches that God Energy is inside everything, breathing or not. Even a stone. It is made of the same basic carbon molecules as everything else in the universe. The cellular makeup of man is not at all different than that of a tree, an ant, a stone. The Loa that lives inside all of us is directly aligned with the energy of the Creator."

"Loa?"

"Yes, Loa energy is similar to Orisha energy. The word "Orisha" originated in West Africa. In Haiti, they refer to Loa or Lwa rather than Orisha. You'll hear me refer to both inter-changeably." Maman's expression changed abruptly. "My goodness, where are my manners? May I get you something to drink? Some iced tea?"

"Yes, that would be wonderful. May I help?"

"No, no. I need all the exercise I can get for these old bones. I do need something to drink, though. I haven't talked this much in a long time and, goodness knows, we have much more to talk about. I'll be back in just a minute."

Melody was fascinated. The idea of God Energy being in everything and everyone made sense, and she desperately needed something to make sense. That's why religion always frustrated Melody; too many intangibles and contradictions, requiring a blind faith.

What Maman spoke of reminded her of Native American spirituality, which she had studied briefly in college. They all tend to use different terminology, but many religions are essentially dealing with energy, on a scientific level. She started to see that, unfortunately, any language or wording that's different can frighten people.

"Okay, where did I leave off?" Maman asked as she handed Melody a glass tumbler filled with amber-colored iced tea. "Ah, yes. Loa. The Loa's energy is so vast and intense that the human body and mind can only contain a small part of it. When you choose to go in, and Elegba opens the door, your ego subsides and you are able to connect to and receive the Loa."

"Elegba?" Melody remembered hearing that name at the Voodoo shop.

"Yes, he is a most powerful Orisha, known by many names: Eshu, Legba, even Saint Michael and Saint Anthony. All rituals begin with an offering to Elegba; sometimes he is even compared to Saint Peter—a gatekeeper. Elegba is the Orisha of the cross-roads, the spiritual connection between man and divinity, our mirror. He embodies all the forces, positive and negative. He tests our humanness and our divinity."

Maman paused to take a sip. In a very solemn tone, she continued.

"There are several very important aspects to Voodoo that are imperative for you, as an initiate, to understand."

Melody wasn't sure she liked the idea of being an initiate or what it entailed.

"First, you understand that Spirit is neutral. The forces of positive and negative are all around, and within all. There is no good or bad energy, per se; it's the intention behind the use of that energy. The responsibility lies with each of us for *how we access and manifest this Energy.*" Maman accentuated the last seven words, speaking each with equal emphasis. She silently held Melody's gaze for several long, uncomfortable seconds.

Having made her point, she proceeded.

"Elegba is also known as the trickster god. A story often told is that one day Elegba walked down the road through a village wearing a hat that was red on one side and black on the other.

Shortly after he left, those who had seen him began arguing whether the stranger's hat was red or black. The villagers on one side of the road saw only the black hat, while the villagers on the other side saw only a red hat. They argued and argued until Elegba returned, clearing the mystery for the villagers. The lesson in this story is the second aspect of Voodoo I want you to understand: *Your perspective can greatly alter your perception of reality.*"

Another pause, another sip of tea.

"Each person normally has one patron Loa that will possess them or guide them. They are then called children of the Loa. I am daughter of Shango; my sister was the daughter of Oshun. That's why we worked so well together. You see, legend has it that Shango and the beautiful Oshun were lovers. Shango is the Loa of fire and justice, his weapons are lightning bolts. He's very intense and charming, a warrior in matters of justice. Oshun is the Loa of the sweet waters of rivers. She's the sister of Yemoja, the mother of the ocean water. Oshun is extremely beautiful and enticing to men, and is sought mostly in affairs of the heart."

Listening intently, Melody didn't know what to make of the beautiful story. While it all sounded lovely, to Melody it was just another fairytale.

It *should* be her Grandmama explaining this. She would know how to explain things to Melody so they made sense. Could Grandmama really have believed these same things, and done the same things, as Maman?

While she grieved, she also struggled with the disappointment that Grandmama had never shared this; that her grandmother had kept a vital secret from her.

Despite her uncertainty and confusion, she grew more and more curious.

Maman announced rather abruptly that she was going to lie down and that, afterward, she would take a purifying bath. She advised Melody to do the same.

A shower sounded heavenly to Melody, but a cool bath would certainly do. The day had been so hot and sticky, she felt as though her clothes were fused to her skin.

"I didn't bring a change of clothes. I didn't know I would need them," she reminded Maman.

"Actually, you won't need them, not tonight at least. It is best to not wear any clothes when you meet the Loa. It symbolizes your oneness with nature and the shedding of worldly belongings. It is a sign of humbleness and purity."

Melody's eyes widened in dismay.

"You do these ceremonies totally naked?!"

"I do. Nowadays some people only undress from the waist up; some don't undress at all, but I feel that in front of the Loa, you should have no reminders of the illusion of worldly life. I adhere to the ancient traditions as much as possible. I understand your hesitation, but I believe you can make a small sacrifice for your grandmother, yes?"

"Well...yes, I suppose I can. Will there just be the two of us?"

"I'm not sure yet. An old, dear friend joins me sometimes, to bring balance."

Melody prayed fervently that this unknown friend would be a no-show tonight. The last thing she wanted was to parade naked in front of *two* strangers, even if they were senior citizens whose eyesight was, hopefully, failing.

"You go ahead and get ready while I rest, so we can make good use of time before sunset falls."

Melody was relieved to finally peel off the sticky clothes. Maman had given her a bottle filled with a greenish liquid and told her to pour it in the tub when it was full. She also told her to shower beforehand. Melody was thrilled to be able to take a shower; she thought Maman's house, like a lot of older homes, might have only a bathtub. But she had not understood why she had to shower and *then* bathe again. Maman said something about the bath being necessary to remove astral debris, not worldly dirt.

Melody was instructed to recite the Twenty-Third Psalm aloud three times, then to lie quietly in the tub and try to clear her mind. Reciting this prayer was the one thing familiar to her in the midst of a world of unknowns.

"The Lord is my shepherd; I shall not want..." She was in the tub a good half-hour. When she got out, she didn't know whether she should put on her same clothes or if Maman would lend her something to wear until the ceremony. She felt fairly sure they were close in size, though she hated not having her own clothes. She wrapped the towel around her body and used Maman's brush to comb through her long brown hair. While she was still in the bathroom, she heard noise coming from another room.

"Maman, are you up?"

Maman's voice arose from a clatter of pots and pans. "Yes, Chère, I'm in the kitchen."

Melody walked to the kitchen, wearing only the bath towel. Maman was busy tending a pot on the stove that exuded a divine aroma. Paul's gumbo was long gone and Melody was famished once again.

"May I wear something of yours until the ceremony? That way I can hand-wash my clothes and they'll dry by tomorrow morning."

"Certainly, I'll find a robe for you. Come with me."

Maman's bedroom was neat and sparsely furnished. The walls were pure white; all the furnishings and accessories, including the bedspread, were red.

Maman explained the decor. "Those are the colors of Shango, red and white. I try to surround myself with those colors whenever I can, but it is especially important in the bedroom. During sleep is when the ego subsides and the subconscious opens. This way I vibrate with the Loa when I'm most open."

At that moment Melody grasped something incredibly significant. This was not only a religion; for people like Maman it was a way of life and permeated every cell of her being and existence.

Melody donned Maman's red silk robe, then washed her clothes in the sink and hung them outside to dry before returning to the kitchen.

"Melody, you shouldn't eat anything before the ceremony. Maybe just a little water, but no food."

Melody's hopes for a good meal were swiftly dashed.

"It's important that you abstain from feeding your body, so that the Loa won't be weighed down by physical chains."

Melody tried not to show her disappointment. "Okay. Is there anything I can help you do right now?"

"You can put wood together for the fire. It's in a pile out back. The fire pit is on the side of the house."

Oh god, it figures she would ask me to do the very thing that terrifies me! Melody had always heard that snakes lurk in woodpiles. "I saw a snake on the sand bank today, when I got here."

"Yes, they often come here to soak up the sun."

Maman noticed Melody fidgeting nervously. "This is a swamp, Melody. Snakes will be seen but they aren't out to hurt anyone. They are quite shy and will leave when they feel someone getting close. Don't worry yourself to death; they won't come close to the fire."

"What about the woodpile?"

Maman had to laugh out loud at the look of sheer panic on Melody's face.

"No, dear girl, I promise. Nothing will hurt you out there."

Melody felt a little foolish but couldn't help it. A lifelong fear isn't easily shed, even with reassuring promises. She changed the subject, trying to delay her chore. "Maman, what was in that bottle you told me to pour into the bath today?"

"Just purifying herbs: hyssop, sage and rosemary. Did you

read out the Psalm I gave you?'

"Yes, ma'am."

"Good. That psalm is powerful in dispelling negative energy. It's all about vibration, Melody. Now please, go take care of the wood for the fire. I have to finish preparing things and we don't have much time."

Terrified yet determined not to show it, Melody walked confidently out of the kitchen and headed for the woodpile. Her eyes were wide as saucers, on full snake alert. A faint noise nearby caused her to jump back and stumble. She had started arranging the wood in the fire pit when she heard the soft rumble of a car engine behind her. *Damn! That old lady must have decided to show up.*

She watched a small pickup pull up to the house and couldn't believe who was driving: the same old man she had seen playing harmonica in New Orleans yesterday, with the smile that warmed her heart.

"Good evening, ma'am. How do you do?" From his casual greeting, Melody was sure he didn't recognize her. "Marie inside?"

Melody smiled, stunned at the coincidence. "Yes, she's in the kitchen."

The man shuffled up to the door and went in without knocking. A few moments later he and Maman came outside together.

"Melody, I'd like to introduce you to my dear friend, Samuel Marlowe. He and I go way back." Turning to Samuel, Maman said, "Samuel, this is Melody Bennet. She's Giselle Baton's granddaughter. Do you remember Giselle? Her mother..."

Maman's voice trailed off as Samuel's eyes widened in surprise and recognition. "Well, well... and what are you doing here, may I ask?"

Maman spoke for her. "Giselle ended up in North Carolina. She passed on recently and had Melody bring her ashes back here and to find me, so I could bless them."

He turned to Maman. "Is that what we're doing tonight?"

"Yes, we'll have the other ceremony another night."

Samuel smiled at Melody. "That's certainly fine, Marie. This child came a long way for this."

Maman looked toward the horizon. "It's almost sundown; we'd better get started."

Samuel returned from the house, first with a record player and then with various bowls of whatever it was Maman had been cooking. To Melody the preparations seemed a well-orchestrated dance the two had clearly performed many times. After setting the smaller bowls to the side of the fire pit, Maman lit the kindling. The flames crackled loudly, sending sparks toward the sky.

Having gathered the last few items from the house, Samuel joined the two women by the fire. Maman picked up a bag of flour and, pouring from a corner opening, drew a wide circle that encompassed most of the yard. She retrieved a stick of some sort from the supplies Samuel had gathered and stepped inside the circle, near the fire pit. She drew what appeared to be a double-edged axe crossed by a lightning bolt, and then enclosed that drawing in a smaller circle.

On the inside edge of the larger circle Maman drew another pictogram. Melody remembered having seen something recently about this and struggled to remember...there had been a book about these voodoo symbols at the shop where she had the reading—*vévé*! That's it! The diagrams were called vévés, and the book's back cover said each Orisha has his or her own vévé.

The one Maman was working on now looked like a cross intersected on the right by a key; an old-fashioned key, a skeleton key. Other small symbols surrounded the cross, including other smaller crosses. This drawing was also encircled.

Maman set down the flour and asked Samuel and Melody to

join her outside the circle.

"Remove your clothes out here. You should enter the sacred space stripped of anything you weren't born with," she said, clearly for Melody's benefit.

Melody was paralyzed. Her mind was the only thing functioning in that split second. From the moment she landed in New Orleans, Melody did her best to go with the flow out of respect for Grandmama. Standing in this very strange setting, with two complete strangers doing very strange things made her life suddenly feel out of control. *What am I doing here?!*

Melody was clearly mortified, her eyes darting nervously, knees shaking violently. Maman and Samuel disrobed silently, without looking at Melody, and waited patiently. Still not looking at Melody, Maman began explaining that she would start the ceremony with an offering to Elegba.

"Elegba is the spiritual connection between man and divinity...he is our mirror. He embodies all the forces within us. He tests our humanness and our divinity. You must pass through the fire to know your strength. What force will test you through that fire?

Melody heard only every third word or so, her mind reeling, struggling for comprehension. When she heard "test you through that fire" something clicked. These were words she had heard Grandmama say many times. She took it as a sign that Grandmama was encouraging her to be brave...that she must participate in order to fulfill her wish.

I'll be brave for you, Grandmama.

Hesitantly, she stripped off her borrowed robe and crossed into the circle. She felt very awkward, but they didn't seem to notice her.

Maman stepped into the circle and started pouring libation while Samuel, still on the outside, placed a record on the player. Melody couldn't understand anything Maman was saying as she poured the ceremonial liquid into the ground. The words sounded African and they flowed in rhythm with the lifting breeze.

A moment of silence followed. Maman explained that she was now making offerings. Melody watched Maman throw different things into the fire: a small dish of yams, morsels of coconut, and a bottle of rum; then she lit a cigar and she took four puffs from it, blowing them toward the sky.

She passed the cigar to Samuel, who took three puffs and also blew them towards the sky. He passed the cigar to Melody who took one timid puff; she tried to imitate Maman, blowing the smoke up towards the sky.

Both Maman and Samuel stood in front of the vévé with the key and motioned Melody to join them with Giselle's ashes. Maman closed her eyes and opened her arms as if to embrace the air in front of her.

"Iba'ra'go Mojuba

"Iba'ra'go Ago Mojuba

"Omode Oni'ko S'iba'go Ago Mojuba

"Elegba Esu Lona."

Melody detected a stronger cigar scent in the air and heard laughter coming from the trees behind them. Goosebumps covered her body. Maman and Samuel exchanged a knowing look and Samuel nodded, then they moved to the other symbol in front of the fire. Maman opened her arms again, embracing the invisible.

"Mo Fori bo rere O Shango to'kan O Ya de

"A Wa'nile Onile O Ku O

"A Wa'nile Onile O Ya."

The flames expanded; one of the sparks exploded, frightening Melody and causing her to jump back.

She heard the faint but definitive rumble of an approaching storm as the breeze grew stronger. The drumming strengthened, pulsating in a constant crescendo, and both Maman and Samuel began moving their bodies to its rhythm. The scene was disconcerting, but Melody also saw stark beauty in the ageless, harmonious fusion between Samuel and Maman and their natural surroundings.

Melody closed her eyes and lost herself in the music, feeling both at peace and simultaneously electrified. She felt light-headed, with things spinning around her. She caught sight of a red rooster being brought in by Samuel but had no idea where the rooster had come from. The animal flapped its wings desperately as he was brought to Maman who was standing by the axe vévé.

Before taking the rooster, Maman lifted the bowl up high, offering it to the Heavens. She then took a sip from it and passed it to Samuel. She held it for him as he drank, since he was holding the rooster, then moved in front of Melody and offered it to her.

"Drink of it, Chère." Maman's voice had a different tone now, more formidable and commanding.

Melody took a sip without protest. The liquid was sticky and sweet; she felt it stick to the roof of her mouth, like peanut butter.

She sat on the ground beside Samuel, serenely oblivious to snakes and lack of clothing. Samuel's face caught her attention: his features were no longer clearly defined and Melody was certain—if she could be certain of anything at that point—that another face merged with his, a stronger but equally loving face, paternal, almost divine. She felt as though she was on a merry-go-round. Everything was blurry, but lightning bolts sizzled nearby. Oddly, she was not afraid at all; it was like being in a dream.

The rooster was in her line of sight again. *Did Maman just bite its neck?* Its wings flapped violently, its body jerked in violent spasm. Blood spurted from the wound on its neck; Maman let it drip on the axe vévé.

Melody looked on, mesmerized. Her awareness began to slip away, when suddenly she saw Grandmama Giselle in front of her, smiling lovingly.

"It is your mission now, Melody. Open your heart and mind. You will find what you need to know. When you find it, guard it with your life, Dear One."

She stared as Grandmama floated away toward the edge of the larger circle, near the key vévé. A shadow materialized from within the vévé, extending its hand to her. In a fleeting moment, the shadow and Grandmama were both gone, as if a portal had opened, letting them in but leaving all others out.

Everything went black.

Melody woke up about one hour later on Maman's couch. Samuel and Maman were seated in chairs on the other side of the living room. When they saw Melody awaken, they both smiled brightly. Samuel disappeared into the kitchen and returned with a glass of water for Melody.

She was relieved that her naked body was now covered by a blanket. Memories of the ritual were like fleeting images from a dream; no matter how hard she tried to remember, nothing came into focus.

"Everything went well, Chère. Giselle moved on," Maman said reassuringly.

Melody sat up, wrapping the blanket more snugly. "I think I saw Grandmama. She was smiling at me...and...then she floated away and disappeared into the vévé with the key on it."

Maman nodded. "Elegba took her across the river."

Melody didn't seem to hear. "She said something about my mission and finding what I need to know...and guarding it with my life. I don't even know what she was talking about."

Samuel and Maman exchanged a glance.

"Maybe Samuel can help with that part."

Samuel took a deep breath and came to sit next to Melody.

"Miss Melody, I knew a woman once, a long time ago. At first she seemed kind, but it wasn't long before she showed her true colors. She was involved in Voodoo, but she worked an evil hoodoo. She would hurt anyone to get what she wanted. It's one thing to embrace the darkness, but that woman drew power only from the negative. She married your great-grandfather, Bertrand, after Yvette left him.

"I last saw her many, many years ago. She claimed to be in possession of a very special book. She never said where she got it, only that it had been in her family since leaving Haiti. She bragged that the book gave her incredible power: a power great enough to change reality."

Melody told Samuel about the strange man who had threatened her earlier on Old Paul's porch.

"Paul was probably trying to protect you, saying you just had a dream. He knows you're leaving soon and probably felt there was no need to alarm you. Plus, if there's something not quite right, we like to...you know...keep the bayou secrets in the bayou."

Maman broke in. "You should not concern yourself about this now, Chère. You need to get some rest. We'll talk more in the morning."

She walked over and held her hand out to Melody, who—very unsteady on her feet—was grateful for the help. Melody was fast asleep as soon as her head hit the pillow.

That night she dreamed of her grandmother running through the woods, clutching a leather-bound book to her chest. Shadows chased her, but could not see her. It was as if the book gifted her with invisibility.

In the dream, Grandmama stopped for a moment and looked straight at Melody.

"The old barn, Melody. Go to the old barn..."

CHAPTER FOUR

The sun was high when Melody awoke. She lay there trying to gather her thoughts but was distracted by the rumbling of her stomach. Sitting up on the side of the bed, she looked around for something to wear. Her clothes were still on the clothesline and the robe she had borrowed from Maman was nowhere in sight.

Dirt and dried blood remained on her body from the night before, so she wrapped the sheet around herself and hurried to wash. After a quick shower, she covered herself with a towel before walking outside to gather her clothes. She found they were dry, though a faint smoky smell lingered in the fabric

Melody could have sworn she heard a storm approaching last night during the ceremony, but the images were too jumbled for her to be sure. Before going back inside to change, she noticed Samuel's truck was gone. She had only been outside a few minutes, but her naked skin already glistened with perspiration. She thought about last night, about dancing naked in front of Samuel and Maman, remembering how liberated she had felt. She felt connected...to who or what she wasn't sure...but she knew something extraordinary had happened.

Melody dressed quickly, energized by the divine aroma radiating from the kitchen, where she again found Maman at the stove.

"Good morning, Maman."

Maman turned around and smiled. "Good morning! Did you sleep well?"

"Most definitely. That was quite a night. What exactly happened? Nothing seems clear."

Maman smiled. "Giselle went back, you saw that yourself."

Melody thought for a moment and flashed to the image of her grandmother floating and disappearing inside the flour vévé by the fire. "Was all that real? Did I really see her?"

"It's all real, child. I watched you last night, Melody. Yemoja was with you."

"Yemoja?"

"Orisha of the oceans. She's good energy, like a mother. She touched your head and your hair became wet." Maman smiled admiringly. "She was behind you the whole time."

Melody had never been around so much talk about the spirit world, not even in church. She couldn't deny something inexplicable had happened last night. She remembered feeling lightheaded, even before drinking the liquid that Maman gave her.

Without warning, an image of the dying rooster popped into Melody's mind.

"Maman, did you kill a rooster last night?"

"No, child, Shango did. That was an offering to him for giving me the wisdom to bless Giselle. The other offerings were for Elegba. Remember, you always honor him first in every ceremony, because he's the one who opens the door. Last night, he also took your grandmother away."

"Where did the rooster even come from?"

"Samuel had it in his truck."

"But I never saw him take it out of the truck."

"Melody, you have more Spirit in you than you know. Your perception was altered by the energy."

"What did you do with the rooster?"

"The head was thrown in the flames as a token; the rest of it is over there, enjoying the company of onions and potatoes in the skillet."

Melody glanced over at the stove and saw the skillet with a lid on, beside a frying pan containing sausage patties. All other questions disappeared in a wave of hunger. "May I please have some sausage? I'm famished."

"I cooked it just for you. There are eggs and biscuits, too."

Melody didn't wait for a second invitation. She piled her plate with sausage, scrambled eggs and two biscuits.

"I'm sorry I don't have any coffee, Melody. I can make you some tea if you'd like."

Melody nodded with her mouth full and waited to swallow before answering. "Tea sounds great. Thank you."

She ate slowly yet steadily, toying with the idea of sharing her dream in which Grandmama told her to guard the book. It was only a dream, but she felt it shouldn't be discussed, though she didn't understand why.

Could she trust Maman? Her grandmother sent Melody to find the old lady, so she saw no reason not to trust her. She felt safe here.

"I dreamed of Grandmama last night. She was holding an old book and running through the woods. There were shadows chasing her, but it's like they couldn't see her. Then she told me to look in the old barn."

"That's interesting, Melody. Maybe that's why Bertrand Baton's people couldn't find her. There may have been a root for the book's protection....strong magick," she said almost absent-mindedly. "Try not to worry about it, Chère. Paul will be here soon. You must get ready."

Melody thought it interesting that Maman acted as though there was indeed such a book. She glanced at the small urn that contained the ashes, then looked up to see an old clock on the wall: it was almost one o'clock in the afternoon! She had slept through the entire morning. *No wonder I'm so hungry!*

"Speak of the devil." Maman saw Paul tying his boat to the old tree at the sand bank. A few minutes later, he walked into the kitchen.

He grinned and pointed to the ashes on the kitchen table. "So, are the ashes all blessed?" he asked sarcastically.

Maman gave him an admonishing look.

"Sorry, didn't mean no disrespect. Well, you ready, Melody?"

"I am, let me just grab my backpack." She took her plate to the sink and went over to Maman. "Thank you for everything, Maman. I won't forget this visit."

Maman hugged her tightly. "Come back and see me, Chère. I'll teach you about Yemoja."

"I will. You take good care of yourself, and thank you again for everything. Please say goodbye to Samuel for me." She lovingly picked up the urn, placed it in her backpack, and followed Paul outside to the boat.

As soon as they were gone, Maman walked back into the house and headed straight for the bathroom. She studied the towel Melody had used and picked two pubic hairs from it, then looked at the brush and carefully untangled a few long brown hairs that stood out from her own gray ones. She carried her collection to the kitchen and put them into a jar,

"These may come in handy some day," she told herself. She closed the jar and put it into one of the kitchen cabinets next to a cloth doll.

Once in the middle of the bayou, Paul turned off the engine and studied Giselle's map. Sweat now dripped freely down his nose, sometimes onto the map. The scorching sun was almost directly overhead, with little vegetation at this point to provide cover.

"Man-oh-man! That ole girl sure 'nough wanted to make certain her resting place wasn't going to be disturbed! Even natives hardly go there. The place is full of 'gators and snakes, and the vegetation so thick you can't see through it. Just keep your hands inside the boat and relax 'til we get there."

Melody wouldn't dare reach outside the boat. She was terrified simply being *inside* the boat. They had taken countless turns through meandering channels, passing under canopies of Spanish moss and vines. They watched alligators perform an ancient courtship dance, writhing and twisting just beneath the surface of the water. Paul told her with a chuckle that it was near the end of their mating season, "...so don't worry much about any 'gators out here...they're gettin' tired."

He was right about the vegetation. By the time they approached the general area indicated on the map, it was so thick Melody couldn't tell the end of one plant from the beginning of another. They looked like bony fingers intertwined in prayer, allowing minimal sunlight and creating a murky, gloomy appearance.

She saw nothing resembling a bank on either side and the plants were now arm's length from the boat. Melody felt rising panic as the water plants moved: she just knew some creature was near. It could be a harmless fish or a venomous snake...at this point she really didn't care. She was petrified of everything.

"Here we are," Paul announced shortly, turning off the engine. He pulled up to a very small strip of sand and looked for a place to tie his boat.

Melody looked at him beseechingly, silently asking if she had to get out of the boat.

"I think it's over there, Melody." He pointed toward a nearby thicket.

Melody was reluctant to move. She thought she heard snakes hissing but realized it was the pounding of her own blood in her ears.

Paul saw how afraid she was. "Stay in the boat, child. I'll take care of the ashes."

Melody was so relieved she wanted to hug him but was hesitant to move. Paul took the urn and carefully stepped out of the boat. Melody saw him stomp on the sand, as she had done upon arriving at Maman's.

"I'm a lot bigger than they are," Paul reminded her with a wink, and disappeared into the thicket.

Returning after several minutes, he handed the empty urn to a very solemn Melody. He carefully rowed the boat out until the water widened, before turning on the engine.

With a single tear trickling down each cheek, Melody closed her eyes and said a silent blessing. *Rest in peace, Grandmama.*

She opened her eyes to see Paul watching her intently. "Thank you, Paul. I was terrified...I didn't think I would be that afraid. Seems my fear of snakes outweighed my grief." She tried to sound lighthearted, but they both knew better.

"Can't blame you none, child. Even folks from here are scared of these remote parts. I'm just happy I was able to help."

"You have helped a lot, more than you can imagine. Maybe I can repay your kindness some day, when I come back to visit."

"I hope so, child. You're a special young lady. I know Giselle's proud of you."

Tears stung her eyes. She had shared a very difficult time in her life with strangers and was surprised how close she felt to them. She almost hated to leave; she had grown to like the part of herself that surfaced in the last couple of days.

They pulled up to Old Paul's convenience store.

"Paul, is it okay if I use your phone? I don't get a signal on my cell phone out here and need to call the hotel so they can come pick   me   up."
"Don't you bother 'bout that. They probably wouldn't be able to get out here 'til mornin'. I've asked Joe to watch the store today, so I can take you back."

"I don't want to put you out like that. You've been so wonderful...I really can't thank you enough."

"Don't you fret none. The pleasure is all mine."

After telling Joe that he'd be gone the rest of the day, he got the truck keys and waited for Melody. After freshening up a bit and saying goodbye to Joe, Melody joined him and they headed for New Orleans.

At first the trip was a silent one. Paul appeared absorbed in his own thoughts and Melody was drained, content to sit back and relax. Since she had slept the entire time on the way here, she was glad to be able to watch the passing scenery on the drive back. It was late afternoon, the heat-generated haze floating just ahead of them on the highway. She noted signs for Highway 190, then Interstate 10, and smiled at the exit name "Whiskey Bay."

She caught glimpses of the cypress swamps and moss-laden bayous, but saw no evidence of the hurricane-splintered trees that punctuated the wetlands closer to New Orleans.

Paul's deep voice broke the silence. "I don't know 'bout you, but I'm plumb tuckered out", he said rather embarrassed. "I'm too tired to talk much, but I thought you might want to read about the Atchafalaya." He gestured to a file folder tucked under the passenger seat, in the midst of a stack of mechanic's bills, maps, and various other papers.

Melody opened the file folder to find a newsletter of sorts, about the Atchafalaya Basin.

"The tourists like to read about the history and what's goin' on...you know, environmentally and all that, 'specially since Rita and Katrina."

"I was just thinking about that. You must be psychic, Paul," Melody winked and began skimming through the sheet.

Louisiana's Atchafalaya Basin, located in St. Martin Parrish, is the nation's largest swamp wilderness at 595,000 acres, with infamous expanses of bottomland hardwoods, swamplands, bayous and back-water lakes... The central area is home to bald cypress trees and presents the "swamp image" most frequently associated with the Atchafalaya. The Atchafalaya attracts hunters, fishing and boating enthusiasts, as well as nature photographers.

She read about the wildlife native to this region and was surprised to see the black bear and bald eagle included.

Melody learned of the controversies affecting the swamps: oil drilling, mulching, dredging. It all sounded rather complicated, with two sides to each story.

Mother Nature was greatly affecting the bayous as well. The

bottom line seemed to be that many influences had been, and were still, damaging this vital area of the world. Melody hoped it would start getting the attention it deserved. One item practically jumped off the page:

"Bear Bayou/Bayou des Ourses continues to be pristine, with no desecration from oil companies or severe hurricane damage as in other parts of the basin."

She smiled, thinking a Higher Power must have protected that particular bayou, knowing Grandmama would eventually return.

She tucked the paper into her purse to read later. Her eyes had grown too tired to pay attention to much of anything as they drove.

When they reached the hotel, Melody leaned over and gave Paul a big hug, which he returned in kind.

"Thank you again for everything. I hope to see you again soon."

"Take care of yourself, child, and forget all that mumbo-jumbo you heard from Marie. She's a sweet old lady, but I think the years have caught up with her"

"No, it was all good. It was...different," she said with a smile.

She got out of the truck and waved as he disappeared around the corner.

The cool, elegant hotel lobby was a welcome sight. Waiting for the elevator, she pondered Paul's comment about Marie. She actually seemed quite sane to her, even normal. *When she isn't running around outside naked, cutting the heads off chickens.*

She laughed out loud at the thought. Now that she was back at the hotel, she felt as though the entire time in the swamp had been an out-of-body experience.

When she walked into her room, she felt as though she weighed a ton. She didn't have the mental or physical energy to do anything, other than get undressed and collapse into bed. She'd have to phone the airline first thing in the morning to book her return flight.

When she rolled onto her side, curling into her favorite sleeping position, she spotted the charm bag the tarot reader from the Voodoo shop had given her. Drifting off, Melody recalled the woman's prediction that she was about to uncover an earth-shattering secret.

I highly doubt it, but I'll find out when I get back to the farm and check the old barn.

CHAPTER FIVE

The sun was just breaking the horizon when Melody awoke. Outside, the world was wrapped in a blanket of haze, with the courtyard lights appearing like fireflies in a dense forest. Odds were that the day would be another scorcher.

After arranging a three o'clock flight for that afternoon, Melody lingered in the shower before dressing comfortably, not bothering much with hair or makeup; the heat and humidity outside would have their way with her appearance.

Venturing out once more, she had hoped to have one meal in the historic hotel restaurant, but they had yet to open, so she opted to revisit the French Quarter. She wanted to immerse herself in it and forget everything for a short time.

As she approached the closest bistro, waves of honeyed air reached out to enfold her. Once inside, the warm, sweet fragrances of assorted pastries battled with one another and joined forces in an effort to override the coffee's distinctive aroma.

Armed with a large "regular" and two beignets—it had been a tough decision between them and crepes suzettes—Melody was back outside, seeking a perfect spot from where she could soak up her last few impressions of New Orleans.

She found an empty bench pushed up against a storefront, and witnessed traffic—motorized and pedestrian—increase by the minute.

She wondered if Samuel was back at Bourbon and Orleans, with his harmonica. There was something about that man's smile.

Melody was still stunned that he had been at Maman's. Samuel and Maman were an inspiration, so confident and self-aware. Perhaps it came with age. It's such a gift to live without caring what others may think; if something is real and right for them, that's all that matters.

After finishing the beignets and going back for more coffee, she wandered through the expanding crowd.

While she would deny it to anyone else—as she had not reached that state of being immune to others' opinions—she had actually enjoyed the ritual at Maman's house, once she got past her initial mortification about the nudity. Amazingly, even the animal sacrifice she witnessed wasn't horrifying.

Maman had explained it very well, in a way Melody could comprehend. She said that the energy exchange was necessary, similar to indigenous peoples giving thanks prior to taking a life for food. Again similar to native traditions, every part of the animal was used and valued; nothing was wasted. Maman further explained that the energy exchange was necessary to "create a catalyst reaction."

Though Melody wasn't sure what had happened, she remained certain *something* had. Never before had she been so captivated and energized.

She thought she might see Samuel but he was nowhere in sight.

When she returned to the hotel Olivia greeted her with a bright smile and cheerful voice.

"Miss Bennet, how are you?"

"Hi, Olivia. I'll be leaving this morning but wanted to thank you again for all of your help."

"You are most welcome. It was my pleasure. I trust you were able to take care of everything with regard to your grand-mother?"

"Yes, thanks for asking. It's all taken care of."

"Well, I hope you'll come back soon. You didn't have time for much sightseeing."

"I hope to. I've fallen in love with what I did get to see, but you're right...there's so much more. Thank you again."

Melody returned to her room to pack. She had barely begun

when her cell phone rang, startling her; it had been silent for days. She hadn't even checked for messages since setting out for the bayou, and wasn't keen to see who might be calling to chastise her.

"Melody, it's Mom."

"Hi, Mom. How's it going?"

"Well, I wanted to see how *you* are doing. You haven't returned my calls. We were worried."

"I'm okay; it's just been stressful. The place where Grandmama wanted to be taken was in a remote part of the swamp. And I found that lady, the one Grandmama wanted me to find to bless her ashes."

"Is that what she really wanted from her?"

"Yes. Seems they knew one another when Grandmama was young. She obviously still felt a close tie to this area and believed in...that kind of thing."

"I just can't imagine my mother still believing in that crazy stuff, even after all the years she'd been away."

"It really didn't seem that crazy."   Her mother's tone was already getting on Melody's nerves, but she had to ask, "Did she ever talk about her life here? About Voodoo or anything like that?"

"Never. Thank goodness!" Changing the subject quickly, "When are you coming home?"

"Tonight. Why?"

"I'd like you to look over some papers. We listed the farm two days ago with a realtor, and someone is already interested. Isn't that great?"

Melody couldn't believe what she was hearing. She knew her mother was impatient—and impulsive—but this was too much.

"You did WHAT?! Why didn't you wait for me to get back?" She could picture her mother on the other end, rolling her eyes in annoyance, not wanting to have to answer to anyone, certainly not her daughter.

"We just wanted to get things moving. Eric said—"

"Eric has no place in this decision, Mom!"   Melody tried to regain her composure. "Listen, I'm sorry I yelled. Please...*please* call the realtor back and put the listing on hold."

"But we've already signed a contract. Besides, Eric said that we may have an offer before the evening."

"Mom, *please*! Call them and tell them you have changed your mind and are no longer interested in selling. I'll handle the breach of contract when I get back."

"But, Melody..."

"For once, I beg you to respect what I am asking."

Annie perceived an accusing tone in Melody's voice and bristled, raising her own voice. "Melody, I have *always*—"

Seeing she had started something she didn't want to finish right now, Melody backed out carefully.

"I'm sorry, that came out wrong. I'm very tired. I'll be back tonight and we can talk about this in the morning. Just for tonight, please put this on hold and don't accept any offers, okay?"

She also wanted to ask her mother to tell Eric, her new husband, to stay out of this, but held her tongue.

"I have to go. I was just in the middle of packing and need to get ready."

"That's fine, Melody. Call when you get in. One of us will pick you up."

"Thanks, but I actually want to go to the farm tonight, so I think I'll just catch a cab."   She was wishing she had parked her car at the airport, rather than let her mom drop her off. Annie had only offered to do so in order to pry, to see if Melody knew more than she did about Giselle's final wishes.

"A cab? From RDU to Clayton? A cab will cost you an arm and a leg, Melody!"

"Mom—"

"I know, I know. You're all grown up now, it's your decision."

Annie's voice had the trademark sarcasm, used when she felt slighted or wanted someone to feel guilty. She was quite the good Catholic, guilt tactics and all. Melody knew this trick well, so she stood her ground.

"That's right, I am. I can take care of it myself, but thank you for the offer."

"Fine. Call me in the morning to let me know how *you* want to handle things." Annie emphasized that last part of the sentence to make sure Melody knew she had stepped over the line, and hung up.

Melody knew it didn't take much to offend her mother. She was like a child, always demanding her way, pouting and playing the martyr when she didn't get it, but Melody was getting better about detaching from the childish manipulations.

While Eric wasn't her favorite person, she was grateful he was around for Annie. Since they married two years ago, Annie's dramatic phone calls to Melody had greatly decreased. Eric gave Annie the attention she desperately sought, and that was a huge relief for Melody. Plus, he seemed to genuinely care for mom, so Melody kept her opinion of him to herself.

After Melody's dad died, Annie had become deeply depressed; it had taken years of therapy and medication to shake her out of it. Eric being a pharmacist was a benefit Melody truly appreciated, since he could counter Annie's tendency to be careless about medication.

Melody's thoughts lingered on her father.

John Bennet was the sweetest dad a child could have. Melody had never seen him cross and he always had a smile for his precious daughter. He had chosen her name, and told everyone he met that the moment he saw her, he heard an angelic melody playing and felt a tug on his heart.

Giselle loved John like a son. When he died of a sudden, unexpected heart attack, everyone was crushed, including Annie, who had come to rely on her husband the way a child relies on a parent. Melody wondered if her mother would ever learn to take care of herself, having found yet another man to indulge her every whim.

Melody finished packing and called the front desk to reserve a cab. With an hour to spare, she decided to go outside one last time.

By this time the streets were fully congested and the temperature was in the nineties. Sweat already beading on her face, she looked for someplace to buy a cold soda. Seeing a corner concession, she made a beeline, rethinking her decision to do any sightseeing after all.

The concessionaire had his back to her when she reached the stand. "Excuse me, sir."

He turned around, a carton of soft drinks in his hand, bound for the cooler. "Yes, ma'am, can I help you?"

As their eyes met, Melody's legs turned to jelly and her heart stopped. It was the same man who had been on Old Paul's porch the other day! He looked at Melody with a sinister sneer.

"Well, well...hello, Ms. Bennet."

He knows my name! Melody backed away, bumping into a group of people, losing her balance and falling.

The man walked out from behind the stand and towered over her. From the ground he looked gigantic—and menacing. She wanted to scream but her voice and body seemed paralyzed.

"If you're smart, you'll return the book to me."

"I don't know what you're talking about!"

He spat on the ground beside her and returned behind the counter. Melody scrambled to get up, trying to ignore the people staring at her.

She walked away as quickly and calmly as possible, but was rather dazed and unsure what to do. Should she ignore it? Should she return and confront him? Should she go to the police, since he had now threatened her twice?

A wild idea crossed her mind. Her feet responded instinctively and, before her common sense could protest, she headed quickly toward the voodoo shop.

She alternately walked briskly and jogged, again glad she had dressed comfortably. She was sure she looked a fright, with sweat running down her face and neck, soaking through her shirt. When she arrived, they were just opening. Stephanie, the young woman who had been there before, let her in.

"Hi, I was wondering if Madame...I never got her name, but she gave me a tarot reading a few days ago. Is she in?" Melody spoke quickly, clearly out of breath.

"I'm sorry, but she won't be here until this afternoon. Is there anything I can help you with?"

"I was hoping...wondering..." She was suddenly too embarrassed to continue.

"Yes?" The young woman gently encouraged her.

"I was wondering if she could make me something for...protection. And something to help me see the truth of things...secrets."

"Please, come sit down and tell me what's going on."

Melody sat on one of the two chairs near the counter and, without being too specific, told the girl about Giselle's passing, about talk of a mysterious book, and about the man who had now threatened her twice.

The young woman seemed unfazed by the story.

"I can help you with protection and clarity, but I can't tell you much about this book. I will say that many of us within the Louisiana Voodoo community have heard that such a secret book exists, that something in it contains powerful magick. But it has become more of a legend; gossip, almost. Madame may know more about it. If you want, I'll have her call you when she gets in this afternoon."

"I'll be on a plane then. May I leave you my phone numbers? I would really appreciate it if she would call me."

While Melody wrote down her information, Stephanie disappeared into the back room for a few minutes. She returned holding a small leather bag, opened it, and handed it to Melody. Choosing two straight candles from the shelves, one black and one white, Stephanie placed them into the bag. She next selected a small bottle of oil, a container of powder, and a business card.

Staring steadily into Melody's eyes, she gave very somber instructions. "When you get home, draw a line at your doors or around the perimeter of your house with this dragon's blood incense powder," she said, holding up the jar of red powder.

Melody was about to ask what dragon's blood was, but stopped. Asking questions about these things led to more questions. Right now she just wanted to be told what to do, so she listened intently as the woman continued.

"Then stick four knives into the ground, one for each direction, to break the winds that can carry your enemies to you. Burn the candles together. Burn the black one upside down. As you do, think of all negative energy being taken away and reabsorbed by Mother Earth, where it will be neutralized and recycled. Burn the white candle normally, asking Elegba to open the doors to clarity for you. Place a glass of water between the two candles and let them burn down, near the charm bag— the gris-gris bag—you got the other day. When they are finished, take the wax remains and some offerings to Elegba at a four-way crossroad. Elegba..." she paused for effect, emphasizing the power of Elegba, "... is a most powerful Orisha. He will take care to protect you and bring you clarity. The usual offerings brought to him are green bananas, coconut, yams and strong liqueur. He also likes cigars. All ceremonies begin with an offering to Elegba."

"Yes, I was at a ceremony two nights ago where the woman talked about Elegba...and the crossroads."

The girl raised her eyebrows ever so slightly, surprised that such a novice had already attended a ceremony. "After the ritual, your protection bag is ready. Wear it around your neck and when you feel in need, rub it three times—three is the number associated with Elegba. Follow by calling his power word: Lalupo. Make sure you say the word forcefully; it is the power of your intention and the need of your call that will bring Elegba."

Melody was writing everything down. The woman placed a hand on her shoulder.

"Don't worry about writing everything down. Before you start, sit down in a quiet place and slow your breathing. Allow your conscious mind to relax and meditate for a few minutes. True magick must be felt in the heart, not read from a piece of paper. Remember, you help to create your reality. Your intentions are key."

Melody nodded in understanding and thanked Stephanie repeatedly for her help as she checked out; before she left, the young woman stepped around the counter and hugged Melody. Melody was surprised, and deeply moved by the gesture.

"Remember, it's all in the heart. That's how you connect to the Creator's energy. I understand this is all very new to you...the words we use and our different way of seeing things. Try to trust that your path is unfolding exactly as it should. Follow the rhythms of nature to help guide you. Watch the moon. Anything you wish to grow should be started during a full moon. Letting go of something and releasing should be done during the waning moon. The new moon is a period of darkness, to be used for rejuvenation and rest."

Melody thanked her again and rushed out, clutching the bag in her hand. She took a different way back to the hotel, not wanting to risk running into that man again.

She quickened her pace when she noticed the time. *Damn! Time really is different down here.* It was already ten forty-five and she still had to collect her belongings and check out.

Reaching the hotel, she practically ran to the front desk and asked Olivia to prepare her bill for checkout. Olivia was calm and collected as usual, telling her not to worry.

Melody quickly went to her room and ran a cold washcloth over her face and neck, and tried to make herself presentable. She knew she couldn't sit down to rest at all; she had just sprinted from the north end of the French Quarter back to the hotel and knew that, once she sat down, she wouldn't want to get up for awhile. When she returned to the front desk, Olivia had the paperwork waiting, along with the shuttle.

"God, Olivia, I don't know what I would have done without your help. I'll be certain to write the management about you and tell them how wonderful you've been to me."

Olivia blushed slightly. "Thank *you*, Ms. Bennet. Again, it has truly been my pleasure."

Olivia looked past Melody, signaling to someone by the front entrance. Melody turned around and was pleasantly surprised to see James, the young man who had driven her to the bayou, walking over to gather her luggage.

Melody climbed into the van and settled back, sipping the delicious chicory-flavored coffee she'd quickly gotten from the lobby. She was anxious to get back to North Carolina. The door to Grandmama's intriguing secret was slightly ajar now and Melody was ready to open it a bit further, if not step through it entirely.

After watching the shuttle pull away, Olivia opened the guest register and copied Melody Bennet's home address and phone numbers onto a message pad. She then tore off the sheet, folded it neatly and placed it inside her uniform pocket.

CHAPTER SIX

It was late afternoon before Melody retrieved her bag at Raleigh-Durham International Airport and left the terminal. The air was palpably different from New Orleans. It was still hot and humid, but at least it was thin enough to breathe.

Instead of going straight to the farm, she decided it was better to take a cab to her apartment to get a few things, and drive herself from there.

With the ubiquitous airport taxis just outside the terminal, Melody easily hailed one and within minutes was part of rush-hour traffic heading east on I-40.

Less than an hour later they pulled in front of Melody's apartment building. After paying the driver, she headed inside, knowing exactly what she wanted to get. She still had to contend with commuters heading for Clayton and Smithfield, and wanted to reach the farm before dark.

She gathered a few changes of clothes and put them in a grocery bag, having neither the time nor patience to empty her small suitcase and repack. She had everything she needed in her backpack, including supplies for the protection ritual.

As she left the city behind, office buildings and subdivisions gave way to pine trees, and fields of tobacco and cotton. This view always took Melody's breath away. It lacked the visceral power of the bayou, but she understood why Grandmama had fallen in love with this area.

The occasional pasture, populated by cows or horses, could be seen among the crop fields. Homes were scattered sparsely, running the gamut from dilapidated single-wide trailers to grand old Antebellum homes, their entrances lined with majestic oak trees, boasting magnificent, wraparound porches.

Upon reaching the farm's long driveway, Melody felt like she'd been slapped in the face: A blue and white "For Sale" sign glared at her from the roadside. Without hesitation, she exited the car and ripped the sign out of the ground, tossing it unceremoniously into the trunk.

She sat there for a minute, steeling herself for what lay ahead. Grandmama had been the heart and soul of the farm; without her smiling face it just wasn't the same.

As she neared the house she was surprised to see Charlie, the handyman who had been with her grandparents for more than two decades. He came over to her car, surprised to see her as well. Melody could tell he was not doing well. He smiled for her sake and but looked lost.

"Hello, Mel. How are you, honey?"

Melody gave him a huge hug, her eyes filling with tears. "I'm okay, Charlie. It's been hard...you know."

He nodded in agreement; a single tear escaped which he wiped away quickly.

"You know, for a few days I pretended that your grandma was on vacation somewhere, but this mornin'...it really hit me that she's not comin' back."

"I understand...believe me, I understand."

Melody knew Charlie had loved Giselle; Grandmama knew it, too. But her loyalty to Grandpapa was so strong that even after his death she could not imagine being with anyone else.

"What's going to happen to the farm, Mel?"

"I'm sure you saw that my Mom called a realtor, and supposedly someone already has an interest in buying it. But I think I caught her in time to put a hold on things. I'm going to stay here for a few days and try to decide whether to buy it myself — if I can, that is."

"Some people were here today. They were leaving when I was driving up."

"I guess they're the ones my mom mentioned. Don't worry; if I have anything to say about it, you're not going anywhere. If I buy it, I'll need help."

Charlie smiled. "Melody, I'm an old man. I have a pension, I don't need the money. But you know I love you like my own granddaughter, and I'll do anything I can to help."

Melody fought to control her shaking voice and building pressure of tears. "I know you do, and I'm grateful. In a way, I wish you would have married Grandmama; that way the farm would be yours, and I wouldn't have to worry about losing the one place that has always been home to me."

Charlie hadn't known that Melody was aware of his feelings for Giselle.

"Your grandmother was a fine lady, the finest around. I loved her for many years, always from a distance, because I respected your grandfather. He was a good man; he gave me a job when no one else was willin' and I never forgot that." He swallowed hard, recalling a conversation with Giselle years ago, the one that broke his heart. "When he died, your grandmother made it clear there was no room for any other man in her life, so I respected her wish."

They went inside to sit at the kitchen table.

"Sam, may I ask you a personal question?"

"Sure, ask away."

"Are you a religious man? I mean, do you believe in God?"

"Of course. When you reach my age, you'll realize that there has to be a director behind the play. Why do you ask?"

Not knowing how else to say it, Melody was straightforward. "Did Grandmama ever mention a book to you?"

"A book? What kind of book?"

"A manuscript, an old one of some sort. Her mother may have brought it from Louisiana when they came here."

"I don't recollect ever hearing mention of any such book."

"That's okay, I figured as much."

"Why did you want to know if I believe in God?"

"Charlie, I know it sounds crazy but it seems my great-grandmother was somehow involved in Voodoo down in Louisiana.

And there's rumor about some book she may have had at some point...maybe Grandmama, too."

"Melody, your grandmother was a fine woman. She's with God and there's nothin' that would convince me otherwise."

"I have no doubt either," she replied with conviction. "It's just that so much was thrown at me, so much I need to learn about. I already learned that Voodoo is similar in many ways to Catholicism, so I can see how Grandmama could believe in both."

"I don't know anything about this Voodoo stuff, but I don't believe you should meddle in it. You don't go wake the devil and then tell him that you were just playin' around."

Melody knew Charlie was a Southern Baptist and—as much as she loved him and respected him—she also knew it was useless to discuss this subject. Having grown up in this histori- cally Southern Baptist area, she knew Catholicism was not viewed kindly; praying to saints is seen as idol worship. Grandmama undoubtedly knew this and was wise to not share her spiritual beliefs beyond attending mass on holidays. If she knew anything about this book, there was no one for her to confide in.

"I was just curious, that's all. Don't worry."

Charlie patted her hand and called it a day. "I'll be back in the morning to take care of the animals."

Melody walked outside to the porch and watched Charlie walk to his pickup truck, noting the slowed gait and slouched posture. She wondered how old he was, though she had never seen him sick or injured. She worried how Grandmama's death might affect *his* health. As far as she knew, he had no one else in this world.

She thought back to her childhood and how Charlie always seemed to be around. He was there every Christmas vacation and every summer, and she came to love him like family. Melody promised herself she would do her best to keep the farm, for Charlie's sake as well as her own. Both the farm and Charlie were now her lifeline.

After the truck's taillights disappeared down the driveway, she stayed outside listening to the sounds of the summer night. A breeze had picked up, and it felt like a storm was approaching. Melody looked up to see clouds racing across the face of the moon, reminding her of what Stephanie at the Voodoo shop had said about the moon's phases. A waxing or growing moon is used to create or attract things; a waning or decreasing moon is used to release things.

She wondered which moon phase to work with to attract clarity *and* dispel negativity at the same time.

She was already confused.

She also remembered the young woman's words, telling her to be quiet and follow her heart. As she tried to quiet her thoughts and tune out everything except an inner voice, she heard nothing but the loud serenade of cicadas. She was too tired to focus and decided to postpone the ritual until tomorrow night.

Melody walked back into the house, now eerily quiet. *Is my heart going to ache every time I walk into this house?*

She went upstairs to the guest bedroom, what she had always thought of as "her" room. Despite the two-hour nap on the plane she was exhausted, and was asleep when her head hit the pillow.

She woke at dawn to a cacophony of crows; several dozen roamed the ground just beneath her window. No doubt there were hundreds visiting the farm this morning after the overnight rain. Before showering and dressing, she ran downstairs to make coffee, so it would be ready when Charlie arrived to feed the animals.

She passed her grandparents' bedroom. Stepping in quietly, as though afraid of waking someone, she sat on the edge of the bed. Soft weeping gave way to deep sobbing.

Melody pulled down the covers and laid her head on the white cotton pillow, hoping to stem the pain by breathing in

Grandmama's scent and feeling close to her again, if only for a short while.

She remembered how as a little girl she was afraid of lightning and thunder, and would run to Grandmama's bed during strong summer storms. Melody's fear of storms was long gone; she now had a fondness for them because they reminded her of cuddling with her beloved grandmother.

She got up slowly and went to the vanity to inspect her red, swollen eyes in the mirror.

All of her grandmother's belongings were sitting there as she had left them. When Melody opened the powder compact, hoping to hide her puffy eyes from Charlie, a small key fell out. She saw that the key had been held in place on the compact mirror by a tiny piece of tape. What would such a small key unlock? Her eyes scanned the room, but she saw nothing.

With Charlie due soon, she tucked the key in the pocket of her robe.

Charlie was already in the kitchen pouring a cup of coffee when she came downstairs.

"Good morning. Did you sleep well?" she asked, hugging him tightly.

He tried to smile but Melody saw the sadness. "I slept okay."

"I know...," she knew there were no words of comfort. "It was strange being here alone."

Melody poured herself a cup and they simply sat at the kitchen table together in silence. Almost reluctantly, Charlie stood up and took his cup to the sink.

"I'd better get to the animals. I think they feel it; they've all been very quiet."

Melody watched him with a knot in her throat and decided to fix him breakfast, Grandmama-style, just for old times' sake.

She pulled a frying pan from the cabinet beside the stove and opened the refrigerator to get some eggs. The refrigerator was almost empty, no eggs. She'd have to go out to check the henhouse.

Walking that short distance revealed what a blistering day it was going to be. Her entry caused quite a ruckus with the hens. When Melody reached into a nest, provoking some squawking and flapping of wings, her fingers touched something that was definitely not an egg. Something metallic—a ring—protruded from under the hay. She pulled at it but it wouldn't budge. Removing the hay, she uncovered a small steel case with a lock.

Her heart pounded in anticipation. She carefully picked up the small case and replaced the hay. After collecting a few eggs, Melody quickly headed for the house.

She hid the steel case in the pantry and started breakfast, but was having a hard time focusing after her henhouse find. She cooked eggs and sausage, arranged the food on a tray, and then poured another cup of coffee before heading out toward the field.

Charlie was working on a piece of equipment and didn't hear her approaching. When she called his name, he jumped. "Hey, I didn't expect you here!"

"I just brought you some breakfast—I hope you're hungry."

"You didn't have to go through all that trouble, Mel." A smile tried to form at the corners of his mouth. "But I sure am grateful you did."

Seeing him enjoy his breakfast eased her mind; she was concerned about his health and couldn't bear the thought of losing him, too.

Leaving him to his work, she anxiously returned to the house, retrieved the steel case and took the stairs two at a time to get the little key from the robe pocket.

Her hands shook so much she wasn't sure she could hold the key. She held her breath to steady herself and, when the lock popped open with an audible click, her heart jumped.

What she found inside was not what she expected.

Instead of an impressive ancient book, the box contained what appeared to be an old diary. Melody gently opened the cover and saw that it had belonged to her great-grandmother, Yvette. It dated back to 1941. *Why would Grandmama lock this away?*

Maybe it would uncover some of the mysteries that had surfaced in Louisiana. When she lifted the diary, she was surprised to find a colorful velvet pouch which held a stunning string of rosary beads, crafted of various gemstones. Returning them to the pouch, she set them carefully back in the box for the time being.

Calling the realtor and other items on her agenda for the day were put on hold.

Melody poured herself another cup of coffee, got comfortable on the couch, and started to read.

CHAPTER SEVEN

The pages on the diary were a bit aged but still in good shape, written in a clear though rather child-like script. The first entry was dated May 12, 1941.

Dear Diary,
There is a terrible storm passing over as I write this. I hope it doesn't have any twisters with it, because I'm alone here with the children and it would be hard to run for cover with the two of them.

The weather outside seems to reflect the turmoil in my life right now. People were right when they warned me not to marry Bertrand.

I suppose that my magick kept him in line for a few years — thirteen of them (not bad!) — Louise Devereux helped a little, but I did most of the work. Bertrand seemed to have changed and he was good to me and the children. I know that people all over the swamp had a new respect for me because I was powerful enough to curb the evil streak inside him. Bertrand is a Creole, and comes from a rich family in the city. He moved here to the bayou to hide from the law and never moved back to New Orleans. Most of the people here are Cajun, and that old rivalry was probably the biggest basis for their dislike of him. None of us even knew what kind of trouble he was in — he was a recluse — but I couldn't help watching him from a distance when I went to pull my father's fishing nets. It took me awhile to talk to him and when I did, I couldn't help falling for him. He was so charming, so experienced — and he talked different than the other men here.

He soon began to seem happy when I went over to see him. Do you want to know a secret? I worked a root on him to make him fall in love. It worked and soon we were married. Giselle was born right away, our son just three years later.

Things went well for several years, and then he joined a group of people who were believers of bad voodoo. I think some of them were from Haiti. I sneaked over there one night and watched their ceremony.

Bertrand was naked and covered in blood, like all the others, and they were rubbing their naked bodies against each other to the beat of the drums. They were like snakes, writhing and slithering around each other, their sweat mixing with the blood and foaming over their bodies from the friction.

Some of them had sex in front of the others and the whole thing seemed evil! After that night, I followed Bertrand many times and their rituals were always disgusting. I don't even know the Loas they were calling in and I have never heard the words of power they were shouting out. Bertrand was always in the company of a colored woman. I don't know her name, but I think she had power over the others because she always seemed to lead the rituals. I think she is from Haiti and maybe she worked a root on him, too, because when he's there, his eyes are glued to her. She must do strong magick — stronger than mine — because I feel he is falling for her.

I have to find out what she's done to him if I want to save my marriage.

Thanks for listening to me. Love, Yvette.

So, that's how things played out! If the Haitian woman here is the same one that had gone to work for Bertrand after Yvette and the kids left, then Bertrand had had an affair with her first. Melody learned more about her great-grandfather in those few lines than she had thus far in her entire life.

The second entry was dated the fifteenth of May of the same year, just a few days after the first one.

Dear Diary,
Thank you so much for listening to me, because I have nobody to go to if I need to talk.

Last night, I followed Bertrand again and he went to a house. Well, it looked more like a shack, if you ask me! When he got there, that colored woman from Haiti came to meet him on the porch, and they kissed. Their hands were all over each other. I thought I was going to throw up. I wanted to cry, but I didn't want them to know I was there.

I noticed all the windows were open and there was a light on inside. I hid behind a tree and watched them in the living room, talking and laughing. She poured him a drink and led him to the bedroom.

Bertrand seemed transfixed as she helped him to lie down on the bed and stripped his clothes off. She tied his hands and feet to the bedposts.

He didn't fight her at all. In fact, he seemed excited about the whole thing, because his manhood stood erect as a steel rod while she got off the bed and shed her own clothes.

She seemed to be in a trance, dancing to silent music, swaying her large hips and tossing her head, offering him full view of her naked body.

She slowly straddled him and pulled a knife from under the bed; the blade glistened in the candlelight. I thought she was going to kill him!

I was afraid to be seen so, as I moved to the bush under the window, I was careful to avoid stepping on and snapping any dry twigs that might have given me away.

She cut a tiny slit on his left ring finger and one on her own, then twined her fingers with his, mixing their blood.

I watched them, because I was afraid she really was going to kill him — but seeing them together like that was breaking my heart.

Bertrand was going crazy, screaming out as she rode him. He kept telling her she was the best, that he loved her — while the whole time I was dying inside. I think that was the hardest thing, hearing him declare his love.

He kept crying out in ecstasy, begging her to untie his hands, but she only laughed and threw her head back as she drove him inside herself.

When he climaxed, he let out a scream that echoed through the trees; that's when I ran off.

I had to stop three times on the way back, to throw up. I've never felt so sick. What has she done to him? Why doesn't my magick work anymore?

Please help me. I love Bertrand and I would do anything to get him *back. Maybe you can help me in my dreams? Love, Yvette.*

Melody's heart hurt for Yvette. She had not run off with a rich lover, as people had thought: She is the one who had been betrayed.

The phone rang and Melody reluctantly got off the couch to answer.

"I tried your apartment but got no answer. Did you really take a cab out there last night?" Her mom offered no niceties, a sharp edge to her voice.

"No, I went home first, then drove here."

"Melody, we need to talk about this contract. The realtor called this morning and said that we can't break it."

"Bullshit. Every contract can be broken. There may be penalties, but it can be broken."

"I wish you wouldn't use that kind of language. That's not the way you were raised."

Melody bit her lip to keep from saying anything that would further agitate either of them.

"I'm sorry, Mom. I'll call the realtor and handle this. I have the name and number.

"Are you going back to your apartment today?"

"No, I'm going to stay a few days, to rest."

"Why? Are you sick?"

"No, I just need a little down-time to make some decisions, especially about keeping the farm."

Her mother's voice sounded annoyed now. "It's not entirely your decision, Melody. As her daughter, I'm entitled, too."

Melody fired back, "You're entitled to half the profit from the sale. If I choose to buy it, I will get a loan and give you half of what it's worth. Does that sound fair to you?"

Annie paused.

"Well, I don't know. You know I don't know much about these kinds of things. I need to talk to Eric and see what he says."

"You do that, Mom. You talk to Eric, and I'll let you know what I decide. I have to go now. Can I call you later?"

"Sure. Let me know what the realtor has to say."

Frustrated, she returned to the couch and turned her attention back to the diary, and tried to erase the conversation from her thoughts.

Melody wondered why Grandmama locked this away. *Had Grandpapa Henry known about all this?* And the beautiful rosary! Both of them must have been precious to Grandmama. Had the beads been Yvette's? Had she hidden the diary because she felt it was a family skeleton? No, surely not. Infidelity is sad and painful but all too common.

Had Grandmama resented Bertrand? After all, it was his actions that had robbed her of her beloved bayou.

So many questions...

She thought back on her dream at Maman's house in which Giselle spoke of the barn. For a long time Melody had dismissed dreams, hunches, intuitive twinges and the like, but there was a time when she very much believed in these things. She decided to give it a chance again and follow up on Grandmama's message.

It was only ten in the morning but the thermostat already read eighty-four degrees.

Melody saw Charlie still working on the same piece of equipment and was glad he hadn't seen her. She quickly stepped around back, heading into the barn.

Squinting until her eyes adjusted to the darkness, she soon saw containers full of seeds and tools of every kind. There was no obvious hiding spot that Melody could see but the building was fairly large. It could be anywhere, and she wasn't positive what she was looking for.

The humidity was oppressive; time certainly would have ruined anything made of paper. Choosing to believe that her dream was indeed a message, she was determined to search every corner and crevice.

Neither the heat nor countless spiders deterred her. She combed through the building for what felt like ages. Her heart almost stopped when she reached behind a pile of old cardboard boxes and touched something that felt like a book, but it turned out to be a manual for the lawn mower. Disappointed and drenched with sweat, Melody gave up the search.

She cursed her overactive imagination and dusted herself off. When she left the barn, Charlie was looking in her direction and seemed a little puzzled. She just waved and hurried into to the house.

Melody knew she needed to go through Grandmama's things and decide what to do with it all, but she couldn't—not yet. She wasn't ready to let go completely. As long as Grandmama's things were untouched, it was like a part of her was still at the farm.

Returning to the diary was a good excuse to put off that chore, and all others, so she curled up on the couch again and resumed reading. She was curious about what had led Yvette to North Carolina.

The next entry was dated May seventeenth, precisely two days after Yvette discovered her husband with the Haitian woman.

Dear Diary,
Bertrand seemed in the best of moods today! He went about whistling and even took the kids along to the store for supplies. The children came back so excited because they hadn't had that kind of fun with him in a long time. When I asked what had happened to his finger, he said he had caught it in a fish net. What a liar!

I can't get those images out of my mind. They play over and over again, and I can't stop crying.

I don't know what to do; I don't want to lose Bertrand. I may try some more magick today. Maybe I'll go to Louise Devereux, she knows black magick...and she may know how to get rid of that woman for good. I have tried, but it hasn't worked. I think her magick is too strong for me to fight alone and I don't even know what her name is. That horrible woman! I think that when she mixed the blood of their ring fingers, she was trying to cast a spell on him, but he is married to me, so what good would that do?

Giselle may know something is wrong, because today I caught her several times just looking at me. She looked sad. Should I talk to her? But she is just a child; she wouldn't understand.

Bertrand is acting as if the world is a beautiful place all painted in pink sparkles. I think he is so taken by it that he hasn't even noticed my eyes are swollen from crying.

He said that he has to go put out some more nets tonight. A large restaurant in the city wants to find a fisherman who can supply them with all the catch they need, he said. I wonder if he's really going fishing or if he's meeting that wretched woman again. I'll let you know as soon as I find out. Love, Yvette.

Melody could feel Yvette's pain. She had experienced betrayal, too, and knew firsthand how devastating it was. Granted, had only been engaged, with no children, when she discovered her fiancé's business trips were actually a cover for seeing another woman. She broke off the relationship immediately when a friend reported having seen him sharing a romantic dinner with a petite blonde at a little French restaurant near Raleigh—when he was supposedly meeting an overweight, bald male client in Boston.

It dawned on Melody for the first time that she and Giselle had been essentially the same age when they lost their fathers. Melody wished she knew how Grandmama felt about Bertrand. Had she viewed him as a good father and missed him terribly when they left? Did she know about the situation at the time, or only after reading this diary?

She moved on to the next entry, dated May twentieth.

Dear Diary,

Sorry I've been a stranger the past few days, but I've not been feeling well. Bertrand has been at home the past three days and he seemed okay until yesterday.

Today, he's acting like a caged animal. He paces back and forth from the house to the porch and is very short with the children.

I don't know what is wrong with me. I wonder if that woman has put a curse on me. I burned a black candle, and tonight I feel a bit better.

I think Bertrand is going back out tonight. He's asked several times if I can cope without him, and seems more frustrated each time.

He told me he was going to get me some stomach medicine later, at the emporium. But they close at seven and it is already six thirty, so he must not be going.

He also said that his Haitian friends are getting together tonight, to do some healing for the cousin of one of them, and that he will probably join them.

Of course I know that isn't true, but what can I do to stop him? If I feel better, I'll follow him again. By now I know where the place is, anyway. Yvette.

May 21, 1941

Dear Diary,

I'm just writing this morning because I was too upset last night to do anything. After Bertrand left, I gave the children some supper and told them to stay inside; not to come out for any reason.

I went straight to the woman's house and when I got there, Bertrand had already arrived. It wasn't fully dark yet, so I stayed hidden in the bushes near the house until it was dark enough to give me some cover.

When I was finally able to get closer and look, they were both inside. The woman was in the kitchen, filtering something through cheesecloth. Bertrand was in the living room sprawled on the couch. After a few minutes, the woman came into the living room and handed him a bottle. She kissed him and told him that it wouldn't be long before they were together. Dear God, are they planning to kill me?

I also heard her say she would like to meet Giselle, to talk about her initiation. I wonder what she was talking about, but I know one thing for sure. She will NOT lay her hands on my baby!

Bertrand stood up, put the bottle in his pocket, and told her to hurry up with the ritual because he was burning right out of his pants. She told him to be patient, that voodoo came first. She opened a leather-bound book and scanned some pages, then pointed at something on a page with her finger and Bertrand nodded.

Could that be her spell book?

If it is, I'll have to get it from her so I can do some strong magick on him — as strong as she does. I'll see what I can do.

She lit some candles and set out to trance. After that, she took a wooden doll in a woman's shape and glued something on it that looked like my hair. I saw her sprinkle what looked like graveyard dirt on it. She said some words I couldn't understand and wrapped the whole thing in a piece of potato sack dyed black.

She said that if the medicine didn't work, this surely would, and then set it near one of the candles on the coffee table. She told him to take it home and bury it in the yard, so now I'm sure it was for me. She explained that I had to step over it several times, so he should bury it near the door.

While the candle burned, they went to the kitchen to eat. I waited for them to leave the room, climbed through the open window to get the doll and put out the candle, and then I got out as fast as I could. First, I ripped every strand of my hair off the doll. I scratched my name off its back. Then, I threw it as far as I could into the water.

When Bertrand and the woman came back, she stood there and said that the spirits had taken the doll and put out the candle. She didn't think it was a good omen and said she had to wait a few days before doing it again. She said something about the twin energy being more powerful than she thought. He told her! I always knew he put more stock in that than he let on.

Bertrand said there was no hurry, and then he grabbed one of her breasts. She told him to go to the bedroom and wait for her, and he turned to obey. She picked up the old book and put it on a shelf in the living room.

I heard him finally call her name from the bedroom: Helena. I guess the bastard couldn't wait. Well, now I have something to work with.

She joined him in the bedroom and I heard both of them moaning and screaming. Several times Bertrand said he couldn't wait until they were together for good.

I didn't want to hear any more. I left and came home right away to take a herbal bath. I also put an egg in the tub, being very careful not to break it. When I finished my bath, I buried the egg outside, but I think this requires an animal sacrifice, so later I will go to Louise's and see if she can help me.

When Bertrand came home last night, he woke me up to tell me that his friends wanted to help my illness and had sent a special Haitian remedy. He showed me the bottle that I had seen him put into his pocket and I told him that I would take it in a few minutes. I got up to go to the outhouse and took the bottle with me. I poured the bottle into the hole of the outhouse and threw a bucket of water in after it. Then I went back inside and told him to thank his friends.

Today he kept looking at me, like he was waiting to see the signs of the potion he had given me. I pretended to be sick, so he wouldn't get suspicious.

When he finally left, I went to Louise's house. Her sister told me to come back tomorrow and to bring something that belongs to the children, so she can do a spell for protection for all of us.

He should be coming back soon, so I have to go. Love, Yvette.

Melody eyes grew heavier and heavier as she read. She laid the diary on her chest to rest for just a moment, but fell instead into a deep, almost hypnotic sleep. Her dreams were chaotic and menacing, marred by images of a black woman burning candles and chanting strange, exotic words.

When she awoke, the midday sunlight was no longer streaming

through the living room windows. She jumped up to check the kitchen clock, which read four o'clock. She couldn't believe she had been asleep for over two hours.

She felt bad for not fixing lunch for Charlie, and wondered if he had come in to find her napping while he had been hard at work outside in the heat. She hurried to get a huge tumbler of iced tea to take to him, when she heard a loud thump outside. She thought it was Charlie, but when she looked out the kitchen window she saw that his truck was gone.

As she turned away, she thought she saw two fleeting shadows disappearing behind the barn. The hair on her skin stood on end. She rushed to lock the front door and did the same for the back.

Melody ran through the rest of the house to make sure all windows were locked. She then crept back to the kitchen window and peeked out, looking toward the barn, from behind the café curtain.

Maybe her mind was playing tricks on her. She had just roused from a deep sleep, with crazy dreams. Her nerves had been frazzled ever since the man on Old Paul's porch had threatened her; it only worsened after the encounter with him in New Orleans. A lot had happened...*maybe I'm more on edge than I realized*. The face of the soda vendor popped into her mind and Melody felt a chill.

She leaned against the kitchen counter and tried to calm down. She reassured herself that he couldn't possibly find her here. Grandmama had an unlisted phone number; the only contact information she had left anyone in Louisiana was for her apartment in North Raleigh.

She switched on the television in an attempt to relax but found nothing to hold her attention.

At least her hands had finally stopped shaking. She convinced herself that it had all been in her imagination, and continued to read.

May 30, 1941

Dear Diary,

Things have gone from bad to worse. Bertrand has been going out every night, and even though I tore my hair from the doll before it was completely charged by the candle, and then threw the doll away, I still don't feel well. I went to see Louise Devereux; she passed a black rooster all over my body and sacrificed it to Babaluaye, chanting his power word "atoto" over and over. She offered him strong liquor and coconut and she lit a seven-day candle in his name.

Before I left, she told me to repeat his power word nine times when I don't feel well. She also said I should look under my mattress for a suffering root — three needles tied together as a six-armed cross, using black thread. Sure as I know my name to be Yvette, when I got home, I looked under my mattress and on the side where I sleep, I found the suffering root. I wrapped it carefully, being mindful not to prick myself on the needles, and went back to Louise's house.

She said she would take care of it and I paid her what I could; I'll pay her more as soon as I can save up more money, but Louise doesn't care, anyway. She works hoodoo because she is a true voodooist for healing, not for profit.

Her sister, Marie, and Giselle have become kind of close. Marie is near my daughter's age and she is learning from her big sister. Some day, the two of them may make a very powerful pair.

Louise knows a lot more than me. I wish I could go over there and learn things from her but, with two kids and a husband who is never here, there is never time to do the things I enjoy.

By the way, I went to Helena's house a few times and hid in the bushes to find out what time she is usually not home. Maybe one of these days, I can go and try to get that book from her. I hope she leaves the windows open when I do; that would make it easier to get in without being noticed.

The times I've gone there, she left her house at about noon and came back around eight at night. Of course, I haven't been able to stay there the whole time, but I've looked for her car parked outside. That's how

I've known whether she was home or not.

I wonder what she does during the day. I think she might work in the city. When I go to her house to take the book, I'll look around a bit. Maybe I will find out something about her. Oh, I almost forgot, she has a son. He looks young, maybe about two years old. She takes him with her when she leaves and he comes back with her at night. I wonder where he was the nights Bertrand was over there. Maybe he was asleep.

Well, I hope Louise's magick works fast and that I'll feel better soon. I don't want to waste away — what would become of my sweet children? I don't think Bertrand would take good care of them and I don't want that woman near them! Especially Giselle, because I think that Helena plans to teach her the evil voodoo.

My daughter is an angel and should only learn of angels, never demons or evil spirits. Helena is too evil to like angels. I'm tired now, so I'm going to take a little rest. Thanks for listening. Yvette.

June 4, 1941
Dear Diary,

I went to Helena's house again today and, to my surprise, she was home with her son and Bertrand. Bertrand was actually playing with the boy! He kept hugging him and calling him "son." That really tore me apart, because he's not the fatherly type and I've never seen him playing with our children. What has that woman done to him?

He doesn't even touch me anymore; at night, he's always gone and during the day, he says he's at work. Well, he didn't seem to be working too hard when I saw him. When the boy went to sleep, he and Helena made love. He spent a long time kissing her face and telling her that he loves her. She really has him bewitched.

How do I get him back?

I ache for him to hold me, to tell me that he loves me and that this thing with Helena isn't really love, just sex. Seeing them together like that, though, they looked like a real family. She made lunch; they all ate together and laughed. Bertrand even laughed when the boy made a mess at the table. The last time my son made a mess, Bertrand yelled at him *and then reached across the table to slap him!*

Maybe we aren't really meant to be together, maybe he should be with Helena and her heathen child. 'm sorry, maybe I shouldn't lash out at the boy; it's not his doing. But with a mother like Helena, how can he grow up to be a good, decent, responsible person?

I hope somebody prays for his soul before it is too late. Well, it's actually too late now and Bertrand could be back at any time. Goodbye for now. Yours, Yvette.

CHAPTER EIGHT

Melody reached her arms to the ceiling and yawned, quietly but deeply, as she stood to stretch. Glimpsing the enchanting glow of the full moon reflected by her car, she considered sitting on the porch. It was something she and Grandmama had loved to do, especially on a night like this, with the moonlight like a translucent, silver blanket. She stepped outside, hesitantly, recalling her earlier fright.

Everything was still but for the chatter of locusts enjoying the warm night air. Melody could see most of the yard from the porch; she walked its length twice, like a sentry. She eased into the rocking chair, still alert for any strange noise.

She had to admit that her recent vivid dreams were unsettling. As a child she had been a prolific dreamer, and loved sharing her dreams with Grandmama Giselle. They would sit at the kitchen table or in the porch swing the following morning, talking about the dreams and how they made Melody feel. She loved to ponder the possible meanings or messages.

That all ended when her father died...much of the essence of Melody ended that day.

He had always been the picture of health, vibrant and athletic. Melody had never seen him sick or in pain. One day they were sitting together in the living room watching football when her dad fell asleep in his favorite recliner; a usual occurrence on a weekend afternoon. Melody glanced over, about to ask him something, and her words caught in her throat.

Instead of seeing him dozing in the recliner, Melody saw him lying in a casket, the picture of death to the last detail: rigid body, unnatural expression, waxy skin. She quickly woke him, trying to obliterate that image, and worked very hard to forget it. She never told anyone.

He died of a sudden heart attack one week later.

At the funeral home one person after another walked up to the coffin saying, "It just doesn't look like him." She then confided to Grandmama, in a very matter-of-fact manner, that she had already seen him dead. She saw it ahead of time.

She finally broke down several days later while staying with Giselle, sobbing nonstop for hours, and confessed her fear that it was her fault. Could she have prevented it if she had warned him? Maybe he would have seen a doctor; maybe they could have prevented whatever had suddenly stopped his heart that day.

It tore her apart then and continued to gnaw at her through the years, blind-sided by grief at the most unexpected times.

The past several days had thrown her into spiritual chaos, reviving questions, thoughts and feelings she thought long-buried. Too many practical things needed her attention right now, not the least of which was the decision about the farm. She had no time to dwell on the vagaries of spirituality and the meaning of life. She needed to snap out of it.

There was no question that she was financially incapable of maintaining two households so, if she decided to keep the farm, it would mean being quite a distance from work. Maybe this was the push she needed to start the consulting business she had been considering; she could then work from home.

On the other hand, maybe her mother was right, and it would be easier to just sell the place. That thought was almost physically painful.

Melody wondered if Grandmama had been truly happy here in North Carolina, or was she running from something and the farm seemed safe? The barrage of revelations and events since Grandmama's death left Melody questioning everything.

She replayed the Voodoo ceremony at Maman's house in her mind. It was nothing like what she expected. She had bought into the Hollywood version—or the tourist version—of sticking pins in "voodoo dolls."

She was in awe of its ancient spiritual foundation, one echoed in world history...a foundation based on humans trying to explain the forces of the Universe, to understand our individual roles and the role of humanity. Of the few things Melody had read about Voodoo while in New Orleans, one description stood out: Voodoo is a participatory belief and practice, where the body becomes a metaphorical crossroad between the human and the divine.

A crossroad between the human and the divine. Now *that* made sense. Melody's arms rippled with angelbumps—what she and Grandmama used to call the "good goosebumps"—confirming when she was on the right path.

She was eager to research the origins and variations of Voodoo, to learn the meanings behind ancient symbols and rituals. Even with Catholicism, so many rituals have a powerful history with significant meaning, but most of the faithful no longer know why they perform them; they're simply told to do so.

She had read just enough to see that trying to understand Voodoo is like following a bayou: It meanders and branches off so often, one can easily get lost. While frustrated by the many things she neither knew nor understood, she believed she grasped the essence of Voodoo. Sometimes, the substance of something so powerful cannot be put into words; words can only hint at the truth and at times can inadvertently corrupt the original truth.

She really wanted to share everything going through her head with someone she could trust but couldn't think of a single person among her family or friends.

She even thought about going to see Father Robert, the priest at her family's church and head of the school Melody had attended. If nothing else, maybe he could tell her about the unusual rosary beads she found, though she wasn't sure she should reveal those—or the diary—to anyone just yet. *Grandmama must have kept them locked away for a reason.*

Wide awake, she decided to finish Yvette's diary tonight. She crawled under the covers and picked up where she had left off.

CHAPTER NINE

June 6, 1941

Dear Diary,

I have it! I have the book! I went to Helena's house today and no one was there. The kitchen window was open, so I glanced inside and listened for any noise before climbing in. I'm glad she left that window open, because the screen was broken! I just had to work on it a little to get in. The others have better screens.

God, I was so scared! I wouldn't put it past her, or Bertrand either, to kill me if I'd been discovered.

I looked around the house a bit, but didn't want to stay too long, so I took a peek in her closet. There were some uniforms with a restaurant name stitched on them. Could it be the same restaurant Bertrand provides the catch for? He never told me the name of it.

I looked in the living room, too, and she has a cabinet full of jars and powders. I wonder what all that stuff is for. The book was on the shelf, but I was too scared to look at it there, so I took it and got out. I just got home a little while ago, so I'm dying to read it. I will talk to you later. Love, Yvette.

June 6, 1941

Oh, my God! The chain I had on my neck is gone! I didn't even realize it until a little while ago when I went to take a bath and it wasn't there. If it's at Helena's house, I am dead. I'm hoping that I lost it on the way somewhere, but I'm afraid it got caught on the screen when I went in. If I had noticed it earlier, I'd have gone back to look, but it's too late now; she's probably already back from work.

If it is there and she shows it to Bertrand, he'll know right away it was me who took the book.

I have to get out of here before she notices or he gets back. I hid the book in a hole, in a tree in the woods, so if I have to leave in a hurry, I can get it on my way. I couldn't hide it in the house.

I still want to read it, but I don't know how it can help now. I won't have Bertrand back, not after finding out that he wanted to kill me. I must hurry and pack the things the children need, along with a few of my own.

I hope to write more soon. Please pray for me that the conjure woman does not find me before I can escape. Love, Yvette.

June 15, 1941
Dear Diary,
It was harder than I thought it would be. I took all the money from the house, my mother's diamond necklace and earrings, and the antique rosary Maman Corinne had given me. I hope I won't have to sell them, but God help my soul, I simply don't know what's ahead of us.

Bertrand and Helena both know people in New Orleans, so it wasn't safe to stay there for more than one night. I used most of the money I had to buy train tickets and some food for the children.

We have to keep moving, because they can find us if we don't get far enough. The train brought us to Savannah, Georgia and I found us a room to stay for a little while. I told my landlady that I didn't know how long we could stay and that I needed a job to pay her the rent. She looked at the children and I think she took a liking to them, because she said I could work for her, cleaning her other rentals.

I was so thankful and relieved that I started crying, right there in front of her. She put an arm around me and told me that everything would be all right. I had to lie about why we are running; I told her my ex was trying to kill me and the children.

She looked at me sympathetically, said I could stay as long as I wanted, and offered to help me if I need to stay hidden for some time. What a nice lady! She even brings the children cakes and sweets, and they like her a lot. I'm happy that we have a stable place to be, at least for a little while, but I don't know how long it will last.

Maybe my guardian angel is watching. Are you there? I hope so. After I finish writing, I think I'll pull out that book. Maybe there is something in it that can help me; that would be great! Right now, I need all the help I can get — for me and for my children!

Giselle stays strong. She is so wonderful; she has become a little mommy for her younger brother.

I hope to write more tomorrow, but often I'm so tired when I get back to the room that I fall right to sleep. I feel blessed Mrs. Ritchie brings supper to the children most nights before I come back. Love, Yvette.

June 18, 1941
For the first time in weeks, I feel a little hope in my heart. Last night I read some of the manuscript and I learned some very important things that I didn't know.

I think I will soon learn how to protect us from Helena and Bertrand. At least now I can use her weapons. She is evil and she uses the book to fulfill her evil purposes, but I can use it to find an island of peace for the children and myself.

Please, dear God, let me learn and I promise that I will use it to help other people, too.

I just want my children to be safe and I never want to see Bertrand again. By now, he and his mistress have probably found my pendant — and they are trying to find us. I wonder if he ever loved me, or if the witch just put a real strong root on him. I can't worry about that now, though, because our lives are at stake. He belongs to Helena now, God help his soul.

I'm going to close, so I can read some more of the book. I'm really excited about this. Pray for me that I find a solution. Always your friend, Yvette.

June 19, 1941
I am so happy! I think I have found the key to freedom! Last night I stayed up very late to read, and this morning I got up early to clean two of Mrs. Ritchie's houses, but I wasn't even tired. Mrs. Ritchie noticed my changed mood. She said I'm beautiful when I smile and that I should smile more often. I told her I would try, and then I hugged her.

How Mrs. Ritchie makes me miss my mother! I feel so badly...if she knew I sold the jewelry I was keeping for her, she might not want to see me, anyway. I didn't even tell her I was leaving. I was too scared, too ashamed to face her. One day, I will be strong enough to write to her, but it's not safe yet.

I have to go now. I heard that they are looking for a barmaid at the "Golden Ale" and Mrs. Ritchie said she would watch the children if I have to work at night. She is such a dear! Today she even bought ice cream for the children. What would I do without her? Maybe she's an angel. She even looks like one, with that curly, blonde hair softly framing her face.

She mentioned today that she received a letter from her cousin in North Carolina, who needs help. Mrs. Ritchie said it would be like working for family, because she cares for me like the daughter she never had. Also, because her cousin lost her own daughter to illness a few months ago, which is why she now has her grandchildren and needs help caring for them.

I think I will leave in a few weeks; first I have to save enough money for the train.

I will write again soon. Yours, Yvette.

June 20, 1941
Dear Diary,
It didn't go well at the "Golden Ale." There was another girl going for the job and they chose her.

Mrs. Ritchie called it a sign of destiny and said maybe I should leave right away. I agreed with her, but told her I didn't even have enough money for all of the rent, so I couldn't pay for tickets yet.

Well, do you know what that dear woman has done?

She gave me enough money for the train, plus a little extra — and she told me to forget about the rent, so long as I stayed in touch with her. She has been such a friend and I love her like you would a mother, so I'll write to her for sure.

I suppose we will leave tomorrow, so I may not write for a few days.

Love, Yvette.

June 29, 1941

We are all settled in! North Carolina is so different than Louisiana, but I think we'll be happy here. Mrs. Roberts is like Mrs. Ritchie, and her two grandchildren are so sweet. It is so sad that their mother will not see them grow up! Last night I started thinking about that, and it made me cry. Mrs. Roberts thought I was crying for my own situation and she made me some tea. We had tea together in her living room and I felt like one of those grand ladies you see in fancy portraits.

I have read a lot of the book, and now I am sure we won't be found. I've been trying to put into practice what I've learned and, to my amazement, it seems to have worked!

Yesterday, Mrs. Robert's son, Joseph, came to see her and he seems to be a real gentleman. I really enjoyed his company. It touched my heart to see how gentle he was with his mother and his two little nephews.

Maybe there are nice men out there. I'm still so hurt though, I don't think I can ever love again. In the deep of my heart, I still love Bertrand, though I know I can never again trust him. Still, I dream of him realizing what he has done to me and to his children.

I hope and pray we have finally found a stable place to live in peace, especially for the children. I have to tend to them now, because they seem to be waking from their afternoon rest.

Yvette.

September 15, 1941

Dear Diary,

Sorry I haven't written in so long. Things have changed a lot and I will soon be Mrs. Joseph Roberts. I know I have to move on, despite lingering feelings for Bertrand, because my children need a father. I wrote to tell Mrs. Ritchie the news just yesterday. I'm sure she'll be a bit surprised, but she'll be happy for us.

Joseph has a house in a small town called Smithfield, which is about thirty miles from here. That's where we will live, later on. His mother was very happy, crying from joy...but her tears soon turned to despair when she thought of Tommy and Wayne. I talked to Joseph about it and we decided that for now, we will live with his mother and the children, so she will not have to worry about finding care for them.

I am happy and Joseph is wonderful. I haven't told him the reason I ran away and I don't know if I ever will be able to. He knows I have to stay hidden and he promised he would never betray me. I love him for that, and I love him for all that he does for my children. Imagine that he even took Giselle to a seamstress and had three dresses made for her — brand new ones! She was so happy!

I have finished reading the book and my life has changed. What I used to believe has now grown and come alive. I can control what happens around us. I must guard it now and, later on, I will have to teach Giselle to do the same. The book can never go back to Helena or Bertrand. I would die protecting it. I know God is with me now, and that Bertrand and Helena can't harm any of us unless I allow them. God has sent me Joseph, and I pledge to be a good wife — but still, I must hide all things from my past. Joseph wouldn't understand the true nature of this as I know you do. To understand it fully, you must be born and raised amid the voodoo that lives and breathes.

What I'm trying to say is, I won't be able to write to you anymore. The connection that has carried me throughout my life so far and — as I know now — made Bertrand interested in me to begin with, must be set aside. You must rest. We'll always have a sacred bond, but I must not speak of or depend on it any longer. With much love, Yvette.

Poor Yvette! First, she had to literally run for her life; then she had people thinking she left to indulge in an illicit affair, when it had been Bertrand who had done so; and finally, she had to hide away her past to guard her own safety and that of her children! Melody was surprised she could be so emotional about someone she had never met, but she was reading her great-grandmother's own words from an extremely difficult time.

Now she understood why Yvette kept the diary hidden. She saw the diary as a friend and didn't have the heart to destroy it, but also felt Joseph should never see it, for many reasons. His spiritual views would likely not be open to Voodoo. Melody also imagined Yvette would neither want to worry her new family nor want Joseph to know about her deep feelings for Bertrand.

She wondered how Yvette could legally marry Joseph if she wasn't officially divorced from Bertrand. And what did she mean by "Are you there?" when she wrote of an angel watching over her? Did she truly believe the diary had the power to protect her?

Hopefully Yvette had been happy after that, for the few years she had left; Yvette passed on at around the same time Grandmama married Grandpapa Henry, which had been only about seven years later.

So, there really is a mysterious book. Melody wondered if she would ever find it. What could it possibly say to have changed Yvette's life so drastically? Melody was very skeptical of such things, especially given how naïve Yvette seemed.

However, this was a book others had talked about through the years as being powerful and influential in some way. *There certainly is a lot of intrigue around this elusive manuscript,* she thought to herself. *There seems to be intrigue all around me right now.*

The tarot reader back in New Orleans had told Melody she was about to unveil a potent secret, something that affected not only her destiny, but that of others. Reading Yvette's words made Melody feel it was possible. Melody was impressed with how the book had seemed to trigger a huge change in Yvette's life. For whatever reason, the young mother gained hope for a better life, along with the courage to pursue and embrace it. *Good for her.*

Melody almost envied Yvette in a way: At least she had a confidante.

She longed for someone to confide in, to share her feelings and all the questions bubbling up inside. Not only about

Voodoo, but how she felt about everything that had happened. It was as though something had suddenly taken control…no, that wasn't quite it. More like something greater than herself was *influencing* her journey now, with many surprises and revelations along the way. She was frightened and excited at the same time.

As an avid reader, strongly impacted by books throughout her life, Melody could appreciate the positive effect the manuscript had on Yvette, though remained wary of any hocus-pocus attributed to it. She now desperately wanted to find it but had already searched the barn thoroughly, turning up nothing.

Perhaps Grandmama would come to her in a dream again and show her more clearly where to look; perhaps Grandmama would be her confidante on the other side since she had no one here.

CHAPTER TEN

Melody was startled awake by the distant ring of her cell phone. She ran downstairs, half asleep, to the kitchen table where she had left it. The "504" area code surprised her: New Orleans.

"Ms. Bennet?" A woman's voice.

"Yes, this is Melody."

"Hi! This is Stephanie, from the shop in New Orleans."

"I remember you, Stephanie. How are you?"

"Very well, thank you. Something just happened that brought you to mind."

"Okay…"

"I got a phone call from an old friend. Actually, she used to work here with me. After Katrina hit, she ended up in your area during the evacuation."

Melody remembered how heart-wrenching it had been in the days and weeks following Katrina, seeing people on TV holding pictures of loved ones, begging for someone to call with information. Families getting on planes, with no idea where they were being taken, and learning that wherever they ended up would be their new home.

"Her name is Isabel. I just learned she's in Raleigh and has been there this entire time. I didn't tell her your story, just briefly mentioned I had met a nice lady from Raleigh. But I thought you might want to give her a call. She might be a good person for you to talk to…she's a Mambo, a Voodoo priestess."

Wow…ask and ye shall receive.

Stephanie must have taken her hesitation as disinterest. "You don't need to call her, I just thought you might want to—"

"Oh goodness, yes. Yes! I would love to get her number and get together! I'm a little flustered because only seconds before you called, I was wishing for someone to talk to about all this."

"Ah, well…Spirit works in mysterious ways."

"Evidently so," Melody responded. "Thank you for thinking of me, Stephanie." Melody wrote down Isabel's phone number and thanked Stephanie again for being such a big help.

"Remember, Ms. Bennet...you're being guided toward your destiny. Pay attention to the signs along the way, and pay attention to how you *feel*." She emphasized the last word. "Experience each day like a new page in a book. Make sure to skip nothing along the way; it's all part of the story, and you are the co-writer. Don't be so anxious to skip ahead, and don't give up until you've finished the very last page."

When she hung up, a light bulb went on for Melody. *Grandmama used to say that all the time!*

She ran up the stairs and grabbed the diary from where she had left it. She flipped through the pages until she reached Yvette's last entry, then turned one page at a time, seeing blank page after blank page...

There it was. A message to her from Grandmama Giselle.

My Dearest Melody,

There is so much I want to tell you, child. If you are reading this, I know you've already been plunged into a new world and you must be wondering who your Grandmama really was and why I never spoke of these things.

I can't begin to write everything out. I need you to continue to trust me. Trust that things are happening as they are supposed to and in their proper time.

I know you, Melody, and I know at some point you will visit the library or sit down at your computer with a list of things you want to learn about and understand. Some of them you have heard for the first time only since I died. (Yes, Dear One, it is odd to write those words, since I'm obviously still alive and breathing at this moment.) You've always been eager to learn every aspect of a story, so I know you will gain the proper knowledge and wisdom.

There are so many versions and theories about life, both modern and ancient...things you'll be learning for the first time as you make this journey. So many people have such different convictions, but they're all just viewing the same story from a different perspective, from different experiences.

I know it's complicated. The more you learn— or think you learn— the more confused it will seem at times. This is why you need to follow your heart and discern YOUR truth, Melody.

You have incredible instinct and intuition. I beg you to allow yourself to use it more and more each day. When you have a feeling of wanting to watch a particular TV channel but don't know why, watch it. When you are inclined to drive a particular route for no reason, take it. The signs are there, and you will be amazed where the smallest sign can lead, but you must follow and pay attention. I know this part is especially difficult for you, to stay open like that. I remember what you told me when your daddy died, how guilty you felt about your vision. Baby Girl, there is nothing you could have done. I pray you forgive yourself soon and allow your sight to come through. It's time, and it is more important than I can tell you.

Since you have found this, you've probably already read my mother's diary and found the prayer beads. It's hard for me to write and I don't have much time, so let me ramble about a few things that I must make clearer for you at this point in your journey.

My mother was rather childish and gullible her entire life, but there was a beauty in that. I don't feel the same about many things as she did, especially spiritual things. I never saw anything as good or evil. To me, most things in life are gray. It's how I choose to see.

Oh goodness, I can't get into all that now. What I want you to do is look into something called the Cult of Twins in Africa, maybe Yoruba. Twins are sacred and revered in Voudou. Even when they pass into the Spirit pool, their relatives interact with them as though they are still alive. My mother was a twin, Melody. She was writing to her deceased twin, that's why it seemed she viewed the diary as a living being. It represented her twin to her.

I need you to know something else, something I promised your *mother I'd never tell you as long as I lived. I'm technically breaking that promise now, I suppose.*

As was your great-grandmother, you are also a twin, Dear One. Your twin was stillborn: a little girl. I can remember how heartbroken John and Annie were. They were filled with joy that you were there, but devastated that your sister didn't stay. Throughout my life in North Carolina I never spoke much about my beliefs, but Annie ran across some personal things of mine long ago, before she married. She's a good Catholic, like her daddy, so she was appalled— in truth, she was terrified— and never tried to learn or understand. I know you are trying, Melody. I know.

Annie blamed me for the death of the baby, said I somehow cursed her with my past and my beliefs, and she absolutely forbade me to ever speak of any of this with you. John agreed to appease her, as he always did, that dear man. I chose to honor her wishes, Melody, which is why so much is being thrown at you at one time. There's no need to speak of this to your mother, it would only upset her; and, she knows nothing about any of this and can't help you. I'm sure she is outraged by my instructions which led you to the bayou. By the way, child, that particular spot I mapped out is the site of my first ritual, my secret initiation into Voodoo. My heart came alive that day, so it was a fitting place to release my earthly remains.

About the rosary: Treasure it and keep it safe. Very safe. I kept it hidden my entire life. It was given to my mother by a woman named Corinne. One of my very first message dreams was about the rosary. And I was told then that I must keep it safe. I don't understand why it's so important, Melody—I honestly don't— but I know without a doubt that its safety is of great consequence, and that you must guard it with your life. I don't mean to frighten you, but it is that important, Baby Girl. I trust this will be made clearer to you at some point. I always accepted that I wasn't to know, but I've seen that you are. You will find out. You have the sight, also, Melody. Trust it.

Finally, my sweet Melody, about The Book.

All I can do is repeat myself and tell you to trust. Trust that The

Book has its own path and that you are now its guardian. Stay alert and be aware of where you direct your attention. Things are not as they seem. You will find that authentic power often lies in the shadow, in the unknown, the unseen...

Remember, I am always with you, believing in you when you don't have the strength to believe in yourself. It is my eternal gift to you, along with my endless love. Blessings are sent your way, Dear Melody.

Melody was so stunned she was unaware of the tears trickling down her face. It felt as though Grandmama had been sitting with her as she read, holding her hand, giving her strength and courage.

I am a twin? Cult of twins? Keep the rosary beads safe and hidden? Things aren't as they seem?

Reeling from what she just learned, Melody wasn't sure if Grandmama's message helped or confused things more. She suddenly felt unbearably alone. She knew it made no sense, but she grieved for her twin sister. Everyone hears stories about the bond twins feel, as though they are two parts of the same soul. *Have I always felt so empty and alone because my other half isn't physically here?*

Melody felt tremendous compassion for her mother. The loss of a child must be utterly devastating. And to keep it to herself, as though it never happened...no wonder Annie seemed so odd and distant. Who knows how this affected her through the years?

Charlie's truck broke through her thoughts; it took Melody a moment to identify the sound. She took another few minutes to compose herself before going downstairs. The new revelations set her back several steps, at least emotionally. Things needed to sink in.

They exchanged their usual morning greetings, but Melody's thoughts were far away. She felt dazed. Her eyes wandered as they silently finished their coffee, taking in odd things like tiny cobwebs along the upper walls and dust on the mini-blinds. That gave her the idea to do what Grandmama had done when she was preoccupied or disturbed about something: clean the house.

The farmhouse hadn't been cleaned thoroughly in quite a while, so after Charlie headed outside, Melody changed into shorts and a big t-shirt, turned on the radio and got to work. She straightened, organized, dusted and vacuumed everything in sight. It was like a meditation for her. She set the intention that, as she cleaned each room, something would be cleared on her path.

She worked for hours, feeling better and better as she finished one room at a time.

Finally, only the attic was left. After managing to open the jammed door, she was certain the room had been ignored for decades as a cloud of dust arose, making her cough. The good news was that, aside from boxes of old clothes and a few miscellaneous items, the room was oddly empty.

Melody started with the boxes closest to the entrance. She choked up when she opened the first box. Inside were all the Christmas ornaments that had been displayed proudly year after year. A smaller box within was full of Melody's school art projects. Grandmama had always made a big fuss over them and placed them on the front of the tree where everyone could see them.

The next box had old tools, a broken clock, and several souvenirs Melody recognized from trips her parents took when she was little; times she had stayed with Grandmama.

She opened a third box, full of various house-related papers. The closing papers for the farm were in one folder; she pulled them out and skimmed through. There weren't many pages; buying property fifty years ago was far less complicated.

One of the documents was a blueprint of the property, and Melody absent-mindedly began to study it. Something seemed off-kilter, but she couldn't quite put her finger on it. The layout of the house appeared the same, but something wasn't right...something about the relationship between the buildings. Then she saw it: The barn was in the wrong place, relative to the house.

Melody took the blueprint downstairs, laid it on the kitchen table, and studied it again in better light. The print showed the barn seventy yards from the house. She knew that was wrong; it was nearly half that distance from the house. How could this be?

It just didn't make any sense! Pouring two more cups of coffee, she again went outside, looking for Charlie. He was in the shed preparing feed for the chickens when she found him.

"Hey, I brought you some more coffee."

"What's that you're holding?"

"I found this print of the farm, but the barn is in the wrong place, too far away from the house."

Charlie set his cup down and took a look. "Naw, they're in the right place. At least, that's where they were when your grandparents bought the farm. A twister went through years ago and destroyed the barn and the silos, so when they rebuilt the barn, your grandfather chose to have it a little closer to the house. They went up where they are today. You probably don't remember that storm, Melody, young as you were, but I still remember the mess it made around here. Thank God it just skirted the house with only minor damage."

The dream she had at Maman's house, the one in which Giselle told her The Book was in the barn, flashed in her mind. Grandmama hadn't said "the barn," she had said "the *old* barn." Melody had been looking in the wrong place!

But Charlie said that the barn was destroyed. Had the manuscript been destroyed as well?

Charlie's voice shook her from her thoughts.

"I have to leave early today, Melody, I have an appointment. I'll come back tonight to close up and make sure everything is straight."

"Don't worry about that. I'll close up. Are you okay?"

"Just a checkup. Gonna get a stress test; Doc said it won't take long."

"You take care of yourself, you hear? I'll take care of the farm today, don't you worry a bit."

Charlie smiled. "I know it's in good hands when you're here, Melody."

She was about to say goodbye when a thought struck her.

"Charlie, was the old barn completely destroyed?"

"Well, most of it. The framework was still standing, but the roof was gone and it was gutted."

"What happened to all the stuff that was in there?"

Charlie thought for a moment. "Let me see...the tools and the machinery we recovered; we took them to the shed first, and then to the new barn. Most of the other stuff is in boxes in the new barn, too. It was scattered for what seemed like miles. We had a real time trying to find all of it."

Melody was going to ask specifically whether they had found a book, but decided against it.

Once Charlie left, Melody carefully measured the distance and direction shown in the diagram. When she suddenly found herself on the weed-infested foundation of a building, her heart began to race. She had no memory of exploring in this area, even as a child; Grandpapa had forbidden many areas for fear of copperheads and other snakes.

The foundation was very hard to see, even when right on top of it, due to the erosion of time and vegetation. The skeletal structure Charlie had mentioned wasn't there at all anymore. If the manuscript was still here, where could it be?

Grandmama hid her mother's diary in a steel box. Could she have done the same with the manuscript?

She got on her hands and knees, feeling for anything that was neither concrete nor a plant of some sort. She nearly collapsed when she touched something cold and metallic protruding from the weeds.

At that exact moment, the sound of tires crunching gravel grabbed her attention. Melody stood up to see her mother roaring up the driveway, spewing dust in her wake. Fortunately, Annie didn't see where Melody had been; Melody got to the yard fairly quickly, before Annie had a chance to look for her.

Her mother was on her cell phone, looking distressed; she waved Melody over as she stepped from her new Lexus and ended her call.

"Hi, Sweetheart," she greeted her daughter with a fleeting hug. "I'm sorry to pop over without calling, but I need your help with something."

"Sure, Mom, what is it?"

"I have an appointment with Father Robert this afternoon, about a proper memorial service for your grandmother, but something has come up."

"Can't you reschedule?" The last thing Melody wanted was to leave right now. She was anxious to get back to the old barn area, to see what she had found.

"No, I...I really can't," Annie stuttered slightly, clearly agitated.

"Is anything wrong?"

"I just need to take care of something, and I need you to go to the church for me at five o'clock to see Father Robert. Can you do that?"

Melody knew by her mother's tone and vague response not to question further. It was better left alone, particularly in light of her newfound compassion—and thus, patience—for her mother. She decided to act on it before it ran out.

"Sure, I'll go. Do you have any details of what you want written down?"

Clearly relieved, Annie handed her a list to discuss with Father Robert and gave her a real hug this time, along with a peck on the cheek.

CHAPTER ELEVEN

It was mid-afternoon when Melody pulled into the parking lot of Saint Anne's Catholic Church. Nothing had changed since she last saw it four years ago when she accompanied Grandpapa Henry to Christmas Eve mass. She remembered the icy roads that night, the temperature in the low twenties, and how worried she had been about driving from Clayton to Raleigh. She didn't want to go, but Grandpapa had been beset with multiple health issues and she knew it might be his last Christmas. In hindsight she was grateful to have spent the evening with him; five months later, he was gone.

As Melody got out of the car, she was greeted by the cheerful squeals of small children in the church playground. Crossing the parking lot, she passed by a group of older children being scolded by a very stern-looking nun. She had an instant visceral reaction, remembering her resentment of the nuns when she was a student. Melody continued along the sidewalk leading to the main entrance. She stopped at the vestibule to dip her fingers in the basin of water and cross herself, before proceeding into the chapel to kneel before the altar. *It's amazing how certain things remain second nature.*

She looked around the chapel; there was no sign of Father Robert. Melody took in the familiar surroundings, trying to recapture the feelings she had as a young child attending service. She had been awed by the Catholic faith, everything and everyone connected with it. Its rituals had seemed comforting and unfailing, a source of reassurance in an unpredictable world.

It was when she lost her father and sought an answer to the inevitable "Why?" that she began to question her religion. Over time, she resented being preached to about morality; being told that by confessing her sins and saying so many "Our Fathers" with a "Hail Mary" or two thrown in, she would be forgiven.

"How do *they* know?" she wondered. For Melody, a direct relationship with God made more sense, with no one in the middle. She respected the devout path her grandfather and mother had chosen, but it wasn't for her and she couldn't pretend it was.

Pretending would have suited them fine.

Melody no longer knew what she believed. She knew she believed in Spirit, God, a Higher Power...the words were interchangeable in her mind. She believed in the innate goodness of people, no matter that the world sometimes seemed otherwise. She believed in energy...that all things had energy...whether the things were tangible or intangible, including thoughts.

She found herself growing tense as she contemplated these things. Part of her frustration grew from her inability to convey her beliefs precisely, without ambiguity, even when having a discussion within herself. *I guess that's why I gave up thinking about it, much less talking about it. There are no words; it just is.*

For years Melody had shied away from discussions about these matters. Truthfully, she envied those who believed without a doubt that they knew The Way, and that their Way was the Only Way. She envied their conviction that life's choices were clear, always black and white, rarely gray. It seemed a much easier way to live.

Even when she had begun to question Church doctrine, Melody felt deeply and strongly about spirituality. She sincerely respected others' beliefs, but found it was rarely reciprocated. Religion and spirituality were two vastly different things in Melody's experience: Judgment and hypocrisy were prevalent in religion; spirituality was more intimate and individual, and therefore more tolerant.

As a child, Melody loved stories about miracles, Heaven and Hell, good versus evil, knowing good would always prevail. Once she started paying attention to the world around her, those lovely ideas became more difficult to embrace. The news was full of innumerable tragedies all over the world. How could a loving God allow such suffering? How could she believe angels were guarding her grandfather, when she had watched him suffer so before his death?

In the midst of these ruminations, Melody saw Father Robert entering the chapel through a side door from the sanctuary. He had aged quite a bit in the last few years, but still had the same attractive Mediterranean looks she had always admired. Now, instead of gray, thick white hair provided a stark contrast to aged olive skin and dark eyes. It struck her that he must be around Grandmama's age; he'd been around since Annie was a child.

She got up and quickly made her way to him, before he could disappear again. He didn't realize she was there until she was right behind him.

With an expression of joyful surprise, he reached out affectionately, taking both of her hands in his.

"Melody, how nice to see you!"

"Nice to see you as well, Father."

"I'm terribly sorry for your loss, Melody," he offered, gently squeezing her hands. "I was saddened to hear of your grandmother's passing. Are you here to make arrangements for your grandmother's memorial service?"

"Yes. My mother couldn't make it, so I'm filling in. She wrote down several things to bring to your attention."

Father Robert was genuinely pleased to see Melody. He had always enjoyed her intelligent inquisitiveness, the same trait which annoyed the nuns. He had compassion for her losses and understood how that can challenge one's faith, though he never abandoned hope that she might return to the Church.

"Of course. If you'll wait for me in my office, I will be there in one moment."

His office hadn't changed much since she was little: same furniture, same shelves, same paint. She sat in the brown leather chair nearest the door, facing his desk, and still found it quite comfortable. In her last year of grade school she had found herself here frequently. She never meant to be such a challenge; she simply posed complex questions for a child and had a difficult time accepting some of the answers, or lack thereof.

She recalled that Father Robert had always been fair, taking time to listen to her questions and concerns rather than scold her for upsetting a teacher. He seemed to know that she was genuinely trying to understand, not being disrespectful or disruptive. Melody appreciated his support immensely and because of it, he always had a special place in her heart.

She looked at the clock. She was anxious to get back to the old barn site and see whether the metallic thing might be another safe box. Instead of fidgeting, she tried to convince herself there was a purpose in waiting; that Annie had come when she did for a reason, and that Melody was now here for a reason. Today was her first attempt to follow the "signs." She closed her eyes and breathed deeply, trying to quell her impatience.

Father Robert paused at the door when he noticed Melody sitting motionless, her gaze focused on the crucifix hanging on the wall behind his chair. He thought she might be praying. He cleared his throat to alert her of his presence and took his place behind the desk. "It really is good to see you, Melody. Now, let's see what Annie has in mind, shall we?"

Melody handed the list to him and said, "You do realize this is more for my mom than my grandmother, right?"

He smiled knowingly. "Yes, Melody, I figured as much. We saw your grandmother at holiday services, but your mother...well, she attends mass at least once a week." He continued with a good-natured laugh, "Even when she's been out of the country, she has always found a church!

"Now, the biggest decision to make from the outset is whether you want a formal or informal service. I understand Annie is comfortable with a formal service, but do you feel

Giselle would have been? This really should reflect *her*."

Melody was impressed with Father Robert's fairness, his sense of how important it was to consider Grandmama's wishes as they were known. They went through various items: time of the service, how the public announcement should read, flowers, music, any material to be read, what should be on the prayer cards, and so on.

When they finished, with only a few things requiring Annie's final approval, Melody asked, "Do you have a few minutes to spare?"

"Certainly. What else may I do for you?"

"I seem to recall that you're an expert regarding religious history."

"Well, I'm not sure about the word 'expert,' but I have studied quite extensively and taught religious history."

"Did you and Grandmama ever discuss her beliefs?"

"No, we didn't. She was a very sweet and very wise woman. I was always happy to see her when she attended with your grandfather and mother, but we never had the opportunity to interact much. Annie handled the service for your grandfather and Giselle went along, knowing it is what Henry would have wanted." His face clouded slightly. "I do remember your mother went through a...difficult time years ago, and expressed concern about Giselle's beliefs."

"Really?" Melody was surprised that Annie would reveal anything personal.

"Yes, but your mother was quite distraught, very emotional, so we didn't discuss anything in detail that I can recall. I tried to reassure her that Giselle was a good woman and wouldn't bring harm to anyone, regardless of her religious beliefs."

"Did my mom mention where my grandmother was from originally, and how she was raised?"

"No. I only remember that your mother was very upset with your grandmother—something to do with her faith—but I also remember always liking Giselle and knowing in my heart that she was a good person."

Melody felt that Father Robert was also a good person, and very much wanted to confide in him. Yet she knew she must be selective in what she revealed.

"The last few weeks have been quite an interesting journey, Father. Grandmama left instructions to be cremated and her ashes taken to a bayou in Louisiana, where she's from. And they were to be blessed by, Marie, a childhood friend of hers. She specifically chose me to take care of this."

Father Robert leaned forward, resting both elbows on the desk. "Blessed by a childhood friend?" He asked calmly, with raised eyebrows.

"Yes. It's a long story, but as you may have guessed — especially with what my mother may have told you all those years ago — Voodoo is involved. But wait, Father," Melody raised her hands, palms forward. "It's not as crazy as it sounds."

His expression never changed; he never moved. He simply listened.

"I attended the ceremony and, I admit, it was a shock to the system. I had never been exposed to anything like that and didn't understand much at all. I had the same idea of Voodoo as most people...the whole sticking-pins-in-a-doll thing."

Father Robert nodded, encouraging her to continue.

"This ceremony was nothing like I expected. It was actually very moving, very powerful. Dare I say it?" she asked with a laugh. "It was very *spiritual*."

He laughed out loud, leaning back into his chair. He recalled the lengthy discussions about religion versus spirituality with a very inquisitive young lady many years before.

"But seriously, Father. The main thing I've taken away from this experience so far is that many religions, or spiritual paths, have far more in common than most people realize. There are different ways of worshipping and different words are used, but the original foundations and intent are quite similar. Things just get corrupted through time, by people. To me, it's not so much *who* or *what* is being worshipped that is the problem, it's who is doing the worshipping and how."

Father Robert remained silent, not changing expression.

"For example, they believe in one Creator, just like you and I do. The gods they pray to...it's like Catholics praying to the Catholic saints. The hexes and such aren't part of the original religion of Voodoo. They call that hoodoo."

Melody expected him to interject something, but he continued to sit silently. Melody went on, not knowing whether he was upset or just absorbing what she was saying. "I'm sure there are some who do so-called evil things, but that's not the religion. It seems there's always a small group of crazies who change the teachings to fit their negative purposes. We have the same type of people in Christianity—and the Catholic church specifically."

The elderly priest closed his eyes, weighing his words carefully.

"Melody, I hear what you are saying. All I know is what the Bible teaches and—"

"They use the Bible for their healing rituals!"

"What do you want me to say, Melody? Are you asking me to condone such ceremonies? Practices not sanctioned by the Church?" he asked rhetorically.

"I'm honestly not sure what I'm asking, Father."

"I try not to judge, Melody, but I am also sworn to uphold the positions of the Church."

"Did your study of religions include indigenous practices?"

"Yes, somewhat."

"Including Voodoo?"

There was an awkward pause. "Some. I did missionary work in West Africa and several Caribbean islands, so I know firsthand a little of what you are describing."

"Really?" Melody took this as another sign, that it would be okay to reveal a bit more. "Do you recall any talk of a sacred text?"

"You mean like our Bible?"

"Yes."

"Theirs is an oral tradition, Melody, with very little, if anything written down."

"Yes, but I've been led to believe there is a book. It's all rather hush-hush, but it's been suggested that my grandmother's family may have been in possession of this book at some point. And, based on my experiences, there are people who believe it is very powerful in some way."

There was complete silence. She couldn't tell what he was thinking; there was no expression, no body movement, nothing to give her a hint of his thoughts or feelings about what she had revealed.

He finally shifted uncomfortably in his chair and let out a sigh. "I don't know, Melody. I really don't see how I can help you. Do you have reason to believe Giselle had this book?"

Melody shrugged, unsure how to proceed, fearing she might already have said too much.

"Maybe if you find such a book, you can bring it to me and I can look it over. Otherwise, I'll be in touch with your mother about the memorial service," he said politely.

He stood abruptly, an obvious sign of dismissal. Melody was surprised by how quickly he went from being warm and friendly to sharp and dismissive.

She thought about giving him a hug before leaving, but didn't feel it would be received well. Instead, she walked out quickly, feeling very uneasy.

CHAPTER TWELVE

Father Robert watched from his office window as Melody drove off, stunned and not sure what to make of what had just happened.

He had known Melody since her birth; he had, in fact, administered all of her sacraments starting with her baptism. She was a very bright girl whose compassionate nature had emerged at an early age. He had always admired her probing curiosity, even though it required him to intercede with the nuns on her behalf more often than he cared to count. She had the best of intentions. It surprised him to learn she had dropped out of law school; she would have been magnificent.

In his youth, he had been like her in many ways: questioning, wanting to find the answers for himself until he truly understood and believed them. To satisfy this urge for independence, he volunteered for a missionary trip while still a seminarian, shortly after graduating from college. He chose Africa's west coast, where he could be surrounded by ancient history, immersed in a completely different world and culture. Best of all, he would be serving God by spreading His message among the tribes most isolated from civilization.

The world he found was far different than he had expected.

Sitting in his air-conditioned office in Raleigh, Father Robert allowed his thoughts to drift back in time, in detail, for the first time in what seemed like an eternity.

Seminarian Robert Rudino did not expect what he found in his travels throughout the West African region. He had imagined primitive villages; instead there were cosmopolitan city-states, with businesses, government, and infrastructure. Theirs was a very communal society, with information and stories shared orally rather than through writing.

He had watched the Fon and Yoruba people with fascination. They had developed an intricate system of learning and mastering tasks that seemed to flow from an innate knowledge. The aspect of their society that had enchanted him the most was their vast set of spiritual beliefs. Their religious history was part of their oral tradition, passed on primarily by tribal elders, so there was no sacred text such as such as *Genesis* or *Gita* through which he could learn.

The oral teaching was maintained intentionally, because of their belief that the vibration of sound is pivotal. The energetic imprint of vibration, combined with the intent of the person speaking or drumming, for example, is where the true wisdom and—as the Voodoo practitioners say—the ability to create magick lie. After sunset, he was always aware of the sound of drums; to this day the sound of ritual drumming continued to stir something within him.

They were a very gracious people, allowing him into their lives, patiently listening and trying to comprehend his message. He often grew distressed by their inability to see he was bringing them a new way, a better way. In fact, his greatest frustration was due to the fact that they did not seem to understand he was introducing them to something *different*. They felt that his God and their God were one and the same; that their prayer and worship were the same. Any differences in form were of no consequence. They would simply smile and urge Robert—who they called "Father," even though he was not yet a priest—to take part in their rituals, wanting to include him in their world.

Theirs was a living, vibrant, participatory belief system. Robert saw the beauty in how their daily lives were inextricably bound with their worship; not only the lives of elders and shamans, but of every single man, woman and child. Throughout each and every day, their gods and ancestors were prayed to and ritually "fed."

He learned that the same deities prayed to thousands of years ago are still invoked throughout West Africa and many other parts of the world as a result of the slave diaspora.

Robert never participated, but he was often tempted. What prevented him from doing so was the fear that his faith might not be strong enough. He had heard stories about missionary priests who worked with indigenous peoples, and how they embraced what they described as the beauty and the raw power within these native belief systems—to the extent that they ended up leaving the Church.

He remained there for five years, spending most of his time in the country now known as Benin, bordered by Niger to the north, Nigeria to the east, and Togo to the west, with a small southern coastline. Drawn to the southern coastal town of Ouidah, Robert spent his final year there. One aspect of life in West Africa that surprised him was how many inhabitants were fluent in several languages. Post-colonization, West Africa has become one of the most linguistically complex parts of the world.

Once he had mastered enough of the language, Robert befriended several tribal elders. They would sit around the fire at night, smoking pipes made of animal bone. He listened as they told ancient tales, reciting them in a wonderful sing-song, story-telling manner, and was captivated by every word.

One of these tales was of a meeting of elders who had gathered centuries before; elders who traveled to this tiny village from all corners of the world. The meeting was about a prophecy, one of global proportions. He didn't understand every word, but what he was able to decipher was that this meeting had resulted in a covenant of sorts between various indigenous religions. According to the tale, these spiritual leaders had foreseen a rapidly-approaching time of extreme unrest and imbalance, not limited to any one region.

They developed a plan or a strategy, or maybe they simply came to an agreement about this disturbing future. Robert couldn't tell for sure. What he did recognize was that the tale itself, no matter how vague in detail, seemed to instill great comfort in the elders. They had an unwavering belief that events are moving according to a universal plan as seen in the prophecy, and that any tragedies or blessings are working toward the fulfillment of that prophecy.

It was said this knowledge passed from the women elders to their female descendants. That seemed particularly important, from what Robert could gather.

He was especially intrigued by something he overheard outside the home of an elder who was "passing into the Spirit pool."

Late one evening several elders and their children were gathered outside the home of the former village shaman, who was not expected to live through the night. Robert remained in the background, wanting to be of service if he could. He fell asleep, leaning against the front wall of the small abode, while the others performed their ceremony around the side of the building facing the proper direction for the ritual. He was awakened hours later by several hushed voices that stood out eerily in the stark silence of the night.

The dying man, in a feverish delirium, had told his children to stay vigilant and prepare for *The Book of Obeah* to be revealed. It was evident that none of the children had heard of this book, and they were asking the elders whether there was any truth to their father's ramblings about this mysterious sacred text. The word "obeah"—they pronounced it "ō-bay′-ah"—carried tremendous significance. They spoke the word with reverence and fear.

For a time thereafter, Robert became obsessed with two questions: What was this prophecy about and did any such book truly exist? To his great disappointment, he never encountered anyone who knew the answers or, if anyone knew, they never revealed it. Some time later, an ostensibly chance encounter propelled him in a direction that changed the course of his life.

Shortly before his date of departure, he was asked to go to the home of a tribal healer where he was to gather medicinal herbs and concoctions for a young woman who had fallen gravely ill. By then he was familiar with the rituals and accoutrements of Voodoo, and had previously visited this healer, known to be a Voodoo high priestess. Much to his embarrassment, he was never able to pronounce her name. Instead, he respectfully called her "Mambo," which is the title given to Voodoo priestesses; priests are referred to as "Houngan."

Mambo always smiled exuberantly when she saw him. She radiated pure warmth and he loved being in her presence. Her wisdom and bearing were those of an elder, yet he could not discern her age. Robert found it remarkable that, once these beautiful people matured beyond adolescence, they seemed ageless.

By the time he arrived, Mambo had already prepared a basket for the young woman and asked him to retrieve it from the adjoining room. Stepping through the beaded curtain, he discovered the room was actually a small enclosure, barely more than a closet.

As he began looking for the correct basket, Robert heard someone else enter the dwelling, followed by a gleeful exchange of greetings between Mambo and another woman. His distinct impression was that the visitor no longer lived in Benin and that Mambo had not seen her in a long time. Continuing to search for the correct basket, several words of the women's conversation caught his attention. Some words were in English, others in French; still others were in a language he could not identify. He caught sporadic references to "sacred text," "garde," "prophecy," "Obeah," and "America."

Not wanting to interrupt, but overcome with curiosity, Robert emerged to see a young black woman wearing a traditional, royal blue, full nun's habit standing with Mambo.

"Ah, Father Robert," Mambo beckoned him forward. "I would

like you to meet Sister Elise."

Robert held out his hand to the petite young woman. "It is a pleasure to meet you."

"And to meet you," responded Sister Elise with a melodious Caribbean accent, as she took his hand in a surprisingly firm grip. In his subsequent travels to the islands, Robert would be able to identify her accent as Haitian Creole.

"What Order are you with, Sister?" he asked, recognizing neither her vestments nor the gold medallion she wore. He assumed she was not with the Roman Catholic Church.

"Les Soeurs de Prophétie," she responded.

Father Robert translated silently: *Sisters of the Prophecy.*

In a motherly fashion, Mambo put an arm around each of them and said in a conspiratorial whisper, "Now, it is as it should be."

Father Robert was confused, but both of the women smiled, then erupted in lighthearted laughter.

"We're not laughing at you, Father," Mambo explained. "You were meant to be here, in this place, at this time. One day you will understand more. For this moment, just know that your path will again cross the path of *Les Soeurs*...and the path of The Book...many years from now. It is written."

Before departing, Robert was required to write a report of his experiences and observations in West Africa. He had maintained a journal periodically throughout his stay, so he drew from the more extraordinary entries for his summary. This report was addressed to Cardinal Bonelli, who oversaw the Vatican's West African missions.

Robert shared his genuine respect for the people and their way of life, and described the intriguing legends they had shared. He made no mention of Sister Elise, nor of *Les Soeurs de Prophétie.*

To his amazement, Cardinal Bonelli himself paid Robert a

visit upon his return to the States. The Cardinal—who Robert thought appeared quite young for such a position—wanted to hear more about these legends, specifically the sacred text. Robert explained that he had only general information from the spoken stories, but that the villagers and elders had tremendous faith in the prophecy. The legend of the sacred text—the existence of which, if real, was known by very few—was far more secretive.

Father Robert's reverie was sharply interrupted by the squeal of children running down the hall.

He did not want to relive that long-ago meeting with Cardinal Bonelli, but he was now facing its consequences.

The manuscript's existence had already been recorded in the Vatican, circa 1900, according to the Cardinal. Robert was forbidden to discuss the subject with anyone else. However, he had to vow that, if it was ever again raised, in any form, he would contact either Cardinal Bonelli or his successor and reveal any new development. To seal this agreement and convey the gravity and importance of his allegiance, Cardinal Bonelli singularly expedited both Robert Rudino's elevation to the priesthood, and assignment to his own parish.

Father Robert was reminded of that every time he looked at his beautiful church, with its marble entrance, intricate architecture, and breathtaking stained glasswork. He knew he had done nothing wrong, yet his years of service to the Church had been subtly marred by the feeling that he had compromised his integrity at the very outset. Without a doubt, he had whole-heartedly and gratefully become the lifeblood of Saint Anne's Catholic Church, earning the love and respect of his parishioners through his work and dedication.

Now this. He could not believe the specter of the manuscript was rising again—and through Melody—in Raleigh, North Carolina, of all places!

For the Vatican to have had been so interested for so long, this book must contain something potentially explosive, something that could harm the Church in some way. What if The Book was to surface and its contents revealed? Could he live with the outcome if it was damaging? Was Melody in danger? Would they strip him of his parish if he stayed silent?

He loved his adored Saint Anne's but had vowed to protect the Catholic Church.

Father Robert had often advised others to follow one rule when making decisions, one he tried to follow himself: Makes decisions based on love, not fear.

Fear of losing St. Anne's and his tranquil world would lead him to stay silent, preferring to ignore what Melody revealed today.

Love of the Catholic Church would lead him to call Cardinal Bonelli.

He bowed his head and prayed silently. Feeling faint, he steadied himself by holding onto his desk as he walked around to his chair, then dialed the number to Cardinal Bonelli and waited nervously for him to come on the line.

CHAPTER THIRTEEN

It was almost noon when Olivia Beauchamp arrived at the trendy Black Cat Café to meet her father for lunch. Their conversation ranged from warm-hearted banter about his ratty old fishing hat to a loving, though perpetual debate over whether the bayou or the city was a better place to live. It was nearly time for her to return to the hotel, so she handed him the slip of paper retrieved from her purse.

"This is what you had asked for, right?"

He took the paper with Melody Bennet's address and phone number in North Carolina, and tucked it into his shirt pocket. He then smiled broadly and took Olivia's hand in his.

"Thank you, Olivia. Finally, we are getting somewhere."

Olivia smiled coyly and pulled another piece of paper from her pocket. "Look what else I have," she said, beaming proudly. "It's the registration card, with her signature. Do you think you can do something with that?"

"Are you kidding? A signature is very powerful! It holds the person's vibration. Let me teach you somethin' you won't find in any book, child. Do you have a pen?"

Efficient as always, Olivia produced one immediately.

"When you sign your name, avoid writing the first letter of your first name and your last name until all other letters have been written. This breaks the vibration contained in your name." Writing on a napkin he showed her what he meant. "So, when you write your name, Olivia Beauchamp, you should write livia eauchamp, and then add the O and the B at the end. Got it?"

Olivia nodded her head but wasn't paying attention. She just didn't have any interest in what she considered old-time mumbo jumbo.

"So, now what? Are you going to North Carolina?"

Her father seemed in deep thought, not looking up when he

spoke. "Eventually I'm gonna have to, unless she comes back here. I'll tell you one thing: If I have to die trying, I will get my hands on that book. My time may be soon over, but you're a female descendant, so it's rightfully yours."

"There you go again with the merry talk."

"I'm just being realistic. I'm an old man, but I can make sure I leave you somethin'. I missed out on so many years while you were growin' up...I want to give you the whole world now, child. This would give you the whole world."

Olivia was Paul's life. When his own father would lament about this damned book, Paul never used to pay much attention. It wasn't until Olivia came into the picture that he started having an interest and began to ask questions.

He started putting two and two together and realized his dad may not be crazy, and everything he talked about may be real after all.

Now that he had a reason he, too, was obsessed with getting this book—for Olivia...it was all coming full circle.

CHAPTER FOURTEEN

Maurice Abudah stepped outside onto the rickety porch, filling his decaying lungs with a fresh dose of morning air.

The heavy overlay of fog was barely dissipating; a handful of songbirds called out to greet the day. Soon, the nighttime drone of cicadas would be replaced by countless other sounds, as the inhabitants of Atchafalaya awoke. The bayou in the morning was like a lumbering giant, reluctant to rouse from its deep sleep.

This awakening was pierced by the hunting cry of a marsh hawk; within seconds she landed on her unsuspecting prey, mere yards from the porch.

Maurice was invigorated by the raptor's energy, and knew what must be done.

One week ago he confronted Melody Bennet about The Book. He had dreamed of that moment his whole life.

He was little more than a baby when that Yvette woman broke into his mother's home and stole his birthright. His mother later told him it had been entrusted into his family's care and was to be passed down from mother to daughter. But Helena Abudah had no daughter; Maurice was her only heir.

He had moved into her home—his one material inheritance— after her passing nearly twenty years ago, and continued to talk with her each day. It was vital he remember all she had taught him, but he found it increasingly difficult to recall details these last few years. He challenged himself, playing mental games each morning to stir dormant parts of his memory he was sure held invaluable information.

Some days his mind was clear as a bell; other days, he barely remembered the previous day's events. This particular morning, Maurice revisited the day Bertrand had entered their lives.

Bertrand Baton was kind to his mother and soon they had fallen in love. In those days, mixed-race couples were not accepted, so his mother cautioned him to keep her relationship with Bertrand a secret. She told Maurice that Bertrand had an ex-wife, Yvette, who had abandoned him, taking his two children and running off with a rich man. Before she ran off, this horrid woman came into their home while they were out and stole The Book.

Maurice was so young at the time that he had no direct memory of this. He always wondered how this Yvette—a white woman—could know it was a special book. More importantly, how could this magickal book fall into the wrong hands, especially given his mother's Voodoo prowess?

It didn't really matter. To him, Helena's word was sacrosanct, and if she said this woman had stolen it and it belonged to his family, that was all he needed to know.

Maurice noticed the fog had completely cleared. Preparation for a day of hunting and scavenging had begun in earnest. He spotted two squirrels racing up a bald cypress, and a family of yellow-throated warblers eagerly foraging in the Spanish moss. Other creatures moved about, staking claim to the shade in the great tree's canopy, anticipating another cloudless, sultry day. A rare white dove flew across Maurice's field of vision, evoking another such day long ago.

It had been a day filled with anticipation, as Helena and Bertrand prepared for their wedding. The small ceremony was conducted by a Voodoo priestess, and Maurice recalled being overwhelmed by his mother's beauty, her soft, chocolate skin complemented by the pale, yellow dress she wore. She had chosen the color to honor Oshun, the Loa of love. Helena told her young son the Goddess had bestowed a great blessing upon them, by bringing Bertrand into their lives. She taught him to bring offerings to the Goddess and lay them by the edge of the water, from which her essence would rise to collect them.

Loss of The Book seemed to have been pushed to the backs of their minds as they basked in the newness of their union. They were happy for about a year, but then Bertrand began to drink heavily. Helena alternated between furor and depression. She believed Bertrand was being unfaithful to her, so she started following him. She discovered Bertrand was seeing a woman—and that she bore an eerie resemblance to Yvette. He stayed away for days at a time and eventually stopped coming back at all.

From what Maurice heard over the years, that relationship had failed as well. Bertrand Baton became a recluse, with whiskey his only companion. Maurice would have nothing to do with Bertrand after he left Helena; Bertrand's betrayal was unforgivable.

His mother's passing had not been peaceful. On her deathbed, she feverishly raved on and on about using magick for evil, inviting God's retribution. She repeatedly and fervently told him not to forget The Book and Its power, and to accept his destiny.

Maurice had difficulty understanding exactly what she meant; her hallucinations confused him. He believed she was commanding him to get The Book back for their family, and he devoted his life to that mission.

He had a good spell the last week or so, maybe because he had something solid to focus on, propelling him forward each day. The Book occupied all his thoughts. His mother told him it was magickal, and he believed everything she ever said. He felt it working its magick on him...possessing him...calling him to reclaim it for his family. He could hear his mother speaking to him; hear his Haitian and African ancestors calling. The voice of his son, Antoine, was present as well.

Maurice knew his grandkids thought he had lost his mind for good when Antoine had died over a year ago. To Maurice, his path had never been so clear. The horror of Hurricane Katrina revealed much, uncovering hidden truths all around.

Katrina had been the pure embodiment of Oya, the Orisha of the winds. Many prayed to Oya to spare New Orleans from the raging storm and at the last hour she did, weakening and shifting slightly, not delivering a direct hit. But it was the breach of the levees that wrought chaos. Katrina triggered this breach, exposing the darkness while allowing the possibility of light.

He knew Katrina had come to demonstrate the power of creation—and the power of destruction. Like Oya, like all Orishas, Katrina integrated different aspects of the same energy.

Maurice grew up embracing this duality of light and dark, and had a healthy respect for each. He saw the energetic aspects come to life through his own grandchildren. Antoine had fathered two children, Alex and James. While Alex saw only the illusion of darkness and despair, James found light and joy around every corner.

Antoine was one of the untold many Ninth Ward residents who perished in the flooding, never to be found. James chose to move forward and honor his dad by making a better life for himself, while Alex was consumed with rage.

It was as if Katrina had blown the lid off the volcano that was Alex, with anger and resentment seething at the core of this young life. Alex took on the suffering of all African-Americans and their ancestors, and was determined to make people—mainly white people—pay for centuries of misery.

After Helena's death, Maurice had prayed for guidance to find The Book. He knew that Yvette, the last person known to possess it, had a daughter—Bertrand's daughter—but didn't know the girl's name. A few months ago, while looking through some of his mother's things that had been packed away hurriedly by a neighbor woman almost two decades before, he found a jar containing blonde hair, labeled, "Giselle Baton, age thirteen." He always knew his mother would help him somehow!

After finding Giselle's hair, Maurice set out to work a root that would attract Giselle back to the bayou. Several weeks later James came to see him after dropping off a hotel guest, "a nice lady from North Carolina" who had come to the swamp to scatter her grandmother's ashes. In that moment, shivers ran down his spine and Maurice felt Spirit at work. He asked the name of this "nice lady."

He asked around about a stranger having come to the bayou — not part of a tour — and quickly learned that the girl, Melody Bennet, was Giselle Baton's granddaughter. It seems she was a guest of the man who owned the emporium at the eastern edge of the swamp. He knew where the man lived, so he went to the house and waited for an opportunity to approach her when she was alone. There was no doubt he would have his chance; his mother was walking alongside him, giving him strength.

Maurice confronted the girl directly, not backing down. Her fear strengthened his resolve.

He knew he would have the opportunity to confront her again, and very soon.

Knowing which hotel she was in, he worked another root to bring them together. The little sidewalk vending business he and his grandkids shared would be perfect. Setting up the refreshment stand on one of the busiest streets near the hotel, he had no doubt Melody would cross his path again.

Sure enough, she came straight to him, not recognizing him at first. When she did, backing away and falling, she injured her hand on a small rock on the ground. Maurice noticed a small bloodstain on the rock; he carefully picked it up and wrapped it in a plastic bag. He would use the rock to craft a pendulum to scry for her location.

When James stopped by later that day after his shift at the hotel, Maurice realized James had access to precisely what he needed: the girl's address in North Carolina.

CHAPTER FIFTEEN

Melody woke very late the next morning, already frustrated that she hadn't been able to get back to the farm before nightfall after meeting with Father Robert.

A traffic jam had made it impossible for her to get back to Grandmama's in time to continue her search, so she decided the best use of her time was to stop by her apartment to use the computer to look up several things.

Dragon's blood seemed to be an important item in rituals, yet she had never heard of it. She learned it's a resin derived from four different types of plants that are found around the world, used as medicine as well as in preparing both incense and dye. In Voodoo, it is used to cleanse an area of negative entities or influences and is added to red ink, to inscribe magickal seals and talismans. Interestingly, red brick dust is often used in place of dragon's blood powder, particularly in New Orleans' Voodoo culture.

She found many online resources devoted to Orisha worship, and liked the idea that they were "...there to clear our path or throw stones in our path, whichever is necessary to teach us what we need to know at that particular stage of our development."

She specifically looked for information discussing ancient beliefs about twins.

As Giselle had written in the diary, twin births are revered in Voodoo. Melody read that twins are seen as having godly powers, and are believed to bestow blessings upon the family and the village.

Thinking about this as she lay in bed, trying to awake fully, gave her pause and made her wonder what a twin's death signified. *Is it a curse? Sadly, that would explain a lot...*

She quickly threw on old jeans and a t-shirt, and headed for the shed. Trowel and shovel in hand, she returned to the foundation of the old barn.

Seizing the shovel with both hands, she started digging around the area where she had felt the metallic ring the previous day. It was strenuous; the ground was hard, full of small rocks and debris. As she continued to excavate, Melody was drawn into the rhythm of her work. Then she heard an odd "thunk." Manipulating the trowel carefully, she began to see the outline of what might have been a large, metal box.

At that very moment a shadow was cast over her, completely blocking the sun. Looking up, Melody was startled to see three men; two in traditional priest's garb, the other dressed in red, with a large, gold cross displayed on his chest.

What is a Cardinal doing here?!

"M-may I help you?"

The Cardinal spoke. "Are you Melody Bennet?"

Wiping the dirt from her hands as she stood, she easily maneuvered in front of her work area to obstruct the men's view.

"Yes. How can I help you gentlemen?"

"Can we speak to you for a few minutes, Ms. Bennet? It's a matter of grave importance."

She hesitated at first, bewildered.

"Certainly. Would you like to come to the house? We can sit on the porch in the shade." She did not want them inside, but needed to get them away from where she was digging.

Oddly, no one spoke as the group moved toward the house. She excused herself to get a pitcher of tea; when she returned, the Cardinal came straight to the point.

"Do you know why we're here, Ms. Bennet?"

"No, sir, I don't," Melody answered truthfully.

"We're here regarding a book you discussed with Father Robert."

Her heart sank. She hadn't asked Father Robert to keep their conversation private, but assumed he would do so. It felt like a betrayal.

"I only mentioned the possibility of there being such a book. I have no reason to believe it does."

The Cardinal never took his eyes from Melody. "This is nothing to be nonchalant about, Ms. Bennet. Do you comprehend the importance of my presence here?

His arrogance was irritating.

"With all due respect, what is it you want from me?"

"My apologies for not making proper introductions right away. My name is Cardinal Bonelli, and these gentlemen are Father Lawson and Father Gervasi."

The introductions were followed by a rather condescending smile. Melody knew others might find him impressive, if only by his position within the Church, but not her. His manner continued to annoy her.

She noted that Father Lawson emulated the Cardinal's patronizing smile and demeanor. Father Gervasi did not; his behavior was odd, even cold, with no pretense of friendliness. He was attractive, with dark good looks, but his unfaltering stare was disconcerting.

In a syrup-laced voice, Monsignor Bonelli continued. "We are not here to offend you, Madam. We have come to confirm whether or not you possess this text. It is of the utmost importance that we recover it, before it falls into the wrong hands."

The Cardinal's appearance, less than a day after her meeting with Father Robert, proved the importance of The Book.

"I wish I could help you gentlemen but, as I said, I don't even know whether there really is such a book and haven't given it a second thought. I've been obsessed with trying to find an earring my grandmother had given me...I lost it ages ago...that's what I was digging for."

She realized her explanation was rather pitiful, but it was the best she could do.

"Can you pass along any information to help us in *our* search,

Ms. Bennet? Something you may have found in Louisiana?" The Cardinal was no longer smiling; iciness had seeped into his tone.

"I'm sorry, Father. I'm afraid I don't know anything that could help you."

The three men exchanged a glance and stood in unison. Although Father Gervasi said nothing, Melody recognized the barely-contained anger seething within him.

"I see, Ms. Bennet. I suppose there is nothing more to say. You will alert us if you do find anything of interest regarding the manuscript." It was not a question.

"I doubt there's anything to be found, Monsignor." Melody extended her hand to each in turn. Father Gervasi left the porch before she reached him.

"One last thing before we go." The Cardinal paused. "You seem to be highly resourceful. Should you find something and fail to alert the Church, are you prepared to take responsibility for this information falling into the wrong hands?"

"I can't think of anything that would require the Church's attention, Father. I lead quite a dull life; nothing worthy of anyone's interest."

The Cardinal left his business card, "just in case." As they walked to their car, Melody went inside and watched surreptitiously from behind the living room blinds. Panic flared when the Cardinal pointed toward the area where they had found Melody digging earlier.

I have to get back out there!

She was determined to either find The Book or eliminate the old barn site as its hiding place. She also planned to perform the protection spell that evening.

The words "protection spell" still sounded odd, but she needed to do something, if only symbolic, in the face of a situation she could not control. Today's visit made that quite apparent.

Melody knew she was potentially in danger, though she had

no idea just how grave that danger was.

As soon as Charlie left for the day, Melody returned to her excavation site and prayed she would have no more interruptions. *Maybe the third time's a charm.*

She knelt and began sifting through the rubble of rock and pieces of concrete to clear the metal object's perimeter. Her complete focus was on the task at hand; she was unaware of the time or anything around her.

Her heart pounded wildly as the box was gradually revealed. Only when she could get both hands around it did she take a deep breath, momentarily resting shaking hands on her knees. Carefully, she lifted the container from its subterranean hideaway.

She sat on the ground, the box resting in her lap. A red powder covered her palms, distinctly different from the soil itself and resembling dragon's blood powder.

Here it is, right in front of my eyes. Or is it?

She didn't know what was inside.

Melody was startled to realize it was already dusk; she'd been out here longer than she thought.

She quickly carried the box back to the house. Once inside, she set the box on the kitchen table, then locked the doors and closed the blinds.

A rusted padlock secured the box. She tugged vigorously, but it was intact and strong. Not to be deterred, Melody found a hammer and screwdriver in the kitchen and got to work. After wedging the flat head of the screwdriver between the box and the lid, she was able to start prying it open with the claw-end of the hammer. It was the latch, not the lock, which finally gave way.

Melody held her breath as she lifted the lid. Inside was a weathered black, leather-bound book, with what appeared to be leather cording worked into the hand-sewn binding. A dramatic, bright red symbol adorned the cover. She had seen this symbol at Maman's, but could not immediately recall its significance.

With trembling hands she removed the book from the metal box and set it on the kitchen table. Noting again the color of her palms, it seemed likely the symbol on the cover had been painted with dragon's blood. Almost reverentially, she opened The Book.

The paper was yellowed with age but otherwise in perfect condition. A hand-written title, in the same red ink, stood out atop the first page: *The Book of Obeah.*

She snapped the cover shut and sat down abruptly to steady herself.

Am I ready for this?

But Melody knew she had no choice; given her insatiable curiosity and Grandmama's guidance, abandoning the journey at this stage was not an option.

CHAPTER SIXTEEN

Every nerve was on edge, and Melody felt she needed the sanctuary of Grandmama's bedroom to help calm her. After double-checking that all doors were locked, she held The Book protectively to her chest and went upstairs. She had no sooner settled in comfortably for a long reading session, when she was jolted by an abrupt noise downstairs.

Instinctively hiding *Obeah* under the bed, she grabbed Grandpapa's shotgun from the closet and crept back down the stairs. At the bottom step she looked around, but saw nothing. She stood motionless for several minutes. Hearing no sound but the subtle whirring of the ceiling fans, she ventured into each room.

The farmhouse was old; it was common to hear settling noises in old houses. So why was she so nervous?

It's that damned book—it's Grandmama's fault! Melody was suddenly overcome with frustration. *Why couldn't she just ask to be buried or kept over the fireplace, like someone sensible?*

Part of her wanted to lock The Book up and put it somewhere far away. She wasn't sure she was in the right frame of mind to handle what was in it...not yet. There was so much to absorb and come to terms with first.

Was it even written in English? The title page was, but it was old, maybe it wasn't even in a language she could understand.

Feeling anxious and unsettled, Melody felt the sudden need to protect herself and decided to work the protection spell right away, before she could change her mind. She had no reason to feel self-conscious; no one would know about it. As with most things of import, it was between her and her God.

She went upstairs and removed the supplies from the Voodoo shop from her backpack. As she did, the little silver skeleton key given her by the fortuneteller tumbled out, landing at her feet.

Melody held it in her hand for a moment, unsure what to do with it. She went to Grandmama's vanity and found a silver chain, then slid the little charm onto it.

"Please, Saint Michael, help me. I ask for courage and strength," she whispered softly, as she fastened the chain around her neck.

She retrieved The Book from under the bed, grabbed the small bag and went back downstairs. Placing the black and white candles on the kitchen table, she filled a glass with water from the sink and set it between them. Before lighting the candles, Melody sprinkled a line of dragon's blood powder across all the door thresholds and window sills, as she had been instructed.

Seated in front of The Book and candles, an image appeared in her mind: Maman pouring flour on the ground in a circle. Melody centered the manuscript on the surface in front of her and sprinkled more powder around it. She had anticipated being uneasy with these rituals but, astonishingly, she felt empowered.

She closed her eyes, trying to relax. She focused on the process of breathing, in and out, becoming strangely in tune with the inner mechanisms of her body. Holding this awareness, she opened her eyes, positioned her hands close to each candle, and tried to visualize her fears pouring into the black candle, her hopes into the white one. She turned the black one upside down and lit it first and then lit the white one upright.

With eyelids heavy from staring into the flames for what seemed an eternity—but which was, in fact, less than fifteen minutes—Melody felt a wave of absolute peace and contentment saturating every cell of her being. She wanted to remain in this space...this state of existence...for the rest of her life. She was reluctant to move or even breathe. She wanted to prolong the feeling as long as possible.

The blissful state gradually dissipated; she stood up, stretched, then inexplicably was pulled to walk around the kitchen, touching things, as though to ground herself. After the candles burned out, Melody brushed the wax remains onto a paper towel, along with the powder lying on the table, then folded the paper towel into a tidy packet. Tomorrow, she would throw it into the creek at the far edge of the property.

With the ritual completed, her mood lifted considerably. Whatever the reason, she no longer felt alone in trying to protect the manuscript.

She decided that, if she was not meant to read The Book, it would not be in front of her. With that in mind, Melody sat on the living room couch and began to read.

CHAPTER SEVENTEEN

The first page was blank. The next contained several indecipherable, arcane symbols; it was followed by a second blank page. Melody noted immediately that these three pages were different from the rest. The paper was heavier; the blank sheets obviously meant to separate and protect the middle page with its inscrutable markings from the remainder of *Obeah*.

Melody hadn't studied languages enough to even begin to identify this peculiar writing, but it looked ancient. Not really hieroglyphics—although there were some pictographic elements within the markings—but a system of language she had never seen. Two of the symbols were the same ones Maman had traced on the ground, before summoning the spirits of Elegba and Shango.

With great anticipation, she began delicately leafing through the pages. The first section was in French, all appearing to be in the same hand. A section in English followed, clearly written by someone else. Melody knew enough French to compare the two and feel confident the text was essentially the same, except the English version was longer, as if information had been added to the original French.

"The Book of Obeah"

In the beginning, there was only Energy. In Its immense knowledge and power, the Creator chose to project an image of Itself on a physical plane, so that It could learn of Itself. To realise each aspect, It chose to integrate into innumerable manifestations.

We are God in Its full essence, only prisoners for a speck of time in a package of flesh and bones that we have chosen, to learn of ourselves. We are not a part of the Creator; we are the whole Creator, disguised in a human role.

For all works of magick, look within your heart and listen to the Creator inside of you; when you have reached It through silence, plant the seed of your thought and forget about it, trusting in the fact that the Creator never lets anyone down, the ego's fear of failure does.

More on the techniques of true magick will be explained. For now, accept the reality that God and Devil are one, and accept the overwhelming fact that, in the recesses of your innermost self, you are both of them.

Melody was stunned.

When she was very young she had been taught that God was the Supreme Being and the Devil was a fallen angel. She pictured God as a wise old man with long white hair and beard; a divine Santa. The Devil was a frightening half-man, half-beast creature. They were two separate spirits—one good, one bad—neither of which was remotely associated with her. Even though she outgrew the literal images, she still perceived both as separate, distinct beings.

The idea that they were of the *same* energy...that was something new for her. As she considered it, Melody recognized its similarity to her view of universal energy; it was just stated differently.

She believed in karma and balance, cause and effect, and that there is a reaction for every action. She believed the energy of one's actions, even their intentions—the combination of which she now understood to be magick—would merely intensify the effect.

Was this the Church's fear? That we'll discover we are all created of the same energy, with "good" and "bad" and everything in between as part of our makeup? Or was it the part about people having control over their own thoughts, with a direct line to Spirit; that we *are* Spirit?

This type of awakening would erode a lot of the Church's power; not just in the Catholic Church, but all organized religions. If people lost their fear of Hell, would they still attend church regularly?

Fear is a key weapon for those in power. The surest way to control the masses is to keep them afraid; this fear ensures they will return, filling the coffers. Certainly churches would have less influence if people claimed their authentic divine right. *That must scare the shit out of 'the powers that be'!*

She felt stronger after reading the introduction, glad that there was a positive message and one she understood. The words essentially echoed her basic beliefs and provided a confirmation of sorts. Flipping through, she noted that there were seven more chapters and that the last fifty or so pages were blank.

The first chapter was entitled "Light and Darkness," and the pages were adorned with symbols of the moon and the sun, along with angels and demons at the four corners.

Darkness must be embraced before true light can be found. This is not to be confused with the light that illuminates the world. The latter only makes it possible for us to perceive the reality we have created for ourselves.

Melody was familiar with the saying "the dark night of the soul," and had read about many people who had experienced spiritual awakenings, epiphanies, after moving through their own souls' darkness and pain. Personally, she preferred to avoid the darkness. Even though she had always recognized, in her own way, that both light and dark live within us all, she tried to avoid giving darkness any attention. She associated darkness with sadness and emotional pain, and was weary of these things. The message here was to embrace the darkness.

She glanced at the clock and, seeing how late it was, thought about embracing the darkness in the form of sleep, but really didn't want to stop reading.

The next section was longer and discussed Voodoo in greater detail, though much of it was still unfamiliar to her. She saw a difference in the handwriting here, too. Scanning the pages, they described the different Orishas, who were—as Maman had explained—multiple expressions of God's energy. She recognized a few of the names from conversations at the Voodoo shop and with Maman.

As she skipped over the unknown names, the name "Elegba" caught her eye. She read the description:

Elegba, also known as Legba, Elegbara and Eleggua, is the keeper of the sacred key which opens all doors, he can also bring in or take away opportunities, wealth and love. He is an image of male fertility and is, therefore, a most powerful Orisha. He is associated with the vibrations of Saint Michael, Saint Peter and Saint Anthony of Padua...

He is the first to be called and given offerings in all rituals, because He opens the doors to all other Orishas. His word of calling is Lalupo, but true intention is the most powerful tool Elegba can be summoned with. His power is everywhere, for everywhere there are doors that must be opened. Elegba is strong especially in wooded areas.

On the bottom of the page, two more names were penned in: "Baron Samedi" and "Maman Brigitte." Nothing was written beside either name and Melody wondered if Helena—assuming it was she who had jotted the names down—had simply lacked the opportunity to finish her addition to the contents before it was taken from her. Melody wondered if these spirits were somehow unique to New Orleans, or whether they might be alternate names for Orishas already described.

More questions...

The energy behind each Orisha is one and the same, and each manifestation includes different facets of itself. Some are warriors, some sensual maidens and some are elders, keepers of wisdom and mystery. All are faces of the Creator's energy. They are, therefore, extensions of your true self.

It is important to reward the Orishas because by doing so, you are rewarding that part of your true self which will materialise your wish. The choice of offerings is entirely up to the adept.

The last phrase transported her to Maman Marie's. Melody recalled how, during the ritual for Grandmama, Maman had thrown food and drink into the fire, in honor of the spirits she had summoned. Now she understood why. She had never read anything that explained why ritual offerings are made, not in this way.

Modern society looked down upon ritual offerings, which bring to mind ancient days when both animals and people were sacrificed to "appease the gods." This passage made her look at this practice from a completely different perspective.

Religious rituals have always disturbed her, as they seem to require people to beg of something outside of themselves. She believed Spirit was within, not external.

In keeping with her belief, she now saw that by making an offering "you are rewarding that part of your true self which will materialize your wish."

That's brilliant!

She continued reading...

The colors corresponding with the Orishas are indicative of their natures, but are not always entirely comprehensive. Because an Orisha dominates the elemental forces at the base of human drama, the colors the adept must accept are those communicated by the Orisha Itself through inner silence.

Melody recalled the Orisha seals she had seen at Maman's, and that Maman had referred to herself as a daughter of Shango and decorated her bedroom in Shango's colors of red and white.

Also, Maman had said she saw Yemoja with Melody. At the time, Melody had no idea who Yemoja was, but from the description in *Obeah*, Yemoja was like Mother Mary, for whom

Melody had great affection. According to the text, Yemoja's color was the deepest blue, the color which reflected the light of God's truth in the sea of inner silence.

For some reason Melody also felt drawn to Elegba, the keeper of the key; she felt safe. After all, she had seen Grandmama Giselle willingly go with the shadow coming from within Elegba's seal, before they both disappeared. She gently touched the small silver key on her neck and said another prayer.

"Elegba, or Saint Michael, please open the doors that I need to go through. Help me understand my path. Please protect me and those around me as I make this journey."

There was so much she wanted to understand.

She suddenly remembered the phone call from the girl at the shop in New Orleans, telling her about Isabel, the woman who had relocated to Raleigh after Hurricane Katrina. Maybe Isabel could shed some light and provide the guidance Melody so desperately needed. She decided to phone Isabel first thing in the morning.

CHAPTER EIGHTEEN

Melody already had coffee brewing when Charlie knocked on the kitchen door the next morning.

Rather than come inside, he poked his head through the door, wearing a silly grin.

"I'm glad you're up. There's something out here I want to show you."

She followed him to the small outbuilding where he kept equipment. He opened the door but intentionally blocked her view.

"Charlie, what is it? Is there something in there—is it a snake?!"

He laughed and shook his head, alleviating her fear.

"Are you ready to meet the new family?"

"What are you talking about?"

Charlie stepped aside, pointing to the corner of the darkened shed. All she could see was a pile of fur lying over some old rags. When the fur moved, she saw a litter of kittens! Charlie walked behind her and put his hand over her shoulder.

"I've never seen the mama cat before; seems she decided to do her nesting in here. Must've come this way last night, lookin' for a safe place."

"How precious!" Melody wanted to pick them up and cuddle but knew better. The orange-and-white kittens kneaded and suckled eagerly, their little eyes still closed. The mother, undoubtedly exhausted, seemed totally relaxed with Melody kneeling directly in front of her.

Both Charlie and Melody realized what a gift this was; they just stared, awestruck. Melody was first to break the silence.

"Come on, you ole softie. Let me get some fresh water and food for the mama, and I'll get your coffee."

Charlie followed her inside to the kitchen.

"That's something, isn't it? The funny thing is, I could swear I closed that door tight yesterday. But, unless Mama Cat knows how to pull doors, I must've left it open."

It took a moment for the impact of this casual statement to sink in, but when it did, Melody's blood froze in her veins.

"Are you sure you closed it?"

"When you get to be my age, you can't be sure of nothin' no more, but I'm as sure as I can be."

She thought about the noise that startled her last night, when she first began reading. She also thought of the black man in Louisiana who threatened her, and of the three priests who came to the farm.

"Are you okay, Melody? Is something the matter?"

She didn't want to worry him. "No, no, everything's fine. I was just trying to think how the cat got in. Well, no matter. I need to put that breakfast together for her. She probably needs it!"

"You're probably right. I'll put some old blankets from the barn in there. What are you doing today?"

"Run some errands, mostly. I need to go by my apartment to get more clothes and take care of a few things."

"You plannin' on staying here?"

"For a while. I'll have to return to the world of the living soon and go back to work. I need to stop by there today and talk to Sue, my boss."

"I'll take care of the kittens and then cut the grass. It's gonna be a scorcher again today, so I need to hurry up and get it done." He put his cup in the sink, gave Melody a peck on the cheek, and went off to work.

Melody tried to find something for the mama cat to eat as promised and was relieved to find a can of tuna. She quietly placed the dish of tuna and a bowl with fresh water near the sleeping cats, and returned to the house.

Something from *Obeah* flashed in her mind as she prepared to leave; that a seed of thought must be planted and then forgotten. She had planted a seed by asking for guidance and protection last night. Today, she would release it—along with her worries—and do her best to simply be part of the ordinary world.

Funny how the rest of the world goes on as though nothing has changed, even though my world has crumbled.

She knew she couldn't contain her grief much longer, no matter how busy she stayed and no matter how intense the drama around her. It seeped out every so often, but she knew the worst was yet to come; until then, she wanted to try to get life back to normal.

Melody gathered her things and, before leaving, called Isabel; after several rings it went to voicemail, so she left a brief message. *Hopefully she'll call back soon.*

CHAPTER NINETEEN

Melody's drive to Raleigh was relaxing, which was exactly what she had envisioned as she set her intention for the day. She kept the windows down, letting the wind blow through her hair, which fell loose for the first time in ages. She kept the radio off, cleared her mind, and listened to the sound of the world around her. Everything—color and sound—seemed so vibrant!

According to what she read last night, what we see, hear and touch is a result of thought manifested into reality. Melody had always found the creative visualization concept a little fuzzy, but she had to agree that all manmade creations—architecture, technology, art—had originated in someone's thoughts.

Does everything we intentionally think about somehow manifest in our experience?

She exited the highway and after several minutes realized that the traffic lights were turning green as she approached; not one had been yellow or red. Had her intention actually paved the way?

But what about everyone around her? Melody could accept the basic idea that we create our reality, but if many people are setting intentions and saying prayers, how do the individual realities blend together?

She had always believed in the power of focused prayer. But what about all the contradictions to the whole prayer-intention approach—why does one seem to outweigh another?

A child lying in a hospital bed needs an organ transplant; the family prays for a donor. Across town, a different child goes out with friends for the evening, and the parents sincerely pray for their child's safety…yet that child dies in a tragic accident and becomes a donor for the critically-ill child. Why are some prayers answered and not others?

Stop it, Melody. That kind of thinking will make you crazy!

These questions had struck Melody to the core from a young age, as she struggled to understand *how this life works.* The only explanation that seemed to make any sense at all of life's injustices was the concept of karma. The idea of relying on prayer and setting intentions to achieve a desired result was a difficult pill for her to swallow.

Not having to stop at red lights, she became lost in thought, nearly missing her turn. She had never had such a trouble-free drive, and began to think it might be a lucky day after all.

Since I believe thoughts have energy, it makes sense to concentrate on thoughts that make me feel better.

For the first time in thirty-five minutes of driving, Melody had to stop at a red light. She was now close and had to decide whether to go see Sue first, or go by her apartment. Grocery shopping was last on the list.

Her cell phone rang, displaying the name "Isabel Hebert."

It turned out Isabel was eager to speak with Melody as well, since Stephanie had filled her in on the basics of Melody's story. Both women were anxious to meet and arranged to meet in less than two hours for lunch.

Before seeing Isabel, Melody wanted to check into a few more things, in order to ask intelligent questions. She found the answer to some of her questions the other night when she was researching online but found very little about Obeah.

The mall was nearby, so she decided to give the bookstore a try. When she asked where she might find books on the subject of Obeah, the clerk said, "O-what?"

"Oh-bay-uh. O-b-e-a-h. It has something to do with Voodoo." That was the best Melody could do. She didn't expect to find anything, but followed the woman to the New Age section, nonetheless.

There was very little information about Voodoo, and much less about Obeah. There was brief mention in several books, referring to it as an obscure extension of Voodoo. One book said "its secrets were closely guarded by the few adepts privileged enough to be initiated into its mysteries, and that this knowledge was orally passed down from one adept to another."

Another said it was a branch of black magick that had originated in Africa and taken root in the West Indies, and in Central and South America, through the slave trade.

Black magick? This can't be the same Obeah the manuscript is talking about. There's nothing malefic about it. Could there be two separate branches of Obeah?

She suddenly remembered a metaphysical store not far away; she had been there several years ago with a co-worker who had gone for a reading. She remembered loving the whole ambience of the store, from the relaxing tea room to the soothing, almost ethereal music. It was a completely open and accepting environment where no one would be made to feel silly or be judged in any way, regardless of their questions.

If she remembered correctly, it was only ten minutes away, so she headed in that direction.

Melody pulled into a small strip mall and parked in front of The Dancing Moon. As she entered she was greeted with the soft tinkling of a small chime, and the welcoming smile of a woman with a carefree, bohemian air, and long, wavy red hair.

"Is there something in particular you're looking for?"

"Yes. Do you have any books on Obeah?" Melody spelled it out once again, in case she was pronouncing it incorrectly.

"Obeah? I've never heard that word before. What is that?"

Oh great, even she *hasn't heard of it!*

"It's connected to Voodoo somehow."

"Maybe we can find something in this section." She walked around the counter, leading Melody into the next room.

When they entered, an attractive Hispanic man looked up and smiled. He appeared to be in his mid-thirties, with short, jet-black hair and piercing black eyes. When he looked at Melody, her stomach fluttered. She wasn't sure if he was an employee or a customer; his face was vaguely familiar.

"Excuse me, ma'am, I couldn't help overhear you ask about Obeah."

Melody was relieved that he pronounced it as she did.

"May I ask why you're interested in that subject?"

Melody was taken aback by his direct question. While she had no intention of revealing anything, she was curious what he may know.

"I'm researching alternate religions and stumbled upon the term while reading about Voodoo."

"Well, ma'am, Obeah is a very serious subject. Some consider it dangerous."

Melody and the red-haired woman exchanged a surprised look.

"Dangerous?" Melody asked.

"Yes. If the person working it doesn't know what he or she is doing, it can be *very* dangerous."

"I don't even know what it is," Melody fibbed. "That's why I'm here, to see if I can find some more information about it."

The red-haired woman chimed in. "I've worked here nearly a decade and have never heard the word 'Obeah' before."

"It's not widely known," he explained. "It deals with black magick; it's a secret practice passed down to a chosen few. There's nothing in writing as that would dilute its power. It's a force *not* to be reckoned with."

"So there's nothing here that might help me, beyond what you've said?"

The phone rang and the redhead left to answer it.

"I feel confident in saying no, there's nothing," he replied earnestly.

Melody could tell he was knowledgeable about the subject and wanted to get more information. It didn't hurt that he was gorgeous.

"Do you know if any people practice Voodoo in this area?"

"In North Carolina, you mean?"

"Yes, I'm trying to find people to interview locally for my research."

"Not to my knowledge, but there is a large following in South Carolina and Georgia. The practice of Voodoo is more common than people think."

"Interesting...well, thank you for trying to help," she extended her hand. When he shook her hand, the butterflies she felt when he first looked at her became a flock of birds. He was not only gorgeous, he was quite charming.

Somewhat reluctantly, Melody returned to the main part of the store. She was attracted to a display rack with dried herbs, recalling that Maman had included hyssop, sage and rosemary in the pre-ritual bath herbs for Grandmama's blessing ceremony. Melody picked up a small bag of each and drifted into the candle section.

There were candles for every possible prayer and purpose in a splendid array, some with petitions and medallions attached. She opted for black, red and white, choosing several of each. She moved to the shelf with incense and oils; there, she added dragon's blood powder and a small vial of oil labeled "protection" to her selections.

Awkwardly cradling her armful and heading for the register before dropping something, she spotted a tiny bottle containing powder labeled "Abre camino." She had knew enough Spanish to know this meant "open the way" or "open the path"—something like that—and she immediately thought of Elegba. She gingerly picked it up with her little finger and made it to the counter without incident.

The woman gave Melody a pleading look; she was still on the phone. When the call ended, she apologized profusely. "I am so very sorry! I wanted to come over and help you, but the woman on the phone was in a minor crisis."

"No problem. I didn't get a basket, hoping it would stop me from getting too much," Melody explained with a chuckle. "But it obviously didn't work!"

"I hope that guy in there didn't scare you too much," the woman said, ringing up the merchandise. She then added quite seriously, "I don't know that I'd investigate it any further, though. Life is difficult enough without involving black magick."

"Oh, I'm not going to try anything; it's just for research."

"That's probably best." She smiled while packing everything in a paper bag. "I hope you have a wonderful day."

As Melody walked to her car she wondered if the woman believed her. After all, she had just bought candles, incense and protection oil.

She had just enough time to get to the restaurant to meet Isabel.

When she pulled into the parking lot, Melody spotted the bright yellow Volkswagen Beetle Isabel said she would be driving, with a woman was sitting inside. When she saw Melody get out of her car and wave, she got out, too, wearing a huge smile, as though meeting a long-lost friend. Melody liked her instantly; she could not imagine anyone who wouldn't.

After exchanging greetings, they headed inside before the lunch crowd grew. Melody suggested this restaurant because of its high-backed booths, so they would have a little privacy to chat freely. Both knew what they wanted, so their order was taken immediately.

"So, how do you like Raleigh?"   Melody asked.

"It's nice. Different, but nice."

"Why did you choose to move to Raleigh? Do you have family here?"

Isabel erupted in laughter. At first it startled Melody, but it was one of those genuine belly-laughs and Melody couldn't help but smile.

"I didn't exactly *choose* Raleigh. And, no, I have no family here. They were loading evacuees onto planes, when we finally got some help after Katrina hit. We had no idea where we were going."

Melody wanted to kick herself. *What a stupid question!*

"I am so sorry! I completely forgot that was how you ended up here. Stephanie mentioned it and I should have remembered."

"No, no, it's okay!" Isabel assured her. "Really. I've been around long enough to know there are things we can't control. Going with the flow is the way I've lived my life for a long time now. I'm alive, so I feel blessed."

"But you do have family elsewhere?"

"My nephew is still in New Orleans." Isabel's concern was plain to see. "He's of age, so I couldn't force him."

Melody didn't ask for details, but Isabel surprised her by sharing further.

"He lived with his mom—my sister—and our mother, in my mom's house in the Ninth Ward. We had no idea what was coming but, honestly, we couldn't afford to have done things much differently, even if we had."

She paused while the server delivered their meals, then continued.

"You know, most of us who used to live in New Orleans, before Katrina, lived paycheck to paycheck. And I'm *not* talking welfare paycheck."

Normally such a statement would have made Melody uncomfortable, but there was something about Isabel that made discomfort impossible. She knew that many who had been affected by Katrina harbored so much anger, and rightfully so. But Isabel's comment held no anger; it was a simple statement of fact.

Melody nodded and kept eating.

"Anyway, it's not an easy thing to do...just up and leave with no money for a hotel. Plus, my mom wasn't able to get around. Her dog was her best friend and she refused to leave him. She encouraged us to go, but there was no way we would leave her. My nephew went to the Superdome before Katrina hit, but we stayed..."

Isabel talked about how no one had expected the devastation that besieged that area. They thought they survived the worst after the hurricane, but then the levees broke...and all hell broke loose with them. She lost both her mother and sister in the flood.

She fought through the putrid flood waters to get to her house in the Gentilly District—"it took me a whole day to get there, trudging through god-awful things"—to find it completely destroyed.

Isabel's search for her nephew had been fruitless.

"I prayed he was safe, but we all heard about horrible things taking place in there."   She choked up a few times, but on the whole relayed her story to Melody in a very detached way. She shared her experiences, her journey to Raleigh, and how, through others' generosity, she found a roof over her head and a job as librarian in a local high school. After several weeks of working with the Red Cross, she finally located her nephew.

"It's easy to get swallowed up in all the bad—and there was a lot of bad brought out by that storm—but my, oh my, there was so much good, too. The kindness of strangers was on full display in those months that followed. There are angels everywhere, child," she said with a wink. "Now, William...that boy has been a handful! He is eighteen now. He was already an angry teenager, even before Katrina, but now he's eaten up with it, can't let it go. Blames the world for losing his Mama and Granny, and everything he knew."

Isabel shook her head as she thought about her nephew.

"I'll tell you what, William and kids like him have been trouble for a long time, but it's like Katrina gave them an excuse to just blow up and blame every injustice on the rest of the world—especially white people. It's like we're back in the fifties and sixties all over again."

Isabel kept shaking her head; she couldn't mask her disappointment.

"But Katrina was a gift. Within any tragedy there is immense potential to heal…to heal the deepest wounds, and to evolve by preventing the growth of new ones.

"There's a huge lesson about accountability in all this Katrina business, too. From the top on down; every single person can learn a lesson about taking responsibility, if they choose to grow."

Isabel looked at her watch and was surprised by the time.

"Melody, I'm so sorry. I've gone on forever and taken up the whole time and haven't gotten a chance to learn about you at all!"

Melody laughed. "I'm honored you shared your story with me."

Isabel reached over, clasping Melody's free hand in both of hers. "I am a good judge of character, dear girl. I haven't felt instantly comfortable with someone as I did with you in a long time. I enjoy people, and I stay open to new people. I've had to lately, haven't I?" She winked good-naturedly. "But there is something special about you. I felt it when Stephanie told me about you, and in your voice when you left the message. I know you are going through a very difficult time, especially since a lot of it is in unfamiliar territory. Am I right?"

"You're absolutely correct. This is all so foreign to me that I feel lost. I have done some research on my own, but I still need all the guidance I can get. I have a feeling you can help me understand a lot of things."

"Let's do it, then. I'd love to have you over to my apartment. We can relax and delve into the mysteries — right here in Raleigh, North Carolina!"

"Have you met others in the area that practice?" Melody

asked.

"No, but I know they're here...especially in the Hispanic communities. Some others practice and don't even realize it," she said with a grin.

That made Melody think of the gorgeous man she had seen at The Dancing Moon, who had heard of Obeah.

"I do have one question before we go: Have you heard of Obeah?"

Isabel met Melody's gaze and answered bluntly. "I have, though not often. Few in the Voodoo community speak of it, even if they know of it."

Neither spoke for a moment, unsure how to continue.

"Do you perceive it as being negative, Isabel?"

"No. I don't perceive anything as inherently negative; the energy itself is neither negative nor positive. What makes it so is our perception which is often based on our perspective. A change in perspective can allow us to view many things differently, change our view from positive to negative — and vice versa — in a heartbeat."

The server brought their check, which marked the end of their lunch meeting, since Isabel had to return to work.

As they walked outside Melody thanked her for taking the time to meet with her.

"I can't tell you how good it feels to have someone to talk to without thinking I'm crazy."

"Let's do it. We'll make plans. Okay?"

Isabel clasped Melody's hands, and spoke in a much more somber tone.

"We both have the sight, child. Please remember: The heart must break wide open to let in the light."

She hugged Melody and got into her car, leaving Melody confused by her words, waving goodbye.

CHAPTER TWENTY

When she opened the door to her apartment, she saw the whole place had been turned upside down. Drawers and closet doors flung open, all her things thrown on the floor. Someone had been looking for something, and Melody knew exactly what it was. She decided against calling the police, opting instead for the management office.

"Pleasant Woods Apartments. This is Cheryl, may I help you?"

"Yes, Cheryl, this is Melody Bennet in Building C."

"Yes, Ms. Bennet, how are you? How was your trip to the mountains?"

Melody was startled. She hesitated for half a second before going with her instinct and playing along.

"It was great, thanks. But it seems someone was here while I was gone. Did you let them in?"

"Yes, I gave your grandfather a key. He was such a nice man! What a wonderful surprise, for him to fix your TV and stereo while you were away. I didn't think you would mind; he returned the key before he left. He was so cute! Said I shouldn't tell you, that I should just let you be surprised when you got home."

"Hmm…well, yes, I was surprised. Did you ask for any sort of ID?"

"I was going to, but he described you so well when bragging about you that I had no doubt he was your grandfather. I was sure it would be okay."

"Okay then." Melody was too stunned to end the call properly and say goodbye. She hung up the phone and looked around at the total disarray.

She wanted to tell Cheryl that she *should* start doubting things, that her instinct was complete shit, but didn't want to bring attention to anything. Still, the man must have known her in some way for Cheryl to have believed him.

Who the hell could it be?

Confused and distraught, she gathered everything up from the floor, heaping it on the couch and the bed for the time being. She would sort through it all later. She needed to get back to the farm right away, to make sure The Book was still safe.

Melody was so distracted on the drive back that she had to really concentrate to drive safely. She tried to think this through, put it in perspective. It was disturbing, but nothing *truly* tragic had happened. No one got hurt. It simply involved "stuff." Granted, it was scary knowing someone was after The Book—that *had* to be what this was about—and she couldn't help but fear what might come next.

For now, Melody was determined not to let it overwhelm her. She just had to focus and figure out what to do next. There was a reason this was all happening...there had to be. *I won't let this get to me.*

The remainder of the drive was spent convincing herself to maintain her newfound glass-half-full outlook; searching for the silver lining, so her prayers of late wouldn't feel like a sham.

"Maybe the fact that I wasn't there is the silver lining?" she mused aloud. "Who knows what would have happened if I'd been home."

It was dusk when she turned into the driveway, so she was surprised to see Charlie's truck still there. She hoped he hadn't fallen ill, working in the heat. She sped to the house and pulled up beside the truck.

She called his name several times, but there was no response. She made sure before leaving that he had his key, telling him she was going to lock the door. It was locked now, too, so she doubted he was inside. She checked anyway, in case he had gone in to cool down and had fallen asleep.

Charlie was nowhere to be found. Melody quickly checked to make sure The Book was where she had left it, and it was.

Back outside, she looked around. Still no sign of him. She shouted a few more times. Nothing. Maybe something was wrong with his truck and he had called someone to pick him up. That had to be it.

She decided to check on the kittens before doing anything else. She lifted the latch gently, not wanting to startle them in case they were asleep. As the door swung ajar, letting in a little light, the distinct odor of wet, rusted metal hit Melody hard. Pushing the door wide open, Melody took one step and recoiled in horror.

Charlie was lying on the dirt floor, his face a grotesque mask of shock and agony, and his denim work shirt stained reddish-brown. Blood covered his hands and face, and had seeped into the dirt around and beneath him. His final seconds were revealed in the tortured expression. The slight creaking of the door seemed amplified, reverberating in Melody's head along with the pounding of her heart, as every horrific detail was seared into her memory.

Trembling violently, she knelt near Charlie, delicately placing her right middle and ring fingers on his carotid artery but knowing she would feel nothing. She stood and backed out of the shed, trying desperately to suppress a wave of nausea, and rushed to the house to call the police.

"Nine-one-one. What is your location and the nature of your emergency?"

Melody's voice sounded odd, even to her. She felt like she was in a tunnel as she provided the necessary information.

"You found a dead body?"

"Yes, I just found a friend's body," Melody reported roboti-cally. "It looks like he's been stabbed."

Her trembling intensified.

"Please hurry!" she pleaded, slumping to the ground, her

body racked with sobs.

"Stay calm, Ms. Bennet. Are you hurt?"

"No," she whispered.

"Help is on the way. I need you to stay on the line and talk to me until they get there. Is anyone else with you?"

"No." Melody barely managed this one syllable.

"Is it possible the perpetrators are inside the house?"

Melody froze, new waves of panic welling inside. She hadn't considered this. Grabbing the kitchen counter with one hand, she struggled to pull herself up.

"I'm in the house now," she tried to think what happened before she found Charlie. She remembered doing a cursory search of the house but finding nothing. "No, I don't think anyone is here. The door was locked, but...I just don't know."

"I understand, Ms. Bennet. Is your door locked right now?"

"No, it's not. I don't have a cordless...please wait." She put the phone down, ran to the door and locked it.

"Okay, I locked it."

"Good. Keep it locked until the police get there, Ms. Bennet. I can stay on the line with you until they arrive."

Melody said nothing. She slid to the floor again, her back against the wall and the phone cradled against her right ear. Arms folded protectively in front of her, knees pulled to her chest, she sat there silently. Periodically the operator would ask whether she was still there, to which she would reply "yes" in a whisper. She remained unmoving for what seemed an eternity until, at last hearing sirens, she dropped the phone and ran to unlock the door.

Two patrol cars raced up in the driveway, followed by an unmarked car and a van. She opened the door and stood on the porch, waiting. A uniformed sheriff's deputy walked up the porch stairs and caught Melody as her legs completely gave way. He helped her sit on one of the rockers and gestured for help. Melody felt dizzy and nauseated. She stumbled to the railing of the porch, leaned over on wobbly legs and vomited. Her heart was pounding; her hands felt clammy. She was grateful when a second officer stepped onto the porch and the two of them, each supporting an arm, helped her inside to lie on the couch.

"Are you all right, ma'am?"

She couldn't speak; she simply shook her head. She was sweating profusely. One of the two deputies stepped outside and returned with a paramedic. He pulled a throw blanket from the couch and placed it over her body, telling her she was in mild shock. He then went to the kitchen, ran water until it was warm, and brought back a glassful.

Melody propped herself up on an elbow to drink a few sips of water; she glanced up when two more men walked in. She caught her breath as she saw the Hispanic man from the metaphysical store. She knew he recognized her, too; she saw it in his eyes.

"Ms. Bennet," he said in a very business-like tone. "I'm Detective Hernandez, and this is Detective Jarman, from the Johnston County Sheriff's Department. You indicated in your phone call a potential homicide?"

Melody could only acknowledge him with a weak nod.

"I'm sorry, Ms. Bennet. I know you're in shock right now, but there are some questions we need to ask. We need to act on any leads while the trail is still warm."

Melody nodded, her lips trembling, heralding a breakdown.

"Are you the person who found the victim?"

She nodded.

"Did you see anyone around the premises at all?"

Melody shook her head. She spoke with care and deliberation, trying to calm her voice. "No, I returned home to find his truck still parked here. Charlie usually leaves much earlier in the day, so I thought that was odd."

He encouraged her to continue.

"I called to him several times before checking to see whether he had come inside to rest. The door was locked and he wasn't here, so I thought maybe his truck hadn't started and he'd called someone for a ride."

"Did you say his name was Charlie?"

"Yes. Charlie Broughton."

"What made you decide to go to the barn, if you thought he left? Was the door open?"

Melody felt her throat close as she relived finding Charlie.

"It was the small shed, not the barn. This morning Charlie discovered a mother cat with a newborn litter in there. I was going to check on them."

"Can you think of anyone who would want to harm Mr. Broughton?"

"No, not one single person."

"Can you think of anything that might help us? Anything at all?"

Melody hesitated, not sure how to proceed. Her mind was a jumble, but her instinct told her to be cautious and not reveal much, for her own safety. She didn't feel she was betraying Charlie; in a strange way, she knew he'd want her to keep some things to herself.

"This morning Charlie told me he had found the shed door open. He thought it was odd; he was quite sure he had closed it the night before."

"Is there anything else?"

Melody obviously paused this time.

"Ms. Bennet, anything—even something you may consider totally irrelevant—may help us find who did this. Please don't hold any information back."

She drew a deep breath. "Today, I discovered someone had entered my apartment while I was gone. Nothing was missing, so I didn't notify anyone."

The detectives exchanged puzzled glances, as Detective Jarman politely excused himself for a few moments.

"Somebody broke into your place and you didn't call the police?"

Melody could only nod. She frankly didn't know what to say.

"Did you let anyone know?"

"No," Melody said, shaking her head and reaching for a tissue from the end table.

"Ms. Bennet, do you have any idea what the perpetrator was looking for?"

Melody felt blood rush to her face but shook her head in denial.

"No, no idea. No one really broke in; management gave him a key, thinking he was my grandfather."

"Your grandfather?"

"That's what the man told the girl in the office, but that's not possible. I don't think anything was taken, though."

"Do you have any idea who this person might be?"

Melody honestly did not.

"Do you think the person who broke into your apartment and the person who killed Mr. Broughton are one and the same?"

Melody wanted to answer yes, but doing so would inevitably lead to The Book, and she wasn't prepared to reveal that. While she would not rest until Charlie's murderer was caught and brought to justice, something sinister was at work here. She was uncertain who to trust and so would say nothing of its presence just yet.

"Detective, there is something...and it may sound very strange."

"Okay, I'm listening."

"You know more about this Obeah thing than I do, but..." she paused, unsure how to word it. "I agree with you when you say it's dangerous. I think my apartment was broken into because some people mistakenly believe my grandmother possessed a sacred book, and that she passed it on to me."

Detective Hernandez glanced around nervously, hoping no

one had overheard. Melody sensed he didn't want anyone to know they had already met. She herself was taken aback by the coincidence of Detective Hernandez being the man assigned to this case.

Was meeting him a coincidence, or was it planned? Could he be after The Book, too?

He could have easily gotten her license plate information earlier and called it in to get her address. She tried to think about the timing of today's events but her mind was too foggy.

He held her gaze as though wanting to say something important, but stopped himself. Melody expected him to ask *something* after disclosing her theory, but he remained oddly silent.

"I'm not dismissing what you just said, Ms. Bennet, but I think that's all for now. You've been traumatized and need some rest. Here is my card; please call me if you think of anything else."

He laid his card on the end table beside the couch and headed toward the door. Before opening it he turned to her and said, "By the way, you may want to stay with someone tonight. Is there anyone you would like me to notify?"

Melody shook her head. "No, thanks, I actually feel safest here, strange as that may seem."

She got up and walked the detective out to the porch, shock deepening as she witnessed the drama of the farm becoming an official crime scene.

As she watched the detectives leave, she saw the coroner's van pull out behind them. Charlie was leaving the farm for the last time.

CHAPTER TWENTY-ONE

The days after Charlie's death were some of the hardest Melody had ever known. She should be numb, her grief for Giselle still raw. Yet this fresh loss seemed to intensify her pain, bringing the others to the fore as though they had just happened.

Her father and grandparents died of natural causes, so she could at least make sense of their deaths. Charlie died at the hands of a monster; the brutality of his murder pulled the rug completely out from under her.

The police search turned up nothing at the farm. They inspected her apartment, finding nothing beyond Cheryl's very limited description.

Annie tried to get her to come to her house, but Melody chose to stay at the farm. Everyone she had ever loved was part of it in some way. She wanted to cling to the farm and the memories of those who had come and gone. She could still feel her Grandmama there, and now she felt Charlie's presence, too.

Melody moved about in a surreal haze.

To her surprise, she was listed as the executrix of his will. This required no real work on her part: Charlie had his life—and death—in order, including pre-paid funeral arrangements. Melody was grateful for his thoughtfulness.

Isabel was the only person she thought about calling during this time. They had met just once, but she felt the same instant connection she had experienced with Maman Marie. Isabel and Maman had similar energy, although one was more modern and the other more traditional.

She felt a little odd calling with such grim news, but Isabel was very kind and sympathetic. Melody got the impression, however, that she was not surprised.

Melody accepted Isabel's invitation to visit the following evening.

She was instantly struck by the apartment's décor. The walls were deep purple, accented by copper hangings; the couch and loveseat were burgundy with purple throw pillows.

Isabel explained that the colors were those of her patron, Oya, Orisha of storms and wind. She showed Melody her altar, set up in the small laundry closet. It was an ingenious use of space, with offerings of eggplant, red wine and various coins placed in copper bowls.

Melody asked if Oya had always been Isabel's patron Orisha.

"Yes. I've always felt scattered to the winds and drawn to her, but it can change as a person goes through different phases of life."

While she prepared drinks and a snack, Isabel talked a bit about the energy during Hurricane Katrina, how palpable it was. "Oya's energy is formidable...I knew something mighty was upon us."

She put a plate of cheese and crackers on the small dinette table along with several bottles of liquor and wine.

"Have you ever been in the eye of a hurricane?" Isabel asked, taking a seat and inviting Melody to do the same.

"No, thank God."

"There is a distinct smell. I've never been able to describe it, but anyone who's been through it knows. You're standing there, with a wall of clouds swirling around and you're in the middle, in stillness. This wall is filled with particles, debris, and you know it started on the other side of the ocean, off the coast of Africa. Everything it scoops up stays in those walls and travels thousands of miles. Most hurricanes carry the seeds of Africa."

As Isabel spoke, Melody sampled spiced rum and also tried cinnamon schnapps. She welcomed the sensation flowing through her, the liquid warmth calming her frayed nerves.

"There I go again, not giving you a chance to talk," Isabel apologized. "How do you like those drinks?"

Melody raised her glass for a toast. "Y'gotta love Voodoo folk;

there's always good liquor on hand!" It was the first time she had laughed in a long time.

Melody felt comfortable pouring her heart out. She talked about her childhood and the early interest in spirituality; she described the horrible vision she had before her father's death.

"I knew you had the sight," Isabel commented.

Melody talked about her closeness to her grandmother and distance from her mother; about her failed relationships; about losing Grandmama, and now Charlie.

She then told Isabel all that had transpired as a result of Giselle's final request, from her arrival in New Orleans to returning and finding Yvette's diary. She included the reference to a mysterious sacred book, but didn't elaborate further. As much as she liked Isabel, Melody did not feel comfortable revealing the manuscript to anyone. It would take an Act of Congress for Melody to completely trust someone, especially now.

When Isabel asked no questions, it crossed Melody's mind that she might already sense something about The Book.

She finished with the details of that fateful afternoon when she found Charlie, after having met Isabel for lunch.

When Melody stopped talking, Isabel confessed she had had a premonition when they met. She said she frequently had "visions" when connecting on a deep level with someone.

"I knew you were going to face something awful that day." She looked down and shook her head sorrowfully before meeting Melody's eyes again. "But I meant what I said: The heart must break wide open for the light to shine in."

Melody doubted any light would be shining in; she doubted everything now.

"I don't know anything right now, Isabel. I'm just reacting to everything around me; I have no control over anything."

Isabel reached for her hand and squeezed it. "I know you're angry and in pain. But this life is like being in a rowboat. You paddle along, knowing where you want to go, but lots of things affect your course. Other boats make waves or get in the way, Mother Nature creates havoc. It's not easy and it's tiring as hell. How you react to these things is up to you. It's your choice; you're still steering."

Melody was too tired to take in what Isabel was saying; exhaustion set in out of the blue and she had to cut the evening short since it was a long drive back to the farm.

They exchanged a long hug before Melody left. Both women seemed to want to say something more, but hesitated.

The day of the funeral was one of the rainiest on record. It was a humble ceremony, befitting Charlie, and the small gathering quickly dispersed after the graveside service. Melody vaguely remembered seeing Detective Hernandez standing in the rain while others were seated under the awning, scrutinizing each person who had come to offer condolences. She had done the same thing, studying the faces; she recognized everyone there, though some only slightly. Her anger and determination to catch the filth that had done this was matched only by the searing pain in her heart.

When everyone left and she had said goodbye to her mother and Eric, Detective Hernandez appeared with an umbrella and walked her to her car.

"Ms. Bennet, for what it's worth, I'm very sorry for your loss. I promise I'll do everything possible to make sure the person responsible is brought to justice."

Melody appreciated his efforts to keep her informed about the case. In the week after the funeral, the detective called several times, either to ask innocuous questions or offer disappointing updates. Once, he called simply to see how she was holding up. His concern seemed a bit unusual, but she appreciated the kindness.

He even stopped by the farm one afternoon, saying he was in

the area and wanted to check on her. Despite her despondence, Melody could not deny her attraction to him. When she shook his hand as he left, she actually blushed when he seemed to prolong the physical contact a little longer than normal.

Sue had also been wonderful, reassuring Melody that her position was safe and to take all the time she needed. She encouraged Melody to branch out on her own if she decided to, and added that the firm would provide enough contract work to keep her going until she could build clientele.

Melody had barely spoken to her mother. She couldn't help but feel Annie's main concern was whether a crime having taken place at the farm would prove a deterrent to selling the property. Melody was leaning more and more toward keeping the farm but was still undecided.

Charlie had bequeathed a small nest egg to Melody with a note—evidently written rather recently—that she should use it as a down payment, if she chose to buy it. This was such an extraordinary act of generosity, and it certainly strengthened her desire to keep the farm.

It had only been one week since Charlie's funeral when Melody had to steel herself for Giselle's memorial. In one way it seemed Grandmama had passed away ages ago; in another, it seemed like only yesterday. The thought of returning to the church and seeing Father Robert again was unsettling; even more, she dreaded the service itself. The weather reflected her mood, the relentless rain continuing.

She sat with her mother and Eric at the church. Father Robert never made eye contact with her, not even while greeting family members. Melody never took her eyes off of him.

While she was glad this service made her mother happy, the entire morning felt like a charade to Melody, and she could not wait to get back home, to the farm.

Once there, she felt a knot in her throat as she opened the

door. It's strange how ceremonies and rituals make things seem so final. Even though she believed that, in some form, Grandmama and Charlie were both present, Melody suddenly felt more alone than ever.

She put the tea kettle on and listened to the rain become a torrential downpour. *Thank goodness I don't have to take care of the animals.* One of the neighbors kindly offered to buy them and had taken them away fairly quickly, the day after she found Charlie.

The kittens! She'd forgotten to check on them all day yesterday and suddenly felt an irrational sense of panic.

Despite the rain and how she was dressed, she had to be sure they were okay; she felt responsible for their safety.

Holding a raincoat overhead, Melody ran to the shed, high heels sticking in the mud several times. The familiar sense of trepidation was present as she reached for the door.

As always, she opened the door slowly, so as not to frighten them; she was already drenched, though the downpour was starting to taper off.

They weren't there. All of them were gone!

There was no sign that any harm had come to them, but her knees weakened just the same. She couldn't bear the thought of anything happening to those babies.

With the rain softening its cadence on the tin roof, a soft mew could be heard.

She searched inside the shed, hoping the mother had simply transferred them to a safer, quieter spot in the shed. Sure enough, she found mother and babies safely tucked between two old storage cabinets, sleeping on a pile of old rags.

Melody collapsed to her knees.

The ever-present fear that another tragedy was around the corner had taken its toll; the relief in finding the kittens safe and unharmed had been overwhelming, and had unleashed a torrent of emotion.

She stayed in that position, disregarding the mud and

physical discomfort, her body racked with silent sobbing and soundless screams so as not to frighten the babies.

Her breakdown continued until she was finally spent.

The shrill whistle of the tea kettle could be heard from the porch. She was weak but rushed to turn the stove off before washing off and changing clothes.

She wrestled with the idea of returning to the manuscript.

The last time she had touched it, she was filled with a hope missing since childhood. She left the house feeling upbeat, believing her prayers and positive intentions would take form— not right away, but eventually.

Later the same day, she had found her apartment vandalized and her beloved Charlie murdered.

"What am I supposed to do with that?!" she screamed at the top of her lungs, arms raised, hands outstretched, pleading for an answer. She had taken two steps forward, only to be shoved ten steps back. It felt like the Universe had knocked her down intentionally.

Melody did not want to read the manuscript. She didn't want to do a damned thing other than stare at the walls until she fell asleep. She wanted to stay asleep.

But she felt she owed it to Grandmama. Reading this book was part of Grandmama's wish; she had no choice. She knew Giselle would not want her to feel so much anger—certainly not toward God or The Book—but she couldn't help it.

I'll try to keep an open mind, Grandmama, but I'm having a hard time right now.

"Spells and Rituals"

Since we all share the same subconscious mind, our existence may sometimes be affected by the choices or intentions of others. Its path falls into the clutches of the ego mind, which will try to dominate the

Creator's mind by creating circumstances or events that are undesirable. Whilst it is true that we learn most from conflict and trial, the conscious mind is a limited vessel, only able to sustain a small amount of pressure before falling into complete blindness and beginning to self-destruct through the fabrication of negative thoughts and images. To alleviate that pressure, we can use rituals and spells, which have the power of creating for our conscious mind an image of what we are trying to achieve, thereby laying the foundation for our subconscious mind to create a better reality.

Through her thick wall, Melody grudgingly connected with the last paragraph, acknowledging that the human mind "can only sustain a limited amount of pressure before it falls into complete blindness and begins to self-destruct." *Yep, I'm almost there myself.*

Rituals open doors for the mind, creating a channel between the conscious mind and the timeless mind of the Creator.

Spells are important because they forge a link between the conscious and the subconscious. As the conscious ego mind works to physically create a likeness of the desired object, it sends the image to the subconscious mind for creation.

The practitioner should also concentrate on forming a clear image of the final object, as if it had already been achieved; never should he try to determine the course of events. By doing so he would, in fact, allow the ego mind to seek control over the perfect intelligence of the true self.

Before beginning any spell, the conjurer...

Melody stopped cold. *Okay, right there: The word "conjurer" sounds so odd.* She remembered Isabel's words about perception and staying open; they were Maman Marie's words of advice as well. *Okay, Mel, it's just a word, a label, written a long time ago. Don't let the words turn you off.*

"Before beginning any spell, the conjurer should observe a period of meditation to reach the inner silence, shifting the predominant energy from ego to true self.

For example, if you perform a spell to attract a man or woman, and after the spell spend every moment of the day looking out the window for their approach, you are hindering the progress of the spell. You are giving the ego control, by accepting only that which you can see with your limited human senses.

Using whatever tools you accept as powerful toward that end, build a clear image in your mind of the final object. Hold that image as long as possible, then, releasing it, rest assured that your dreams shall soon come true.

Melody looked up and addressed the same invisible target she had screamed at earlier.

"Bullshit! I'm tired of these promises! Tell people 'whatever is for your highest good' will come true, not what they prayed for."

Definitely not what they prayed for.

It was easier to channel her anger toward *Obeah* than on recent events in her life, so she kept reading.

One important part of root-working is to incorporate personal objects of the target into the work itself. If the object is a piece of clothing, then it should not be washed, because the subtle stimulus to the senses of the conjurer and the vibrations of the target will pinpoint the right person to the Creator's mind, rather than all those who share the same name and possibly same date of birth.

The final recommendation is to alert the person if you have worked a root for hexing, but to remain silent if you have worked a healing or love spell. The reason for this is very simple. If someone is told that a root has been worked against them, whether they are believers or not, the seed of that revelation will spark a chain reaction of symptoms that the person will believe they are suffering.

Their subconscious fear of the unknown will activate their conscious fear and they will begin to feel ill. As they experience the first symptoms, they will write them off as coincidence, but by then, the seed is planted and it can only grow.

Melody closed The Book and put it down.

So, this is where the black magick comes into play.

She stood up to stretch, then began pacing and talking to no one.

"Why would someone who believes in the core goodness of Voodoo provide instructions on how to harm others, especially in such detail? Who wrote this?"

Melody also wondered why Grandmama would have dealt in such things. Or had she?

While knowing next to nothing about black magick, it seemed as though what was written here—disturbing as it was to her— was neither revolutionary nor earth-shattering. Spells to harm others had been used by people of different beliefs for eons.

But maybe they've never been written down in this way...or is there something hidden in this book that makes these words, and this knowledge, somehow more dangerous? Is The Book meant to test the person in possession of it?

Melody unconsciously twirled the little skeleton key on the chain between her right thumb and index finger as her mind raced. The sound of her cell phone interrupted her thoughts.

"Hello, Melody. This is Detective Hernandez."

She was surprised by his use of her first name.

"Hello, Detective. Have you found anything?" She held her breath for a moment, hopeful.

"I'm afraid not, Melody. We do have the autopsy results; if you want me to share, I will."

"No...no thank you," she replied weakly. The cause of death had been fairly obvious.

Melody closed her eyes and swallowed hard, trying to dispel the image of how she had found Charlie.

"So, we have a murder but nothing that we can tie to a murderer. We've combed the place but found nothing. Same with your apartment. If I didn't know better, I'd say a ghost did it."

Melody wasn't surprised.

"Listen, Melody, I was wondering if maybe you'd like to meet me for dinner tonight? Nothing fancy, but it would give us a chance to sit down and talk. Maybe you could tell me a little more about the book you mentioned before. This may be our only hope of tracking down the murderer. You said you'd been threatened over this book."

Melody was caught off guard.

"That's very kind of you, but it's been a rough day. My grand-mother's memorial was this morning..." She didn't finish the sentence, assuming he'd understand.

"I'm sorry. I'm sure it was difficult, but you need to get out."

Melody was ready to politely decline, when he spoke again.

"How's seven?"

She laughed, still not knowing what to say.

"Perfect, I'll take that as a yes. Should I pick you up at the farm?"

"Geez, you are persistent." She felt miserable and knew she looked awful, and wasn't sure any amount of makeup could fix it.

"Please, call me Mario. So, where do I pick you up?"

"All right. Seven it is," she relented. "I could meet you halfway."

"Now what kind of knight asks a maiden to meet him halfway?"

Melody was charmed by his sense of humor. "Okay, Mr. Knight. I'll see you at seven. Here at the farm."

When Melody hung up, she felt an unexpected twinge of excitement. Checking the clock, she saw it was only four, so she had plenty of time.

Grandmama didn't have cable television, and the last thing

she wanted to do was watch the news, so she returned to reading.

The next chapter was "Sacred Symbols."

The right side of Elegba's seal displays a skeleton key, but the most important feature represented within the seal is the repeated pattern of equal-armed crosses. These symbolise the crossroads we encounter on our life journey, as well as the meeting point of all four elemental forces, which is the home of Spirit. The crossroads represent the conflicted events requiring decisions on our part, thus setting in motion the power of using the gift of free will.

Melody had always been drawn to symbols. She knew they represented different things to different people; even the cross has had varied meanings for peoples throughout time. She learned long ago to pay attention when a symbol came repeatedly into her awareness.

Several weeks before her sixteenth birthday, she found herself drawn to Celtic crosses—equilateral crosses—with each arm of the cross coming to a point. At the same time, white roses suddenly seemed to appear everywhere. One day, she drew the image that had been in her head: an emerald green Celtic cross with a white rose in the center. She framed it and hung it over the bed. When her mother saw it, all color drained from her face.

Annie left the room, went into the attic, and returned with a large gift box. Inside was a beautiful, knitted afghan. When she unfolded it, Melody saw the image she had drawn: It was the afghan's central design.

Annie explained that this was a family heirloom, passed down by Irish ancestors on Melody's father's side. Only days before he died, John told Annie he planned put it in Melody's hope chest, a surprise for her next birthday. Annie had completely forgotten about it until she saw the picture.

Melody took it as a sign that her father continued to watch over her.

This memory made Melody long for another sign to comfort or guide her. She yearned for some grand insight. She had suppressed her spiritual side for so long; now, doubt and anger had taken hold, with a corrosive effect on her soul. She felt empty and lost.

When you lose hope, you lose everything...

Melody asked Spirit for a sign. She knew it was probably blasphemous in some way to "test" God, but she needed to know someone was paying attention.

She clutched the charm and asked for an undeniable sign from Elegba, something she couldn't dismiss. She had no specific request; she only wanted a reason to feel hopeful about life again.

Finished reading for the day, she needed a safe place to hide The Book and thought of the perfect spot.

She went to the pantry and opened a small door on the back wall. Grandmama Giselle had hidden money back there since Grandpapa Henry didn't believe in banks. Grandpapa and Charlie together had built it; it was indeed a masterpiece. Blending seamlessly with the wall behind the flour vat, its small latch was concealed by the shelf underneath, where Grandmama kept sugar and shortening. It was virtually impossible to detect unless one knew of its existence; Melody knew The Book was safe there.

CHAPTER TWENTY-TWO

In New Orleans, another young woman was asking for a sign. Olivia Beauchamp had tried in vain for three days to reach her father. She wondered if something had gone wrong during his trip to North Carolina.

Maurice Abudah continued to spiral into an abyss of anger and resentment. Even before his dementia had taken a firm hold, he was obsessed with striking back against those who had stolen The Book, destroyed his beloved mother, and his family; those who were defiling his revered bayou; those who had killed his son and prevented his grandchildren from living their dreams.

During the past few days he had been feverish, often shaking uncontrollably. Rage had overtaken his body.

His mind was often as foggy as a bayou morning, but not during his mother's visits, which were increasing of late. She always wore the beautiful yellow dress and looked as she did the day of her wedding, vibrant with youth. Whenever she came to see him, Maurice calmed down and listened closely. His mother always soothed him, and he clung to her words.

She told him not to give up, that the time was soon coming when he would save their family. It was important that he not let anyone get in his way, as it was his destiny to retrieve The Book.

Helena told him it was a disgrace for white people to be in possession of his heritage and that he must rectify it.

CHAPTER TWENTY-THREE

Mario Hernandez pulled his black Ford Explorer into the driveway and parked beside Melody's car. He flashed his dazzling smile when he saw her on the porch.

"Kind greetings, Milady. I apologize, as I had no time to shine my armor, so I hope Your Majesty will accept an outing with a poor knight in civilian attire." His playfulness put Melody at ease.

"'Tis quite all right, Sir."

Melody hated being shallow, but she really could not get beyond how incredibly attractive he was. He was about six feet tall, with a toned body that was subtly revealed in his form-fitting pullover and jeans. The brightness of his smile contrasted sharply with the dark eyes and raven-black hair.

"And where will my knight escort me this evening?"

It was Mario's turn to laugh. "If it is not too common for your royal taste, I'd like to take you to a favorite little place of mine. Do you like Mexican food?"

"That sounds wonderful. Let me get my purse and I'll be ready to go."

She came back outside to find Mario in one of the porch rockers, obviously relaxed and enjoying the scenery, which was backlit by the approaching sunset. Birds jockeyed for position, enjoying the soft breeze through the trees.

"You've got quite a place, Melody. It reminds me of my grandparents' home, when I was a little boy."

"Did you grow up around here?"

"No; I grew up in Florida and came to North Carolina to go to college. For years I couldn't stand that farm life, but now I miss it. It was so uncomplicated..." his voice trailed off with a hint of melancholy. "I see so much ugliness in the world every day. Having a sanctuary to retreat to would be a relief. You're really blessed."

"Thank you, but it's not mine yet. I still have to make that decision and see if I can manage it."

Since he didn't seem in a rush to leave, she tried to make conversation, not one of her strong suits.

"What is your degree in?"

"Criminal justice."

"What made you want to go into that?"

A subtle shadow crossed his handsome features. "It's a long story. We should go before it gets too late." He led her to his truck and courteously opened the door for her.

It was a short drive to the restaurant, during which they engaged in very casual conversation about the area in general. They arrived at Nuestra Casa twenty minutes later and were greeted by a beautiful young hostess, who led them to a room toward the back of the restaurant.

"Will this be all right?" she asked Mario. Melody noticed the look in the girl's eyes and understood it. He was quite striking.

"This is perfect. Thanks." The hostess gave them each a menu and said their server would be by shortly. After an awkward moment of silence, Mario spoke first.

"What's the situation with the farm? Are you living there now?"

"I have been, since my grandmother passed away. I still haven't packed her stuff away yet. I'm beginning to think it will never get done."

Mario smiled knowingly. "It will get done when the time is right. It took me years to pack up my father's things after he died."

"Were you close?" Melody asked.

"Sadly, no. He and my mother divorced when my brother and I were very young. We hardly saw my father while growing up."

The server came by with tortilla chips and salsa, and took their order. Mario encouraged her to try sangria for the first time.

"When I was fifteen, I found out my dad was a drug dealer. Three days before my seventeenth birthday, I found out he'd been shot, reportedly over a deal gone bad. They never caught the killer."

"I am so sorry," Melody whispered.

"When I got out of college I decided to join the police force. I think deep down I'd always hoped to catch my father's killer."

"Do you stay in touch with the rest of your family?"

"My mom died a few years ago; my grandparents have been gone a long time now. There's no one."

He didn't mention his brother, but Melody got the distinct impression this was intentional, so she left it alone.

"Have you ever been married? Any kids?" Melody blurted, surprising herself.

"Nope, no kids. I was married. We separated two years ago; the divorce was final last year." He took a long drink. "Truth be told, this is the first social interaction I've had in two years."

Social interaction? Is that the same as a date? Melody wasn't sure whether he considered this pleasure or business. Either way, she was enjoying his company, and the sangria.

"Am I boring you yet?" he asked.

In the midst of eating a salsa-laden chip, she put up her index finger, indicating that she needed a moment to swallow. After a big gulp of wine she said, "Goodness, no, you're not boring me at all. I like to learn about people! I'm all ears."

"I really think all this has helped me be a better detective. I can empathize with families, both criminal and victim."

As he continued to talk, intermittently taking a bite or a drink, her eyes never left him, taking in every movement in intricate detail. The simple act of him dipping a tortilla chip into the salsa aroused something in Melody that had long lain dormant.

"What about you? I've done all the talking. It's your turn, Milady." When he winked she felt a warm, quivering sensation.

"There's really not much to say. I've led a fairly ordinary

life…went to NC State for business, decided I wanted to go to law school, then realized it wasn't for me after all. I've been working as a paralegal for several years, and now I'm thinking about going out on my own as a research consultant."

"What made you realize you didn't want to be a lawyer?"

"I came to terms with the fact that I don't deal with people very well…all the game-playing." She took a drink of water, cutting herself off from more wine. "That's why I enjoy research. It's me and books and the computer. I rarely have to interact with others. It works out well," she said with a laugh.

"And your parents? Any siblings?"

"I lost Dad when I was twelve. My mom is remarried and lives here in Raleigh. I'm an only child."

Well, I always thought so, anyway. Learning she had a twin, even one who died at birth, still rattled Melody.

"And you are thinking about buying the farm?"

"Yes. My mom wants to sell it, so I would need to buy her half out if I decide to stay. I have to decide soon, because I can't afford two households.

"A lot of changes for you."

Melody sighed, rolling her eyes. "You have no idea. It's been a little over a month since my grandmother passed, and that turned my whole world upside-down. I was still trying to wrap my mind around her death, then Charlie…"

"It's a lot to deal with in such a short time." Mario reached for her hand. "I don't want to upset you further, Melody, and if you'd rather talk about it another time, I would understand. But can you tell me why you believe you are in danger because of a book?"

The waiter came to deliver their meals, providing Melody with time to gather her thoughts.

"When my grandmother passed, she left instructions for me to go to New Orleans— actually, the bayou—to scatter her ashes. This led to quite an interesting journey, which was *exactly* what

Grandmama intended. I discovered my great-grandmother was involved in Voodoo, and there is some sort of legend about a sacred book. Somehow my family is rumored to be involved." Melody kept her voice even and maintained eye contact, trying not to betray that she wasn't revealing everything. "A crazy old man threatened me twice while I was in Louisiana, saying the book was stolen from his family and that he intended to get it back."

"Did you tell anyone about the threat?" Mario asked.

"Only the people I was with, my grandmother's friends. I didn't tell any authorities, if that's what you mean."

He gave her a chastising look and she knew he was thinking about her not reporting the break-in at her apartment right away.

"When I got back to Raleigh, I began to wonder if there was even a grain of truth to this, and whether my grandmother ever said anything about this to anyone. I casually asked the family priest if he'd ever heard of this mysterious book and he said he hadn't, nor had Grandmama ever mentioned anything. I thought that was the end of it."

"It wasn't?"

"No, the very next day a Cardinal and two priests showed up unannounced, at the farm."

Mario looked at her in disbelief. "Priests came to see you? What did they say?"

"Only the Cardinal spoke. He was so arrogant! Said that if there was such a book and I found it, it was my duty to let him know. He said tragedy could befall the world if it got into the 'wrong hands.'" She rolled her eyes, emphasizing the absurdity of the implication. "Those weren't his exact words, but that was the basic message."

They stopped talking to enjoy their dinners, both deep in thought. Mario softly broke the silence.

"This book, legend holds that it contains mystical truths...truths beyond the grasp of the human mind."

Melody visibly tensed. "How would you know that?"

Mario laughed. "Melody, I grew up in a Voodoo family. I was initiated as a son of Shango. We held quite a few ceremonies at the farm. To this day, I love to drive through those fields...you can still feel the energy. It's absorbed in the land, in the trees, and especially the small creek where my mother brought offerings to Oshun."

"What do you know...a respected member of society, in law enforcement no less, involved in Voodoo," Melody teased.

The rest of the meal was spent chatting about food, travels, likes and dislikes. Melody genuinely enjoyed Mario's company.

After dinner, they went to Starbucks and then headed back. As he drove, Mario picked up the conversation where he had left off earlier.

"Have you come across anything of your grandmother's of interest? Anything about a book?"

"No, nothing." Melody crossed her fingers as she blatantly lied.

"But you felt threatened by this man in New Orleans, and by the Cardinal?"

"Very much so. It was overt with the man in New Orleans; more implied with the priests."

When they arrived back at the farm, Melody was so absorbed in her thoughts that she jumped when Mario spoke.

"I'm sorry, Melody. I didn't mean to startle you."

"No, don't apologize. My nerves are a bit frazzled, that's all," she said.

As she walked up the stairs ahead of him to unlock the door, part of her hoped he would stay awhile. Taking a chance that she'd be rejected—and humiliated—Melody invited him in.

"I know we already had coffee, but can I offer you something else?"

What the hell else does he think you're offering, Melody? She cringed at her own awkwardness, but was relieved when he accepted.

"I could use another cup of coffee before driving back to town. I worked late last night and didn't get much sleep."

Once inside, he immediately excused himself to use the bathroom, while she went to make coffee. Measuring the grounds into the basket, her mind again wandered into more lustful territory, this time without the influence of sangria. She imagined his mouth on hers, his strong hands caressing her...

"So, have you concluded anything from your research?"

Mario had come up behind her without making a sound.

"Research?" she asked.

"Research into Voodoo," he clarified, with a concerned look on his face. "Are you okay, Melody?"

Melody laughed nervously, embarrassed by her thoughts. "I'm fine. I just have a lot on my mind."

They sat at the table as the coffee brewed.

"What have I learned about Voodoo? If I told you the whole story, you would probably have me committed."

"Try me." His face was serious, so Melody leaned back and began to talk.

She told him what she had learned in Louisiana and what she witnessed the night at Maman's house, including seeing Grandmama's soul departing with a shadowy figure near Elegba's seal.

Mario listened attentively. After all, he had been raised in a Voodoo home, living through his own unusual situations and experiences. Mario told her about the first time he had been allowed to participate in a ritual, rather than just watch from a distance. He was terrified. As it turned out, he saw absolutely nothing, because he'd been too nervous to relax. The next time, he spent two hours in meditation before the ceremony. "That night, I felt it...felt it spreading throughout my body. It was the most exhilarating experience of my life."

His gaze had moved to her chest. She felt her nipples harden and prayed it didn't show through her light cotton blouse.

"Do you still practice?" she asked, clearing her throat.

"Yes, I do practice, usually alone, though occasionally I join friends."

"Do you practice hoodoo?"

Amused, he replied "Do I stick sharp pins in a doll to hex people?"

"I don't know what the hell I mean any more," she replied nervously.

Mario leaned over, smiling, and his hand moved toward her chest. Melody held her breath.

"Where did you get this?" he asked, his hand wrapping around hers, which was clasped around the skeleton key charm. "You've been holding it most of the night. Did you realize that?"

"No, I didn't. I guess it's become a kind of security blanket for me."

"Where did you get it?"

"At the Voodoo shop in New Orleans I told you about."

"You know it's a symbol for Elegba, right?"

"Yes," she answered, paying more attention to the fact that his face was inches from her own. Her body begged for his touch while her heart and mind resisted.

Mario pulled his hand away and moved it toward his left arm. "I think you'll like this." He pulled up the shirt sleeve to reveal a black and red skeleton key, tattooed on his bicep.

Holy shit! Melody was astounded. She had asked for a sign, specifically from or involving Elegba, and here it was. It was undeniable.

Something instantly shifted within her. It was as though an ice wall was melting; a barrier she had erected long ago began to dissolve. Receiving this sign, proof that someone or something was listening to her, began to soften her heart.

She couldn't deny her physical attraction to Mario, but there was more to it, and his tattoo was confirmation. They had a connection; an unusual, intimate connection, through Elegba and Voodoo. In her head that sounded odd: *a connection through Elegba and Voodoo.*

"Can you believe that? What are the odds we'd both have a skeleton key symbol?" He sounded excited, like a small child on Christmas morning.

She was glad this was significant to him as well.

They both shook their heads and laughed in disbelief. Mario reached over and brushed her cheek with his fingertips.

"You are so beautiful, Melody. I love when you laugh."

Allowing him to be this close was a huge step for her. Though she craved his touch, the intimacy terrified her; she had to restrain her instinct to pull back.

He sensed her hesitation. "Are you not attracted to me?"

She couldn't look him in the eyes. "I'm more attracted to you than I've ever been to anyone in my entire life."

"Then what's wrong? Did I do something?"

"God, no! It's not you, it's me." Her voice was strained. "I'm going to tell you something I wouldn't share with many people. But I have a feeling you'll understand."

He listened attentively.

"I'm the kind of person who needs to *believe in something*," she said emphatically. "Something more than just what we experience with our five senses."

Her eyes became emerald, brimming with tears. Mario reached over silently, placing his hands over hers, encouraging her to continue.

"I read something earlier today and it made me want to *try* to have hope. I took a chance and asked for a sign; a sign that I'm on the right track and that everything will somehow be okay." She looked up and their eyes locked; she felt heat rising from her heart to her throat. "I asked for a sign from Elegba."

Mario stood and gently pulled her to him, tenderly lifting her face and brushing her lips ever so lightly with his own.

He led her to the living room, pulling her down onto the couch beside him. Melody was spellbound by his eyes; two deep, shimmering pools in which she would gladly drown. He took her face in his hands, and this time when he kissed her it was more urgent. Their mouths parted, seeking one another.

Melody had always repressed her sexuality, never unleashing it to fully explore its depths. She felt a rush of sensation, like a dam breaking under the strain of a flood. As his tongue teased hers in a sensual dance, she became dizzy. Every inch of her body was on fire.

She pulled back to catch her breath; he began kissing the side of her neck, his tongue flicking her ears as his hot breath drove her to the brink of madness. He stood to pull off his shirt, revealing a muscular torso that glistened in a light sheen of sweat.

He knelt before her and gazed into her eyes, where he found desire mirroring his own. As he unbuttoned her blouse, he kissed her almost imperceptibly. Melody strained to feel his lips on hers, but he kept pulling back, teasing. With ease and fluidity, he removed her blouse, then sat back to look at her.

"God, Melody, you are so beautiful."

His mouth took possession of hers; they remained locked together as the rest of their clothing disappeared. When their naked bodies touched for the first time, the sensation left them gasping.

Savoring each kiss, each touch, they joined in the ancient ritual of two souls becoming one through their physical union.

Melody moaned when she felt him enter her, shifting slightly to welcome him further. Mario moved unhurriedly at first, caressing her face and breasts, kissing her deeply, in rhythm. His thrusts became insistent, his body seized by more passion than he could control.

The movements grew faster, harder. When Melody climaxed, she felt as if a lightning bolt had struck the base of her spine and pelvis, the heart of her sexual center, its electricity spreading throughout her entire body, nearly convulsing her.

Mario joined her a moment later, holding tightly to the back of her thighs, digging his fingers into her flesh.

They eventually moved to the bedroom and made love several times that night, exploring one another more slowly and intimately each time. Mario introduced her to tantra; taking their time, postponing climax, heightening the sensation and taking it beyond the physical.

Hours later, finally spent, they allowed sleep to take over.

CHAPTER TWENTY-FOUR

Melody awakened to the smell of freshly-brewed coffee.

Opening her eyes, she saw sunlight filtering through the curtains, casting a dreamy glow over the bedroom. The blue-and-white quilt was scrunched at the foot of the bed, but there was no sign of clothing anywhere. She then remembered their clothes were strewn about the living room. After retrieving her robe from the closet, she brushed her teeth and hair, and headed downstairs.

Mario was fumbling around in the kitchen, clad in boxers. She panicked when she saw the door of the pantry was open. *Does he know about Grandmama's hiding place in the pantry? Is that why he's really here?!*

As soon as the thought came to her head, she dismissed it as paranoia.

When he heard her, he turned and flashed one of his knee-buckling smiles. "Morning, beautiful."

She walked over to the stove, placing a light kiss on his soft, moist lips. He set down the spatula and seized her about the waist, transforming her gentle morning peck into an ardent, fiery kiss. Her robe opened and Melody felt him hard against her, erasing all thoughts of morning coffee.

He turned off the burner, where bacon was loudly popping, and pushed her against the table, his warm hands roaming across her naked body.

"No tantric fusion this morning?" she teased.

His response was to press his body against hers with an urgency and passion that was all the answer she needed.

Their encounter was raw and fierce, reaching a crescendo in minutes.

After normal breathing resumed, Mario took control of the spatula once more and Melody poured them each a big mug of coffee. Within minutes, a breakfast of bacon, eggs and toast was served and devoured with great pleasure.

It was hard to wipe the smile from her face this morning. Even if their story ended when he left today, Melody was grateful for what they had shared. For this moment, she was happy.

She knew it was more than freeing a passion held captive for years. Mario had been a catalyst, enabling Melody—if she would allow it—to release the anger and fear that had paralyzed her for so long.

She felt good; alive and content. She poured another cup of coffee and took it outside to the porch, while Mario ran upstairs to shower and get ready for work. Rather than stay on the porch, she sat on the steps to feel the sun's warmth on her skin. The morning was magnificent, the sky a deep blue eclipsing everything in its brilliance. Several puffy, cumulus clouds dotted the sky, inspiring a childhood memory.

Melody had loved searching for animal shapes as a child; she would lie in the field for hours gazing at the sky, finding enough animals in the clouds to fill her imaginary zoo.

Mario found her in this very act when he came outside, keys in hand and a smile on his handsome face. "I have to run now and stop by my house for a change of clothes. Thank you for a wonderful evening, Milady."

"Oh no, thank *you*," she grinned, accepting the hand he offered. He pulled her up, and they exchanged a long hug and goodbye kiss.

Watching until his truck disappeared, Melody brought the key charm to her lips and thanked Elegba for the sign and for the courage to act upon it.

Melody was anxious to tell Isabel about the synchronicity of the tattoo and the charm, and about the rest of her evening. *She'll be so proud of me!*

With a satisfied smile, she went inside to warm her coffee and figure out the rest of the day. Though sadness was still present, she was able to acknowledge it without allowing the pain to overtake her. Today she wanted to wallow in the sea of well-being she had plunged into last night.

She probably wouldn't change out of her robe until later, if at all; she wanted to enjoy the sensuality of the satin against her skin, the nerve endings still tingling and deliciously sensitive.

Melody opened the small door hidden in the pantry and retrieved the manuscript.

It was a perfect day to leisurely sit back and read. She knew she had to return to the productive world soon, but wanted to put it off a little longer. Armed with a box of Godiva chocolates and a full mug of coffee, she went to the couch and opened the text to the point where she had left off yesterday.

Before reading she decided to light a candle, inviting Spirit to guide her. She was also moved to play some background music. Melody had given Grandmama a small countertop stereo for the kitchen. There were CDs in a drawer, and she was delighted to see one with a Mardi Gras scene on the cover: "A Collection of the Best New Orleans Blues." *Cool! Way to go, Grandmama.*

The setting was now perfect; the jazzy, soulful blues returned her to the liberating freedom she had felt in New Orleans.

Some humans have become so enlightened that they are able to channel through themselves the Creator's message of perfect love, light and truth. Such divinely inspired and enlightened words have been recorded in books such as the Bible and the Koran, but have been misinterpreted or exploited by people to control others, thereby feeding the need of the ego to establish supremacy.

When a prayer is raised after silence, an image of the object prayed for should stand clear in our mind. The sounds that spontaneously rise from the heart to the throat — the ones not belonging to any human language and which bypass the ego's understanding of them — those are the true words of Spirit language.

The adept realises that when allowed to spontaneously surface, those sounds create a harmony that raises mystical vibrations. As the bird is not trained to develop its melodic voice, but sings nevertheless, the human mind that truly chooses to connect with the Supreme Mind of the Creator can do so through the power of sound. The result is a melodic and angelic vibration, the notes of which are aligned with the rhythm of nature itself.

This is indeed a significant tool for the adept, because once this connection is created through Spirit language, he will feel a most powerful surge of heat rising through the palms of his hands, and he will be able to use the Creator's Energy to alter his world.

It was not lost on Melody that she had been inspired to play music right before reading about the language of Spirit.

Spirit language. Vibration. Energy. She had always instinctively known the vibration of sound, including words, has a tremendous impact on everything. Not being a scientist, she didn't understand the physics, but her intuition told her the vibration of sound had the power to heal.

Even as a child, whenever her body ached with fever, she would moan...sort of. It wasn't really moaning; she would inhale deeply and then exhale slowly, making a sound until she found a particular tone or vibration or whatever that "felt" right. It drove her mother crazy, but it soothed Melody, helping her sleep.

The next section, "Magical Power of Psalms," was a lengthy list of psalms and corresponding prayers, which ended by saying: *Each Psalm is a coded message, delivered from the conscious ego mind to the subconscious mind of the Creator.*

Melody recalled Maman and Stephanie telling her about the Twenty-Third Psalm. According to them, by reciting it with focus and a clear mind, one could dispel negativity. She turned to the next page and found several blank sheets. She assumed they were there so The Book could be added to over time.

That's it?

She felt some disappointment that there were no undeniable, irrevocable revelations. On the other hand, she had resigned herself to the reality that, whatever power *The Book of Obeah* truly held, it was probably only recognized by those much wiser than she.

She lost herself in the sultry song now playing in the background, wondering again about the strange page at the beginning of The Book, with the peculiar, ancient writing. Too sleepy to think, Melody put *Obeah* down, closed her eyes, and drifted into dreams of making love with Mario.

CHAPTER TWENTY-FIVE

When the front desk phone rang, Olivia Beauchamp jumped. She had been busy clearing registration cards from guests who had checked out, but her mind was elsewhere. She had been gripped by worry for several days, wondering why there was no word from her father. Paul had left more than a week ago for North Carolina, and had called her when he first arrived; she had heard nothing since.

Olivia did not share her father's belief in this secret book. She had been raised in New Orleans, with Voodoo all around, but she had come to regard it as merely something offered for tourists. Paul had invited her to participate in a ritual with him, telling her she needed to get involved to understand. Olivia politely refused, having absolutely no interest. She understood it was part of who he was, but it was not part of who she was.

She answered the phone on the first ring, hoping to hear her father's voice, but it was a guest needing directions back to the hotel. Olivia did her best to sound professional and hoped the disappointment she felt was not reflected in her voice.

She hung up the phone and turned back to the registration cards, surprised to find James, the shuttle driver and on-call bellhop, behind the counter looking at the cards. She liked James, he was a good guy; a little unrefined for her taste, but definitely a nice young man.

"Hi, James. Can I help you?" she asked with a smile.

"Do we still have the registration cards from last week, Miss Olivia?"

"Yes, over there, already filed." She pointed to the corner of the back counter. "Are you looking for something in particular?"

Olivia noticed that James seemed jumpy, but he was always shy and fidgety around her.

"I'd really like the card for Melody Bennet. She was a guest

211

here a couple of weeks ago."

Olivia felt heat rising from her neck to the top of her head.

"Yes, I remember Ms. Bennett. Why are you looking for her card?"

James seemed unsure how to answer. "She gave me such a good tip before she left and then another when I brought her luggage out. I just want to send her a note to thank her."

Olivia thought it odd that he wanted to write a guest, but she knew James wasn't out to hurt anybody.

"James, you're gonna owe me a coffee and croissant. You know we're not supposed to give out guest information like this."

"I'll bring you two, Miss Olivia."

She found Melody's card and was going to write down the information, but decided to photocopy it instead. It would be unwise to have any more guest information in her handwriting leave the hotel. She returned with the copy for James, who tucked it in his jacket pocket.

"Thank you, Miss Olivia. You're the best."

As soon as James went out the door to help a guest, the phone rang again.

"Good morning—"

"Hello, child," Paul cut off her prepared greeting.

"Dad, is that you?!"

On the other end of the line, Paul was jovial as usual. "Of course, it's me. How many dads do you have callin' you?"

"I was worried sick about you! I called so many times, but your cell phone just kept ringing and ringing. I thought something had happened."

"I left that aggravating contraption at home."

Olivia knew there was no point badgering him about it; the man didn't have a television, or even a home phone.

"Okay, okay. So what happened, why didn't you call?"

"I couldn't call before now."

She knew by the tone of his voice that prying would be

useless. "So, did you find the manuscript?"

"No, she must have taken it somewhere else." Paul didn't want to tell Olivia about the murder at the farm. It had made the news in North Carolina but he doubted it would reach New Orleans. No sense worrying the girl even more.

"When are you coming home?"

"I don't know. I'll call you in a couple of days and let you know."

"Okay, Dad…please be careful. Thanks for calling. I love you."

"I love you, too."

Olivia hung up with tears stinging her eyes. She didn't want the damned manuscript; she wanted her father back home and safe.

CHAPTER TWENTY-SIX

The ringtone rousing her from a sound sleep, Melody reached over to the coffee table to get her cell phone. When she flipped it open, the sound of Mario's voice quickened her pulse and a warm rush engulfed her body.

"Hey there, beautiful. Did I wake you?"

"I can't believe it, but yes." She couldn't believe it was nine P.M.! It was five o'clock when she put The Book down and fell into a luscious daydream.

She sat up and stretched, allowing a sultry yawn to escape. "But I had the most delectable, yummy dreams."

"About me?"

"Of course about you! I must say, you've unleashed something." She was half joking, half serious.

"Well, I'm honored. And *very* glad."

She laughed softly. "No, I don't think you understand—"

"Believe it or not, I do," he said rather seriously. "I had my own walls up, but we smashed them to hell last night. Have you had dinner?"

"No, I haven't eaten since you left this morning, and I'm famished."

"Is it too late for me to come over?" he asked. "I could pick up Chinese food."

"I would love for you to come over, as fast as you can. Food or no food!"

Since he was coming from the office, they settled on him being there in about an hour.

Melody jumped up, energized and eager to see him again.

She took a leisurely bath instead of a shower, wishing she had sexy lingerie to wear. Not that she had much of it at her apartment; there had been no need in a long time. Still, she would definitely need to decide soon about where to live; having her things in two places was wearing thin.

It dawned on her as she soaked in the lavender-scented bath that she had never been intimate at her grandparents' house before last night. At first she cringed a little, thinking of what they had done, and where; but then she relaxed, knowing it didn't matter. She was certain Grandmama would approve—and just as certain her grandfather wouldn't have stayed around to watch. Melody giggled at the thought.

She had just come downstairs when the doorbell rang.

The sight of Mario made her catch her breath. As he stepped inside, she threw her arms around his neck and met him with a sizzling kiss.

"Wow! Now *that's* a greeting!"

They had a relaxing dinner, chatting about his day and inconsequential things. It was as though they'd done this hundreds of times.

"What did you do today?" he asked.

"Not much, but tomorrow I'm going to get back on track." She lightly pounded her fist on the table in mock determination.

"Come on, you had to do *something*."

"I'm just catching up on reading these days."

"What are you reading?"

Melody wasn't sure what to say. What if he wanted to see what she was reading? Grandmama didn't have any books here; she couldn't say she was reading online, he knew there was no Internet connection.

"I saved a variety of things on my laptop to read when I had a chance."

"You haven't looked through your grandmother's things yet?"

Melody was a little embarrassed that she appeared so unproductive and lazy, as it's so unlike her.

"I'm not trying to push you, but it will weigh on you every day until you do it. I know it's hard, though." He leaned over and kissed her forehead.

They ate in silence for a few minutes.

"I hate to bring this up again, Mel, but part of why I think it's important for you to go through her things is from an investigative perspective. You might find something to help the case; something that would explain why people believe she had something of value, like that manuscript."

She didn't want to lie to him, but she also did not want to discuss it. At this point, she had no intention of revealing the existence of *Obeah* to anyone. She was adamant about it. How she would help them catch Charlie's killer while keeping The Book a secret was beyond her at the moment.

Mario thought he had upset her; he came up behind her chair and began massaging her shoulders, murmuring an apology. He loosened the robe to expose her neck and shoulders and within seconds his hands were sliding down the front of her robe as he lightly kissed her neck.

It was the prelude to another night of bliss.

After Mario left early the next morning, Melody prepared for a busy day. She finished reading the manuscript, so now it was time to get on with the business of life.

She listed the things she needed from her apartment, including financial documents; her first priority was making an informed decision about buying the farm. With the money Charlie had left her, she felt it was feasible without undue hardship.

Determining her work options was a priority today as well, so she would call Sue to discuss details.

Melody knew Mario was responsible for her revitalization. He had come along just in time to save her from sliding into a major depression, though she would never tell him so. She would not want him to feel pressured, and she did not want to be seen as vulnerable or weak.

Her attitude about Mario was straightforward and simple: She was grateful for his presence, but was taking life hour by hour, expecting nothing. While diving into the physical aspect of their relationship with abandon, she was determined to keep the emotional aspect reined in.

As for The Book, there was nothing for her to do right now. She needed time to absorb what she had read and not take in any new information.

By early that afternoon, Melody had accomplished what she set out to do. Her finances were organized, and her work situation started to take shape. During her long conversation with Sue, they both realized it would be mutually beneficial for her to work as a consultant rather than an employee. Sue also kindly provided referrals to other firms that might have need of her services.

It was agreed that she would return to work in this new capacity in two weeks, giving her time to organize her new life in earnest: Move things out of the apartment into the farmhouse, get set up to work from there, and finally go through Grandmama's things and pack them away.

After laying out her finances and feeling more confident about her income, Melody felt like celebrating. She knew she could buy the farm without hardship, thanks in large part to Charlie.

As if on cue, Isabel called, inviting her to an early dinner.

She arrived at Isabel's with the ingredients for a great gabfest: a large bottle of red wine, a bottle of Captain Morgan's Spiced Rum, a liter of Coke, and two large Chicken Caesar salads from one of her favorite delis.

"I love that you get off work before five!" Melody exclaimed, wearing a big smile, when Isabel opened the door.

They laid everything out on the kitchen counter and each

made a rum and Coke

"It feels so decadent having drinks at three-thirty in the middle of the week, doesn't it?" Melody asked.

"You forget I'm from New Orleans—decadence is a way of life." Isabel winked.

Melody knew Isabel missed her home and admired her ability to move forward, creating a new life while grieving her former one.

"But those of us from New Orleans are now spreadin' the love." With a sly grin she added, "And that includes spreading our love of Voodoo all around the country, wherever we landed."

"Wow, I never thought of that." Melody imagined little pockets of Voodoo practitioners spread out all over the United States. "I'd love to visit New Orleans with you. We'd have so much fun."

Melody paused and cleared her throat with a dramatic flare. "Speaking of decadence…" She intentionally let the sentence trail off while she took a drink.

Isabel's curiosity was piqued. "Yes?"

"Let's have a seat. I have a story to tell you…and it involves sex!"

"I want details!"

Excited as schoolgirls, they transferred to the living room and got settled.

Melody disclosed details, from Mario's first phone call inviting her to dinner, to their tender, unhurried lovemaking this morning.

"You seem much lighter, Melody. How do you feel about Mario?"

"I think you'll be proud of me. I'm staying in the moment with this, no expectations. And it's weird…it's not that hard to do. I enjoy him *thoroughly* when I'm with him but I'd be fine if I never saw him again. It's not like I'm looking for my soulmate or anything."

CHAPTER TWENTY-SIX

"You should be proud of yourself," Isabel commented.

Melody nodded, with a self-satisfied smile.

She changed the subject entirely and talked about reading something that made her curious about the power of words, the power of sound—the whole idea of vibration. She mentioned the synchronicity of putting on music and, within seconds, coming upon a passage about the vibration of sound.

"That's one of the reasons I became a librarian, along with it being sort of a...family tradition," Isabel said, a little mysteriously. "I love the power of words. But one thing I've learned is how the intention is key. I can use the "f" word in a funny way or I can use it in a mean way. And it's not just how I *intend* it to be used; it's how it's *perceived*. I think that may have happened with the word 'Obeah'."

Melody stopped eating, fork in midair; she put her fork down and gave Isabel her undivided attention.

"My great-grandmother was a High Priestess, from Haiti, but we can trace our family back to West Africa. I remember overhearing talks between her and my aunt, who had been a missionary nun in Haiti. That's when I heard 'Obeah' for the first time. What stuck with me is them saying the elders planted a seed using that word, something about the word being a trigger for something. I feel the word's vibration is powerful. It may have started off with a certain intention and became distorted over time."

She got up to get more wine and shrugged. "But what do I know? It's just a feeling I have."

Melody struggled, wanting to tell Isabel about The Book, especially after what she had just shared.

Isabel sat down again and met Melody's eyes. "You know, the last time you were here, you were in a much different space, emotionally and vibrationally. I suggest you tap into this feeling; hold it strongly and for as long as possible. Make it a habit. It sounds obvious, but what I mean is that the more you can hold onto this feeling, the less likely you'll be tripped up by any hurdles."

Isabel finished off her wine and said with comedic effect, "And as sure as I'm sittin' here a black woman, something'll surely come along to knock you on your ass!"

The way she said it made Melody nearly choke from laughing so hard.

"Okay, enough of the serious talk," Isabel proclaimed. "How about a reading?"

"Seriously?"

"Sure!" Isabel disappeared into her bedroom, returning with a deck of cards and a white pillar candle, which she set on the kitchen table. She lit the candle, then instructed Melody to clear her mind and breathe deeply. She took the cards out of the box and sat back to clear her own mind and regulate her breathing. Several minutes later, she told Melody to shuffle the deck and pull out five cards, one at a time. Holding each card in turn for a moment, eyes closed, Isabel placed them before her on the table.

The deck looked like nothing Melody had ever seen—not that she'd seen many tarot decks. She had no idea what each card represented but knew it would be useless to ask Isabel to explain. The cards were indecipherable to Melody, just like the first page of *Obeah*.

Isabel rather dramatically cleared her throat, though she appeared not to be joking. She examined the cards for a long time, then closed her eyes again. Her face remained expressionless. Melody hoped she was kidding around and would start laughing any second, but the longer Isabel remained silent, the more nervous Melody grew.

She was relieved when Isabel finally opened her eyes, but her relief quickly turned to apprehension.

"I'm not going to say this is meaningless, that these cards are just in fun. And I'm not going to pussyfoot around this."

"What is it?" Melody wasn't sure she wanted the answer.

"I'm...I can't begin to explain what I'm going to tell you, but I hope you'll trust me. It's not just the cards, it's...it's what I'm feeling and seeing."

Melody was concerned about Isabel as she began to speak, her eyes closing again. It didn't sound like her; she mumbled in a rambling, disjointed manner. The thought that she might be having a stroke entered Melody's mind.

"He's coming after The Book."

Melody froze.

"You must guard it, Melody." Isabel's breathing became more rapid and labored. "Things are not as they seem...people are not who they seem." She cocked her head to the side, as though listening. "Alex?"

Her eyes snapped open and she seemed startled, confused. Melody still hoped Isabel would smile and say, "just kidding," but that didn't happen.

"I'm sorry, but I couldn't have stopped it if I'd wanted to. That hasn't happened in a long time, and never like that. I didn't expect that at all."

At least she sounds like herself again.

Isabel excused herself, obviously unsettled by what just occurred.

Melody still hadn't moved. *Things are not what they seem? Why do people keep saying that to me?*

When Isabel returned, she was back to her old self and suggested they each get another glass of wine.

Isabel recounted what she had seen and felt, trying not to interpret anything, only relaying what happened. Melody trusted Isabel and believed in her sincerity.

Though unclear about much of what she had seen, Isabel proceeded to describe the cover of *Obeah* to perfection. Melody neither confirmed nor denied having The Book; she kept quiet.

Isabel had the distinct impression Melody was in danger, from several directions.

"Do you know an Alex?"

"No, I don't know anyone named Alex."

"It was audible. Everything else was an impression, but I heard a man call out that name. There was a lot of fear. I don't know what to make of it or how to help you, Melody. I'm sorry." Isabel shook her head, growing more upset. "I invite you over here to relax and get away from the drama, and look what I do to you."

"Please, don't apologize. I'm sure this happened for a reason; we just don't know what it is yet."

"You really do need to be careful, Melody. I don't understand what just happened, but I know I felt the fear and danger, and you were the focus." She leaned over and reached for Melody's hand. "Watch out when you come across an Alex."

Isabel never asked one question about The Book.

CHAPTER TWENTY-SEVEN

Over the next two weeks, Melody tried to pretend the tarot incident never happened; Isabel seemed to do the same thing. They spoke a few times and met for lunch, Melody keeping Isabel filled in about Mario and the progress of her move.

The paperwork was underway for Melody to buy the farm. Annie and Eric were once again on vacation, so Melody arranged to have her mother fax the necessary signed paperwork.

She saw Mario fairly often, and they continued to take pleasure in exploring one another, both in and out of the bedroom. Mario asked nothing further about the manuscript, though he knew she was packing Grandmama's belongings away, room by room.

Melody was feeling much more in control. The big decisions were now behind her, and she was productive and efficient, making progress. Her daily life was finally stabilizing and returning to normalcy.

It was the end of a long day. Cardinal Bonelli sat at his desk, scribbling on a piece of blank paper and trying to decide how to proceed. His seniors in the Vatican continued to demand daily reports, growing impatient.

Years ago they had worked overtime to conceal the scandal which threatened to destroy him and would have been another black eye for the embattled Church; this was his last chance to make up for the distress his previous actions had caused.

In a fit of hysteria, a young nun in his diocese had confessed to drowning her newborn baby, naming him as the father. Her attorney requested a DNA paternity test; when the results were positive, they planned to prosecute him and hold him accountable for the infanticide.

The nun revealed that Cardinal Bonelli had repeatedly

molested her throughout her childhood; she described how he had convinced her that he carried the essence of God, that to be spiritually joined with him she should take her vows. He told her that in this way they could be together in God's eyes, though legally they must keep it secret.

Her state of mind had become so fragile from years of mental and physical coercion that the pregnancy caused a psychotic break, ending in tragedy and another potential mess for the Church.

He now had the chance to redeem himself, to show that he would go to any lengths to save his beloved Church. By finding the manuscript he could pay them back for burying the ordeal, and saving him from certain prosecution.

Father Rudino had been contacted several times but insisted he had heard nothing from the girl. The Cardinal was convinced she had The Book and was hiding it. On impulse, he picked up the phone and dialed the grandmother's number, provided by Father Rudino. The phone rang four times before a female voice answered.

"Ms. Bennet, this is Monsignor Bonelli."

The irritation in her voice was evident. "Yes, Monsignor. How can I help you?"

"You already know how you can help me."

Neither had any patience for pleasantries.

"As I have already stated, Cardinal, I have no information for you. Now, if you will excuse me, I have work to do."

The line went dead.

He was infuriated. He would go confront the girl again. Considering himself an expert in reading—and manipulating—people, he vowed he would find out whether she was lying or not.

The specter of this damnable book had been a thorn in his side for years. He deplored the heathens who had written it and those who protected it, and would do what he must to prevent it from seeing the light of day, destroying what the Church had worked centuries to build and maintain.

The Cardinal knew being seen at the farm would be risky. He was aware a murder had taken place there and, with the crime as yet unsolved, it remained a local news item. The last thing he needed was to be implicated in another scandal. Should anyone happen to see him in the area and ask about it, he would say he was there to offer spiritual guidance, after being contacted by the family priest.

Fathers Gervasi and Lawson were summoned to his office, where he informed them that they would join him early the next morning to eradicate this threat. He was certain success was imminent; he was doing the work of his God.

CHAPTER TWENTY-EIGHT

Many miles away, Marie Devereux wiped beads of sweat from her forehead as she dialed Melody's number from the phone inside the emporium. She wondered where Paul was. This business was his baby; he never left it for more than a day. This was the second time in the past few days she had noted his absence. She had ventured out two days ago for a few groceries. Returning today and finding him still gone, Marie wondered if he had taken ill.

Something was wrong all around; she could smell it in the air.

Last night she had barely slept. Hazy images of Melody running, bleeding from numerous wounds, haunted her dreams. At one point she awoke, covered in sweat, with Giselle standing at the foot of her bed, begging her to help Melody.

She got up and pulled Melody's hair out of the jar, placing a few strands in a bowl of clean water with nine drops of olive oil, to wash out the evil. After reciting the incantation, she sat back quietly and retreated to inner silence. That was when the vision began to haunt her.

Melody was lying on an altar, surrounded by candles. A man was standing over her holding a knife, the candlelight reflected in its blade.

Marie knew she must protect Melody. It was imperative the girl return to the bayou *now*.

The moment the emporium opened at five-thirty, Marie was there to use the phone.

Melody had left the phone number for her cell, her apartment, and at the farm. Marie tried the girl's home number without success. She next tried the cell and prayed to Shango to help her get through. The phone rang three times before Melody's sleepy voice came on the line.

"Melody, this is Maman Marie."

"Maman?! What a surprise! How are you?"

Marie's heart beat faster and she couldn't breathe. The vibrations she was picking up just by having Melody on the phone confirmed her feelings of danger.

"Chère, you must listen to me very, very carefully. I can't give you details right now, but I feel you are in danger, child; grave danger. I can't say it more strongly."

Melody's blood ran cold.

"What kind of danger, Maman?"

"I don't know. What I do know is we have no time—you must get here right away, Melody. I told Giselle I'd protect you."

"Come there? You want me to come to your house?" Melody was flustered.

Melody knew something was dreadfully wrong. Maman was one of the most stable people she'd ever met; her hysteria was a huge red flag.

On the other end of the line, Marie took a deep breath, relieved to have reached her.

"Giselle came to me in a dream and begged me to protect you. I can't come to you, Chère; I'm too old. You must come here." She paused, clearly winded as she tried to speak forcefully enough to convey her message.

"In another dream, you were scared. You were running and..."

"And what?"

"...and you were bleeding. Someone was after you, Melody. Someone *is* after you."

Melody believed her; Isabel's warning echoed in Maman's words.

"I'm pretty sure I can get on a flight today or tomorrow."

Maman was insistent. "You must get here as fast as you can. *Today*. Can you drive here?"

Melody's head was spinning. She pressed her hand to her forehead to counter the mounting pressure.

"Yeah, I guess so. I have to think—"

"There's no time to think—you must leave NOW!"

Marie couldn't hide her fear. It had been years since she had felt so strongly about anything; she had never been so frightened. She barely knew Melody, and had barely known Giselle, but this connection was beyond anything she had ever encountered.

Melody threw logic out the window and agreed, saying she'd leave immediately.   "I'll be on the road within an hour or two. I think I can make it by late tonight."   She looked at the clock; it was nearly six and the sun was rising.

"Good, good. I'll light a candle to keep you safe. Do you remember how to get here?"

Melody hesitated.

"I'll have Samuel wait for you at the emporium. Do you remember the way there?"

"I'll find it, Maman, don't worry. Let me think just a second, please."

Melody knew it would take about thirteen hours to reach New Orleans from Raleigh. She should easily arrive by midnight at the latest. That would give her time, in case she got lost or delayed along the way.

"Ask Samuel to meet me around midnight and to please wait for me."

"I'll see you tonight. I'll have everything ready by the time you get here."

"Suddenly Melody was terrified, like a small child, and had to fight back a rising sense of panic. "Please...pray for me."

"Don't you worry, I will, Chère. You just worry about getting here—and don't talk to anyone."

"Okay. I'll see you soon."

Melody sat on the bed for a moment, trying to slow the torrent of thoughts flooding her mind. Maman had said not to talk to anyone, but she had to let *someone* know, didn't she?

Knowing she couldn't stop to think, but instead had to act, she dressed quickly and packed the bare minimum. She grabbed her purse, phone, and The Book, locking everything safely in the car while she tended to the cats. That done, Melody locked the house and jumped in her car, *The Book of Obeah* resting on the passenger side floorboard, her backpack carefully placed over it, concealing it from view.

She then sped out of the driveway, picturing the route she would take in her head. She could get as far as Atlanta before having to check her atlas for directions. Preoccupied with these thoughts, she didn't see the black sedan approaching the driveway.

Monsignor Bonelli watched the white Ford Taurus speed out of the driveway, and wondered where the girl was headed in such a hurry, away from Raleigh.

He ordered Father Gervasi to follow her; he had a strong feeling whatever she was up to involved the manuscript. No one could tell him differently at this point. Last night he convinced himself Melody Bennet had the evil book; all the signs pointed to it. With a kerchief, he lightly dabbed at the perspiration beginning to bead on his forehead, his eyes never leaving the girl.

She weaved in and out of traffic, apparently in a great hurry, making it a challenge for Father Gervasi to keep up. They managed to follow her for several hours, along Interstate 40, then I-95 South, and next on I-20 West. Time passed fairly quickly as they maintained constant focus on their target. Approaching Augusta, Georgia, Father Gervasi warned that they were running out of gas, though he assumed the girl would have to stop soon as well.

About thirty minutes later, their "check engine" light came on. The temperature gauge showed the car was indeed running hot. They knew they were in trouble when they heard a hiss and caught the odor of burnt fluid, signaling a blown radiator hose.

Before they could exit the highway to find a service station, steam began pouring from beneath the hood. They had no choice but to pull onto the shoulder and call for help.

Meanwhile, Melody Bennet's car disappeared over the steamy asphalt horizon.

Cardinal Bonelli conceded this battle but had no intention of losing the war. He knew without having to follow her further that she was headed back to Louisiana.

Arrangements were made for the two priests to be picked up and return to Raleigh; Cardinal Bonelli would be taken to the nearest airport for a flight to New Orleans. Somehow, he would find the girl in that godforsaken place.

CHAPTER TWENTY-NINE

Maurice Abudah was trying to escape the scorching heat of bayou afternoon. He had drawn all the blinds and lay on the floor in the middle of his living room, under the ceiling fan. Physical relief was the only thing he hoped for now. His thoughts, both waking and asleep, were tortured, filled with dark images and foreboding. Helena had come to him last night and warned that time was running out. Her voice was angry, no longer sweetly encouraging. She ordered him to go to North Carolina and get The Book from the girl.

Maurice was too distraught to undertake such a trip. It required planning and his mind just couldn't handle that kind of detail right now. He had believed Melody would return soon to Louisiana, but now he was worried. Helena's frustration added to his anxiety; the last thing he wanted was to disappoint his mother.

He lit a black candle and sat in front of it with his eyes closed. There was so much confusion. He had to somehow find his way through the mist of worries and fears that clouded his thinking. As the candle burned, the tension in his muscles slowly released its grip, and in a few moments he was in deep trance.

He saw Melody Bennet again. She was driving this time. He could sense that she was scared and distraught. He also saw a black car following her, and was certain that whoever was in it sought the same thing he did. The convergence of anger, frustration and fear was so intense that he began to sweat profusely, becoming feverish again.

The vision changed, and now Maurice saw an old woman with gray hair, her aura also overlaid with anxiety. But there was something different about her—she was stronger than the others, her inner light very intense. Maurice saw her gathering wood and arranging it in a circle outside a house. There was water and he saw cypress trees, so he knew it was in the bayou. He had seen this house before, but where?

At the end of his vision, Helena appeared again, looking different this time; older, much as she had before moving into the Spirit pool. She smiled gently and, before disappearing, pointed toward the ritual knife he kept on the end table.

When he returned to full consciousness, he knew what he had to do. He must take back The Book and avenge the spirit of his mother and ancestors by killing the white woman.

Now he was sure Melody Bennet was coming back here. The vision was very clear. He also knew the old woman had been shown to him for a reason. He walked outside and climbed into his old Camaro, leaving the black candle to burn itself out, along with any doubts he may have had.

Where had he seen that house before? He hated that he couldn't remember things any more, and his frustration led to anger that made the problem even worse.

He drove for awhile, ending up at the emporium where he bought a pack of menthols and a cigar for later use. While in the store he overheard the young man behind the counter telling a friend about seeing someone earlier, an old lady he called "Maman." He said he was surprised to find her here as soon as the store opened. She had come to use the phone, and he heard her talking to that lady who came to scatter her grandmother's ashes a few weeks ago.

Maurice pretended to be browsing and listened carefully. The young men gossiped, saying the old woman must be two hundred years old by now and that they wouldn't mind seeing the pretty young woman around here again. He decided to play a wild card and approached the counter with a few canned goods.

"Say, man, I couldn't help overhear 'bout that young lady. Last time she was here, she said she was interested in my artwork. Any idea how to get in touch with her?"

The younger man shrugged. "I wouldn't know nothin' about that, but maybe Maman knows."

"Know where I could find her?"

"Yeah, everyone knows Maman. You never heard of her?"

Maurice shook his head.

"Man, I thought everyone knew that ole Voodoo lady."

Maurice suddenly recalled where he had seen the house in his vision, and he knew exactly who Maman was. She was one of the Devereux sisters. His mother pointed out her house one day as they took their boat through the swamp, looking for herbs and vines.

He paid and managed to keep from sprinting to his car, not wanting to draw attention to himself. He drove home like a madman and ran to his boat.

Knowing the fingers of the bayou like the back of his hand, he cut off the motor well before reaching his destination. He didn't want the old woman or anyone else to hear him approach. Leaving the boat tied to a tree about a quarter mile away, he walked through the thick brush covering the path to the old woman's house. When he finally saw it, his heart began to race; it looked just as it had in his vision.

Careful not to be seen, he hid behind a tall bush bordering the yard. Maman was nowhere in sight at first but soon walked out the back door. She carried bowls to a large circle made of cypress logs. Outside the perimeter was a larger circle of stones and in the center was a red cloth large enough for someone to lie on.

Suddenly overcome with fever and a hot poker sensation in his solar plexus, Maurice felt his legs giving way and had to fight a strong urge to urinate. He waited for the old woman to return to the house before relieving himself, fearing any sound might alert her. Maurice watched the house for a little longer, then decided to return home for a while.

This Maman was obviously preparing for a ceremony with Melody Bennet, and he would bet it involved The Book.

Back home, he could barely contain his excitement and couldn't wait to tell James and Alex when it was all done and over with.

He poured a generous glass of rum and downed it in a few gulps, knowing he needed all the rest he could get. He noticed the black candle from earlier had just finished burning, gray tendrils of smoke swirling in ascension.

The liquor took effect quickly and soon he was fast asleep, dreaming he was a little boy walking along the streets of New Orleans with his mother. Helena was radiant, smiling down and telling him what a good boy he was.

Maurice Abudah slept peacefully, knowing justice was finally at hand.

CHAPTER THIRTY

Melody made calls from her cell phone as she drove, but no one answered. She left messages for the real estate attorney handling the closing, for her mother, and for Mario. In each message she mentioned having to leave town for a few days, without elaborating further. She spoke briefly with Isabel, but lost connection before she could give any details.

As she drove through Mississippi, along a stretch highway where the signal was very weak, Mario called. She could hear the concern in his voice, but the static made conversation nearly impossible.

She had to shout into the phone before losing signal altogether. "I'll be in Louisiana for a few days. Don't worry, I'll call when I get back." She didn't know if he heard her.

Melody felt guilty about revealing her destination, against Maman's specific request, but she didn't want to lie to him again. Not telling him about *Obeah* already nagged at her. She wasn't ready to tell him, though she wasn't sure why. Something still didn't feel right. It took her a long time to trust people; she was surprised how close she felt to Isabel and Maman already.

For the remainder of her drive, Melody did the only thing she knew to do when feeling helpless and afraid: She recited The Lord's Prayer. Over and over and over again.

It was almost eleven before her tires bit into the gravel parking lot of the emporium. Thirteen straight hours of driving with only three quick stops had exhausted her.

Turning off the engine, Melody looked around but saw no other vehicle. Samuel hadn't arrived yet.

Stepping out of the car into the quiet night, she was happy to have her feet on solid ground, though still heard the hum of the engine in her ears. To clear her head and get blood flow back into her cramped body, she walked a bit. Rounding the corner of the building, she nearly jumped for joy when she saw Samuel asleep in his truck.

Melody lightly tapped on his window, wanting to wake but not frighten him. True to form, as soon as he opened his eyes, he smiled. He jumped from the truck to give her a big hug.

"You're here, little lady! It's good to see you."

Melody didn't want him to let go. She felt like a small child, needing the comfort of someone wiser and stronger.

"It's good to see you, too. How is Maman?"

The perpetual smiled faded.

"She's worried, Melody. She's very worried about you."

"I know. She sounded frantic on the phone. I got here as soon as I could."

"Her instincts are usually good. I've known Marie a long time and can tell you that she doesn't panic easily. For her to venture out to the store first thing and call you, then come looking for me…well, it's not a good sign."

Melody's anxiety escalated. "Okay, let's go. The sooner we get to her, the better."

Maman had seen the approaching headlights and was in the yard waiting for them.

Melody stifled a gasp. Maman had aged dramatically in the weeks since Melody saw her last.

She flung her arms wide open for Melody, who ran over the moment she was out of the car.

"You're here, Chère! Everything will be fine now."

Samuel had already gone inside and put on water for tea. At the door, Melody excused herself and ran quickly back to the car for the manuscript and her backpack. She wouldn't leave The Book unattended. A few minutes later, the three of them were seated around the kitchen table.

"Any trouble driving down here, Chère?" Maman asked.

"No, I only stopped when it was absolutely necessary."

"Did you tell anyone you were coming here?"

"I told two people, Maman. I know you asked me not to, but I needed to tell someone...in case anything should happen. I told a friend, Isabel—she's from Louisiana—and...another friend."

Though clearly troubled, Maman didn't reprimand Melody.

"I have everything prepared for the ritual, but I think we should wait until tomorrow. It's been a long day; we're all too tired. I'll sprinkle some powder outside to keep you safe."

Melody was happy that whatever needed to be done could wait until tomorrow. She could barely stay awake; her eyes burned and her entire body ached.

Maman's eyes fell on Melody's things in the middle of the table. She looked at Melody, eyebrows raised, silently questioning. Melody had placed the backpack over the manuscript, so all Maman could see was the binding of a leather-bound black book. When Melody lifted the backpack, *Obeah* was revealed.

She observed Maman and Samuel closely, curious how they would respond. Both looked slightly shaken; Samuel whistled softly.

"So she *did* take it from Helena." Samuel's voice was a mixture of awe and surprise.

"She did, but not for the reasons everyone believed. I found Yvette's diary, too."

Melody pulled the diary from the backpack and showed it to Maman, who seemed more interested in it than The Book. Maman noticed Melody's puzzled expression and explained.

"I'm old, and I know my time is short. I have no need for that book. Authentic power comes from true communication with Spirit. A true voodooist learns how to use the power of Spirit for inner growth; to create a peaceful world *inside*, where Truth resides. We don't spend energy trying to change things *outside* that are part of an illusion."

"Have you already read this?" Melody asked with a smile.

Maman managed a weak laugh and shook her head. "No, child, but when you get as old as I am, you realize most knowledge comes from living life and paying attention. No amount of reading can help you walk that road. You just have to do it. You'll learn that even what you perceive as obstacles are really opportunities—gifts from Spirit—for you to grow and learn."

Samuel nodded his head in agreement. "Marie is right, Melody. Young people think it's not worth listening to old people. We may not understand computers and such as well as you young folk, but we know more about how this life works; how to be in this world. When your body wears out and you're not motivated by physical needs as much, you develop a different understanding of things. A deeper understanding."

Melody was so touched by Maman and Samuel. As each imparted their wisdom and watched the other do the same, their faces magically lit up. She'd never seen an aura, but she swore she saw light emanating from them. The respect and devotion they had for one another was almost tangible; it filled Melody's heart to witness such love.

"It does seem arrogant to think our modern technology helps us control anything, or understand anything. More and more I see most things are just illusions."

"You're learning how to keep an open mind, to learn as you go. That's good; it's what you need to do. It's why you have the manuscript." Maman looked directly at Melody, smiling. "And another thing about illusions, child: Unless you rise above the ego, rise above how you see things, you'll fear everything. When you start to see yourself as a victim, well…you then become one. And it's no one's fault but your own."

Despite the gravity of the situation, Melody was grateful she was here. She treasured this, sitting in the comfort of Maman's kitchen, listening to them. They reminded her of Grandmama and Charlie.

She realized neither Maman nor Samuel were aware of all that had happened since she had returned to Raleigh. They knew nothing about the visit from the priests, the break-in at her apartment, or about Charlie. They knew nothing about Mario, and she had only mentioned Isabel's name in passing. There was much to tell, but not tonight.

The relaxing effect of the tea hit her all at once and Melody could hardly keep her eyes open.

"Go to bed, child. Your room is ready. I'm going to do a few things around here to make sure you're safe until tomorrow night."

After saying goodnight and blowing a kiss, Melody headed for the same bedroom where she had stayed before.

Several minutes later, Maman went in to make sure she was comfortable, and found her sound asleep. Maman then burned sage throughout the house and sprinkled red brick powder on windowsills and doorsteps. She threw sea salt in every corner of the house, with the most care given to Melody's room.

In the kitchen she smiled when she saw Melody had left her things on the kitchen table, including the manuscript and diary; this meant she trusted them and felt safe.

"That's good," Maman thought to herself. "She needs to trust, if I am to help her. We can't let fear get in the way, not now."

She thought of a few more supplies that would be helpful and asked Samuel if he would go to the city tomorrow to get them. Before he left for the night, the couple sat in silence for several minutes, holding hands, simply cherishing one another's presence

After securing the property, Marie Devereux went to bed. She was extraordinarily tired tonight, bone-weary.

Marie was certainly not afraid of death, for she knew it was merely a rebirth. From an early age she held great respect for the aging process, having known relatives who lived more than a century. She watched their mental and physical capacities diminish, regressing back to childlike behavior.

To her, elders were "old babies," ready to be born again in the other dimension, though sometimes struggling as they passed through the "death canal." Once there, the growth process began again, as the soul remembered all its lessons from its earthly life. With remembrance and assessment completed, the soul allows itself to forget, in order to be fresh and receptive during its next incarnation.

Marie understood this; she was comfortable with the idea of going through the death canal, knowing she was being reborn. She also knew it would happen soon, but not until she helped Melody. She didn't understand how she was to help, only that her role was to be with Melody now and do her best to protect her. Marie had long since accepted that she need not know the hows or whys. This would be her last task, and she would die performing it.

Completely at peace with this knowledge, she slept soundly until morning.

Melody was caught in a nightmare. She was being chased through the bayou, surrounded by trees draped in moss and wading through waist-deep black water. Snakes, alligators, vultures, and shadowy figures were steadily converging on her from all directions. An old boat backed toward her, threatening to run her over, its backup alarm ringing in her ears until she was ready to scream.

At that moment she awoke to the incessant beeping of her cell phone alarm.

It took a minute to remember where she was.

She reached for the phone and saw she had messages.

That's odd. She knew there was no signal here and that she could neither send nor receive calls, but perhaps she could access messages. When her sleepy haze fully cleared, she saw there was one voice message and one text message.

Melody accessed the message inbox and displayed the text, and was mystified. The sender was unknown; she only recognized that the 504 area code indicated a New Orleans number.

Then she saw the message: Watch out for Alex.

Alex?! Who in hell is this Alex?!

Isabel's warning came rushing back. Confused and alarmed, she quickly listened to the voice message. It was Mario, sounding tense and worried, telling her he was coming to Louisiana and that there had been a break in Charlie's case, and said something about a suspect in the New Orleans area. He gave the flight information and said, "I trust you'll get this message, Mel. I hope to see you at the airport tomorrow. If not, don't worry...I'll find you somehow. Be safe."

Melody stared at her phone, incredulous. *Is this another coincidence?*

She was torn between relief that there was a break in the case—though afraid that the murderer was now very close by—and disbelief, thinking Mario was coming here to find her for other reasons. She tried to dismiss the doubt, blaming it on her conditioned response to men, keeping her distance for fear of being hurt.

That was when Maman walked in.

She proceeded to relate everything that had happened since being here last. Melody was surprised she could get through it without crying, especially the part about finding Charlie, but assumed she was finally numb. It was like recounting something that had happened to someone else.

When she confided how close she felt to both Isabel and Mario, Melody felt Maman's body tense. She then told her about Mario coming to Louisiana, and saw her face darken with concern.

"Isabel reminds me a lot of you, Maman. She did a reading about a week ago and saw things similar to your dream, about me being in danger, people coming after The Book. She specifically heard the name Alex. Do you know any Alex?"

"No, child, I don't. I can't think of anyone by that name."

"I could go to the emporium and call the number..."

"NO!" Marie's forcefulness surprised them both. "No, Melody, you can't leave here, not yet."

Mario will be able to trace the number. Maybe his cell phone will work here. Maybe this Alex guy is the lead he's following up on?

Maman shook her head to clear her thoughts. She stood with great effort, sighing deeply. "I hear Samuel's truck. I'll tell him to pick your friend up from the airport when he goes into town."

After getting Mario's information, Maman then turned to Melody and said sternly, "Be careful, child. Beyond me and Samuel, I don't know who you can trust."

While Melody showered, Maman spoke with Samuel about what she just learned. She asked him to pick up Mario from the airport when he got into New Orleans, giving him the flight information and Mario's description. Melody was out of the shower, drying off, when she heard them.

"I don't feel good about this, Marie. I don't feel good about any of it," Samuel said before he left.

Melody's heart sank. She had never heard him sound so worried.

The day had already taken on a strange, dream-like quality. It seemed events beyond her comprehension had been set in motion, as though she was watching a movie that switched jaggedly from scene to scene, character to character. There were too many actors in this movie for her to follow any longer. Oddly, she felt very detached, surrendering to what Maman advised was her only plan at this point.

She dressed and went to the kitchen, finding *Obeah* on the table, exactly as she had left it last night. Melody saw her fatigue reflected in the old woman's face when she entered the room.

"Oh, Chère." Maman heaved a huge sigh and patted Melody's

hand.

"I have so many questions, but those messages this morning were the last straw for my poor brain." Melody tried but couldn't muster a laugh.

"I know, I feel it, too." Maman went to the cupboard where she kept root-working herbs. "But we need to talk. Maybe it will give us energy."

Maman was mixing some sort of concoction as she spoke, which she placed in a tea diffuser.

"After all, magick is energy and energy is a constant flow, from person to person, right? We'll energize each other," she said with a wink. "If not, maybe this tea will help us out. I don't have much time, but I'll use what I have left to work with you, child."

The last comment, echoing a similar comment from last night, jolted Melody. *What is Maman saying?* She couldn't lose her, too. She hid her face in her hands, not wanting Maman to see her distress. The poor woman was already worried and obviously not well; Melody didn't want to make it worse.

But Maman knew Melody was in pain. She came over and placed her hand on Melody's head, then gently stroked from the crown to the nape of her neck as one would a small child. It was a loving, maternal gesture that gave Melody permission to release her emotions and let it all out.

CHAPTER THIRTY-ONE

Cardinal Bonelli was finally in Louisiana. He had spent the night in Atlanta after the car broke down, but was on the first flight to New Orleans the very next morning. All of his arrangements went like clockwork and by lunchtime he had reached his destination.

After checking in, he phoned Father Robert Rudino.

"This is Father Rudino. May I help you?"

"Father, this is Monsignor Bonelli speaking."

"Yes, sir. What can I do for you?" Father Robert recoiled at the sound of the Cardinal's voice but kept his voice even and cordial.

"I am in New Orleans. I neglected to ask you earlier whether you might recall any names of people here...anyone this Melody Bennet might have mentioned during your talk. Some of her grandmother's friends, for example?"

Father Robert thought for a moment. "I'm not sure...I'd have to think about it."

"Do try to remember. It is very important—to all of us."

The veiled threat wasn't lost on the priest.

"I do recall one name. She only mentioned one person, a woman known as Marie, a childhood friend of her grandmother. I got the impression she lives in the bayou."

Monsignor Bonelli snorted. It was like looking for a needle in a haystack.

"Are you sure she didn't mention any specific area?"

"I'm sorry, Monsignor. That's all I know. I think the woman in question is a fairly well-known local Voodoo practitioner."

"A witch?! I knew that girl was up to no good. You can smell the devil at work here."

Monsignor Bonelli's rant seemed to go on and on, but Father Robert was no longer listening. He knew Melody, and he knew she wasn't evil. A bit confused perhaps, in need of returning to her Catholic roots, but definitely not evil.

Once off the phone, Monsignor Bonelli sat on the bed, trying to devise a viable plan.

He went back to the front desk and asked how he could obtain information about a woman who lived in a remote region of the bayou. The clerk told him that most of the tours were conducted in the Atchafalaya Basin and that one of the locals there might know the woman. Since he had few options, he asked her to book him on a tour for that afternoon. She politely informed him that the tour shuttles left at around five each morning, with nothing available after that time.

"I must get out there today, young lady. Any suggestions?"

"Well, it would be quite expensive, but you could take a cab to where most of the tours launch and see who might be available to help you."

"Good. Please arrange that for me right away. I'll be waiting outside."

He was impressed with her demeanor and professionalism. Before leaving, he glanced at her name tag: Olivia Beauchamp. What a pleasant girl, most likely a good Catholic; one of the few worthy children of God in this wretched place.

Outside the hotel, the sidewalk teemed with people, noise, and innumerable distractions. This was surely a true haven for sinners.

CHAPTER THIRTY-TWO

In her heart of hearts Melody knew Maman was right—that their time together was limited—but hearing her say it was too much.

"I'm sorry. I thought I was getting things under control but then something else happens…"

"No apology needed, Chère. I had no idea what all you'd been through since leaving here. I felt energy building, but I couldn't see clearly."

She took a sip of tea and encouraged Melody to do the same. "Maybe this will help us get through the rest of the day."

"I need you to listen to me, Chère." Maman's eyes had a distant look as she began to speak again. The tone of her voice drastically changed, as if preparing to deliver the sermon of her life, pulling from the inner depths of her wisdom.

"Death is hard to accept, especially for those left behind. Our fear of death—and grief—comes from our ego, always trying to control things.

"But if you truly and unconditionally love, you don't need to connect on the physical plane; you connect at the soul level.

"People often mistake fear for love. Some fear losing others because they're afraid of being alone. Other people fear losing someone because they need to take care of others and distract from themselves; they need to be needed. Either way it's about control, which originates from the ego, not from the soul."

Maman looked at Melody, and resumed talking in her soothing, velvet voice.

"It is always a miracle when two spiritual beings connect. It's tangible. We are connected, Melody. If our purpose to teach and learn from one another isn't completed in this lifetime, then we'll meet again. I believe we're so close that we'll never truly be apart.

"Each of us is here for a purpose, and all of us must fulfill many tasks in order to achieve that purpose in the manner we choose. I believe that helping you is my final task on Earth, in this body."

Melody nodded, her heart full of gratitude for having met this amazing woman, though heavy with the thought of losing her.

"I know what you're saying, Maman. In a perfect world we could all see things that way and never feel pain. But it's human nature to fear losing loved ones and to grieve the loss." Her voice cracked as she defended her pain. "It's comforting to know we're never apart at the soul level and to know our loved ones are fine, but people long for a hug, a physical connection. I know it's selfish, but it's human."

And the heartache of losing those we love can be absolutely unbearable.

"Melody, where is your focus?" Maman asked, confusing Melody.

"Focus?"

"What were you thinking about?"

"I was thinking how devastating it is to lose a loved one, how it rips my heart to shreds every time."

"Okay, that's perfect. Try to shift it. Instead of focusing on the pain of loss, focus on a joyful time spent with your loved one. When you think of the loss, you are sad; when you think of time together, you are uplifted, right?

Melody nodded.

"Shift your focus to where you feel joy, Chère. It's a matter of vibration. Try to hold thoughts that fill you with happiness. It takes effort to shift your mind this way, but to move beyond the pain—not just put it aside, but truly move *beyond* it—you must learn how to shift your focus.

"Recognize also how joyful your loved ones are once they've passed on. Yes, you miss their hugs, but when you find yourself missing them, think of their soul, the very essence of them you cherished and always will. Think of them entirely free from pain or distress....they *are* free.

"It's important we do that as a gift to our loved ones. Sometimes our prolonged grieving interferes with the soul's ability to pass completely into the Spirit pool. That energetic pull of the person reluctant to let go is like a chain, tethering them here."

The idea that intense grieving could hinder a loved one's soul hit Melody hard. She would never want that. Believing in energy as she did, she understood how such an emotional chain could affect someone, whether or not they were in physical form.

"And, child, another thing to consider regarding pain: Sometimes people will subconsciously hold on to pain long after their grieving has subsided. Some people hold on to the pain for so long they identify the pain with their loved one, as though the pain of grieving is the only thing they have left of the departed soul. They fear that by releasing the pain, they are releasing their connection to that person."

Maman was right. Melody had done that with her father's death. She had held on to the gut-wrenching pain, identified with it. She remembered thinking that letting go of the grief would somehow be a betrayal.

Melody laid her hand on *The Book of Obeah*.

"What is Obeah, Maman?"

"Obeah is the knowledge from within; the one true, eternal power and strength that no one and no book can teach you."

Melody grinned. "Not even this book?"

"I haven't read it, but I'm certain even a special book like this can only show you the path. Maybe it shows several paths from which to choose, but it can't walk the path for you."

"So, Obeah is a positive thing?"

"It's not a *thing*, child, and it's neither positive nor negative. It's just power; raw, undiluted power from Source. Anything can be positive or negative; it all depends on the intent."

"Why do you think people associate it with black magick? Even Mario does."

Maman arched her eyebrows, puzzled. "Mario knows Obeah?"

Melody explained that they had met in the metaphysical bookstore, and that their relationship was not merely professional, but personal. She said they had discussed Voodoo and spirituality quite extensively.

"But I haven't told him about The Book."

"That's good, Melody. Obeah has been kept a secret because it holds the key to great power. Only a few people know its true meaning. This secrecy serves two purposes. One is that, by keeping Obeah secret, the essence of its power remains undiluted, uncorrupted. The other is to reveal a critical aspect of the human ego. Humans will label anything they don't understand or can't comprehend as negative, even evil. They attach a stigma to anything their conscious mind can't grasp.

"This is why I tell you, Chère: True power is in the unknown. The *word* Obeah may have been corrupted because of the limitations of human consciousness to grasp certain knowledge, but the *energy*, the *essence* of Obeah remains untouched and pure."

"What about black magick—hexes and roots to harm people? The Book even gives details about this."

"Well, I would suggest you keep in mind that all books, even sacred books, have been written by humans; humans who, whether they realized it or not, influenced the outcome in some way." Maman was pacing now, wanting to phrase her words so Melody would understand. "Take channeling; you understand what that is, right?"

Melody nodded.

"Even when a powerful adept channels a message from Spirit, it is almost impossible for the outcome to be free of their imprint. Each person interprets words and visions and sounds uniquely, translating them in their own way. So, a channeled message is often worded in a way that is understood by the person channeling. Another person may interpret the same message differently. Even if it is a very slight difference, those slight differences are like snowballs; they can end up being tremendously different down the line. Do you understand?

"Yes, Ma'am." Melody thought this described the Bible perfectly. The original text had been translated countless times through the centuries, with innumerable interpretations of the translated text.

"Other things to consider are the intention and perception of the person writing, and how these influence what is written. The same is true of the person reading; their perspective and intention color their interpretation. Rare is the human who is a pure vessel for anything. As far as The Book is concerned, I would imagine that the real power lies in what cannot be clearly understood."

"You mean the writing has a double meaning, like a secret code or something?"

"I don't know, Chère. I don't have any guidance beyond what I just said."

Maman took another sip of tea, followed by a deep, cleansing breath.

"Back to hexes and black magick. Power is energy, Melody, and energy is not positive or negative, it is both. All elements, and therefore all Orishas, have a nature of duality and can be used to for healing or destruction.

"It is easier to do effective works of magick with a positive object, because one need only hold to their alignment with the mind of the Creator. To work magick intending harm, while not harming oneself in the process, one must align with the true mind within, both to raise power and to hold it as protection for oneself. At the same time, the conscious mind must split a part of itself to concentrate on the intent to harm. It takes a tremendous amount of skill to do that, and very few people are able to."

Melody didn't completely grasp that last part, but she was still spellbound. Maman continued.

"The easiest way a conjurer can do harm with a so-called hex is by making the target aware of it, planting the seed of fear. If the seed takes, the conjurer's work is finished. The target will self-destruct by envisioning pain, harm, or loss. The real Obeah men and women who can access true power have no need to hex anyone. They know obstacles are only illusions, created by the ego to blur true vision.

"Always consider that things happen for a reason that may not be visible to us. The situation may carry a lesson for you or others; it may be a crossroad where you need to decide to part with something or someone, including something within yourself, before you can move forward on your soul's journey. Allow the Creator mind—*not* your ego side—to have power over the details and circumstances. If your desire is meant to manifest, then it shall. The process of desiring something may be no more than a stepping stone, leading you toward your life purpose. With that in mind be grateful for the desire, even if it never manifests."

Maman finally sat down to rest.

Melody remained silent, absorbing and processing the insights imparted in Maman's words. It was surreal, as though Maman was attempting to share a lifetime of wisdom in one morning. Melody was honored, yet it left her with a sense of anxiety, and urgency.

"Goodness, child, look at the time! We need to prepare a few things before Samuel and Mario get here. Are you sure we can trust him?"

Thinking of Mario made Melody feel warm inside. "I believe so."

Maman was not so certain, but she knew Melody would have to find out on her own, one way or the other.

CHAPTER THIRTY-THREE

Samuel Marlowe lit a cigarette outside the American Airlines terminal.

Since the flight Mario Hernandez was supposed to be on was delayed, Samuel had gone back outside, rather than wait in the terminal. He figured he had time to enjoy both a smoke and the distraction afforded by the hurrying airport crowd. Smog or no smog, Samuel preferred the outside air to artificial indoor cooling systems any day. He had arrived at a point in life where he could flow along wherever the current took him and smile through it all.

But he hadn't always been this way.

Many years ago, Samuel Marlowe was a polished and well-respected banker, who seemed to have a sixth sense about financial matters.

Samuel had been raised in a staunchly materialistic, "old money" New Orleans family. The Almighty Dollar was the only god in their household; Samuel was taught to serve this god at all costs. The stellar reputation he had built held the promise of a long, successful career. Samuel's gut feelings about investments had thus far proven invaluable. Unfortunately, his boredom led him toward increasingly risky investments.

One particular catastrophic decision made from a position of youthful arrogance destroyed his career.

Having been entrusted with portfolio of one of the firm's wealthiest clients, he took a known risk, convincing himself he was infallible. In less than forty-eight hours, the risky investments crumbled like a house of cards, taking the client's entire portfolio along with it.

Samuel quickly discovered that he was *persona non grata*. Unable to find work and unaccustomed to curtailing his lavish lifestyle, Samuel soon ended up with nothing.

He impulsively packed his few belongings and turned his back on New Orleans, hitchhiking all the way to the bayou. While fishing one day he met Marie Devereux, who was out gathering herbs for her sister. Samuel was instantly stricken by her beauty; her incredible blue eyes were like two bottomless oceans, in whose unknown depths he would gladly spend an eternity. They talked for some time and, much to his delight, she invited him over for tea.

Samuel didn't even like tea, but he would have sipped mud to see Marie again.

He was surprised the first time he went to her house and saw all the Voodoo paraphernalia on full display. Not only was he unfamiliar with Voodoo, he had to adjust to the idea that white women were practicing it.

Over time their relationship blossomed. By the time he became comfortable with the idea of romantic involvement with this beautiful woman, Samuel had also come to appreciate the beauty of Voodoo. Marie and her sister slowly showed him the truths of their path. He moved to the bayou for good and became an avowed voodooist.

He and Marie became lovers, and he wanted nothing more than to seal their relationship in matrimony. But Marie told him that her first commitment was to Voodoo, and she felt she would not make a good wife. Samuel silently disagreed, but respected her decision without arguing.

Their sexual relationship gradually ended, but their souls united. Samuel did not know how much time he or Marie had left on this Earth, but knew their bond would never break; they would always be together.

Finishing his cigarette, he made his way back into the terminal. He enjoyed watching people; it was one of the few reasons he still came into New Orleans every so often, to play his harmonica on the street in the Quarter.

Along the way he noticed how many people were rushing

around, afraid to miss their flights, fearful of losing their luggage, worried about not finding those whom they were here to meet.

Humans spend three-quarters of their time worrying. They regret what has happened in the past, and they worry about the future, fearing what it may bring. Thanks to Marie, Samuel learned to live in the present; it amused and saddened him at the same time to see how many had yet to discover this simple truth.

He scanned the crowd of arriving passengers and saw one man who fit Mario's description: mid-thirties, Hispanic, about six feet tall. He raised the small sign he had made and waited to see if the man responded. Mario was surprised to see a stranger instead of Melody, but flashed a warm smile as he extended his hand.

"Hi, I'm Mario Hernandez."

"Samuel." The older gentleman shook his hand. "Nice to meet you. Any luggage to pick up?"

"Yeah, sorry. I had to check my bag...couldn't carry it on."

Samuel waited outside while Mario collected his luggage at the carousel. Both men were uneasy, thinking about the day that lay ahead.

CHAPTER THIRTY-FOUR

Maurice Abudah's fever was intensifying. He wiped his forehead with his shirt and then checked the knapsack he would take to the Devereux house. He had been there very early this morning and tried to break in, but felt sick every time he got near the doors and windows. He had no problem walking through the yard, so he was sure the old woman had done something to protect the house. He knew he couldn't get The Book or the girl until they came outside. Maurice wasn't worried. He was certain they would come out; it was obvious they were preparing for a ritual.

Having readied his own house for the sacrificial ceremony, his heart raced, envisioning the girl's blood soaking the urn that contained his own mother's ashes. The sacrificial knife was resting in its red cloth beside the knapsack. Maurice picked it up and tucked it gently into the sack. He planned to sacrifice the white woman here, but in case the plan changed, he wanted to be prepared.

He placed his hands lightly on the urn and closed his eyes, trying to connect with his mother. She was there almost immediately, smiling peacefully and nodding her head in approval. She had been there during the night, wiping his forehead as he lay burning with fever, telling him it would all be over soon.

"Maurice, you know the girl is coming back. You know what you must do. It's up to you: Get The Book for your grandchildren so they can have a better life, the life they deserve."

Returning from the Devereux place just after dawn, he had been surprised to find James waiting for him. The boy was alarmed by the ritual supplies scattered around the living room and was worried about Maurice, begging him to go to the hospital.

"Please, Grandpa, you're going to hurt yourself or someone

else! Have you gone insane?!"

The boy just didn't understand at all. He didn't recognize Maurice's fever as possession by Spirit, giving him the strength of the righteous. Other than his mother, Maurice needed neither the help nor blessing of anyone to do what must be done. He would convince James of the honor in what he was about to do when the time came. Alex had no time for the old man lately and chose to stay away, but seemed to understand.

Samuel and Mario left the airport, heading for a little botanica near the French Quarter, the only place where Samuel could find everything on Marie's list. It was mid-afternoon, before rush hour, so they expected to get back to Marie's by dinnertime.

After purchasing the supplies, the men headed out of the Quarter and back toward Atchafalaya, cutting through a neighborhood that had been hit hard by the levee breach. A hotel van caught Samuel's attention. He had seen this same van and driver on the back road from the emporium this morning. That same young man stood outside a small clapboard house now, arguing heatedly with a young black woman. She looked so familiar it jarred him, and he braked abruptly. Mario was on the phone but looked over curiously, wondering why Samuel had slowed to a crawl.

Samuel stared at the girl, trying to place where he'd seen her before. His memory was still good, but not good enough to place her face right away. He nearly got out of the truck when he saw the boy grab her arm, but she jerked away and ran inside. Samuel saw the boy walk back to his van, distraught and clearly worked up about something.

Maurice hoped the old woman would not be there; he didn't want to shed the blood of an innocent, and the old lady had nothing to do with what happened all those years ago. He led the boat to the inlet where he had left it before, following the same path toward the house.

Only moments after he got situated, hidden behind a tall bush, the old woman walked outside carrying a basket. She placed the basket within the circle of logs and looked up at the sky. The sun had begun to relinquish some of its power, and the evening breeze was already teasing the leaves with its breath. Twilight was the time to move between worlds, and Maurice knew Helena would join him here soon. When the light fades and shadows appear, the bayou fills with illusions, but a true voodooist sees through the illusion to the truth.

Maurice's pulse quickened. He knew that by the time the moon rose high in the sky, Helena's spirit would be avenged. He would have what he needed to free his family.

He heard the old woman call out to Melody, and he quietly slipped closer. Maurice shifted only slightly, but it was just enough to get Marie's attention. Hearing a noise behind her, she turned to see what it was.

Her reflexes were not fast enough. Before she could scream and alert Melody to stay inside, two strong hands closed around her throat, squeezing the life out of the ocean-blue eyes.

Daylight rapidly fading and storm clouds rolling in, Melody hoped Samuel and Mario would arrive soon. She was anxious to hear about the new lead in Charlie's case; she was just as anxious to feel his arms wrapped around her. He would never meet Giselle and Charlie, but she was glad he would get to meet Maman and Samuel.

The time spent with Maman earlier had calmed her for a while, but as the afternoon wore on she felt more unsettled. She had become nervous, even frightened.

It was apparent Maman was lost in her own thoughts as she got things ready. Melody didn't know exactly what the ceremony was for, but assumed it was to protect her and *Obeah*.

Melody hated to interrupt her, but really wanted to get her

thoughts about the first page in The Book, the one written in what seemed an indecipherable language. *She might recognize something about the symbols, or be able to pick up something psychically.*

She picked up The Book from the table and went looking for Maman.

Maurice laid the Devereux woman's lifeless body on the ground and quickly moved out of view. He pressed his back against the side of the house so the girl wouldn't see him; he heard her moving around and knew it wouldn't be long before she came outside.

As he expected, Melody Bennet opened the door after only a few moments, protectively clutching *The Book of Obeah* to her chest. She had only taken a few steps beyond the small porch stoop when she saw something out of place on the ground ahead. Daylight and darkness were converging, creating deceptive shadows and making it difficult to see clearly. Melody thought she saw a crumpled robe on the ground, but as she came closer a silent scream rocked her as she realized it was Maman Marie.

She dropped The Book and ran to her. Marie's head was grotesquely twisted, perpendicular to her lifeless body; her eyes stared into nothingness and the color had already drained from her weary face. As Melody leaned over the body a shadow appeared, towering above her. She felt sudden, blinding pain in the back of her head and everything went black.

CHAPTER THIRTY-FIVE

Samuel couldn't erase the young woman's face from his mind, trying to recall where he had seen her; Mario was on the phone with his partner for much of the drive to the bayou, discussing two ongoing cases. About forty-five minutes from the Whiskey Bay Exit, they found themselves at a bumper-to-bumper stand-still.

Getting antsy because of the unmoving traffic, Mario dialed Melody's number again. It went straight to voicemail.

"I told you, it's no use out there."

"How can you stand not having a phone? What if there's an emergency?" Mario didn't mean to sound rude, but he was frustrated with the whole situation. He couldn't stand being unable to reach someone. He didn't know exactly why Melody was here, but knew it had to be urgent for her to leave in such a hurry.

"You just get used to it, son."

Samuel recalled Marie telling him about the weird phone message Melody had found this morning and knew Mario was unaware of it. He had a gut feeling it may be important. His instinct also told him he could trust Mario with that information, but nothing further.

"Listen, Melody got another message this morning. It wasn't a voice message like you left; it was typed out."

"You mean a text message?" Mario asked.

"Yeah, I guess that's what you call it. Anyway, it really upset Melody. All it said was something about watching out for Alex."

"Alex?"

"Yeah, that's what she told Marie. She said it warned about some 'Alex' person and it was from a 504 area code. New Orleans." Traffic at a halt, he turned to look at Mario. "You think it could be that old man who threatened her when she was here

259

last time. You know about that, right?"

"Yes, I do. Maybe...it's hard to tell." Mario was going over everything in his head about Melody's case—the break-in, Charlie's murder—but no Alex came up anywhere.

Traffic limped along for another thirty minutes or so, but at least it was moving.

"We're not far from our exit now," Samuel said.

As traffic opened up in earnest, Samuel caught sight of some commotion in his rearview mirror. There was a little red Nissan, faded and beat up, weaving through the lanes of traffic, horn blaring and causing a ruckus. When a lane finally opened up, the car darted into it, speeding dangerously.

What Samuel saw next set off warning bells.

It was the hotel van, with the driver he had seen earlier, obviously chasing the red car. Samuel hadn't seen who was driving the car, but wondered if it was the young woman involved in the argument he had witnessed. Something was up with these two, something no good. Samuel felt it in his bones. It suddenly dawned on him who the girl reminded him of: She was the spitting image of Helena Abudah, the woman who had worked the evil hoodoo so many years ago.

Samuel knew it was an omen and began to pray.

Paul had gone straight to the store when he returned to town late in the afternoon. He was very disappointed by not having found the manuscript in North Carolina but knew everything happened for a reason. Joe saw him coming and met him at the door, running down the list of what had happened during his absence. The most peculiar was that a "fancy priest" had come in to take a swamp tour only a couple of hours before. According to Joe, he seemed mostly interested in asking where people lived in this "godforsaken region."

The hair on the back of Paul's neck stood on end. His suspicion was heightened when Joe added that the old priest had asked about the whereabouts of Marie, the "heathen voodooist."

Then Joe dropped the real bomb.

"Oh, yeah. The priest also asked if I knew where a young girl from North Carolina might be staying."

Paul placed his hand on the wall to steady himself. "Is she here?"

"Gee, Paul, I dunno. I haven't seen her."

After Joe left, Paul closed the store so he could think in peace. He waited, hoping the storm would pass soon; he hated to be on the water during a storm. By the time the worst of the storm was gone, so was the daylight. Untying the pirogue from the pole behind the store, he rowed until the water was deep enough to start the motor. He then set off for Maman Marie's, surrounded by trees that stood like sentinels in the night, guarding the ancient secrets of the bayou.

As Maurice carried Melody's flaccid body toward his boat, Helena appeared to him. Shango was stronger at the old lady's house, she said, so the sacrifice must take place there.

He took the storm approaching in the distance as a sign that he must begin. Placing Melody at the center of the circle, he removed her clothing and continued his preparations.

As she regained consciousness, Melody became aware of the pain in her head and her bound hands. When she tried to move, the pain intensified sharply. Taking it more slowly and allowing her eyes to gain focus, she saw the black man who had threatened her at Paul's house and again in New Orleans. He was setting logs on fire all around her.

Maurice stood in front of her in the circle and stretched his long arms toward the sky, intoning strange words. The storm came upon them quickly; Melody could feel the ground shudder every time lightning struck nearby. She heard the man invoking Shango, and she shivered as the lightning drew closer.

Then the rain came.

It started as a few large drops and increased to driving rain. Lying on her back, face up and fearing she would drown, she struggled frantically to move. The water had softened whatever was binding her hands; she could turn her wrists slightly, but could not move them enough to uncross them.

Desperate to break free, she glimpsed the blade of a knife reflected in a lightning flash lying just beyond the circle. She gathered all of her strength and struggled to her knees. She staggered toward the edge of the circle where the drenched logs were now only barely burning. Before she reached the edge, the man seized her arm, blindly stabbing at her with the smaller knife he held. At that point, he wanted only to stop her from leaving the circle.

Ritual sacrifices require precision.

Melody screamed, stumbled over a log, and fell back into the circle. The man stepped toward her. Towering over her naked, bleeding body, he raised the knife high above his head and prepared to strike.

In a split second, a lightning bolt struck the tip of the knife and Melody saw sparks fly from the man's body. He fell to his knees, hands pressed over his ears, squeezing his head in agony.

The combination of rain and sweat had finally loosened the thin binding about her wrists, allowing her to free her hands. Propelled by fear, she snatched up *The Book of Obeah* and fled toward the woods. Her leg was injured; she limped heavily, adrenaline keeping the pain at bay for the moment. Not knowing whether the man was dead or alive, Melody kept moving, her wounds leaving a bloody trail.

Her hands were slippery from her own blood running down her arms, and the leather binding was now covered in blood. Pain spreading throughout her body, her mind spun wildly; she knew she might pass out at any moment. Still terrified the man with the knife would catch up with her, she had to hide the manuscript.

An image of Yvette Baton hiding The Book in a hollow tree

flashed through her mind. She frantically searched for such an opening, but found nothing suitable. Instead, she set The Book on a flat rock out of view of the path, covering it with branches and leaves until it was completely hidden.

After spotting the speeding vehicles on the highway, and having alerted Mario to his suspicion that something was wrong—something that had to do with Melody and Marie—Samuel did his best to follow them. Mario didn't feel comfortable calling the state police; it was only a vague hunch at this point. But he was certainly glad to have brought his gun, even though it had meant checking his bag rather than carrying it on the plane.

Samuel's inner alarm grew louder when both vehicles got off at the Whiskey Bay Exit. At this point the rain let loose, creating dangerous driving conditions. He managed to keep up with them until they reached the turnoff for Bear Bayou. At that point the drive became nearly impossible, with very little visibility and almost no light. The downpour hid the road like a dark, impenetrable blanket.

Obeah was hidden. Melody tried to get to her feet and continue running, but she became severely disoriented. She stumbled along the path, having covered only about thirty yards before her legs simply could take her no further. She leaned against a tree, unable to keep from falling to the ground.

She remained there, in and out of consciousness, as the rain pummeled her body. She became vaguely aware that the rain had stopped. Through the monotonous sound of water dripping from the leaves, she heard something else. There were footsteps, loud and fast as the wet leaves were crushed beneath the weight. She heard mud splashing. There was more than one person, and they were running, getting closer and closer.

As they approached, Melody heard a voice repeatedly calling, "Alex!"

She had no energy to fight or even be afraid at this point. Melody curled into a fetal position, one arm weakly attempting to cover her exposed breasts, the other her head. Mouthing the words, she silently prayed: *Our Father, who art in heaven, hallowed be Thy Name...*

She continued to pray, becoming almost catatonic and shutting out everything around her.

Paul's journey through the bayou was treacherous; he couldn't wait for the storm to pass before he set out.

As the pirogue approached Maman's stretch of property, he heard wailing and then shouting. He saw at least one person running, maybe two. They were headed along one of the paths leading away from the house. Thinking one of them might be Melody, he set off down the same path.

CHAPTER THIRTY-SIX

The rain finally let up as Samuel's truck approached Marie's property. When they rounded the bend of the narrow drive and the house came into view, they saw the Nissan and the hotel van parked askew in the yard. Samuel was out of the truck and running toward the house, almost before the truck had come to a complete stop; Mario was right behind him, after grabbing his gun and a flashlight from his bag.

They first came upon the circle of logs, where they noticed a large, dark mass on the ground. Mario shone the flashlight on the area and, as the light hit the ground, both men jerked back in unison. In front of them was a dead man.

It looked as if his clothes had been burned, and he had scorch marks on his hands and face. He looked like a photo that had been in a fire; once touched, the image would dissolve to ash.

"Oh, my God. He must have been hit by lightning." Mario was repulsed by the image and the odor. Samuel didn't recognize the dead man. What he did recognize was the ceremony which had been disrupted here: the circle of logs having been set afire at some point, a ritual knife...

His heart filled with dread, Samuel ran into the house with Mario at his heels. The house seemed untouched, with no sign of a struggle. They ran through quickly, but found no one and rushed back outside. When the beam of Mario's flashlight hit the bushes on the opposite side of the circle, he paused and motioned for Samuel to follow him. There they discovered the body of Marie Devereux.

Her head was positioned in such a way that Mario instantly knew her neck was broken. Her eyes were open and fixed on unknown realms. The rain had soaked her hair and clothes, making her look like a discarded rag doll.

Samuel dropped to his knees and let out a heart-wrenching

howl of agony. He gently lifted her from the ground, burying his face in the wet clothing that clung to her lifeless body. He placed a hand under her wobbling head and carried her tenderly into the house.

Mario's first instinct was to stop Samuel from moving the body from the crime scene, but there were too many things colliding in his mind for him to concentrate. He also felt compassion for the old man and did not want to intrude on his pain.

He tried to establish what had happened here. The dead man had clearly been struck by lightning; the woman could have broken her neck by falling in the dark. This entire macabre scene could be the result of two freak accidents. If so, then where was Melody? He needed to find her, fast. And where were the drivers of those two vehicles?

Turning to inspect the property, he quickly spotted a woman's shirt. Though it was saturated by the rain, he noted a faint blood-stain. Casting about with his flashlight, he picked up the faint but still visible trail of blood.

As he made his way on the path leading away from the property, he heard a man's voice distinctly yelling out, "Alex!" Taking off at full speed, ready to draw his gun in an instant, Mario ran down the path.

He followed the trail, the voice, and the sound of more than one person running. He ran until the flashlight shone on Melody.

But she wasn't alone.

The scene before him was confusing. They were at a cross-roads in the woods, with several paths intersecting at this one spot. Melody was curled up, motionless, at the base of a large tree; Mario couldn't tell if she was alive or not, but he saw blood.

A young black man and woman stood in front of her, shouting at one another, wrestling over control of a gun.

Mario had both his gun and flashlight pointed directly at them. He ordered both to drop the weapon and back away.

Consumed in their struggle, the pair either did not realize he was there, or did not care.

Mario stood immobile, letting neither the gun nor the beam of light leave them. His focus was more on the young man since he had heard the name Alex and knew someone by that name was a threat to Melody. The girl seemed maniacal, possessed by a venomous rage; the boy was trying to reason with her, begging her to let go of the gun. The boy put all his weight into wrenching the gun away from her; in the process, it discharged.

Everything was happening so close to where Melody lay that Mario felt helpless; he couldn't move in without endangering her. Before the boy had fallen to the ground, indicating who had been shot, the girl sprinted into the darkness of the woods, the skirt of her pale yellow dress billowing behind her.

"Miss Melody?" the young man pleaded, turning toward Melody, who was unresponsive.

"Don't touch her!" Mario commanded. "Put your hands up!"

The young man did as told, revealing that he did not have the gun. The girl had run away with it.

With the boy unarmed and injured, Mario dropped every-thing and ran to Melody. He checked her pulse and breathing; both were faint but present. He put the flashlight in his back pocket, tucked the gun at his waist, and picked up her limp body.

Mario froze when he saw a startled expression on the boy's face as he stared over Mario's shoulder, fearing the girl had returned and now had the gun pointed at them.

Instead, a baritone voice pierced the scene.

"Let me help." Old Paul emerged from behind a clump of trees, removed from the chaos that had just ensued.

Mario turned to see a very large, burly man, tears streaming down his ruddy face, standing with his hands at his sides.

"I don't know who you are or what you were doing back there, but I've got a gun and I'm going to be walking behind you." Mario didn't have time to question the man; he didn't know how badly Melody was hurt.

Paul nodded in understanding. He went over and helped the boy up off the ground, propping him up so he could hop on one leg. It was a slow procession back to the house, with Paul assisting the wounded young man and Mario following behind carrying Melody, still motionless.

As they neared the house, Melody's eyes began to flutter. She tried to speak, but no sound emerged. Trying once more, she managed a faint whisper, nearly drowned by the soft rustle of the breeze through the trees.

"You're here."

"Shhh...don't talk, honey. I'm here now. Let's get you into the house."

When they entered the backyard and Melody saw the circle of logs, her eyes flew open and her body was gripped in a fresh wave of terror.

"No!" she yelled, though it was still a hoarse whisper. "That man's trying to kill me!" A vision of Maman crumpled to the ground entered her mind and she became hysterical. "He killed Maman, I saw him!"

Mario stopped, trying to calm her before they went inside.

"I know, I know. Hush...it's okay now. The man is dead, Melody."

"Are you sure?'

"Yes. You're safe now."

Mario carried her inside and set her gently on the couch, wrapping a light throw around her to cover her nakedness. He turned on a light in the living room and looked around for Samuel; he found him in Marie's bedroom, kneeling beside the lifeless body he had lovingly laid on the bed. Mario decided not to disturb him.

After pouring Melody a shot of rum from one of the bottles he had found inside a kitchen cabinet, he brought it to her. He then went in search of first-aid supplies and some clothing. As he wandered through the house looking for these things, he checked his cell phone for a signal; there was nothing. "What do people do in emergencies out here?" he wondered aloud.

Mario returned with a woman's robe and inspected her wounds, relieved to see they were only superficial. One of the cuts had severed a secondary vein, which explained the loss of blood; the blood had coagulated on its own by now, so he cleaned and dressed it.

With Melody stabilized, he went to check on the other two men.

He found them sitting outside, the young man in a lawn chair, the older man wrapping the wounded leg with a bandage from a first-aid kit. He looked up when he heard Mario.

"It's just a flesh wound; this kid is really lucky. He'll still need to get to a doctor, though." Paul hesitated before asking, "How's Melody?"

"How do you know Melody?" Mario asked, still unsure of their role in this whole mess.

"I'll explain to both of you, once she's okay. I think this young man wants to do some explaining of his own first, when she can listen," Paul said, looking at the boy in the chair.

Mario went back in to check on Melody. He sat down on the floor in front of her and kissed her forehead.

"Where is Maman? And Samuel?"

Mario nodded in the direction of the bedroom.

"He took her in there, Melody, but I think he needs more time alone with her."

She insisted, so Mario helped her take several steps so she could look into the room, where she saw Samuel on his knees by the bed, eyes closed and head resting on Maman's womb.

She began to cry softly, but didn't intrude. Mario helped her back to the couch; she sat down, trembling, and took another sip of rum.

"Mel, there are two men outside who witnessed what just happened in the woods. One of them was shot. They both seem to know you."

Mario leaned against the wall where he could see everything: the bedroom with Maman and Samuel, Melody as she sat on the couch, and the doorway, should anyone come in or go out. He watched her face as the two men entered the living room, the younger man wincing in pain and limping.

Recognition flashed instantly for both. She seemed happy to see them, though confused. Old Paul sat down next to her and took her hand.

"Melody, I owe you an explanation for why I'm here, and I'm going to do that. I have quite a story to tell you. But I really feel this young man needs to talk first. He needs to speak his piece and explain what happened, at least as much as he knows."

"James?" Melody looked at the young man inquiringly.

In addition to being in physical pain, the young man looked devastated and near tears.

Melody explained to Mario how she knew these two men. She told him that James worked at the hotel in New Orleans where she had stayed and had driven her out here to the bayou the first time, and that Paul owned the emporium and had introduced her to Maman Marie.

James then told what he knew.

He started by saying that the dead man out back was his grandfather, Maurice Abudah. James described a very different man than the one who had committed murder earlier that evening. He told how his grandfather had raised both him and his sister, Alex...

"Alex is a girl?!" Melody exclaimed.

"Yes. I'm the one who texted you about Alex. I'll explain..."

James went far back, relating how they had come to live with his grandfather when they were little and how the death of their father had sent Maurice over the edge. The old man hadn't been well since the death of his own mother, Helena, and had steadily declined since then.

"We started to think they both had some of mental disease where they de..deter..." he stammered, trying to find the right word.

"Deteriorated?" Mario helped him out.

"Yes, deteriorated. He would have weird fevers, just as his mother did before she died. And they would see things, have delusions and stuff."

James went on to explain that, when he and Alex had visited Maurice about six months ago, he had been going through old family things. He was highly emotional and showed them his mother's belongings, including her yellow wedding dress; then started talking about her, about her Voodoo and this mysterious book. Maurice told them it had been stolen from their great-grandmother and that her soul wouldn't rest until he got it back for the family.

Neither he nor Alex paid much attention at the time, but Maurice became increasingly obsessed with getting this book back. Alex gradually grew more interested, talking with Maurice about it in detail. She started to believe there really was such a book. "The idea that there was some family heirloom out there and—pardon me for being so blunt, Ms. Melody—well, Alex couldn't stand the idea that a white family had it, and had taken it away in the first place."

James paused, asking politely for some water, which Paul went to get for him.

"Alex is angry. Always has been," James said, shaking his head sadly. "But when dad died and Pappy started to go crazy, she took it to a whole other level. She came up with this plan to use Pappy to get this book back, so she could have it—he told her it's supposed to be passed down to the women in the family."

Mario noted with interest that Paul, perhaps inadvertently,

was nodding in agreement, as though he had some knowledge of this.

"Anyway, I didn't know what she was doin' until early this morning; that's the first time I realized what was goin' on and how dangerous it all was." James hung his head, ashamed. "Please believe me, Ms. Melody. Honest to God, I didn't know what they were doin' until this mornin'."

Melody carefully got up and went to James; she knelt down and took his hand. She could tell the pain he was in; he had just lost his grandfather and his sister had run off to who-knows-where.

She squeezed his hand. "It's all right, go ahead."

He recounted having gone to his grandfather's very early this morning, just after dawn, and being surprised to see Alex leaving the area so early. She hadn't seen him, but he saw her; she was wearing Helena's yellow wedding dress.

"I couldn't go straight to my grandfather's house 'cause I had a group of people I had to take to two different tour companies. But as soon as I was done, I went over there to find out what was goin' on."

Maurice wasn't there, but what James saw when he walked into the living room made him physically ill. He knew his grandfather was planning some kind of ritual. He saw knives and binding materials—things to restrain and hurt people—and knew it was bad. When he confronted his grandfather, they got into a big argument. Maurice talked about Helena coming to see him a lot lately, wearing her wedding dress and looking so young and pretty. He said she was pressuring him to get The Book, telling him people needed to pay for what they did.

"That's when I knew Alex was playin' him."

When Maurice told him about Melody being back here and the plan he and "Helena" had come up with, James became frightened. He knew Melody was in danger. He thought the danger was mainly from Alex; he was sure he had talked his grandfather out of doing anything crazy.

"That's when I texted you, to warn you," he said to Melody.

Melody wondered fleetingly how he had known her phone number.

After helping Melody get situated back on the couch, Mario turned to James and said, "I'll need you to tell the police what you just told us."

James nodded, then hung his head, sobbing.

Melody wondered when someone would call the police or the coroner; she knew it had to be done, but dreaded seeing Maman taken from her home and from Samuel.

Mario had been eyeing Paul almost the entire time they'd been gathered in the living room; he chose this moment to ask rather mysteriously, "Now, what is your name again?"

Old Paul went over to the couch and sat next to Melody. She looked at him, slightly perplexed and a little frightened of whatever he was about to say. "Everyone here knows me as 'Ole Man Paul', but my real name is Paul Francois Baton."

Melody stared at Paul, mouth agape, the words not quite registering in her brain.

Paul knew she was stunned; it would take a few minutes for her to absorb the magnitude of what he had just revealed.

"Let me ask you this, Melody: Have you found my mother's diary?"

"You mean Yvette's diary?"

Paul nodded in response to her question. Melody nodded in return. The exchange seemed to be in slow motion as they stared at one another.

Mario noticed the oddity of the exchange and interrupted.

"Melody, what's going on? Who is this man to you?"

She couldn't get the words out of her mouth at first. She stuttered a few times and finally said, "He's my Grandmama Giselle's brother."

Saying it out loud gave Melody angelbumps; for a moment it was as though Grandmama was sitting there with them, orchestrating this very bizarre, dramatic reunion.

Mario sat down abruptly, also astonished. This was not at all what he expected to hear. Clearly, there was something he wanted to say, but he couldn't find the words. There were several minutes of awkward silence, broken only by the tick of the old mantel clock reverberating throughout the small room.

Mario walked over and knelt in front of Melody. "Are you okay to stay here for now, while I take James and call for help? I also need to secure things around here." Turning to Paul, he added, "I think you know that we need to talk later." It was not a question.

Melody assured Mario she'd be fine. Paul said he would take care of her, and also promised Mario they would talk when he returned. Melody found their exchange very odd but chose to let it go and not ask questions.

As Mario helped him toward the door, Melody hugged James and thanked him for trying to help her.

Once they had gone, Paul took her hands in his and said, "I am so sorry I deceived you, Melody."

He knew she had read most of the story in Yvette's diary, so didn't bother rehashing that family history. He told her how he came here to the bayou a long time ago, to be closer to Bertrand.

"Is he still alive?" Melody asked incredulously.

"If you want to call it that," Paul answered sadly. "He is a bitter shell of a man, an alcoholic. I rarely see him any more."

He told her how he'd fallen in love with the bayou and stayed here, hiding his true identity in order to live peacefully, without people asking questions and unearthing ghosts of the past. He'd been around long enough now to be part of the scenery.

"Did Maman know who you really were?"

"I think she suspected it, but she always respected my choice to keep it quiet. That was Maman. She never tried to pry or impose her will on others; she knew things would work out as they were meant to."

Melody felt tears building; she blinked and swallowed hard.

"Would you mind checking on them, please, Paul?"

Paul went into the bedroom, returning after a few long minutes.

"How is Samuel?"

He took a deep, ragged breath, struggling to find the right words. "Samuel is with Marie."

"I know he's in there with her, but should we let him stay by himself so long? The poor man must be devastated."

Paul sat next to her once again, taking hands in his. "I meant that Samuel is *with* Marie, Melody. His heart couldn't bear parting from her. He is lying beside her, at peace. She was everything to him."

"What?! Are you telling me Samuel is dead, too?"

Melody already knew the answer.

I can't believe this is all happening. Will it ever stop?

Closing her eyes, she tried to remember everything Maman said earlier, about death and grief. Maman and Samuel had known a special bond. Neither would have felt complete on this journey without the other; now they could continue on together.

"What are we going to do with Marie and Samuel, Paul?"

"Neither one of them has any family left that I know of, child. I know they would like to be buried together here."

Melody had so many questions for Paul, but they would have to wait. Her head had begun to throb; with the light from the lamp increasing her discomfort, she recognized the beginning of a migraine. She asked Paul to please find something in Maman's medicine chest for pain. After swallowing some aspirin, she turned off the light and tried to get comfortable on the couch. Paul, exhausted as well, slumped into the closest chair. They remained in the dark, in silence.

Melody was startled out of a light doze by the sound of a car door slamming. She sat up, confused, thinking she had just awoken from a horrendous nightmare.

When she saw Mario walk in, his silhouette visible in the dim glow from the stove, and then saw Paul sleeping in the chair next to her, the events of the day rushed back like a tidal wave. Mario came in and sat with her, at which point Paul sat up, rubbing his tired, reddened eyes.

"How's James?" Melody asked.

"He'll be fine. I drove to the nearest pay phone and called for an ambulance. I'll sort through the legal things tomorrow with the local police." He rubbed his face vigorously with both hands, trying to shake off the fatigue that had set in on his way back to Marie's. "Can I get you anything?"

"I could sure use some coffee, but I know Maman doesn't have any. I'll put some tea on."

While she put the kettle on the stove and rummaged through the cupboards, she heard Mario and Paul talking quietly, though couldn't hear what they were saying.

She stared mindlessly at the kettle until the water started boiling. After several sips of tea, Melody felt her brain attempting to revive.

She offered a feeble smile as Mario and Paul came in and sat with her at the kitchen table, looking even more somber than she expected.

Oh God, now what?

"Listen, Mel, there's more you need to know and some things I need to take care of." Mario wore the same look of compassion mixed with business he had the day Charlie died. "I came down here because there was a lead in the case—"

Paul interrupted. "If it's okay with you, I'd like to tell her."

Mario agreed, reaching for Melody's hand, which made her even more nervous.

"I didn't tell you who I was when I first met you because I

wanted The Book, too. I knew Giselle had it, and figured it had been passed to you." His voice was shaking, ashamed. "God help me, the idea of getting hold of The Book blinded me, just like it did these other people."

Paul went to the sink for a glass of water and stayed there, leaning against the counter. "I even went to North Carolina to look for it. I'm the person who broke into your apartment."

Mario squeezed her hand and spoke before she had time to react.

"That's what brought me down here. We finally got a hit in the database on some of the fingerprints lifted from your apartment. They matched Paul's."

There was only so much her mind could take in at once, and it already felt overloaded. A sudden realization made her audibly gasp. *Did Paul murder Charlie?*

She looked at Mario with panic in her eyes and he seemed to know what she was thinking.

"No! No, Melody...not Charlie. There were unidentified prints there, but not Paul's. He was never at the farm, only your apartment. Paul's prints were in the system from something minor a long, long time ago."

Melody nearly collapsed with relief. Paul came and pulled a chair next to her.

"Child, I can't tell you how ashamed and sorry I am. I was obsessed, but when I saw you in the woods tonight, your life in danger, I came to my senses. I just wanted to make everything right. You're the only family I have, besides Olivia."

"Olivia?"

"Yes, my daughter. You know her already; she's the girl who works at the front desk of the hotel where you stayed."

Melody could clearly picture the attractive young woman who had helped her weeks ago. The same feeling she had earlier, that she was watching a movie with too many characters, hit her hard.

Mario explained that he and Paul had spoken about this, and said he felt comfortable making the whole North Carolina thing "disappear," as long as Melody agreed to drop the charges.

"Yes, of course," she said without hesitation.

She was shocked and confused about many things, but she felt Paul was good at heart. His coming forward and revealing everything tonight meant a lot to her. Right or wrong, she believed in his goodness. Maman had seemed to genuinely care for him as well, which solidified her belief in him.

As the truth of their relationship sunk in more and more, she was grateful to have a connection to Grandmama's past and treasured that.

"There's a lot more to fill you in on Melody, but we'll do that later." Paul patted her knee reassuringly. "It's nothing bad, just details you might want to know...about Olivia, for example."

"Now," Mario's voice continued to hold its authoritative tone. "We need to figure out what to do with..." his voice trailed as he nodded toward Maman's bedroom, as well as the backyard, where Maurice lay as they had found him.

They discussed various aspects of the situation: legal implications, their personal feelings and beliefs, and what Maman and Samuel would have wanted. They all agreed it was best to bury Maman and Samuel together. Paul knew a local doctor who he was sure would issue death certificates without having to involve any authorities. "Doc Barrow always held Marie in high regard. I know he'll feel it's a privilege to do this."

Mario felt strongly that the police should be called regarding the Maurice-Alex situation. Since Alex was still out there, she was a danger. He covered Maurice's body and left the rest of the crime scene as it was, planning to call the police first thing in the morning. Before then, he would think of a way to explain why they hadn't called tonight.

Later that night, by the glow of candlelight, Mario and Paul reverently carried the bodies of Maman and Samuel to a clearing near the woods, away from the yard. Melody had spread Maman's red quilt on the ground. The men placed the couple on the quilt, side by side, and wrapped them in Shango's love. A shallow grave had been dug, where they gently laid them inside. Melody set Samuel's prized harmonica on his chest and gave Maman a few small items from her altar, a few token treasures to symbolically take into the Spirit pool. After they were properly covered, Paul and Mario traced the seals of Shango and Elegba over the fresh dirt.

That one simple act by these two strong men was filled with incredible love and power, and Melody felt blessed to have witnessed it.

The following morning Melody and Mario awoke to the hearty aroma of coffee. Shuffling into the kitchen, they were surprised to see Paul cooking sausage and eggs. Two large mugs of coffee were waiting for them on the table.

"I went to the store way before dawn and got a few things for you," he said with a pleased smile. "And I arranged for Joe to watch over things while I go see Doc Barrow."

The disembodied feeling one gets in the aftermath of a tragedy had again taken hold of Melody. They all sat at the table, Mario eating heartily while Melody savored the coffee, with Paul sitting there watching, happy he could do something to help.

He told them about Olivia; she was obviously his pride and joy, and Melody understood why. She recalled liking Olivia very much.

"I can't believe I have a cousin!" she exclaimed at one point. "I hope to see her again soon...I'd like to get to know her better."

"We'd like nothing more, child," Paul smiled broadly.

When they finished eating, Mario got ready to find a phone and take care of police matters. Paul left to see Doc Barrow and get that detail taken care of, so there would be no problem with the police. Not wanting to leave Melody alone, especially with the specter of the man who had tried to kill her still outside, Mario asked her to go with him.

"No, I'm really fine, Mario. I need to shower and organize my thoughts. I'm not even close to thinking clearly…yesterday was such a nightmare."

He gave her a peck on the cheek and drove off in Samuel's truck.

Melody couldn't wait to get into the shower. The hot water pouring over her head always helped to clear the spider webs from her mind.

She had been through enough drama recently to recognize she was in shock, numb. She knew tears would come—they always do—but for now she felt detached, emotionless.

As the water cleansed away the physical debris, Melody envisioned it also clearing away emotional debris.

Melody thought of Yemoja, Orisha of the oceans. She flashed to her hands being bound yesterday and not being able to move, then remembered how the rain had loosened the binding so that she could break free. Melody believed Yemoja and Shango had brought in the rain and the lightning bolt that took Maurice's life.

Together they had saved Melody and *Obeah*—

The Book!!!

Melody clutched the skeleton key charm instinctively with one hand and braced herself against the wall of the shower with the other.

How could I have forgotten to get The Book?!

She got out of the shower, dried off and threw clothes on in minutes, nearly frantic. She was glad to be alone; unless she had said something in her delirium, she hadn't acknowledged having The Book to either Mario or Paul. So much drama and danger had revolved around it that Melody wanted to have a clear game plan before revealing she had it.

She retraced her steps from her terror-stricken escape, praying she could find where she left it. She knew it wasn't far from where she had collapsed; she also knew it was off the path, not directly in sight.

She prayed it hadn't been destroyed by the rain.

Relieved to recognize the area where she left it, Melody squatted down to remove the debris from the smooth rock she had chosen as a hiding place.

There was no book.

She wiped leaves and moss from several rocks in that small area, finding nothing. Frenzied, she began raking the leaves and mud with her fingers, but *Obeah* was nowhere to be found.

She sat on the wet leaves in disbelief. A wave of nausea threatened her, and she had to focus on her breathing to control it.

I can't believe this!! I let everyone down…Grandmama Giselle and Maman Marie.

Melody wanted to scream but didn't have the energy. She felt hopeless and worthless…abandoned. People had died, some protecting her, but she still failed to do her part.

She looked to the sky and spoke through tears to her loved ones, apologizing for disappointing them, apologizing to Spirit and to any souls affected by the loss of this sacred text and its messages. Melody had no idea how long she sat there, sobbing and pleading for forgiveness.

She had no idea how long she had been in the woods. By the time she made her way back to the house, both Paul and Mario were there, getting ready to search for her. When they saw her red, swollen eyes, and her filthy clothes, they knew something disastrous had happened.

"The Book," she managed to choke out between sobs. "It's gone."

Paul got a warm washcloth to wipe her face, while Mario once more offered rum to calm her nerves. Neither understood what she was saying through her hysteria.

Melody finally calmed down enough to tell them about The Book, admitting having had it this entire time. She went through the previous night's events step by step, with her running away clutching it for dear life and then hiding it when she heard voices.

Once she returned to some semblance of normalcy and they felt she'd be okay, Paul and Mario decided to go look for themselves. "It couldn't have walked away on its own," they assured her.

But, returning half an hour later, the dejected looks on their faces matched Melody's.

Sitting at Maman's kitchen table, they were forced to accept that it was indeed gone.

"Maybe it's for the best. No power in the world is worth this much loss of life and tragedy," Paul said. "Giselle wouldn't have wanted you to go through so much grief."

Mario agreed. "Honestly, I'm glad we didn't find it. You've been through too much already. Who knows what else might have been in store if you still had it with you?"

Melody reluctantly agreed. She had no choice; there was nothing she could do.

God only knows what had happened to it...

The rest of the day was spent taking care of things: providing Doc Barrow the needed information for the death certificates; filing police reports and giving statements; and, at last, cleaning up the house after everyone had left. By early evening, all three of them were ready to fall into bed.

Paul decided to sleep at home, in his own bed. "I'll take care of everything else here at Marie's. Don't fret about that none."

Melody walked him to his car to say goodbye. "Hey, I just realized you haven't used your boat in the last day. Are you getting old?" she asked with a wink.

"Nope. Just needed a car to get to Doc Barrow and bring him here. He isn't a fan of my pirogue," he chuckled. "Speaking of noticing something..."

"Yes?"

"Child, do you realize you've been roaming all over here, in the woods and everything, and you haven't once mentioned being afraid there'd be a snake?"

Melody hadn't thought of that and her face lit up, obviously pleased with herself.

"I'm proud of you!" Then, with a more serious tone and nearly choking up he said, "Giselle is proud of you, too. So is Maman. Don't you ever doubt that, you hear?"

He opened his arms wide to give her a big hug and she gladly went into them. They didn't need to say anything. So much had happened and they had shared so much; they knew they would stay in touch.

After all, they were family.

CHAPTER THIRTY-SEVEN

Melody and Mario spent that night alone together at Maman's. They agreed she would drive back the following morning while Mario wrapped up a few more police matters; he would fly back to Raleigh later in the day.

On the long drive home, Melody had plenty of time to think, which was not necessarily good for her.

The past few weeks had been the most hectic, most devastating, most intense of her entire life. She had been led along a path where she met a few angels on Earth, impacting her life in a wonderful way; she also witnessed how the ego's hunger for power can turn a decent soul into a murderous thief.

Melody still marveled at the fact that Paul was her great-uncle. She had lost so much recently that anything positive was a welcome blessing. Maybe the old saying "when one door closes, another opens" had some merit.

The events of the last couple of months starting playing through her brain like a movie reel. Her mind started going a mile a minute, with thoughts and questions arising about so many things.

She couldn't shake her anger and frustration about losing The Book. She had done her best to protect it and was crushed by having failed so dismally. *Does it contain something that could truly cause harm in the wrong hands? Is that part of my karma now, too?*

Melody had gone through this stage frequently enough of late to know that if her mind took over, with her trying to understand the impossible, her emotions were at a breaking point.

And I'm so tired of breaking down.

She just wanted to make the drive with as little thinking and feeling as possible; she just wanted to get home.

She opened the windows and turned on the radio but couldn't find a good station. Instead she listened to the sounds of the highway and tried to calm her thoughts.

The distant but distinct sound of a harmonica filled the air. She was certain of it. About to pass a rest area, she quickly exited. She shut off the engine to listen and still heard the harmonica, though it was growing fainter. Within seconds, it was gone.

A bittersweet smile replaced her look of bewilderment. Melody knew exactly what it was: It was Samuel, saying goodbye.

Part of her did not want to say goodbye; saying goodbye was the last thing she wanted to do. Another part recalled Maman's wisdom about letting go: *When the soul is pulled energetically by someone reluctant to let go, it's hard on the soul as well.*

Resigned to what must be done, Melody pulled her car around and parked at a more secluded area; she sat at a picnic table near the edge of the park, bordering the forest. Eyes closed, breathing in and out in controlled rhythm, she restrained the ever-present emotional dam threatening to break free.

Maman's voice echoed in her mind: *Move beyond the pain...truly move beyond it...release it...*

Melody accepted that she would have to dive into it in order to move beyond it.

She thought of her father and how she had felt after his death, how the pain threatened to devour her. It was a raw, rip-your-heart-out pain, and she had wanted to die.

That was her first great loss, so she immersed herself in the pain of her shattered heart, allowing it to seep into every pore. She had always suffered so deeply, as though there were lifetimes of emotion built up inside, never relinquished.

She stayed still, the only movement being a slow trickle of tears down her face. It was time to let go.

When she was ready, she drew in one long breath to fill her lungs and strengthen her for the task at hand, then began.

"I love you, Dad. I want your soul to be free, not held back. The pain I feel in this moment, I honor it so it can be released.

Please forgive me for not warning you about my vision." Her voice cracked and she paused for a brief moment to compose herself. "I honor *you* and release you, Dad."

She imagined cradling a white dove, holding it to her heart in gratitude, then releasing it with love; giving her blessing for it to soar to its greatest, most brilliant heights.

For a split second she experienced the joy a dove must feel when set free. She breathed, in and out...in and out...releasing her father, setting him free from the chains of her grief.

Melody went through this same process, one by one, with everyone for whom she grieved, giving herself wholly in the pain and loss. Tears flowed steadily as she sat with her memories of Grandpapa Henry, Charlie, Maman, and Samuel.

Finally, she allowed herself to feel the loss of her beloved Grandmama, and asked her forgiveness for failing to protect *Obeah*. Deep down, Melody knew the only person from whom she needed forgiveness was herself.

She envisioned releasing pain and fear, freeing each of her loved ones in turn from the confinement of her grief.

Melody then continued her journey, much lighter, unburdened of the weight of a lifetime of sadness.

CHAPTER THIRTY-EIGHT

Today was a horrible morning to look for anything interesting. The leaves were crunched and the bird feathers were wet from the heavy rain that had fallen the night before; the whole place had been turned into a mud pie.

Sylvie Checconi hated living in the bayou and spent every free second dreaming about the day that she would break free.

She had nearly given up hope of finding something the tourist crowd in New Orleans may want, when she stumbled over a rock and noticed something that stood out against the rest of the ground cover. Kneeling, she brushed aside wet leaves to uncover what looked like an old book. Sylvie picked it up and examined it closely. The title was in red, over a dirty black leather cover. It was called *The Book of Obeah* and the binding appeared bloodstained. Sylvie thought the word "Obeah" sounded vaguely familiar, but she didn't know what it meant.

She thought it looked old enough to be worth at least ten dollars from a tourist. Placing it carefully into her backpack, she headed home.

Cardinal Bonelli was packing in preparation to check out of the hotel and return to Raleigh. This trip had been a fiasco; an embarrassing, complete fiasco. He had let the Church down, leaving the faith of millions of people—people who relied on their sacred religious foundations—in peril. What would he tell the Vatican?

The manuscript had ruined his life. His failure in finding it would never be forgotten by his superiors. The Cardinal could only hope the horrid book had been swallowed by the murky depths of the swamp.

He had no idea where the Bennet woman was hiding or where the wretched old Voodoo lady lived. It was like people in

287

the bayou shielded each other and enjoyed pulling the curtain closed so those on the outside could not see in. The man at that pathetic excuse for a store in the swamp probably knew where the old woman was, but he had acted like an ignorant fool.

Cardinal Bonelli had been left with no choice but to take the swamp tour; that, or sit in the smelly old store until the shuttle came back to pick him up. He opted for the tour, where he saw firsthand how the evils of Voodoo had overtaken the region. It was a wasteland, full of snakes and other wicked creatures. The water was murky—impenetrable to the eyes—and he just knew lost souls were anchored to the bottom.

He finished packing, then called the front desk to alert them that he was checking out and would need a taxi to the airport. After taking care of the bill at the front desk, he went outside and sat on a bench to wait for his cab.

He became irritated when a young girl set up a vending station next to him. Casting a disgusted look at the Voodoo dolls on display, he crossed himself, convinced this place overflowed with the children of Satan.

The girl mistook his scrutiny for interest, so she smiled.

"Are you interested in my dolls, sir? They're authentic; they do work magick."

Cardinal Bonelli couldn't believe his own ears! Could the girl not see that he was a man of God?

"Stay away from me, you heathen!"

Sylvie had developed a hard shell in dealing with people; the tourists, even men of the cloth, often had too much to drink, saying things to intentionally hurt her feelings. She persisted.

"I'm sorry, sir. If you don't like dolls, how about this unusual book? I found it today by the swamp. I believe an old witch owned it."

Ignoring her, he was about to leave when his eyes fell on The Book.

"Where did you find that?"

"I found it in the swamp. It looks old pretty old."

Cardinal Bonelli's chest felt tight, he could barely breathe.

"How much do you want for it?"

The girl seemed unsure. "I don't know... ten dollars?"

Monsignor Bonelli pulled out a fifty-dollar bill and handed it to the girl.

"Here, keep the rest. And go to church!"

"Yes, sir. I will."

Sylvie picked up the book but hesitated when she saw his eyes. She had the strange feeling that allowing him to take it was a big mistake. It was as if The Book was talking to her, sending small shocks through her body, telling her it did not belong to him.

Sylvie had never felt anything like this before. She was frightened but dismissed the odd sensation. *Books don't give off "vibes." That's crazy!* She shook her head before forcing a smile. Despite being unable to shake the queer feeling lingering in the pit of her stomach, she released the book to the old clergyman.

His taxi arrived and Cardinal Bonelli got in as fast as he could, anxious to leave this area. Throughout the trip to the airport, he held The Book tightly, as if some unknown force may rip it away from him. Once within the safe perimeter of the airport, he pulled out his cell phone and rapidly dialed the three-key shortcut to connect him with his office. Father Gervasi answered.

"It's Monsignor Bonelli. Listen carefully: I'm on my way and will be there in a few hours. But as soon as I get home, I must leave again. Book me on the first flight to Rome. I have it. Call Rome; arrange for my arrival there."

Monsignor Bonelli carefully placed *Obeah* in his bag and headed toward the gate.

On the plane he allowed himself to relax slightly. All the activity had taken the wind out of him, so he leaned back against the headrest and closed his eyes. This had been another war between good and evil; as usual, God had won. But then, didn't He always?

As he fell asleep, Monsignor Bonelli felt himself surrounded by white light and knew Jesus was proud of him. After all, the Church was now safe and he Its savior.

EPILOGUE

It was close to six P.M. when Melody pulled off in Columbia, South Carolina, to get gas for the car and use the restroom. A small restaurant was connected to the service station, so she decided to get a sandwich before making the final stretch of her trip.

She opened the front door and heard the pleasant tinkling sound of a small bell. A familiar song played in the background, but she thought it sounded rather odd; the tempo was a tad slow, probably not noticeable to most.

As she made her way toward the ladies room, her eyes wandered over the people seated at the tables. There was an older, heavyset man with a short, white beard, wearing a paint-stained, white t-shirt. When she passed by his table he was taking a drink of coffee, and he stared at her from between the mug and the visor of his baseball cap. A woman in her mid-thirties sat staring out a window, covered with a blanket of melancholy. Her dyed yellow hair was held in place by a flashy red barrette that seemed to throb when Melody looked at it. The woman wore tight, revealing clothes; her makeup looked caked and old. She was alone, stirring her coffee and making a "clink, clink, clink" sound.

After using the restroom she walked to the counter to look at the menu board, then waited for someone to take her order. Feeling someone was standing behind her, Melody hesitated before turning around, fearing it might be paint-stain man or sad, red-barrette lady.

Unable to ignore it any longer, she turned to see an older man; he appeared to be about seventy years old, his skin a warm chocolate color. He was flamboyant, dressed in a black pinstriped suit and red silk shirt, with a red carnation in his lapel, topped off with a black fedora. His right hand gripped a

291

black cane; on his index finger shone a large, gold ring in the form of a snake. Black sunglasses gave him an even more dramatic flare.

He was smiling, completely at ease. Melody smiled in return, though her eyes widened when he removed his shades.

His eyes were deep black but incredibly warm, and soft as velvet. Melody stared, mesmerized, and saw that his pupils were not dilated; the irises of both eyes were like tar, with no flecks of color at all.

"Hello, Melody."

Melody's breath caught in her throat, unable to reach her lungs. *How does he know my name?*

The old man sensed her discomfort. "I'm sorry, *chère enfant*. I didn't mean to startle you. I expected you."

His smile was disarmingly magnetic and inviting.

"You wouldn't know who I am; actually, my name is not important. I would like to speak with you about a matter of great importance, however." The stranger smiled and pointed his walking stick to a table in the far corner. "Would you be so kind as to have coffee with me, Melody? I'll explain everything."

"What do you mean, you expected me?" She had no idea she was going to stop here; how could anyone else?

"Please, Chère." He motioned with his cane once again. "Join me."

Melody hesitated, but curiosity got the best of her. She was in a public place so there should be no harm in talking to this gentleman. This was just another odd encounter in a series of odd encounters.

She followed him to the table, observing that he walked with a limp. Melody had just taken a seat across from him when a waitress came over for their order.

Her voice was guttural and tired. "What can I bring you today?"

The old man said nothing; Melody ordered coffee. He lifted

his index finger and nodded his head, indicating he'd like a cup as well.

"Make that two cups of coffee, please," Melody said.

The waitress walked away, a heavy trail of cheap perfume in her wake.

Melody looked at the man and saw her own reflection in the sunglasses he had donned again. "So, you were about to explain?"

"It's important that you know *The Book of Obeah* is where it belongs," he said matter-of-factly. "You did your part beautifully."

"How do you know about The Book? Who are you?" Melody was alarmed, the same fear of the last few days returning full force.

He reached over and touched her hand, hoping to calm her. At that moment she became aware of the key charm against her skin, hidden under her shirt. The silver charm suddenly felt warm against her skin, as though it had been near a fire.

"In a way you know me very well, but it really doesn't matter. You took The Book back and fulfilled your part of the prophecy. "What are you talking about?" Melody was becoming agitated, thinking he was playing with her. She was too tired for games.

However, she didn't move her hand from his; there was something calming, even comforting, in his touch.

"I know you think you failed because you did not keep *Obeah* in your possession, but things were meant to unfold as they did. When your Grandmama sent you to Louisiana, she knew you were the next person tasked with safeguarding the prophecy, but she did not know what your role was to be. As she had been the last guardian, she assumed your task would be the same; however, your task was only to bring The Book back to Louisiana. As you can see, you succeeded."

Over the last few weeks Melody had learned to accept these odd, mystical encounters, not knowing what insights complete strangers may offer.

When she heard him say "Grandmama," she knew something powerful was at work and she must pay attention. His message brought tears of relief that burned her eyes; she was dabbing at them when the waitress came to the table with their coffee. She smiled at Melody and left without a word.

Pouring sugar into her cup, Melody watched the old man put a handful of sugar packets into his jacket pocket.

"You do know I lost The Book, right? I didn't give it to anyone. I have no idea where it is."

"No, Melody, you didn't lose it. It simply appeared that you did. The Book has its own journey, its own preordained path; it is on its way to the next segment of its journey. The Book is only the first part of this Divine Plan. You have served a great purpose; you have also served your own soul well by opening your perceptions as you safeguarded the prophecy."

Melody stared at the swirls as she stirred her coffee. "You've mentioned a prophecy. I know nothing of a prophecy."

He sat back with a content, peaceful expression as he explained. "The prophecy was written long ago. It states that powerful natural events around the world are signs for which the elders have watched and waited. Some of these events serve as catalysts, opening of important doors of awareness which must take place within the human consciousness before the shift can begin.

"Hurricane Katrina was such an event, as was the Indonesian tsunami. These events served to expose imbalance and lack of unity within Mother Earth and Humanity.

"Long ago, it was told that a new world would arise and that the Southern part of this new world would be the center stage for the beginning of a shift in human awareness. The exact location of this new land was shown to elders, who were also forewarned of the unraveling of their own cultures. The descendants of four of those elders, now elders themselves, have been compelled to take residence in the four points of the cross which centers in the middle of the Atlantic Ocean. The elders are located in London, England; Benin, West Africa; Carolina, Brazil; and New Orleans. As they are led by Spirit, they will begin the sacred drumming. They will synchronize the drumming at the four cardinal points, and the ripple effect of the vibrations caused by the sacred drumming will trigger the shift.

"Returning *The Book of Obeah* to Louisiana is believed to be one of the signs."

He leaned forward for emphasis. "You will know when the shift begins. You will recognize the signs. It is very near now, but you must not worry, because a greater design will manifest."

Melody listened, watching him closely.

"A new world has opened for you, Melody. You see the world differently. It's time to remove the veil which has hidden you from yourself."

Melody took a sip of her coffee, trying to understand what he was saying and wondering how *Obeah* fit in with this alleged prophecy.

"I want you to remember three things, okay, Chère?"

Melody nodded, feeling as though she had fallen down the rabbit-hole.

He leaned forward again and raised one finger at a time as he recited three things. "First, protect the rosary. Second, remember what you read about the Language of Spirit. Third..." he paused as he began to rise from his chair and finished with emphasis, "remember, Melody. You are the new Rosetta Stone."

She sat there in stunned silence.

"Would you excuse me for a moment, child? I must use the men's room."

Melody nodded as she watched the old man get up from the chair and limp to the restroom. Before closing the door, he turned to her and flashed a brilliant smile, then raised his left hand to the middle of his chest.

Again, Melody felt her silver charm grow hot against her skin.

She waited quite some time for the man to return before growing concerned. Eventually, she walked over and knocked on the door, but there was no response. When she heard no sound coming from inside, she timidly opened the door. It was a single-stall arrangement, just like the ladies room. And it was empty.

Melody stood there puzzled until her gaze fell on a large, gold skeleton key resting on the chipped sink. Next to the key lay a red carnation, a black fedora, and some empty sugar packets. She was certain they belonged to the eccentric gentleman.

Beneath the pedestal sink, she noticed something else. A large circle had been drawn on the black linoleum floor with sugar. An equal-armed cross drawn inside the circle divided it into four equal sections. In the right half of the circle was a shape similar to the skeleton key.

She walked out of the bathroom, items in hand, and went to the counter where their waitress stood brewing a fresh pot of coffee.

"Can I help you, Hon?"

"Yes, I was wondering if you saw that older gentleman I was sitting with leave? He forgot some of his things."

The waitress raised her eyebrows and opened her heavily made-up eyes a bit wider.

"I don't know where you found those things, but you weren't sitting with anyone."

"But you brought coffee to both of us," Melody reminded her.

"I brought coffee to *you*, honey; I wondered why you had asked for two cups."

Melody thanked her and paid the bill, leaving rather quickly to get away from the woman's concerned gaze.

As she walked to the car, understanding of what just happened dawned on her. She clutched the objects tightly to her chest.

Back in the car, she pulled the necklace from beneath her shirt and wrapped her hand around the charm.

"Thank you Elegba. It's time to go home."

Melody felt as though she had flown on invisible wings. She covered the rest of the distance without stopping, Elegba's gold key clutched in her hand as she drove.

She sighed with relief as she turned onto the gravel driveway of the farm. She parked, turned off the engine and sat for a moment with her eyes closed.

She was relieved to be home, but also looked forward to what the future held; this was new, she couldn't remember ever having felt that way before.

By releasing so much, on so many levels, she knew she had opened the energetic door for good things to come into her life.

As Giselle and Marie both told her, "Have faith in the Creator...everything will work itself out."

At that same moment, Cardinal Bonelli was in his Raleigh office, wiping his forehead with a cold cloth. He had planned to fly straight to Rome, but began to feel terribly ill while at the airport. He called the office staff and they postponed his departure for Rome to the next day.

He was certain exhaustion was the culprit, so he came here only long enough to secure *The Book of Obeah* in the safe. The moment he walked in he felt dizzy, so he left The Book on his desk and crossed the room to sit down. He was sweating profusely, his mouth parched.

He tried to stand, but a sharp pain shot across his chest and took his breath away. He was barely able to call out for help when another wave of pain, more severe than the first, washed through him. He collapsed on his leather couch.

Within seconds a member of his staff walked in and found him. An ambulance was called and soon there were people everywhere.

Father Gervasi walked in quietly and unobtrusively, and took advantage of the commotion. He took *The Book of Obeah* from the desk before leaving the building unobserved. Jumping into his car, he sped off toward the Interstate.

He opened the window and tossed out the white collar he had been wearing. He no longer needed to play the role of Father Gervasi; he had lost his faith long ago. Now he could resume his true identity: Federico Hernandez. He had changed his name when he was legally able, intending to wash away any association with the shameful life his father had led.

He practically sneered when he thought of his brother, Mario. They had never been close, even as children. Mario scorned him when he took his priestly vows, never understanding how Federico could take that path when they had been raised in Voodoo. He, on the other hand, never understood how Mario could join the police force with the naïve hope of catching their father's killer. The old man didn't deserve it.

Mario wouldn't laugh any more; not when he learned *The Book of Obeah* was in his little brother's possession! With The Book resting on the seat beside him, Federico Hernandez already felt like the most powerful man in the world.

He almost couldn't believe it was real when he first heard the old Cardinal talking about it. After seeing the girl, though, he knew she had The Book. He had gone back to the farm the next day, alone, to find it. It was unfortunate that the old farm hand had walked in and surprised him, but it was a small price to pay for what was on the seat next to him now.

The Book was all that mattered to him, and whether it was God or the Devil that had led him to it, he couldn't care less. His life would change from this moment on.

He switched the radio on and scanned the stations, until he found one that fit his mood. As Ozzy Osbourne's "Mama, I'm Coming Home" filled the car, Federico sang along. He felt powerful...so powerful that he closed his eyes while singing, believing nothing could harm him now.

He was unaware that he had cut directly in front of a car in the next lane. The other driver could not stop in time and slammed into the left side of Federico's car. It spun out of control; he found himself across the median, where his wild ride finally came to an end. With a shaky hand, he reached for *The Book of Obeah*, still on the seat beside him and, amazingly, unscathed.

He never saw the truck coming. He heard a tremendous crash and then everything went silent.

BOOKS

O is a symbol of the world, of oneness and unity. In different cultures it also means the "eye," symbolizing knowledge and insight. We aim to publish books that are accessible, constructive and that challenge accepted opinion, both that of academia and the "moral majority."

Our books are available in all good English language bookstores worldwide. If you don't see the book on the shelves ask the bookstore to order it for you, quoting the ISBN number and title. Alternatively you can order online (all major online retail sites carry our titles) or contact the distributor in the relevant country, listed on the copyright page.

See our website www.o-books.net for a full list of over 500 titles, growing by 100 a year.

And tune in to myspiritradio.com for our book review radio show, hosted by June-Elleni Laine, where you can listen to the authors discussing their books.

mySpiRitRadio